THE PRIDE OF A GENTLEMAN

LINDA RAE SANDE

Twisted Teacup
PUBLISHING

The Pride of a Gentleman

ISBN: 978-1-946271-01-3

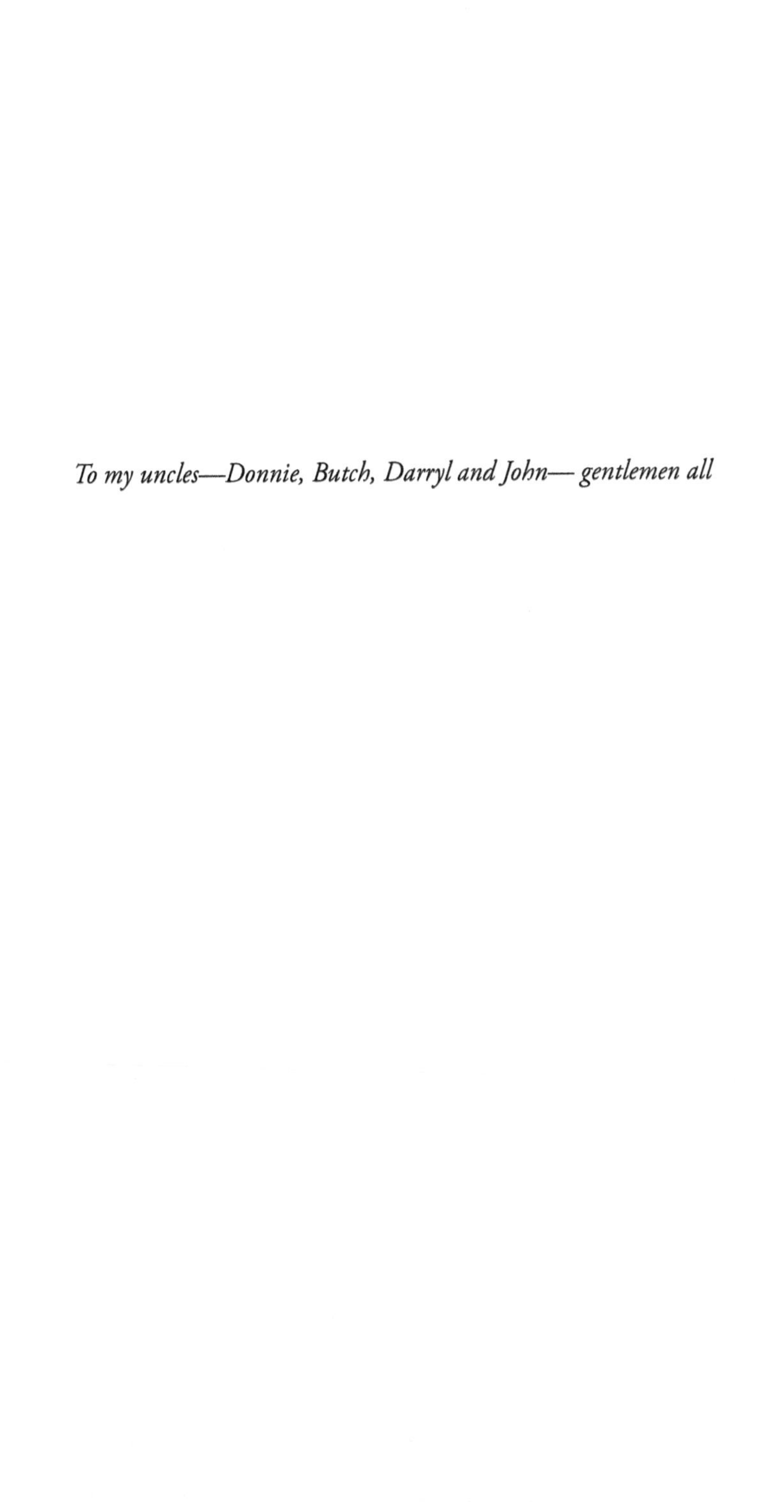

To my uncles—Donnie, Butch, Darryl and John— gentlemen all

CHAPTER 1

A MORNING BEGINS IN THE
VERY BEST WAY

The first day of autumn, 1802

Gregory Grandby stared up at his wife and allowed a grin. "Well, good morning my beautiful bride," he whispered, lifting his head to determine that, yes, indeed, Christiana was straddling him in their marriage bed.

His turgid manhood was about to disappear inside her when Christiana said in a quiet, breathy voice, "You don't mind, I hope." She sounded as if she'd been involved in some activity that had her struggling to catch her breath.

Gregory blinked and considered the question as a grin appeared on his handsome features. "Am I to play a *horse* this morning?" he asked in delight, the last of his question turning into an, "Oof," as his wife impaled herself.

"Oh, would you, dear? I find it so much easier when you do the bouncing."

Blinking several times in an effort to ensure he was really awake, Gregory allowed a chuckle. "No... foreplay?" he countered, rather stunned at how ready she seemed for him. He glanced about with suspicion, as if to look for someone else in their master suite—for whoever had seen to making his wife so ripe for him.

He wouldn't have been surprised to find someone else there. A construction crew had been working on the west wing of the house for over two months. Their bedchamber had been the first room on the renovation list, the majority of it finished the day they were married.

Had that been just two months ago?

Christiana sighed. "The workmen will be here in a few minutes. For just this one morning, I would like us to do this without having to match our moves to the sound of hammering."

Rather surprised by her words, Gregory slid his hands up the sides of her petite body, finally pulling her down until he could kiss her lips. "Understood," he whispered. He was about to start the bouncing she had referred to when Christiana lifted her head.

"Perhaps it would be better if I were on my elbows and knees," she whispered as she moved to get off of him.

"Wait, what?" Gregory watched as she repositioned herself. "Why?" he asked, his suspicion evident.

Christiana sighed as she turned her head to regard him. Her bottom, high above her arched back, was bare as was the rest of her body. Her pert breasts barely grazed the bed linens. "Mrs. Dawes says I should do this if I wish to conceive a boy," she explained quickly. "Hurry, please."

Desire slammed into Gregory even as he questioned why she would offer herself as if she were some doxy in a brothel. "Yes, my sweeting," he managed to get out before he stepped off the bed and positioned himself behind her. "Just so you know, I'm only doing it this way because you've demanded it of me," he whispered. He let his manhood seek out its favorite place as he held onto the globes of her bottom. He groaned as he buried his member into her, glad he wasn't playing a horse that morning.

And he was ever so grateful when her mewling turned into the unmistakable sounds of intense pleasure just one moment before the first hammer struck a nail. On the second blow, he allowed his own release. On the third, he cursed happily and tumbled onto the bed, bringing Christiana with him on the fourth so she ended up tucked into the front of his body.

Gregory supposed he should be glad Christiana was determined to conceive a child so early in their marriage, but his last thought before falling back to sleep was of how exhausted he would be until she did so.

*W*hen the waves of pleasure finally subsided and Sophia Simpson's breathing returned to normal, she smoothed the palm of one hand down the side of her husband's torso. She delighted in how his own breath hitched as her fingertips caressed his skin, in how his body jerked, and especially in the words he whispered next to the whorl of her ear.

"You saucy minx!"

Sophia giggled, her joy at their early morning coupling evident in her flushed face. "As I recall, *you're* the one who started it," she murmured, her other hand joining the first to slide over his heated skin until it reached his hip.

"Careful, my lady, or I shan't allow you to take your leave of this bed for the entire day," James Simpson warned in a hoarse whisper.

His wife's expression betrayed her confusion. "Why do you say that as if it's a bad thing?" she asked, a grin still in place. She felt the vibration of his chuckle even before the sound erupted next to her ear.

James lifted his chest from hers, his arms straightening on either side of her body as he regarded her with bemusement. "You're so beautiful," he whispered. He ducked his head down, capturing her lips in a quick kiss. "And I am a very lucky man."

Sophia blinked as she regarded her husband of nearly twenty-one years. "How much did you win?"

His face screwing up in confusion, James shook his head before his eyes widened. "All of you," he finally answered.

The fifth Duke of Ariley's youngest daughter sighed. "I thought you went to your club last night," she countered, her thumbs moving to lightly brush over his nipples before smoothing the crisp, graying curls on his chest.

Nodding, James finally pulled his body from hers and

landed in the mattress next to her, rather liking how Sophia mewed a sigh of disappointment at the same time. "I did, but not to gamble," he replied in a voice that sounded far away. "I needed to speak with your brother."

Sophia's eyes widened. "Sir William?" she questioned as she raised herself onto an elbow and regarded him in alarm. The motion allowed James to snake an arm beneath her and pull her body on top of his.

"Indeed."

"Is anything... wrong?"

James opened one eye and gave his head a quick shake. "Not at all. And why is it every time I seek out your brother's advice, you think something is wrong?" he asked before a yawn took away his ability to speak.

Sophia considered the question, realizing she did seem to jump to the same conclusion every time. Conditioned to it, she supposed. After all, her brother, Sir William Burroughs, had been the one to use his skills as a banker to help her escape a life as a widow at Merriweather Manor and begin a new one with the household's butler. A life that had now passed its twenty-year mark.

Her inheritance from her late husband, Roger Grandby, as well as the funds she received from her father upon reaching her majority, had funded the purchase of an entire street of town-houses in Kingly Street in London. The properties had given her the means to live a modest but comfortable life with a man she loved. And it allowed her to hide in plain sight, for her sudden disappearance from Merriweather Manor on the last day of 1781 had set the *ton* in a twitter. Some thought she had run off to the Continent with a secret lover, while others were sure she had left for the United States to begin a new life there. A few thought she had simply moved to the country to live a quiet life away from the censure of the *ton*.

Who would have thought to look for her closer to home? To the middle of London? To a modest townhouse in Kingly Street?

"Did he provide you good advice?"

James struggled to open his eyes, but found sleep about to take him under. "He did."

Aware of the moment James succumbed to sleep, Sophia sighed and lowered her head to his chest. Although she was curious, she knew she would have to wait to learn whatever it was that had her husband asking a banker for advice.

Thomas Wellingham watched his wife as she pulled on a silk wrapper and moved to open the drapes concealing the bedchamber's only window. Early morning light filtered through the sheers still covering the glass and cast her tall figure in silhouette as she made her way back to the bed.

"Good morning, handsome," she murmured as she removed the wrapper and slipped back into the bed. Given the warm, late summer nights, she had shed her nightrail even before climbing into bed the night before.

"Indeed it is," Thomas whispered in delight, realizing she only returned to the bed because she wished for his amorous attentions. Given how aroused he had become just watching her remove her wrapper, Thomas needed little in the way of encouragement.

Although they had only been married ten weeks, Thomas could hardly remember what his life had been like before he finally met Emma Fitzsimmons. There was his work, of course. Running the import business his late father had begun still took up most of his days, but back then, his nights had been spent in quiet desperation. An occasional dinner in town with friends, a visit to Boodles now and again, but otherwise lonely evenings spent in the library with a book and a brandy.

As his sister's roommate at Warwick's Grammar and Finishing School for nearly two years, Emma was certainly known to him. Christiana spoke of the woman often when Thomas took his sister to dinner or when she was home from school for a holiday.

He didn't have the occasion to meet the woman until earlier that year, though. In February, he had paid a call at his sister's boarding house to join the young ladies there for dinner. Unlike every other time he had done so, Emma was actually present that evening. The capable woman had seen to directing her fellow housemates in making that night's roast beef dinner—the cook had taken ill and died earlier that night— and she had, in the process, impressed him with her culinary skills. Later that night, she had endeared herself to him with her knowledge of cost accounting.

Who knew that talk of numbers could have him so enamored?

Just the month before they met, he had come to believe someone at Wellingham Imports had been embezzling funds. Needing to learn the identity of the guilty party, he offered her the position of auditor for his company's books the night of the dinner.

Working in Woodscastle's library for several months following the end of finishing school and her night classes in accounting, Emma audited the company ledgers Thomas brought home. She determined not only who had stolen money, but how much.

In the process, she had stolen his heart.

Thomas hired her to replace the fired employee, and now she was responsible for the company's payroll as well as his renewed enthusiasm for making the trip to the London offices every day.

They would be late in arriving that morning, he decided. Although Emma would have been satisfied with a quick tumble, he wanted to make that morning's encounter last as long as possible.

*D*eborah awoke to the soft snores of her husband and a brief case of morning sickness. Finishing off the biscuit her lady's maid had left on the nightstand helped in that regard, and she settled back down into the mattress.

"Are you ill?"

The sound of her husband's voice had given her a start— she

hadn't thought him awake. "I am fine now," she answered, moving her body so she rested against his side. The warmth of his tall body permeated her nightrail, and she allowed a satisfied sigh. "It's barely light out."

Todd Vandermeer inhaled deeply, the scents of honeysuckle and lemon from her hair and nightrail a heady combination. "Thank you for joining me in my bed," he murmured. "And for staying the entire night."

Angling her head where it rested in the small of his shoulder, Deborah allowed a grin. Was there another man in all of London who thanked his wife for sharing his bed? "I am glad to do it, of course. Perhaps you'd like to visit me in my bedchamber this evening?" she hinted.

Todd wrapped an arm around her shoulder and pulled her atop him. "I'd like that very much. Your bed is far more comfortable than this one."

Deborah frowned. "I hadn't noticed," she remarked with an arched eyebrow.

Grinning, Todd allowed a chuckle. "Then I must be doing something right," he murmured as he pulled her hand to his lips and kissed her fingertips. When he didn't make a move or offer another comment, Deborah lifted her head again, thinking perhaps he had fallen asleep.

"Are you well?" she asked in concern.

Todd's eyes were closed, but he allowed a grin. "I am, my lady. I am merely... thinking."

"Good thoughts, I hope," she countered.

Inhaling slowly, Todd finally sighed. "Possibly. Right now they are rather... unsettling. But I will know more later this morning. Should they result in what I hope they do, then I will wish to speak with you about them when I return tonight."

Although the words were spoken in a near whisper, Deborah couldn't help but think they sounded rather ominous. Perhaps her husband sensed her sudden discomfort, for he allowed a chuckle before adding, "Nothing bad, I assure you. Possibly something very... very good, in fact."

Relieved at his words, Deborah lifted herself from the

mattress and placed a kiss on his lips. "Then, by all means, get lost in your thoughts as I return to slumber," she murmured.

She settled her head back into the small of his shoulder before Todd gave a start. "Slumber?" he repeated. "Why, I thought..." He allowed the sentence to trail off before another sigh escaped, this one sounding of disappointment.

"What is it?" Deborah asked, sensing his sudden distress.

"I merely thought you were about to have your way with me," Todd replied in dismay.

Deborah allowed a giggle. "Am I allowed to interrupt your serious thinking in such a manner Mr. Vandermeer?"

She heard the slap from the palm of his hand intersecting his forehead and lifted her head again to regard him in shock.

"I was rather hoping you would *save* me from thinking, my lady," he replied, his lack of humor giving Deborah pause.

Another moment passed before she lifted herself onto an elbow and stared at him. "Does that mean you *wanted* me to... to suggest we make love?" she asked in confusion.

Todd chuckled then, his other arm wrapping around her hips to pull her body more firmly atop his. "It means I wanted you to *demand* I tumble you. Or that you should simply mount me, and ride me like the humble steed that I am," he replied happily.

A moment later, Deborah was straddling her rather startled husband, her nightrail having been stripped from her body in a quick movement that belied how ill she had felt only minutes ago. "I apologize for not understanding your meaning," she whispered before she impaled herself on his engorged manhood.

Not able to stifle his growl of astonishment, Todd moved his hands to her hips and gave them a gentle squeeze. "I shall be sure to make my meaning more clear next time," he managed to get out before his wife's ministrations and her bouncing on his balls had him seeing stars.

He wasn't able to form a coherent thought for some time, thank the gods.

Or rather, his goddess.

CHAPTER 2

RENOVATIONS LEAD TO A DISCOVERY

Woodscastle, Chiswick, September 23, 1802

Humphrey closed the front door and studied the names on the three envelopes he held. Before Gregory Grandby had taken up residence in Woodscastle, an estate home about six miles from London, the household usually received only one or two posts a week. Now, they seemed to come in clusters of three or four every day, sometimes by post and sometimes by courier. At one time rarely used, the silver salver set aside for mail was now employed on a daily basis.

Today's delivery required all the spare pence kept on the small table next to the front door. Although Thomas Wellingham, his other master, usually saw to it that there was a collection of coins left to cover postage, the butler had no intention of asking him for more funds given most all the mail these days was for Gregory. He would simply make mention of the depleted postage money when he delivered the day's mail to Mr. Grandby.

As he made his way in search of the man, Humphrey considered how different the household was now that both Thomas and Christiana Wellingham were married.

For over ten years, the siblings had lived in the east wing of the dilapidated home. Their late father, Graham Wellingham, had been the black sheep of an aristocratic family. His father and then his older brother had been the third and fourth Earls of Trenton. Despite having married the sister of the Earl of Everly, Christina Tennison, Graham eschewed the *ton* and insisted he wanted to build and run a business. He did so with the blessing of Christina.

Since his father's death, Thomas had built Wellingham Imports into a rather prosperous firm. Once Gregory Grandby announced his intention to marry Christiana and then bought half the house from Thomas, Humphrey realized Woodscastle would never be the same.

A good thing, he decided. Although he currently delivered the mail to the library—a long room adjacent to the vestibule—there would one day be a room designated as Gregory's study to which he would do so.

Apparently, Thomas would continue to use the library as his study.

There would also be more servants, a situation he found rather exciting, since he and a housekeeper, a part-time maid and laundress, a cook, a groom and a stableboy had been the extent of the staff for the past ten years. Despite the rumor of a baby in the household within the year, a nurse hadn't yet been hired. Once Gregory and Christiana returned from their upcoming trip to Europe, though, a nurse would be added to the staff.

At least, Gregory had promised Thomas' wife, Emma, one would be hired. The mistress of the house had a background in such matters but, given her position as an accomptant at Wellingham Imports, she had little time to see to the care of an infant.

The sounds of pounding and sawing assaulted his ears as Humphrey made his way to the library. In its third month of renovations, Woodscastle was slowly transforming from a shabby and somewhat dilapidated hulk to an estate home worthy of its name. Although the east wing had been in a livable state for many years and had hosted Thomas and Christiana as well as their late parents, the west wing suffered from neglect—no one had lived in that part of the house for nearly a half-century.

Having purchased half of Woodscastle from his best friend and brother-in-law, Thomas Wellingham—the bad half, if one believed the story—Gregory Grandby insisted on footing the bills for the renovations. It was his intention to create a wing in which to raise a rather large family. Christiana had grown up with only the one brother and insisted she wanted ten children.

Since Gregory grew up in the nearby estate home Merriweather Manor among dozens of cousins, and since he wanted a large family of his own, who was he to argue?

But ten children meant the need for a nursery, multiple bedchambers, bathing chambers, a salon for his wife, a study for him, and servants' quarters. Hence the extensive renovations.

The sound of pounding from above, which had been going on all day, was a constant reminder that the roof was undergoing replacement as well. It would be another week before that project would be completed.

Drawings for the finishing woodwork for several rooms lay spread out on a library table. Several more were in the process of being rendered by a draftsman who had taken up residence in the library where accomptant Emma Fitzsimmons had spent several months working on ledgers earlier that year.

Christiana, surrounded by stacks of fabric samples and bits of trim and tassels, sat in silence whilst holding a fanned display of fabric samples. Her look of exasperation suggested she was looking forward to Emma's return from Wellingham Imports. She obviously needed help in making the final decorating decisions, the butler realized.

Humphrey nearly collided with Gregory as he stepped into the library. "Several posts arrived for you, Mr. Grandby," the butler said as he recovered his composure and held out the salver for the tall man. "And I gave the last of the money for postage to the postman, I'm afraid."

Gregory eyed the collection of envelopes and plucked the top one from the salver, examining the puddle of red wax that sealed the four corners of the missive together. "You can leave the others on my desk," he murmured as he reached into his waistcoat pocket and pulled out a fistful of coins. "This should cover what arrives whilst I'm gone. Mrs. Grandby and I will be back in a few months, I should think."

Humphrey's eyes widened at the collection of coins Gregory dumped into his palm. Despite knowing the man was one of the wealthiest in all of England, Humphrey required an occasional reminder as the man's easy-going manner belied his station in life. The grandson of a duke and cousin to the Earl of Torrington, Gregory could one day inherit the earldom if his cousin, Milton, died without issue. Given Milton's relatively young age, Gregory rather hoped he could avoid the responsibility.

He regarded the envelope a moment before he slid a thumb beneath the seal to break it. Before he could open the letter, though, a construction worker appeared behind Humphrey.

"What is it?" Gregory asked as Humphrey moved to leave the salver on his desk.

"We've discovered something, sir. Could you come take a look?"

Gregory blinked. The entire time the west wing had been under reconstruction, at no point had any of the workers approached him with such an intriguing invitation. Usually the foreman was apprising him of potential problems or warning him that some new request was going to cost more money, to which Gregory would often simply shrug and say, "It costs what it costs."

Having been told something had been discovered was exciting. Curiosity had him wondering just what might require his attention. Intrigued, he replied with, "Lead the way."

Following the foreman's assistant to the west wing stairs, Gregory opened the letter and intended to at least determine its author, but the foreman stood at the top of the stairs and appeared rather anxious.

"It should not take much of your time, sir," the man said in an apologetic tone. "It's just that when we measure this room and the one next door, there seems to be a rather large space missing in between."

Gregory's eyebrows arched up as he followed the workman into the room that would eventually be his study. "Here, sir," the foreman said as he pointed at the paneled wall on the south end of the long room. Water damage from a leaking roof had ruined most of the moldings in this room and others on the second story, but the carpenters were busy installing paneling in the rest of the study.

Another carpenter stepped into the room. "Hey, Henry, there's definitely a space..." He stopped in mid-sentence when he took sight of Gregory examining the wall. "Oh, pardon me, sir," he said as he gave a short bow and stepped back.

"Quite all right," Gregory replied absently, studying the details in the room's original paneling. He walked up to the wall and allowed his eye to follow the pattern of the moldings until he found a place where the wall wasn't quite connected. Pushing against the panel near the vertical crack didn't result in any movement, but when he moved his hand across the wall about three feet to the left, where another vertical moulding was located, the wall pushed inwards several inches.

"A secret door!" one of the workmen exclaimed as he moved closer to the south wall. "A passageway, do you suppose?"

"Or perhaps a priest hole," Gregory murmured as he glanced around the room. "Can you get me a torch?" he asked as he pushed open the door, its unused hinges creaking in protest.

One of the workmen grabbed a kerosene lamp from near the room's entrance and lit it. Holding it in front of his body, he offered it to Gregory. The taller man took it, his attention on the space behind the secret door.

"This is most curious," Gregory said as he walked into the hole. Directly across from him was evidence of a matching door from the adjacent room, and to the left, a set of stairs that led down into inky black darkness. No water damage was evident, although the light from the lamp barely reached the unadorned ceiling. "Mr. Thompkins, can you see if you can find a similar door in the next room?" he asked as he contemplated where the stairs might lead.

"Right away, sir," the carpenter replied before he hurried out of the room. Despite the muffled pounding from above, Gregory could hear the man's footfalls in the corridor and then through the wall. After a few seconds, the door from the other side opened and Mr. Thompkins stood staring at Gregory, a look of delight on his face.

"These doors are well hidden in the old paneling, sir," Mr. Thompkins remarked with a nod.

"Indeed," Gregory replied as he directed the lamp's glow to the stairs. "See to it the new paneling accommodates these doors, if you would," he murmured.

"Aye, sir."

"Well, nothing ventured," Gregory commented before starting down the stairs, careful to check to be sure each runner would hold his weight before stepping onto the next.

There were seven steps before a wall and a landing forced him to take a turn. He slowly descended the next set of seven steps and again reached a wall and a landing. At the bottom of the last set of stairs, Gregory faced a door at the end of a short corridor.

Listening, he tried to determine what might be on the other side and was amused when he heard the curses of Mr. Tanner, the cook, as he prepared luncheon. The door at least had a handle. Noticing the hinges on his side of the door, Gregory gingerly turned the handle and pulled hard. The hinges protested at first, but the door opened to reveal a rather startled cook staring at him in fright.

"Good afternoon, Mr. Tanner," Gregory said with a satisfied grin. Then he realized he couldn't actually walk into the kitchen. A large, oak table blocked the doorway. Located along the west wall of the kitchen, the door was quite evident as it included trim molding and a handle.

"Mr. Grandby," the cook acknowledged with a half-bow.

"Where ...?" he started to ask before he leaned around

Gregory to stare at the open door. "Where did you come from?" he asked as his bushy eyebrows did a dance.

"The west wing study," Gregory replied with a nod. "Seems the original owner of this house wanted a quick access to a midnight snack," he added with a grin. "Capital idea, wouldn't you say?"

Mr. Tanner screwed up his face. "I suppose so, sir. Does this mean I'll have to move my table?" he asked, his tone of voice suggesting disappointment.

Chuckling, Gregory said, "Not yet. In a few months, perhaps." He set the kerosene lamp on the kitchen table.

Still holding the letter, Gregory took the opportunity to study the handwriting and the embossed wax seal on the back. *Sir William Burroughs*, he realized as he read the letter by the brighter light of the kitchen. He flattened the folds.

To my dear nephew, Gregory Grandby II, I hope this letter finds you and your bride in good health. I fear I must ask that you delay your departure to Rome on the occasion of a matter of Utmost Importance regarding a business matter to which you must attend with great Speed and Authority. The nature of this matter is too important and private to express in this letter. I ask that you come to the Bank at your earliest convenience. Yours truly, Sir William Burroughs.

Frowning as he read the letter, Gregory wondered which of his investments could require such immediate attention. He had dozens of business ventures scattered throughout Great Britain. There was no telling which one his uncle thought so important that he would need to not only make a trip to the Bank of England, but also change his travel plans.

As for delaying his departure for Rome, Gregory realized just then he hadn't made his updated itinerary known to his uncle. He and Christiana wouldn't be leaving for Rome on the morrow as originally planned, but rather the following week. Although Gregory would have suggested the change in departure first—renovations still required his presence, it seemed—Christiana had been the one to put voice to the request.

He hoped it wasn't because she feared being away from her best friend and sister-in-law, Emma, or from her only brother, Thomas. He certainly hoped she wasn't fearful of being in his company—and only his company—once they departed for Italy. They had never been alone as a couple for more than a night at a time since they met one another. Besides, a lady's maid would accompany them on the trip and provide Christiana with a companion should she require one during the voyage and whilst they visited the ancient sights of Italy.

Gregory could hardly wait to return to his favorite city. He rather hoped Christiana would agree with his assessment of Rome.

Refolding the letter, Gregory gave a nod to the cook, lifted the kerosene lamp so it lit the stairs, and headed back up to his study. Ten minutes later, he was on a horse and headed to the Bank of England.

CHAPTER 3

AN OFFER IS ALMOST ACCEPTED

Meanwhile, at Wellingham Imports

"There you are," Emma said as she hurried to meet Thomas at his office door. "I was about to send Master Billy in search of you," she murmured.

The owner of Wellingham Imports wrapped an arm around her waist and pulled her into a quick hug, bussing her on the cheek as he did so.

"Mr. Wellingham!" she admonished him, her face blooming with a shade of pink he hadn't seen since the spring.

Rather surprised by her scold, Thomas blinked. "It's not as if anyone paid witness..." He turned around when he noticed that Emma's eyes were darting off to one side. There, in front of the upholstered chair facing his desk, stood one of his best friends. "Todd!" he exclaimed, quickly moving to join the tall man, his right hand extended. "Pardon my... indiscretion."

"Good morning, Thomas," Todd Vandermeer replied, shaking Thomas' hand at the same time he aimed a wink of amusement in Emma's direction.

At one point earlier that year, Todd had set his cap on Emma, convinced she would make him the perfect wife. Then Emma had introduced him to her best friend, Deborah. A midwife at Mrs. Dawes' Home for Unwed Mothers, Deborah stood nearly six feet tall and proved the perfect match for a man of his unusual background—and taller-than-normal height. She also played nursemaid when it came to his ever cranky knees.

"So glad to see I am not the only one who enjoys kissing his wife," Todd added with an arched eyebrow.

Emma angled her head. "I'll be down in the accomptants' office," she said in a quiet voice, a signal to Thomas that she wouldn't be going back to her desk. Located behind the wall that separated her space from Thomas' office, her elaborately designed escritoire was where she spent most of her time seeing to the payroll for Wellingham Imports.

With a window overlooking the Thames and a stove on which a teakettle stayed hot most of the day, the office was a rather cozy place to spend her days. But Emma's work as a payroll clerk sometimes required she spend time with the accomptants who saw to the accounts payable and receivables. Given the increase in the products Wellingham Imports brought in from all over the globe, the staff in the clerks' office had grown by four in just the last few months, but Emma still needed to help on occasion.

Thomas gave a bow in her direction and moved to sit at his desk. Once Emma curtsied and took her leave, Todd settled into the wing chair across from Thomas. A sigh escaped his lips as he did so, as if he were relieved to be sitting down.

"From the looks of things both in here as well as downstairs, I am of the opinion that you, sir, are doing rather well," Todd remarked with an arched eyebrow.

Leaning forward, Thomas rested his forearms on his messy desk and nodded. "I am. Can't say I have the time to enjoy the success, though. It seems as if I am here most of the day, as is Emma," he complained lightly.

"Perhaps I can be of some help, then," Todd said as he leaned forward. "I've given your offer of employment a good deal of thought. Especially since... since I tendered my resignation with the John Company."

Thomas blinked as he straightened in his chair. "Truly?"

Todd nodded. "Yes. I felt it was time, and I wanted to leave there on good terms. If I had stayed much longer, I fear I would not have been able to do so."

Furrowing his brows, Thomas regarded his friend for a moment. Todd was known as one of the East India Company's best brokers. He was eminently well-liked. Whatever could have the man leaving the company he had worked at—since he was a tyke—on less-than good terms? "Whatever happened?"

Embarrassed, Todd shifted in his chair. "One of the brokers... he's never been very good at the position—"

"The one that ordered the transparent gowns from Paris?" Thomas broke in, remembering the hubbub that had happened when a huge shipment of see-through gowns had a hard time finding buyers. A bit of creative marketing had solved the problem, though, resulting in a sudden demand for them from several modistes and ladies' shops. Worn over an unadorned gown, the transparent gown instantly enhanced the dress, and provided a woman the means to create several fashionable ensembles.

Apparently, the experience had taught Todd not to trust the other broker. Perhaps not to trust anyone else should they seek his help in matters of the import business.

"Yes. Him," Todd agreed with a sigh. "Anyway, despite that situation having been sorted—rather satisfactorily, I might add —he has taken my marriage to Miss White as an affront to his sister." He didn't add that Hughes had been let go from the John Company, a development that he found rather surprising.

Thomas blinked, not quite sure he understood. "Who is his sister?"

Todd cleared his throat. "Miss Charlotte Hughes. I hosted her in my home for tea one afternoon..." He held up his hand as if to stave off Thomas' immediate sound of protest. "I didn't know any better at the time. She didn't come with a chaperone, but given her apparent age, I didn't think it was out of the ordinary for her to show up without one. But from the time she arrived for afternoon tea, she took stock of everything in Grace Park as if she were determined to move in and redecorate the place. I made a comment that she found... offensive, and she left quite suddenly. Much to my relief, really."

Thomas managed to avoid putting voice to any response, knowing his friend tended to make an occasional *faux pax* when in the company of those better educated.

The man had grown up an orphan, after all, and had never been formally schooled in proper manners. Having befriended him when he was but a caddy for the John Company, Thomas and Gregory hosted him in their respective homes on multiple occasions. A quick study, Todd quickly learned what he needed to know so he could at least pass in polite Society. He learned even more about the import business and used his instincts to figure out which products could find eager customers in Britain.

Now that he was an adult and had been employed in a position of some importance, traveled to India—twice—and owned a prestigious home in Cavendish Square, Todd seemed to have overcome his disadvantageous youth.

He still committed the occasional *faux pax*, but now he had people around him to help cover the mistakes.

"Mr. Hughes is an ass," Thomas stated. "Do not concern yourself with him. Besides, Miss Hughes recently accepted an offer of marriage from Michael Merriweather," he added with a wave of his hand.

His eyes widening at this bit of news, Todd finally allowed a grin. "Michael Merriweather once owned my house," he claimed. "One of Gregory's cousins, if I remember correctly?" he half-asked, his brows furrowing. He sobered. "Didn't he go to debtor's prison? I was quite sure I ended up with the house because he had to sell it. To cover his gambling debts."

"Indeed," Thomas replied with a nod. "The lucky bastard won a bet and made enough to get himself out of debt. Runs the Sans Souci Theatre in Leicester Square."

Todd chuckled as he considered the irony. If Michael Merriweather hadn't had to sell Grace Park, the mistress of the house he now owned could have been Charlotte Hughes. "I'm happy to hear things have worked out for him," he murmured.

He glanced up to find Thomas regarding him with a serious expression. "What is it?"

Thomas took a breath and held it for a moment. "Do consider my renewed offer to work here."

Todd regarded his friend for a moment. "Can you... can you offer a regular salary instead of merely... incentives?" he asked, obviously uncomfortable putting voice to the query.

Thomas blinked, realizing he may have misunderstood how Todd Vandermeer was paid by the East India Company. "I can offer a salary, of course, and a bonus based on the new business you bring into Wellingham Imports," he stated. "Fifteen-hundred a year. What say you?"

It was Todd's turn to blink. And blink again. "I'll be a rich man," he murmured.

Thomas straightened, a frown appearing. "I thought you already were," he countered.

Todd angled his head first to one side and then the other. "True, to some extent. However, I spent most of my funds on my house, and I find myself spending... just to spend. Deborah does not join me nor encourage me in such endeavors, although she has agreed to wear the jewelry I have purchased her as gifts."

Inhaling sharply, Thomas wondered if perhaps his friend had been encouraged to spend simply to appear as if he belonged in the Beau Monde.

Although Deborah had grown up in a middle-class household in Whitechapel, she had spent her adulthood—until her marriage to Todd—in relative squalor. As a midwife in a home for unwed mothers, she'd had a bare-bones, unheated room in which to sleep and nothing else. As her wedding gift, Todd had seen to buying a hotel to replace the old Home for Unwed Mothers in Newport Street. After a few weeks of renovations, the old Cooper Hotel in Oxford Street was now the new Mrs. Dawes' Home for Unwed Mothers, and Deborah was simply one of several midwives on staff.

Compared to the old home, living in a Cavendish Square mansion with twelve servants was probably a shock for the modest woman.

"Does that mean you'll accept my offer?" Thomas asked hopefully.

Todd allowed a wan smile. "I hope to. I wish to discuss this with Deborah."

Thomas didn't bother hiding his disappointment. He rather hoped the tall man would simply accept his offer outright and begin work on the morrow. "But, why?" he asked in a hoarse whisper.

Giving a slight shrug, Todd sighed. "She is my wife. She will be left alone for hours whilst I am here—"

"But it's not as far for you to travel to get here," Thomas countered. "Certainly your time on a phaeton will be far less than having to make the trip to the John Company and back every day."

Todd considered the comment. "True," he acknowledged. "Still, I promised I would speak with her about this. I wish to keep that promise. I will have my response for you by next week," he said with a nod.

Realizing he wasn't going to get the answer he was hoping for that moment, Thomas finally gave the man a matching nod. "Agreed," he replied.

With that, the two shook hands and Todd Vandermeer took his leave of Thomas' office.

As Todd made his way along the raised walkway to the stairs, he couldn't help but notice the name on the next office door down from Thomas'.

T. Vandermeer was painted in bold letters with the words, "Senior Broker" beneath.

A grin lighting his face, Todd almost turned around to let Thomas know he would accept the offer. His words to Deborah gave him pause, though, and he instead took his leave of Wellingham Imports.

CHAPTER 4

A MEETING WITH A BANKER

Meanwhile, at the Bank of England in Threadneedle Street

Gregory approached the doors to his bank and paused as a footman hurried to open one of them. He gave a nod to the liveried man, briefly wondering how long he had been in the bank's employ.

Although he didn't have an appointment with Sir William Burroughs, Gregory figured the summons he had received via that day's mail was enough to gain him entry into his uncle's office. He expected to have to wait a few minutes, given how Sir William's schedule was usually filled with meetings, but his knock on the banker's door was met with a gruff, "Come in!"

He turned the handle and opened the door enough to poke his head through the opening. "Reporting as ordered, Uncle," Gregory stated as he regarded the knight—and youngest son of a late duke—who sat behind a massive mahogany desk covered in a mess of papers.

"I was beginning to wonder if you'd already left London," Sir William said as he waved in his tallest nephew—the only son of the late Roger Grandby.

"Not as yet," Gregory replied as he moved to take the chair in front of his uncle's desk. Movement to his left had him pausing as he glanced in that direction and recognized one of his cousins. "Max?" he asked, his voice filled with disbelief when he realized the identity of the man seated behind a small clerk's desk in the front corner.

"Aye," replied the dark-haired man. He stood up and regarded Gregory with a huge grin. "Although I go by 'Andrew' these days. I haven't seen you in an age, Cousin."

Gregory regarded his younger cousin for a moment, stunned to find Maximilian Andrew Burroughs dressed in clothes and shoes better suited to a clerk than to the youngest son of a duke. "Whatever are you doing here?" he asked, his attention going to the small desk where his cousin had been seated.

"Finishing up some details before I return to Brighton on the morrow," Andrew replied, extending his right hand to Gregory. The taller man took it and gave it a good shake. "I have a position at the bank down there, but I sometimes find a reason to make an occasional visit to London," he added, as if he did so deliberately.

"You're a banker?" Gregory questioned in surprise. Given he had spent a good deal of the past few years traveling all over England in search of investment opportunities and to meet with clients and owners of companies, Gregory hadn't kept up on what his dozens of cousins had been doing. But to learn the youngest son of the Duke of Ariley was engaged in a trade was a surprise.

"I wasn't suited for a career in the military or the church," Andrew said, as if he could read his cousin's mind. "Uncle took me under his considerable wing a few years ago and taught me all about the banking business. I'll be taking over the head position at a bank in Bath by year's end."

Gregory shook his head, stunned by the man's words. "And your... family? I heard you married. Lady Bess Craven, wasn't it?"

The younger man nodded. "Indeed. They're all in Brighton at the moment. Two sons," he murmured, his eyes darting to one side as if he were trying to decide how much information to offer. He brightened. "I heard you've just been leg-shackled yourself."

The taller man smiled. "It's true. I married my best friend's sister. Bought half his house—Woodscastle—and now I'm shoulder deep in renovations and the mess that goes with it," he said with an arched eyebrow.

Andrew grinned. "Have you been back to Merriweather Manor recently?" he asked, referring to the estate home all the Grandbys, some of the Burroughs and, before that, the Merriweathers, had called home for the past few generations.

Gregory shook his head. "Been by it several times, of course. It's just down the road from Woodscastle, but I'm afraid there's only one family left living there, and I find I cannot bring myself to request a tour. I'm not sure of their plans for the place. It's become... shabby of late," he said with a hint of disappointment.

Indeed, ever since his stepfather, James Simpson, had left his position as the butler of the household in 1782, the place had begun to deteriorate. In the meantime, a particular street of townhouses in Kingly Street had been undergoing a transformation that made those townhouses some of the most sought after properties in London. Given his mother (and Sir William's sister), Sophia, owned that particular street, Gregory was quite sure James was responsible for overseeing the improvements. The man had an uncanny way with carpenters and construction crews, and he seemed to possess a vision for how buildings and their interiors should look.

"Such a shame," Andrew murmured, giving his uncle an arched eyebrow. "Why didn't you mention Merriweather Manor's condition when we spoke of it last night?"

Sir William gave his nephews a shrug. "Until it's vacated, there's little we can do about it, Max," he replied in his own defense. "If you truly feel it worthy of renovation, we can see to it when we have the funds," he said simply, not adding that the manor home was actually an entailed property of the Torrington earldom. Milton Grandby, Earl of Torrington, had only recently inherited the earldom and probably didn't know he owned the pile. Given the man's easy-going manner, however, Sir William was quite certain Grandby would welcome someone taking on the responsibility of renovating the property at some point.

Andrew gave his uncle a reluctant nod, as if he were disappointed to hear the man's answer. "I had rather hoped I would be raising my family there," he said, his response directed to Gregory. "But my work has me elsewhere these days, I suppose." He paused a moment. "Oh, my. I guess you're here because you have business with Uncle. Pardon me for having taken your time," he added, his crestfallen expression at odds with how happy he had been only the moment before.

Gregory shook his head. "It's quite all right, Max. I rather wish we could spend some time catching up," he remarked. "I'm actually here because I was summoned by our uncle," he added as he held up the missive that had come in that day's post. "But before you say anything, Sir William, please know that I am not about to delay my wedding trip another day. Christiana and I will be on a ship to Italy a week from today."

Sir William rolled his eyes and indicated the chair in front of his desk. Swiveling around in his own chair to snag a crystal decanter and some tumblers from the credenza behind him, Sir William waited until Gregory was seated before he spoke. "I may have... *exaggerated* the situation when I had my clerk write that letter," he hedged, pouring a finger's worth of brandy into the tumblers. He gave glasses to both nephews before holding up his own in a salute. "Cheers," he said before drinking his brandy in a single gulp.

Gregory and Andrew exchanged uncertain glances before repeating the word and taking sips from their own glasses. The younger man gave a nod to Gregory before he returned to his desk, apparently aware his input wouldn't be required in whatever Sir William had to say.

"Exaggerated?" Gregory repeated. "What the hell is going on, Uncle?" he asked, unable to hide the annoyance he felt at having to make what might be an unnecessary trip into London.

Sir William regarded his nephew for a moment before allowing a sigh. "I have reason to believe your mother will be considering an addition to the family," he stated finally.

Gregory blinked. And blinked again. *An addition to the*

family? As in... ? "Is she considering adopting a child?" he asked after a moment of stunned silence. "Am I to gain a brother or a sister?" he asked in a whisper. *Good God!* His mother was old enough to be... well, she wasn't too old to be a mother, he supposed, but if Christiana gave birth to a child within the year, as he wholly expected she would, given how often he paid attendance on her in their marriage bed, Gregory thought Sophia Simpson would soon be a grandmother. Another thought struck him and his eyes widened. "Is she... expecting?"

The older man interlaced his fingers and leaned forward as far as his rotund belly would allow. "Not as far as I know. Your stepfather mentioned it last night. At the club. Seems he's... he's feeling his mortality. He has no heir, and although he claims you're a better son than most, he admits he would welcome a child."

Several thoughts raced through Gregory's mind just then. What made James Simpson think that just because he wanted a child, Sophia would be able to provide one? The two had been married for...

"One-and-twenty years," Sir William stated, as if he could read Gregory's mind. "I have reason to believe they've been careful to avoid the very situation he finds himself desiring now."

Embarrassed at hearing his uncle speak of his mother and stepfather's private affairs, Gregory held up his hands in front of his body, palms out, and shook his head. "Am I expected to provide input on this? Because, truth be told, it's really none of my business," he murmured.

Sir William sat back in his leather chair and regarded his nephew for a moment. "So, I can't persuade you to talk the man out of it?" he asked in surprise.

Gregory blinked. "You're speaking to a man who is doing all he can to get a child on his bride—the sooner, the better— given we've decided on ten of them," he countered with an arched brow. "I am the very last man to persuade another not to at least *try*."

His expression rather contemplative, Sir William finally

nodded. "I suppose, when you put it like that, I can see my brother-in-law's point of view," he said with a sigh. "At least he only wants the one," he added with a slight grin.

It was Gregory's turn to roll his eyes. "Then let's hope my mother delivers a boy," he replied with not the least bit of humor. *If she can even conceive a child at this stage in her life*, was his last thought before he took his leave of the bank.

He was about to head back to Woodscastle, but realized he had the time to pay a call on his mother.

CHAPTER 5

A TOWNHOUSE TOUR

Meanwhile, at #4 Kingly Street, London

The sound of the front door opening and closing had Sophia setting aside her embroidery hoop, the needle safely tucked into the silk. She glanced at the clock on the mantel, rather surprised to see it wasn't yet time for the late luncheon she had requested of the cook. "I'm in the parlor, dear," she called out.

James Simpson appeared on the threshold a moment later, giving her a bow before he hurried to join her on the settee. His topcoat bore the unmistakable look of having been brushed out just the moment before. Given the renovation projects the man had been overseeing on one after the other of the townhouses they owned in Kingly Street, his boots usually displayed a layer of dust. Most days, the fastidious man was quick to wipe them upon entry into their vestibule, but Sophia noticed he hadn't yet cleaned them.

"You look rather lovely today," James remarked, lifting one of her hands so he could brush his lips over the back of it. He didn't release it, though, which had Sophia giving him a quizzical glance.

"And you're as handsome as ever," she countered, using her free hand to reach up and spear her fingers through the short hair near his graying temples. "With a bit of mischief mixed in, I should think. Whatever are you about?"

James had always been a handsome man, his short-cropped black hair and dark brows framing a face that featured a square jaw, a thin blade of a nose and eyes that were almost sapphire in color. Topped with long, dark lashes, those eyes had first captured her attention when she was a new bride in the Merriweather Manor household. She hadn't done anything to betray her husband, of course. Even after his death due to pneumonia, it was nearly six months of widowhood before she realized there might be something more to the man than his charm and good looks. Given their class difference, she had to be the one to make the first move, however.

James had taken the position of butler a few years before her arrival at Merriweather Manor. Although he was far younger than the man he replaced—there were concerns among some of the Grandbys in residence that he was too young to hold the lofty position—James' efficient but friendly way with the existing staff and all the children that lived at the manor soon silenced their concerns. Rather than ruling the household with an iron hand and an unyielding clock, he instead encouraged the servants to perform their duties at the times it made the most sense to do so.

Not only did the house seem cleaner as a result, but necessary maintenance was scheduled and performed without disruption to the day-to-day routines of the five families who lived there. It came as no surprise the man was missed when he resigned his position after seven years in service. It would have been a scandalous surprise if anyone learned exactly why he left Merriweather Manor.

"I do think you are the most debonair man I know," Sophia stated.

James allowed a grin, and Sophia thought for a moment a touch of red colored his face. "Ah, compliments! Should I be expecting a request for something?" he teased.

Sophia's eyes widened before a blush colored her face. "I cannot help that I find you desirable," she whispered, aware a maid was setting the dining table in the next room. "Especially after how you behaved this morning." This last was said with an elegantly arched eyebrow.

The back of her hand was bestowed with another kiss. "I find my thoughts going to you far more frequently these days," he said in a quiet voice. "Especially now that, well, I have something to show you, and something rather important I wish to discuss with you."

A mix of excitement and dread filled Sophia just then. She, too, had something important to discuss with her husband, but at no point in the past month had there been an appropriate time to bring up the topic. "Show and tell, then?" she answered as brightly as she could muster.

James straightened and allowed a smile. "Agreed. First, though, I must explain myself."

Sophia swallowed, the weight of a stone having dropped into her stomach. "What have you done?"

Shaking his head quickly, James said, "Oh, it's not *bad*, my sweeting. At least, I think you will like it very much. You see, I know when you first bought these townhouses—"

"We," Sophia interrupted.

James angled his head.

"When *we* bought these townhouses," Sophia amended.

It was hard for James to think he had anything to do with the acquisition of the entire street of properties in Kingly Street. The purchase had been made with Sophia's inheritance money. Then, when she reached her majority, her father, the Duke of Ariley, had given her additional monies, funds she and James could live on for the rest of their lives if they did so modestly. For his part of the bargain, James had merely agreed to see to the renovations and maintenance—an arrangement that suited his skills perfectly. "When *we* first bought these townhouses, I know that you chose this one to live in because it was the best of the lot at the time."

"And the perfect size for the two of us," Sophia agreed with a nod. "Cozy. Easily maintained. We only require a few servants," she added with a nod.

James' eyes darted to one side. "Well, now that it's been twenty years, I am of the opinion it's time for you to have a house better suited to your station in life," he continued, giving the back of her hand another kiss.

Sophia's eyes widened before she frowned. "Whatever—?"

"You're a duke's daughter. You deserve far better than what a man who worked in service can provide," James interrupted. "But I believe I've found a way. Will you take a walk with me? It's not far. Just across the street. You won't even require a pelisse as the weather is perfect just now."

Her curiosity piqued, Sophia gave a reluctant nod and stood when James helped her from the settee. "Is this about the last townhouse? The one that's had you so vexed these past six months or more?" she queried, remembering how he seemed to be spending an inordinate amount of time on the renovations of the last townhouse.

The tenants of the others had always been pleased with his renovation results, even if it meant they had to vacate for part of their lease. When they returned, some made offers to buy the houses. Although they had never sold any of them, the idea that they could assured Sophia that they could fatten the coffers and make it possible for James to continue seeing to the maintenance and renovation of the others if circumstances required it. Lease income helped pay for their living expenses and afforded them a rather comfortable lifestyle.

"I wouldn't say it's been vexing, exactly," James replied as they made their way out the front door. He turned to lock it before offering his arm. "I merely wanted it to be perfect, since I would like us to live there."

Sophia nearly stopped in the middle of the street, but a horse and rider might have run her down if she had. "Live there?" she repeated as they reached the walkway in front of the house in question.

James allowed a grin as they approached the bright white townhouse across the street and down one from their own. Redone from its Georgian roots, it now looked like a modern house in the Palladian style. Wrought iron railings, curved to hold decorative flower boxes beneath each window, had been installed the week before, and the boxes had just been filled with a variety of autumn flowers that very morning. The front doors were painted a dark green. A brass knocker featuring the head of an elephant was polished to a high shine, its curved trunk providing the knocker. A shallow portico was supported by two Grecian columns on either side of the doors.

"There's not much of a yard, I'm afraid," James said as he used a key to open one of the front doors.

"But the gardener has done a remarkable job with what's here," she countered, noting how the boxwoods lining the wrought iron fence didn't even look as though they had been transplanted from somewhere else—they were already filled in and trimmed flat along their tops. Despite the row of late summer flowers blooming along the front of the house, there was still a strip of lawn separating the shrubs from the flowers. "And it's more yard than we have across the street." Indeed, their townhouse's only claim to greenery was a series of large flower pots positioned on either side of their front door.

Just as Sophia was about to enter the house, James lifted her into his arms. He ignored her yelp of protest and carried her over the threshold, closing the door with a swift kick of his boot before finally setting her on her slippered feet when they were in the middle of the vestibule. One of his hands moved to take hers, as if he thought she might turn and run away.

"This is... *huge*," she murmured as she slowly turned in a circle. Her eyes took in the dark green silk-covered walls and a series of framed paintings before they traveled up to the ceiling, where cherubs played in puffy clouds. Despite the closed front doors, light still filled the vestibule from the transom above the entry.

"Well, that would be because part of this room used to be the parlor," James remarked with an arched eyebrow. "And because it is the largest townhouse on the street," he added, watching closely for her reaction to the decor. "Although it's still not quite as grand as those in Park Lane."

Sophia tore her attention from where it had come to rest on

the table just inside the main hall. One of her favorite crystal vases displayed a bouquet that looked as if it contained every red rose from all the greenhouses in Chiswick. "Grand?" she repeated. "Why, this is more beautiful than any of them."

James allowed a proud grin. "I do hope you still hold that opinion when you've completed your tour," he said as he led her to room after room on the main floor. The library already displayed leather-bound books on the shelves and smelled of vanilla and vellum. The repositioned parlor was completely furnished in cherrywood and green velvet and floral-upholstered chairs. Lamps had been placed on several tables, and some of Sophia's favorite miniatures decorated the fireplace mantel. The study, furnished with a rather masculine desk and overstuffed chairs, looked as if it was already in use.

"So, this is where you've been hiding," Sophia murmured as she moved around the mahogany desk to glance at large, curled sheets displaying floor plans. Stacks of fabric swatches and paint colors littered the remaining desktop.

"Indeed," James replied, rocking on his heels. "There's a kitchen, of course, and a dining room and a breakfast parlor..."

At the mention of the breakfast parlor, Sophia whirled to face him. "Oh, James, is this what you've been doing every day for the past... six months?" she asked in a whisper.

He nodded, not about to admit it had been far longer. Once he knew the tenants intended to move to the country, he had set to work on the plans and ordered the furnishings. "Yes, but it didn't start out that way. The work was halfway done when I realized I wasn't doing it for anyone but you. I cannot abide anyone else living here but you. Us," he amended with a sigh.

Sophia blinked. She raised herself up on tiptoes and kissed him on his lips, rather happy when his arms moved to wrap around her waist and keep her pressed against the front of his body.

"You like it, then?" he whispered before returning the kiss.

Sophia sighed. "Well, I rather love what I've seen so far. I suppose I won't know for sure until I've seen the bedchamber," she added with a teasing grin.

"Yours or mine?"

Blinking as she settled back to her feet, Sophia regarded James for several seconds, a look of disappointment crossing her features before she offered a reply. "There isn't just the *one?*" she asked, suspicion evident in her voice.

Separate bedchambers.

Had she taken to snoring these past few years? Tossing about so the bed covers left him exposed to the cold? He hadn't said a word of protest, but then, James would never do such a thing. He was far too accommodating. Far too polite. Far too loving to say anything that might offend her.

James realized his mistake immediately and allowed an audible sigh. "You have to *choose* a bedchamber for us, my sweeting," he said in earnest. "I will merely use the other when I am dressing." After a moment, he added in a whisper, "If you think for one moment I will allow you to sleep alone, let me assure you, I still intend to warm your bed."

Allowing a wan smile, Sophia realized then just how badly James wanted to impress her. But to what end? She had never found him lacking in any regard. He had always been attentive. Accommodating. Loving. So what had him so nervous? So eager to please. So...

Eager to earn her approval?

"Show me, then," she ordered lightly, realizing he was acting as if he were her servant. He had always said working in service was an honor for him. *At least I can honor him*, she figured.

James led her out of the study and up the stairs, heartened to hear her compliments about the white Italian marble that covered the floors and made up the stairs and the series of caryatids that lined the main floor hall. At the first bedchamber, he paused before opening the door. "I thought I might use this one," he said cautiously. "But if you prefer it, then it shall be yours."

Sophia regarded him a moment before stepping over the threshold into a bedchamber obviously meant for a man. Deep blues and a few dark-wood furnishings, most notably a wardrobe, were set upon a patterned carpet of blues and browns.

Although it wasn't completely furnished, she knew it would only require a chest of drawers and possibly a bed to make it usable. "Definitely yours," she murmured. She started to turn around, but James gave a slight shake of his head and pointed to a door in one corner. "Through there," he said quietly.

Making her way into the dressing room, Sophia gave a start when she noticed most of her winter gowns had already been hung up on a series of pegs. Cubbyholes contained most of James' shirts, breeches, and waistcoats, and shoes were lined up beneath it all. "Goodness. It looks as if we're already moved in," she murmured.

Two doors featured in the dressing room, and Sophia gave him a glance before opening the one in the middle of the long wall. A bathing chamber with a huge tub, tiled floor, and a Brahma toilet appeared. She inhaled sharply, about to inform him she didn't need to see anything else when he murmured, "There's a gas-fed hot water heater in the corner."

Sophia giggled, her delight bringing a smile to James' face. "Oh, James. You do know you had me at 'breakfast parlor,'" she murmured happily.

He frowned. "But you haven't even seen the mistress suite," he complained.

Guessing the mistress suite was through the other door in the dressing room, Sophia quickly made her way there. She stopped short on entering the bedchamber, her gasp rather loud in the quiet house. "Oh, James," she breathed as she took in the sight of a room decorated entirely in deep purples and lavenders.

"It is your favorite color, is it not?" he asked carefully, watching her closely as her hands went to her throat and her body spun about as if she were trying to take it all in as quickly as possible.

Her arms were around him in an instant, her lips on his in a crushing kiss he had barely begun to return when she suddenly pulled away. "Of course, it is," she breathed before relaxing into his hold. "Oh, James, thank you," she murmured. "I've a mind to make love to you right this very moment..." She turned around and realized that, although a counterpane covered the bed, there were no bed linens beneath. "But I suppose I can wait a few minutes."

Taking a deep breath of relief, James sighed. "You're welcome, my sweeting," he murmured. A new nervousness gripped him though. "Would you be up to seeing just one more room?" he asked. "It's just across the hall."

Sophia considered what she could tell him then. What she *should* tell him. His idea of a larger townhouse was a good one, considering the situation. "And what room might that be?" she asked lightly, deciding now wasn't quite the right time.

James placed a hand on her arm and led her out of the mistress suite and across the carpeted hall. He took a deep breath before opening the door.

Sophia gave him a nervous glance before leaning in to discover a bassinet, a rocking chair, and a crib in a room that had been painted a pale yellow. Inhaling sharply, she straightened and regarded him with a look of surprise. "How... ? How did you *know?*" she asked in bewilderment.

James blinked. And blinked again. "Know what?" he countered in confusion.

Feeling light-headed, Sophia welcomed his arms around her waist. Appreciated how he lifted her into his arms and quickly moved back to the mistress suite. He had her settled onto the bed in a moment, his worried gaze concentrated on her face. "Sweeting? Are you all right? It certainly wasn't my intention to have you fainting during the house tour!"

A burble of a chuckle sounded. Sophia grasped one of his hands and moved it to her middle. Holding it there, she allowed a sigh. "How did you know I am with child?" she asked in wonder.

James blinked. And blinked again. "I... I didn't." After another moment, he added, "But given that I was about to ask you if you would give me an heir, I do believe I am the one who is about to faint."

Giggling with relief at hearing his words, Sophia pulled her husband down to the bed and held him close. "Then let us hope

I am carrying a boy," she said happily. "But if I am not, then I shall demand your services until I bear you an heir. You will service me, will you not, husband?" she asked in a voice full of amusement.

James responded with a hearty laugh. "I am always honored to serve you, my lady."

Despite the lack of bed linens, James saw to his wife's pleasure well into the late afternoon, until hunger forced them to dress and return to their old townhouse for a very late luncheon.

CHAPTER 6

MARITAL DISCUSSIONS

Later that night

"So, tell me your thoughts."

Deborah stared at her husband for a moment before she allowed a rather large smile. "It sounds... wonderful. It sounds exactly like what you had hoped."

"It is," Todd agreed, one of his hands gripping hers as they sat next to each other in the back gardens at Grace Park. Although it wasn't yet dark, the lanterns lining the path through the formal gardens were already lit, the slight wind making them appear as if lightning bugs provided the light.

"So, why didn't you accept the offer?" Deborah asked in alarm.

Todd blinked and straightened on the stone bench. "I distinctly remember telling you that I would discuss it with you. This change in employers will make a vast difference in my life," he replied quickly. "Working for Wellingham Imports won't have the same... caché as the East—"

"Caché?" Deborah repeated in surprise. "I hardly think caché is as important as how much you'll earn or how you will be treated by your superiors. Aren't those considerations more important?"

Frowning at her question, Todd considered how to respond. To someone who had grown up in Whitechapel, perhaps caché wasn't important. Perhaps the other considerations were more important. But he had spent his entire life working for a firm known throughout the world for the products they imported. For their importance in politics and trade policy. For their fleet of ships and the new docks that were still under construction. The East India Company had resources. Influence. Money. Wellingham Imports had... well they had two docks, at least. And an overland transport network.

"You don't work there anymore," Deborah whispered, as if she could read his mind. "You helped to get them where they are now, but even you said they are becoming more important politically than they are as a trader."

"So you agree it's time for me to move on?" Todd asked, squeezing her hand again.

It was Deborah's turn to frown. "I was under the impression you already had," she replied.

Todd lifted his head and finally nodded. "I can start any time at Wellingham's. They already have an office set up for me," he said with the hint of a grin touching the corners of his mouth. "My name is painted on the glass in the door."

Deborah blinked and straightened on the bench. "And yet you thought you had to discuss it with *me?*" she whispered in surprise. "Mr. Vandermeer—"

"Todd," he insisted. He glanced around where they sat, the greenery hiding them from the neighboring townhouses and those who strolled in Cavendish Square.

"I rather think you were a fool to have said you would think about it—"

"A fool?" he countered, the grin disappearing.

Allowing a sigh, Deborah realized he had taken offense at the comment. "I didn't mean it like that. I didn't mean to offend. I just... you're finally getting what you deserve. Recognition for your abilities. Commensurate pay. Better pay, if what you said is true," she added, remembering how shocked she'd been at hearing what his annual salary would be at Wellingham Imports. "It hardly matters if Wellingham Imports is small now.

You shall help make it a large company. You shall be the one to give it caché," she added with an encouraging grin.

Her husband allowed a long sigh. "I knew you would know what to say," he whispered, lifting her hand to his lips to kiss her fingertips. "And I probably was a fool not to simply accept—"

"I love you," Deborah whispered, her free hand moving up to cup his cheek as her lips took purchase on his. The kiss was interrupted when she let out a squeak, though, his arms around her middle, pulling her up onto his lap so his face was pressed into the side of her neck. A moment later, his kisses trailed down to her shoulders and then along her collarbones. When he pulled away, he allowed a sigh. "I love you."

Although he intended to tell her more, to ask for her opinion about something else entirely, Todd found his thoughts entirely redirected.

CHAPTER 7

A STEPSON PUTS VOICE TO
HIS CONCERN

Meanwhile, at #4 Kingly Street

James and Sophia had just returned to their old townhouse when a maid hurried from the dining room. "A letter just came for you, Mr. Simpson," she said as she held out the white missive and bobbed a curtsy. "From Mr. Grandby. I was just about to leave it next to your plate," she added as she handed it over to the man of the house. She turned to Sophia, "And Mr. Grandby says I was to tell you he'll be by to take you for supper tomorrow at one o'clock."

Sophia blinked, realizing right away the maid referred to her son and not one of her brothers-in-law. "Did he say anything else?" she asked in surprise, rather disappointed she had missed her only child's visit and that his missive was directed to her husband. She glanced up to find James already reading the letter.

"No, milady. Other than he wished me a happy day." The young woman beamed in delight, as if Gregory Grandby's simple words had accomplished the task all by themselves.

"Is it too late for luncheon?" Sophia asked then, her attention back on the servant. "We were across the street far longer than we planned."

The maid shook her head. "I'll let cook know you're ready to be served, milady. Oh, and when would her ladyship like the rest of her clothes to be moved to the new house?" she asked.

Sophia blinked. *Am I the last to know?* She gave James a quelling glance. "Tomorrow will be soon enough," she replied. "Or even the next day."

"Very good, milady." The maid curtsied again and hurried off to the back of the townhouse.

James kissed the top of Sophia's head, knowing the maid's words had upset her. "The servants were sworn to secrecy, my sweeting," he whispered. "And they are ready to make the move whenever we give the word. Please do not be angry with them."

Sighing, Sophia angled her head to one side. "I'm not *angry*. I just feel..." She brightened at the thought of moving into the other townhouse, of the breakfast parlor, and the nursery, and her bedchamber.

Their bedchamber.

"A bit overwhelmed, I think," she finally added. "I'm getting an entirely new home, and I haven't had to lift a finger. Why, someone could accuse me of being my mother," she complained lightly.

James blinked. "My sweeting, at no point—at any time in the past, present, or future—could anyone confuse the two of you," he said. He had met his mother-in-law only the one time, and that had been a year or more before he married Sophia.

"Now, what had my son visiting, pray tell?" she asked as she indicated the note James still held in one hand. "I thought he and my daughter-in-law would be off to Italy by now."

Her husband ushered her into the dining room. "It seems your son wants to meet me at White's tonight. And he and his bride are not off to Italy until next week. Your new daughter requested a delay so she could finish choosing the fabrics and colors for some of the children's rooms," he explained as he pulled a chair out for her.

Sophia frowned. "That seems rather odd. She's had weeks to choose—"

"It's vexing, I tell you," James interrupted her with an arched eyebrow, amusement evident in his voice. "Positively vexing.

Every decision feels as if you're making a mistake," he added as he took the carver at the other end of the table. "Every decision feels as if it weighs too much. As if you'll be crushed under the enormity of it. When you see it after it's all done, you wonder how it came together so well. Except for the nursery. I now find myself wishing I had chosen a robin egg's blue rather than the pale yellow."

Giggling, Sophia regarded James for a moment. "If it matters that much, you can certainly change it, darling," she murmured. "It is just a visit to the colorman." She paused a moment, still curious as to why her son had paid a visit. "Do you suppose he just wants to play cards?" she asked lightly, hoping it wasn't something more serious. She had always been glad the two men in her life got along as well as they did, Gregory respecting James' position as his stepfather despite the man having been born to a lower class. But then Gregory spent his days in a form of trade, earning a living by investing his inheritance in all sorts of British-based businesses. Although he occasionally lost money when a firm suffered losses due to fires or the weather, he usually made money. Indeed, his earnings were seeing to the upkeep of the family estate in Derbyshire as well the renovation of Woodscastle and the wedding trip to Italy.

"I've absolutely no idea," James replied, giving the missive another read-through. "But I'll find out at seven o'clock." He paused a moment. "May I tell him our good news? Or would you prefer to be the one to tell him?"

Sophia considered the question a moment. "I suppose he should know before he leaves," she reasoned. "I can tell him tomorrow at supper if you don't do so tonight." She angled her head and a small grin appeared. "Why, it's possible he'll have a younger sibling even before he returns to these shores."

James nodded, although his expression grew serious. "I do hope ours will be born before his first child," he remarked. "I shouldn't wish to be a grandfather before I'm a father, after all."

Almost giddy at the thought, Sophia had to suppress another giggle. "I am so relieved you want to be a father," she murmured. "I've spent the past month wondering how you would react to the news."

"A month?" he repeated in shock. "I knew you were good at keeping secrets, but—"

"I was... unsure of how you would react to the news," she reasoned, one shoulder lifted slightly.

"Likewise, I'm sure," James replied as he lifted his wine glass. "To us," he whispered.

Sophia grinned. "To us," she repeated. "All of us."

CHAPTER 8

AN EVENING AT WHITE'S

#17 St. James Street, London

The crowd at White's was rather subdued at seven o'clock in the evening. The older gentlemen enjoyed brandy and cheroots before departing for their homes and their dinners or the theatre while the younger bucks played cards or studied the betting books. James arrived to discover his stepson already seated in a wingback chair, the bowl of a lit pipe held in one hand.

"A penny for your thoughts, Mr. Grandby," James said as he approached the younger man.

Gregory grinned as he stood and shook the man's hand. "You'd go broke, I fear," he replied. "I don't believe I've had ten minutes to just *think* for the past month," he added in complaint. "And now I'm attempting to make up for it all at once."

James frowned. "Problems with an investment?" he asked in concern as he took the chair adjacent to Gregory's. A small side table in between held a drink and a pouch of tobacco.

The taller man shook his head. "No. All those seem to be going rather well," he replied. "It's the planning for the wedding trip—I want it to be perfect, you see, and... well, the renovations on the house..." He paused and angled his head. "Have you finished yours yet?" he queried. Although James had far more experience with renovating old properties, the man had second-guessed himself on several decisions and put voice to his concerns on a number of occasions with his stepson.

The older man nodded. "I gave her the tour today."

"Ah. I thought that's where you might have been," Gregory replied with a grin. "So? What did she think? She loved it, didn't she?"

James nodded. "Turns out, it could have just had a breakfast parlor, and she would have been happy. Well, that, and..." He stopped and wondered how to broach the subject of the nursery.

"Did you ask her about an heir?"

His stepfather blinked and stared at him a moment before he rolled his eyes. "Sir William spoke with you, didn't he?" he half-asked, his manner more serious. "Damn that man."

"He was... concerned," Gregory replied. "And I can't say I blame him, but... you two have been married twenty—"

"One-and-twenty."

"—Years, and I find it hard to believe the subject is only now an issue," the younger man continued. "However, I told Uncle it wasn't really any of my business anyway. I'm busy with my own bride..." He stopped, his face coloring when he realized how his words could be interpreted.

"I should hope so," James replied, not the least bit offended by the topic of conversation. "Mrs. Grandby made it very clear she wanted ten children, and I find it admirable you're of the same opinion. Your mother and I were *not* upon the occasion of our marriage, however," he explained. "We'd both had quite enough of being surrounded by all those children—all your dozens of cousins—and just wanted to make our properties the best they could be."

Gregory blinked, realizing he might have misunderstood what his uncle had said to him earlier that day. "What changed?"

James inhaled slowly and sighed. "Except for the townhouse we currently occupy, all the renovations are complete. I've given your mother the home of her dreams. Our dreams. And I woke up to discover we have no one to share it with." He paused, a rather sad expression crossing his face. He brightened, though. "Well, at least, not yet."

His eyes darting to one side, Gregory straightened in his chair. "So, you spoke with her, then?"

Taking a sip of the brandy a footman had just delivered, James allowed a moment to pass before he shook his head. "I didn't have to. Your mother has already seen to it, bless her heart. Turns out, she didn't know how to bring up the topic, either, so it took seeing the nursery before she told me she's expecting. If all goes well, you'll have a sibling within six months."

A slow smile spread over Gregory's face. "You dog!"

James nodded quickly. "I am, indeed. And rather relieved. Those French letters are damned expensive and hard to come by," he whispered. He didn't add that he found the odor of vinegar not the least bit conducive to lovemaking, but the fact that Sophia had been willing to use sponges when he had no French letters was a testament to their initial commitment.

"She's six-and-forty," Gregory stated, a look of worry crossing his face.

"Four-and-forty, actually. I'll be fifty in a couple of years,"

Gregory sighed. "You do realize you'll be a grandparent and a father about the same time."

James smiled broadly. "I can hardly wait!"

Surprised at his stepfather's enthusiastic response, Gregory finally allowed a nod. "Well, then, I suppose I need to do what I must to see to my own heir," he murmured before knocking back the finger's worth of brandy in his glass. He squeezed his eyes shut as the amber liquor burned the back of this throat.

"You've got time, Gregory," James said quietly. "Go on your wedding trip. Enjoy yourself. Eat well, and make love, and you'll be a father before you know it."

Gregory resisted the urge to snort. "You do realize these will be the longest five or six months of your life," he stated as he leaned forward. *And mine as well,* he thought, given the travels he had planned for his new bride.

James nodded. "I am well aware," he replied, uncertainty betraying his words. "Well aware."

CHAPTER 9

A FUTURE IN THE PLANNING

Later that night

"You're home early," Sophia said as she met her husband in the vestibule. "I didn't expect you for hours."

James bussed her on the cheek. "Your son just wanted to talk, my sweet. No cards tonight," he replied, wondering if he would have to tell her about their conversation.

He had to tell her.

"I know it isn't any of my business, but will you tell me why he wished to speak with you?" she asked carefully. "I admit to being *worried*. Is Christiana all right? Has something happened—?"

"Sir William told him I wanted an heir," James stated as he placed a hand at her back and led her to the parlor.

Sophia nearly stopped in her tracks as her eyes went to his. "What? How does my brother know such a thing?" she asked, and then allowed a huff when she realized James must have spoken with Sir William. "I suppose he's not too happy with you," she murmured as she sat down. James joined her, his arm still at her back.

"He is not. I think your son is concerned as well," he added. "But just a bit."

"Because I'm old."

James couldn't help but allow a grin. "You're not *old*, my

sweet. You're perfect," he countered. "At least he'll have a sibling before he's a father, and I had the distinct impression he's rather looking forward to it. By the way, he and Christiana will be leaving for Italy in a week."

Sophia stared at the flames in the fireplace, rather heartened by her husband's quick rejoinder. "You'll be a father before you're a grandfather," she murmured. "It is better that way." She turned to find James staring at her, his eyes darting to her middle. "What is it?"

"May I?" he asked as he moved a hand beneath her bosom and pressed lightly.

Sophia placed one of her hands over his, interlacing his fingers with her own so she could move his hand down an inch or so. "It will be some time before you'll be able to feel anything," she warned.

James moved his hand to her shoulder and pulled her into a hug. "I do hope you know just how much this means to me. That you would give me a child. It doesn't even have to be an heir," he added before kissing her temple. "Although I shall feel greatly outnumbered if you have a daughter. There are only so many fingers I can be wrapped around."

Giggling, Sophia returned the hug and settled her head onto his chest. "Are we really moving into the other house on the morrow?" she asked, vaguely aware the servants in the house had been busy surreptitiously wrapping and placing knick knacks into drawers. Several pieces of furniture were missing from the parlor, and some paintings were no longer on the walls.

She felt his nod and sighed. "I didn't even look at the guest bedchambers—"

"There are three of them," James stated as he lightly rubbed her back. "And I rather imagine it will take more than just a day or two to complete the move."

"Or give the parlor a glance—"

"There's a salon for you, as well, with a new escritoire and a fireplace and a Grecian lounge." The escritoire had been a splurge. He didn't dare tell her he'd ordered it from Chippendale's studio.

"Sounds divine," she murmured, her voice sounding far away.

"Servants' quarters are on the top floor, and there's an attic above that." He waited a moment for her to respond, but knew she would not. The tell-tale rhythm of her breathing had him allowing a grin and a sigh.

She was sound asleep.

CHAPTER 10

ON THE EVE OF A TRIP

October 1, 1802

"Was it your intention to take everything you own?" Gregory asked as he took in the sight of the two large Louis Vuitton trunks and three valises that lined one wall of the mistress suite.

Having just come from a tour of his mother's new residence, he was well aware of how much could be stuffed into a trunk. With several new servants hurrying about setting up the household and a parade of footmen sent from an agency in Oxford Street, the move would no doubt be done before the dinner bell chimed. Lady Sophia Simpson finally had the house he had always thought she deserved, and he had his stepfather to thank.

He was still finding her other news rather difficult to believe. At least they'd had supper together the week before. It gave him an opportunity to assure her of his support. He knew she wouldn't get it from her brother, Sir William, and probably not from any of her friends, either.

Christiana gave him an uncertain glance. "Do you think I've forgotten anything?" she countered, worried. "My maid saw to the packing —"

Gregory interrupted her reply with a kiss on her lips. "I was teasing, dear heart," he murmured. "I didn't think you owned enough gowns to fill two trunks."

"Oh, I don't," she replied with a shake of her strawberry blonde curls. "One of those has slippers, and reticules, and bonnets, and fans, and..." She allowed the sentence to trail off when she noted his look of shock. "But neither trunk is full, I promise. Emma said I should be sure to leave room in case I acquire anything in Italy. I mean, in case *you* should buy me anything," she corrected, one eyebrow arched in a tease.

For a second, Gregory thought he might have to thank his sister-by-marriage for her recommendation. He rather doubted there would be room in their ship's cabin for yet another trunk should they need to acquire one for the trip home. They were only scheduled to be gone four months, and that was down from the six-month tour he had originally planned. Given their late start, he had decided to forgo a visit to Greece. At least there would be porters to see to their luggage when they landed at the port near Rome. He couldn't imagine having to manage all the pieces they were taking as it was.

"I'm quite sure we'll come home with more than we're taking," he acknowledged with an amused expression. He sobered though and placed his hands on either side of her head. His fingers explored her neck and the space below her collarbones before he dropped to one knee and placed an ear against her chest. He listened a moment and finally pulled away to look up at her. "I do hope you're feeling better than you were last week," he murmured, concern evident in his voice.

Christiana's eyes widened. Although she was used to his examinations—Gregory had studied anatomy and could have been a physician if he'd chosen the profession—she was still surprised by his last comment. "I feel fine," she replied. At least, now she did. For a few weeks, she had felt terribly tired and avoided spending too much time in the dining room during breakfast.

"I'm rather glad to hear it. I do hope you won't suffer from sea sickness."

She blinked at the comment. Not ever having traveled on a ship before, she had no idea how she would react to the week or more they would be on the Mediterranean. "Me, too," she agreed. "What about you?"

Gregory shrugged. "Depends on how rough the seas get, I suppose." He paused a moment, deciding now was as good a time as any to tell her of the conversation he'd had with his mother whilst they toured the house. She had dropped her *on-dit* the moment after she opened the door to the nursery, her other hand moving protectively to her belly. *I do hope you're not terribly vexed at the idea of a baby brother or sister*, she had murmured, her face taking on a pink blush that made her look almost like a young, blonde English miss at her first ball.

What could he do but allow a shake of his head and a shrug? At least his stepfather had given him the news the night before, so he'd had some time to think on it. Now he thought it best to tell Christiana the news. "By the way, it seems I'll be an older brother a month or so after our return."

Pausing in her attempt to loop earrings through her pierced earlobes, Christiana glanced at his reflection in the looking glass above her dressing table. "Whatever do you mean?" She turned around to regard him directly, her eyes widening.

"My mother is expecting a baby. Could be late March or early April," he stated before finally allowing a grin. The more he thought about Sophia Simpson having a child, the more comfortable he felt with the idea. Perhaps holding her babe would help prepare him for whenever Christiana gave birth to their first.

Christiana sat down on the bed, her mouth open and her eyes darting about nervously. "Oh?" she managed to get out. "Oh, my. Well, this is unexpected." She brightened after a moment. "But she'll certainly be in good company."

Gregory frowned. "Whatever do you mean?"

She shrugged. "Although she has not yet admitted she is having a baby, Emma and I are of the opinion that Mrs. Vandermeer is due to have a baby about that same time," she replied. "And mine is probably due a month or so later." She held her breath, curious as to how Gregory might react to her news.

Although she had been tempted to tell him she was expecting, she thought to break the news whilst they were in Italy, perhaps during a tour of one of his favorite ancient locations. She rather liked the attention he was paying her in their marriage bed and feared he wouldn't sleep with her once she was *enceinte.*

"Jesus. Todd will be over the moon," Gregory replied with a grin. "I wonder when Deborah will tell him?" He gave the thought another moment and added, "Probably the very day he finally starts a position at Wellingham Imports..." His voice trailed off before he frowned. "Mine is due?" he repeated.

"Well, *ours is due*, I suppose I should have said," Christiana replied, angling her head to one side. "I'm well past the time I had the miscarriage with the first one, so I'm quite sure..."

Her words were swallowed up as Gregory's hands gripped her shoulders and his lips took purchase on hers, his kiss almost punishing in its intensity. He pulled away nearly as quickly. "Why... why didn't you *say* something?" he asked in alarm.

"I just did," she replied, her expression one of wide-eyed innocence.

"Who else knows?"

Christiana blinked, rather surprised by the question. "Well, no one." She sighed and rolled her eyes. "Well, Mrs. Dawes knows. I went to see her at Grace Park a few weeks ago. Just to be sure, you see, but I've told no one else." Although the midwife had married the Grace Park butler just the month before, everyone still referred to her as "Mrs. Dawes".

Gregory sat down on the bed—hard—and regarded her with a mix of shock and happiness. "You've known for three weeks, and you're just now telling me?" he asked, annoyance in his voice.

Lifting her fingers to run them through his short hair, Christiana gave him a peck on the cheek. "I wanted to, believe me, but you've been so busy with the renovations on the house and planning our trip, I didn't think it fair to burden you with one more thing to be concerned about."

"You *minx!*" he nearly shouted. An arm snaked around her

middle and pulled her atop his lap, his chuckle of delight swallowed up by her kiss. When she pulled away, she regarded him with an arched eyebrow.

"You still have to make love to me every night," she stated in a whisper. "Or, almost every night."

Gregory blinked. "I do?"

"Mrs. Dawes says I'll have an easier delivery if you do."

Gregory blinked again. "Does she now?" he replied before clearing his throat. Did the midwife really know of what she spoke? Or did she think that, as an expectant husband, he would seek a different bedmate until the babe was born? He had certainly known of a few gentleman who did, although they were some men who weren't particularly fond of their wives—pregnant or not.

He allowed a grin before giving a one-shouldered shrug. "If you insist, then I shall continue to be at your beck and call," he said in a voice that suggested it would be a chore. "I rather imagine I shall be *exhausted* the entire time we're in Italy."

"You bounder!" she accused happily. Then she sobered. "Let's not tell anyone just yet. Then, I shall be round with child when we return from our trip."

His eyes darting to one side, Gregory wondered if he could keep her condition a secret for the rest of the day. "I'll try not to say anything, but I might accidentally let it slip that I'm about to become a father," he warned. He paused a moment before adding, "And a brother."

"And a godfather, if Mr. Vandermeer gets his wish to have you take on that role for his child," Christiana said in a teasing voice.

For a moment, she was quite sure her husband was about to faint, for Gregory's face took on an expression of bewilderment she had never before seen him display.

"Perhaps we can simply *move* to Italy," he suggested before he lifted her into his arms. Christiana squealed in delight as he tossed her onto the bed.

A moment later, she was squealing in delight for an entirely different reason.

CHAPTER 11

FAREWELLS

The next day

"Whatever you do, don't get lost," Thomas ordered as he gave Gregory's hand a shake.

The taller man huffed. "I have been to Italy before. Twice, in fact," he countered with an arched brow. Impeccably dressed in Nankeen breeches, a scarlet topcoat and a navy waistcoat, and sporting a short top hat and a pair of black Hessians, Gregory looked as if he would be having dinner at the Carleton Hotel instead of at the captain's table.

His attention went to the deck of the *Fair Winds*, where Emma and Christiana were standing at the railing under colorful parasols. One of the sails had just been released from its moorings, the canvas slowly filling with that morning's breeze. "With any luck, we shall be back on British shores by the end of February," he added.

"I can't say I'm very comfortable with you traveling during the winter," Thomas countered, his brows furrowed.

"It won't be winter where we'll be, though," Gregory claimed. "Not like here." He allowed a shrug. "I'll write when we arrive." With that, Gregory moved to the ramp and hurried up, Thomas at his heels so that he could collect Emma.

Thomas gazed at his sister, reminded of their earlier

encounter. Before they had departed Woodscastle, he had reached out and pulled his sister into a hug. "I can hardly believe it," he had whispered. "This will be a first for us, you must know."

Christiana had pulled out of the hug and looked up at him in bewilderment. "Whatever do you mean?" she had asked.

"We have never been as far apart as we will be when you are on the Continent," he reasoned, a smile appearing at the end of the comment.

Smiling in return, Christiana had hugged her brother again. "We won't be gone long," she had said with a grin before climbing into the barouche.

"I'll send a letter with a list of everywhere we've been," Christiana was saying as Thomas came into earshot. He pulled Emma's free arm onto his.

"Do bring back some glass baubles, if you're able to pack them well," Thomas murmured before he leaned down to buss his sister on her cheek.

"I'll try," she replied, her eyes widening when she realized some men on the dock were about to lower the ramp from the side of the ship. "You have to take your leave of the ship, or you'll be joining us," she said with some alarm.

"Good-bye," Emma managed, tears filling her eyes as she gave Christiana a quick hug. She and Thomas nearly ran down the ramp, their attention on Gregory and Christiana as the two waved from the railing. Within minutes, the ship disappeared from the dock.

"I can't decide if I'm happy or sad," Thomas murmured as he led Emma back to the barouche. Mr. Larsen had brought the trunks in another carriage earlier that day so that only the valises had to ride with them. Now the barouche seemed empty.

"I am relieved," Emma offered, knowing the changing travel schedule had unsettled her husband.

"Indeed. Humphrey assures me he has the renovations well in hand, so we shouldn't be bothered with any queries from workmen," he commented.

"Christiana claims she made every decision possible with respect to paint colors and fabrics," Emma said. "Although I expect there will be an occasional query." She dared a glance back toward the docks. "I do hope she'll be all right on the water."

Thomas helped her up into the barouche. "Are you referring to sea sickness?" he asked as he stepped in behind her, joining her on the same seat so they faced the direction of travel.

Emma considered how to respond. "I was thinking morning sickness, but I suppose it will seem the same."

Jerking his head to regard his wife, Thomas blinked. "Morning sickness?" he repeated in a hoarse whisper.

Nodding, Emma swallowed. "She hasn't said anything to me, but I'm quite sure she's with child," she whispered.

"Nor me," Thomas replied, his brows furrowed. "May I ask how it is... you suspect?"

Allowing a slight shrug, Emma listed the reasons. "She hasn't had her monthly courses since the wedding, she picks at her breakfast, and Gregory looks as if he's harboring a secret he can barely contain. I'm rather surprised he didn't tell you."

Thomas blinked and regarded Emma for a moment before allowing a sigh. "Well, damn him. How is it I haven't noticed?"

Allowing a giggle, Emma turned to give him a kiss on the cheek. "Because you, my darling, have entirely too many other things on your mind."

Thomas inhaled sharply, as if he intended to argue with her, but he realized he had been too preoccupied. "I expect to hear from Todd in the next day or so," he said as he lifted her gloved hand to his lips and kissed the back of it. "He has to accept my offer."

"He will," Emma said with certainty. "Deborah is more excited about him working for you than I am, especially since she is expecting a baby."

Thomas blinked. "Does Todd know?"

Emma frowned. "Oh, dear. You cannot say a word to him," she whispered. "I think she was saving her news for when he started work at Wellingham Imports."

"I won't," he replied. Regarding his wife a moment, Thomas wondered if he should bring up what he had been thinking ever since the day they were married. "Are you of a mind to—?"

"Goodness, no," Emma interrupted him. "At least, not until..." She allowed the sentence to trail off, wondering if Thomas was considering the possibility of children right away. At first, they had been so careful in their marriage bed, employing French letters Thomas had been able to procure and hide in shipments of other products. Mrs. Dawes had provided Emma with instructions and the sponges she could soak in vinegar, but she loathed the odor and the time it took to prepare herself.

"Not until... ?" Thomas prompted.

Emma sighed, wondering if she were being selfish in not wanting a child right away. "The time is right," she whispered. "Are you—?"

"God, no," Thomas replied, shaking his head and allowing a sigh of relief. He pulled her into his arms.

"Then, will you continue to use the French letters?"

Thomas stiffened before allowing a sigh. "I suppose I must. At least, when it makes sense to do so."

Her face brightening with his response, Emma kissed him on the lips. "I know you don't like them—"

"They're not so bad," he managed between kisses. "But should you change your mind, simply put voice to your desire and we shall see what we can do." This last was said with a hint of humor before he kissed her again. "And if I do not stop these kisses this every instance, you will find yourself being tumbled in a barouche," he warned with a grin. "Without so much as a French letter in sight."

Emma sighed, the idea of being tumbled just then not at all unwelcome. Before she could reply, though, the barouche came to a sudden halt and she realized they were at Wellingham Imports.

"Do have a good day, my darling," she said as she stepped down from the barouche.

"And you, as well, my sweeting," he replied.

The two walked into the front doors of Wellingham Imports arm-in-arm, prepared for whatever the day might hold.

Or so they thought.

CHAPTER 12

VENGEANCE TAKES ITS TOLL

Three o'clock in the afternoon

Busy transcribing payroll numbers into a ledger, Emma didn't immediately notice Master Billy standing next to her.

"Mrs. Wellingham," he said, apparently for the second or third time.

"Yes, Master Billy," she replied, carefully setting aside her pen before giving him her full attention. Billy seemed out of breath and concerned. He also seemed at least four inches taller than he had been when she had first met the street urchin.

The day she had been hired to work at Wellingham Imports.

"There's a man ta see you. Ask' for you by name, and gave me a shillin' to come find ye," he said, his brows furrowing behind bangs that were too long and hadn't seen soap in probably a week. Emma wondered when last he'd had a bath.

She returned his frown. "Did he give his name?" she asked as she pushed her chair away from the desk and started to get up.

"No, ma'am," the boy replied. "But there's somethin' off about 'im. Do you want me to fetch Mr. Wellingham?"

Standing up, Emma shook out her skirts and considered the boy's query, "I don't think that will be necessary," she replied, rather more curious than concerned as to the visitor's identity.

"There's no need to bother Mr. Wellingham. I'll see to it," she added as she moved to leave the office.

Benjamin Cunningham, one of the other clerks, overhead the conversation from his desk behind the one Emma used on occasion and gave her a quizzical look. "Anything amiss?" he asked as she passed by. The clerk, hired by Thomas just the month before Emma started working at the import company, had been a fellow student in her accounting classes.

"I don't think so. Someone has asked for me is all," she replied with a shrug. She left the office with Billy in tow.

At the bottom of the stairs, she turned to ask Billy where he had left the visitor, but a deep, raspy voice sounded from the vestibule near the front doors. "Are you Miss Fitzsimmons?"

Emma turned to find a rather tall, large man regarding her with an uncertain expression. His coat was dusty, as if he'd been riding a horse for a long time, and his breeches were worn. A hat dangled from one hand and appeared to have been crushed and reshaped several times. There was something familiar about him, but she couldn't place him or his voice.

Curtsying, she replied, "I am... I was," she corrected herself. "Mrs. Emma Wellingham, at your service." After a short pause, she added, "And you are?" when the man did not immediately introduce himself.

The man moved a few steps closer and regarded Emma for another moment, his gaze traveling down and then up until he made eye contact again. He frowned. "I was expecting someone... older. And not so... comely," he commented, his eyebrows drawn together in confusion. A look of nervousness replaced his curious stares as he nodded. "My name is Cavendish. Harold Cavendish," he said solemnly. "I think you must know why I've come."

Emma blinked. She shook her head. Other than the name associated with the famous square in Marleybone, 'Cavendish' meant nothing to her. But she had seen those eyes before. Over a beard on a brute of a man she had shot in the neck.

One of the highwaymen, she realized as her heart skipped a beat. One of the men who had paid a visit to Woodscastle with the intent of robbing the place and doing who-knew-what with the residents they discovered within. She and Humphrey had made sure none of the highwaymen got anywhere near Christiana. Armed with a dueling pistol, she had shot the first man in the neck. Behind her, Humphrey had used a hunting gun to wound another who later died. Although the entire episode had lasted only a moment or two, Emma had thought it cost her a year or two of her life.

Struggling to allow her face to remain as impassive as possible, she gave a slight shake of her head. "I apologize, but I don't recognize you or your name," she answered carefully, only slightly aware of a sudden movement to her right as Billy left her side. "Have we... have we met before?"

The man shook his head, and a bead of sweat dribbled down the side of his face. "No, miss," he replied. "I just want to say I'm sorry it's come to this, but I'm here to take vengeance on my brother's behalf." With that, the man pulled a muff pistol out of his coat pocket and aimed it squarely at Emma.

Too stunned to move, Emma stared open-mouthed at the man as he raised the pistol. When she heard the pop of the gun as it released its bullet, she wasn't aware of Billy pulling on her right arm, jerking her so hard that she stumbled and nearly fell on top of him as she went down. A searing pain radiated from her left arm, and she instinctively moved her right hand to the source of the pain.

Billy, having taking the brunt of her fall to the wooden floor, struggled out from under her. At the same time, Sean MacGregor, one of the warehouse workers, ran into the man, his bulk knocking him to the floor. Emma glanced up in time to see Cavendish's head trapped in the crook of MacGregor's elbow, and a second later, she heard the distinctive sound of his neck separating from his spine. She watched as the life went out of the man's eyes, and her own vision went gray.

Rather bothered by what he had overheard Billy Overby say to Emma, Benjamin Cunningham stood up from his desk and stepped out of the accounting office. *Who would give a child a shilling to find someone if they knew the person was already here?*

Leaning over the railing of the walkway overlooking the warehouse, he scanned the floor below until he spotted Emma speaking to the visitor. Just inside the vestibule, the two seemed at first to be conversing. But from Emma's guarded stance, Benjamin realized she didn't know the man. Although Benjamin's gaze didn't stray in the direction of the larger warehouse, he was aware of Sean MacGregor glancing up at him and then following his worried gaze to Emma. When he saw her back straighten and Billy make his move, he banged on Thomas Wellingham's door.

"Come in," Thomas replied, startled by the loud thump on his office door. He was even more startled when Benjamin swung open the door, and the sound of a gunshot rang out from somewhere below.

"What the hell?" Thomas exclaimed as he got up from his desk and quickly moved around it. But Benjamin was already back out on the landing, looking down.

"I think Mrs. Wellingham has been shot," Benjamin replied as he moved to make his way down the steps.

The next few seconds brought about a flurry of activity as the general din of warehouse noise was replaced with shouts and men moving toward the front of the building.

Thomas was out of his office and halfway down the stairs when he witnessed Sean MacGregor break the shooter's neck. But his main focus was on Emma, who lay on her side with her right hand covering her left arm. A growing pool of blood already stained the upper half of her yellow muslin gown and dripped onto the floor next to her.

"Billy!" Thomas yelled as he noticed the errand boy staring at Sean and the lifeless head he held in the crook of his elbow. "Take a horse and get Dr. Talbot. *Now!*"

Billy's attention snapped to his boss, and he acknowledged the order. "Right away, sir," he said as he turned and ran through the warehouse and raced to the stables.

Thomas knew it would be fifteen minutes or more before

the boy could get the doctor back to the warehouse. It had taken that long the last time they had needed a doctor, back when a crate fell on one of the workers and left the man with a broken leg.

Pulling a handkerchief out of his vest pocket, he knelt next to Emma and pressed it hard against her wound, moving her hand away as he did so. He could tell the bullet had at least grazed her arm, but in doing so, it had ripped away the skin and who-knew-what-else in its path. When the blood started to flow with his removal of the handkerchief, he quickly replaced it and held it tight against the wound. "Stay with me, Emma," he ordered in a hoarse whisper, his heart racing and his breaths reduced to short gasps.

Benjamin came running from the warehouse carrying several wool blankets. He spread one over Emma and pushed another under her head as Thomas held it up. "She's awake," Benjamin whispered when he noticed Emma's eyelids flutter. Pulling out his own handkerchief, he left it on her arm and said, "I'll get some cotton," as he nodded toward the soaked handkerchief. Then he disappeared back into the warehouse, ignoring the crowd of workers who were lining up to see what had happened. A stunned silence had fallen over the warehouse, as if everyone had been left mute and unable to move.

Thomas bent his head down to find Emma's eyes open. She turned to look at him and frowned. "I think I've been shot," she whispered in awe. "And it hurts like the *dickens!*"

Failing to suppress his grin of relief and the bit of amusement he felt, Thomas kissed her cheek. "I've sent for Dr. Talbot," he whispered. "Just stay with me, all right?" he pleaded quietly.

Mr. Bingham ran up and knelt next to Thomas. "What can I do?" he asked, his eyes at once drawn to and then repulsed by the sight of the blood covering Emma's bodice.

Glancing in MacGregor's direction, Thomas noticed the Scot look down in sudden revulsion at what he had done. While he watched, MacGregor removed his arm from around the dead man's neck and stepped back as the boy fell to the floor in an awkward heap. The gun lay not far away, having fallen from the shooter's hand the moment MacGregor had him in his grasp.

Sure the man would either be sick or flee the scene, Thomas jerked his head in MacGregor's direction. Mr. Bingham caught his meaning. "Send someone for a constable," he murmured, flinching when he realized his best worker might be arrested and possibly transported for what he had done.

The warehouse manager quickly moved to MacGregor's side, placing a hand on his shoulder. "Come with me, MacGregor," he said as he urged the man to step away from the body. "Let's have a seat, shall we?"

The burly Scot simply nodded and walked with the manager to the bench on the warehouse floor. MacGregor sat down hard and buried his face in his hands.

"It will be fine," Mr. Bingham assured the man as he slapped the man on the back. "Mr. Wellingham and everyone else here will vouch for what ye did," he said. But could Mr. Wellingham convince a local constable that MacGregor's actions were warranted?

Benjamin returned to Thomas' side with a brown wrapped package. "I found these in the shipment for St. Bart's," he said as he unwrapped the paper and pulled out a stack of large cotton bandages.

Quickly folding one in quarters, Thomas replaced the soaked handkerchiefs with the bandage, relieved to find that the blood no longer flowed so freely when he removed the cloth.

Emma moved the blood-covered fingers of her right hand back up her arm to cover his hand. He glanced around and noticed the line of workers watching the scene with a combination of horror and curiosity.

"What's next?" Benjamin asked as he took a glance around the entry. "Should I get the robin redbreast?" he asked, referring to the nearest peace keeper on duty.

Thomas regarded the accomptant and bit his lip. "That would probably be a good idea. What time is it?" he asked.

"A few minutes past three o'clock," Benjamin replied after he pulled his pocket watch from his vest. "O'Leary will be on now. He's a good one, right?" he half-asked, not certain who the best law enforcement person would be in this situation. The last thing he wanted to see was Sean MacGregor arrested for murder, but the morning runner would do just that. He had no idea what a Bow Street Runner would do.

"Go get him. Tell him there was a shooting, and tell him MacGregor was defending us all," Thomas instructed. He glanced in the direction of the dead man, attempting to get a look at his face. "Who is he, anyway?" he asked.

"Harold Cavendish," Emma answered in a hoarse whisper.

Thomas exchanged glances with Benjamin, at first shaking his head. "Did you... *know* him?" Thomas asked Emma uncertainly.

"No," Emma replied. "He said... he said I shot his brother."

Biting his lip, Thomas took a deep breath. "Oh, my God." *One of the housebreakers?* He would never forget the day he had discovered Emma's horse in the middle of a field, a dead man lying next to it. He supposed it should have prepared him for what he found when he reached Woodscastle. The fear he had felt for what might have happened to his sister—for what might have happened to anyone in the house—had been palpable. Learning that Emma, merely an employee at the time—had defended Woodscastle only endeared her to him even more.

"Cunningham," he said as he turned to the accomptant. "Get O'Leary and then we'll send word to Sheriff Morgan. Tell him that one of the housebreaker's brothers came for vengeance. He'll know what you mean," he added when he noticed Benjamin's quizzical stare.

Understanding dawned on the accomptant's face. though. "I'll see to it right away," he responded as he got to his feet and headed out the front door. He, like everyone else in London who took a newspaper, had read the headline in *The Morning Chronicle* following the shooting of a gang of housebreakers by a bookkeeper and a butler at Woodscastle in Chiswick. That had been...

Early June?

Benjamin couldn't remember the exact date, but he

wondered why the brother had chosen this particular day to exact his revenge.

Another thought brought him up short. How many other brothers would seek vengeance against the woman who shot their gang leader with a dueling pistol?

Running along the length of the stables that lined the exterior of Wellingham Imports, Benjamin scanned the people making their way along the street up ahead. He spotted the peace keeper, O'Leary, speaking with a rider on horseback. "Mr. O'Leary," he called out as he waved an arm over his head.

The robin redbreast took notice of his approach and bade farewell to the rider. He started jogging toward Benjamin and met him halfway down the street. "What is it?" the law officer asked, breathless after his run from the corner.

"There's been a shooting, sir," Benjamin said between breaths, pointing toward the river. "At Wellingham Imports. A man came in carrying a pistol, and he shot Mrs. Wellingham before one of our workers could take him down," he explained, hoping he was giving the runner just enough information.

"Where is this man now?" O'Leary asked as he hurried alongside Benjamin toward the warehouse.

"He was in the vestibule, sir. I think he may be dead. I'm not sure," he added, hoping he wasn't saying too much.

"Dead?" the constable replied, his brows furrowing. "Did he shoot himself?"

Benjamin struggled to breathe as they ran back to the warehouse. "No, sir, but after he shot the one pistol, I think the man who wrestled him to the floor thought he had another and was about to shoot it," he explained, fabricating only part of the story. Out of the corner of his eye, he caught sight of Billy and a man on horseback, their mount running at a full gallop and heading in the direction of the warehouse. *The doctor*, he realized with relief.

Billy Overby flung open the front doors of the warehouse just before Dr. Talbot hurried in, grimaced at the sight of the dead man, and hurried to Emma's side.

Setting his bag down next to her, Dr. Talbot lifted Thomas'

hand from her arm, studied her wound, and then placed his hand back over the wound. "Who is this woman?" he asked as he opened his bag.

"Good morning, Dr. Talbot," Emma said when she recognized the doctor.

The doctor peered at his patient. "Miss Emma? Is that you?" he asked in surprise. As the doctor who was called upon for emergencies at 'Mrs. Dawes' Home for Unwed Mothers', Talbot recognized Emma from when she had done her charity work there.

"Indeed," she replied with a small smile. "And this is my husband, Thomas Wellingham," she said as she nodded to Thomas.

"We've met," they both said in unison.

"You finally married then," Dr. Talbot commented with a grin as he threaded surgical catgut through the hole of a hook-shaped needle.

"Yes," Emma and Thomas replied in unison. "Nearly three months now," Thomas added as he took Emma's blood-soaked hand in his.

"Honeymooners, then," Dr. Talbot commented with a slight smile as he completed his preparations.

"Will she be all right?" Thomas asked as he regarded the doctor, noting the man's rather calm manner. "I'd rather not be a widower this soon in life."

Despite the serious tone of Thomas' words, the comment brought a smile to Emma's face.

"Well, it appears she's lost a lot of blood, and she will have an ugly scar on her arm, but she should be fine in a few days," he said as he motioned for Thomas to move aside. Reluctantly, Thomas let go of the cotton he held and was moving to the other side of Emma when Benjamin and the constable burst into the vestibule.

The constable stopped short at the sight of the man with the broken neck and the woman covered in blood. "Dear God," he said in amazement. "Who is this man?" he asked as he surveyed the crowd.

"He said his name was Harold Cavendish," Thomas replied as he stood up and nodded to the constable. He offered a hand, unaware it was smeared with blood.

O'Leary absently shook it, his attention still on the dead man. He spoke in low tones. "What happened here?" he asked as he glanced around Thomas and stared at the bloodied woman.

"He came in carrying a pistol. Asked to see my wife," Thomas said as he indicated Emma, "Formerly Miss Emma Fitzsimmons," he said, saying her name slowly in case the constable might recognize the name from the housebreakers incident. "And then he shot her."

The constable regarded Thomas for a moment. "Fitzsimmons? As in the hat shop?" he asked, a look of recognition on his face.

Thomas sighed, disappointed the man didn't make the connection he had hoped he would. "Indeed. She works here as an accomptant now, though," he explained.

"Why did he shoot her?" O'Leary asked, peering around Thomas and screwing his face in disgust when he caught site of the doctor stitching her wounded arm.

"Are you familiar with what happened at my home in Chiswick in June? When my bookkeeper and butler shot a band of housebreakers?" Thomas asked carefully.

O'Leary's eyes opened wide and he stared at Thomas. "She's the one who shot Cavendish!" he said in astonishment. He dared another glance at the dead man. "So this chap was his brother? Out for revenge, I take it?"

At once relieved that the robin redbreast had figured it out and then on his guard, Thomas nodded. "We think so. One of my warehouse workers subdued him, but it was too late for my Emma," he said sadly.

The constable walked over to the dead man and kicked at the body. "He's dead," he said with a shrug. Reaching down, he picked up the pistol and sniffed the barrel. Setting it down, he searched the man's pockets and pulled out another pistol.

Studying the barrel, he nodded and stood up. "It's loaded," he said to no one in particular.

Thomas gave a sigh of relief at the constable's discovery. The loaded pistol would indeed be enough of an indictment of the man's intent and hopefully clear MacGregor of any murder charges.

"I'll get the coroner here as soon as possible. Is the chap still here who... subdued this man?" he asked, using Thomas' word for lack of a better.

"He is," Thomas nodded. "I can take you to him. He's understandably upset," he added as he led the constable to the back of the warehouse. They found MacGregor sitting next to Stephen Bingham on a bench.

"Constable O'Leary, this is Sean MacGregor, the man who saved my wife from certain death and who knows who else had he not taken out Mr. Cavendish," Thomas said by way of introduction.

Bingham had to suppress a grin at Thomas' embellishment while MacGregor gave the constable a worried nod. "I didna' mean for him to die," he said solemnly. "When I saw what he did to Mrs. Wellingham, I... I just wanted ta be sure he didna' shoot anyone else."

O'Leary nodded. "Understood. You're excused," he said as he glanced around the warehouse.

"I dinna think I have ever seen so much blood. Is she gonna live?" the Scot asked, a pained expression on his face.

Thomas nodded and placed his hand on MacGregor's shoulder. "Yes, thanks to you," he said, realizing he meant it. "Take off the rest of the day and tomorrow with full pay, Mr. MacGregor," he added with a nod to Bingham.

The warehouse manager nodded reluctantly, obviously not happy about losing the laborer for an entire day. He slapped MacGregor on the back again. "Off ye go."

The constable motioned for one of the workers to join him. "Did you see what happened?" he asked.

The warehouse worker shook his head. "Just heard the gun go off, and then I saw all that blood," he said in disgust. "Good thing MacGregor got to the guy before he could shoot anyone else," he added, giving a nod in the direction of the Scot.

Pursing his lips, O'Leary rejoined the group around MacGregor. "I'll take my leave now, Mr. Wellingham. I need to report this to my sergeant and send the coroner."

Thomas nodded in reply. "Thank you, Mr. O'Leary," he said as he bowed. He saw the man to the door and then hurried back to Emma's side.

"How is she?" he asked as he knelt down next to the doctor.

"She'll be fine. Very brave," Dr. Talbot said as he continued his handiwork. A trail of black stitches crossed the raw wound. "Hasn't let out a peep even though this has to be very painful for her," he murmured, his concentration on his needle. "Now, she'll need to see me next week to get these out, say next Friday," he said as he used a scissors to cut off the excess catgut. "I'll put a bandage on this and then make a sling for her arm. She needs to keep it dry, and to keep pressure off of the arm. No sleeping on it, no lifting, no writing, no exercise." When he noticed she was paying close attention to his words, he said quietly, "You can walk slowly if you're up to it in a few days." Turning his attention to Thomas, he added in a lowered voice, "And no tumbles."

Emma moaned in disappointment as Thomas' ears turned bright red.

Dr. Talbot resisted the urge to roll his eyes and pulled a large triangle of muslin out of his bag. He had Thomas lift her to a sitting position as he moved the fabric under her bent arm and tied it around her neck. "How do you feel?" he asked then, staring into each of her eyes for a moment.

"Tired," she replied with a weak smile.

"Completely expected given the blood loss," he answered shortly. "She needs to drink a large quantity of tea," he said to Thomas. "I would say water, but not from around here," he added with a nod toward the Thames. "If the pain gets to be too much, then she can have brandy or wine."

"Understood," Thomas replied. "Can I take her home

then?" he asked, rather glad they had ridden in the barouche instead of on horseback.

"Yes, sir, you can," Dr. Talbot said with a nod. "And might I get a ride back to my office?" he asked as he looked around for Billy.

"Master Billy!" Thomas called out. In a moment, the boy was at his side.

Emma reached out with her good arm and took the boy's hand. "Thank you, Billy. You know you saved my life," she said quietly as she pulled the boy close enough so she could kiss his cheek.

The boy nodded, his face taking on a decidedly reddish cast at having been kissed, especially in front of onlookers. "You're welcome, Mrs. Wellingham," he said with a quick bow before turning to see to the doctor.

Thomas stared at Emma. "Whatever did he do to deserve that?" he asked, startled by her statement—and the kiss she bestowed on the body.

Emma turned her attention back to Thomas. "When Cavendish pointed the gun at me, Billy pulled me aside. Even broke my fall to the floor. If he hadn't, I'm quite sure the bullet would have gone into my neck... or my chest, perhaps," she explained quietly. *Tit for tat*, she supposed, given she had shot the man's brother in the neck.

The doctor and Thomas regarded the embarrassed boy with equal surprise. "There shall be a bonus for you on payday," Thomas stated with a nod. "Could you please see to it that Dr. Talbot gets back to his office?"

Billy stood up to his full height. "Yes, sir," he replied with a nod. He led the doctor out the door and back to the stables.

"Payroll," Emma said sleepily. "I didn't finish payroll," she said as she looked up to find Benjamin Cunningham staring down at her.

"I can do it," the accomptant said with a nod. "You get some rest." Turning his attention to Thomas, a look of concern crossed his face. "I have not yet had a chance to ride to Sheriff Morgan's office," he murmured.

Thomas gave a shrug and replied, "Thank you, Mr. Cunningham, but it won't be necessary. The constable came to all the right conclusions on his own." He paused a moment. "I'll see to it in the form of a letter."

Frowning, the accomptant gave his response a thought before finally saying, "Very good, sir."

CHAPTER 13

HOME FROM AN ORDEAL

Later that day

It was nearly five o'clock in the afternoon by the time a groom had the barouche pulled up by the front door of Wellingham Imports. Thomas carried Emma to the equipage, relieved when she was comfortably asleep inside. Another saddled horse was soon tethered to the barouche. Thomas had arranged for the groom to drive them home and then ride the other horse back to town.

As the barouche clattered over the cobblestone streets to Kingsbridge Road, Thomas carefully held his wife against his side and rested his head on hers. After so many months of having Emma with him at work, he found it hard to imagine leaving her at home. Even though they worked at desks close to one another, it was sometimes only at midday when they spent any time together. It was the idea that he could summon her at any time and have her with him in his office that he found comforting. He smiled as he recalled the first time he had done such a thing.

Emma had come in looking as if she had been summoned to the headmistress' office at school. "What have I done wrong?" she asked as she sheepishly approached his desk.

"Made me fall in love with you?" he replied with a mischievous grin. And then he had stood up, took her hand, and led her around the wall behind his desk. When they were safely hidden from sight, he kissed her, told her he loved her, and sent her back to work.

Now, he realized he had nearly lost her. Grief filled him as he considered what life would be like without her. The way life had been just six months ago.

Before February 22, 1802.

That was the day he had finally met Emma Fitzsimmons. How could he go back to life the way it was before that day? *That wasn't a life*, he considered, unconsciously pulling her harder against his body until she stirred and her eyes fluttered open.

"What's wrong?" she asked as she tried to sit up. The sway of the barouche told her they were somewhere on the Great West Road. From the look on her face, Thomas frowned and shook his head to clear it, just then realizing that tears were streaming down his face.

"I... I almost lost you today," he whispered as he stared at her, his brows furrowed in despair.

Emma shook her head. "I promised I would never leave you," she countered with a sleepy smile. Her head fell back into its resting place and she was once again asleep in his arms.

Once at home, Thomas lifted Emma from the barouche and carried her to the house. Humphrey, having opened the front door at the sound of the conveyance in the drive, stepped aside and gave a look of alarm.

Mrs. Werthers, the housekeeper, was on her way from the music room to the library when she caught sight of her master on his way up the stairs. "Would you like tea served in the library?" she asked before she realized Thomas was carrying Emma. A smile crossed her face and she teased, "You needn't carry her over the threshold all the time, you must know, but it's rather romantic that you do."

When Thomas didn't pause in his haste to get up the stairs, Mrs. Werthers realized something was wrong. She climbed the stairs as quickly as her arthritic legs would allow, holding up her skirts past her ankles as she did so. "What has happened?" she asked in alarm when she was finally in front of Thomas' path.

He paused in mid-step but nodded in the direction of the master suite door. "Open the door, Mrs. Werthers," he ordered in a low voice, his breaths coming in gasps due to the exertion of carrying Emma.

The housekeeper did as she was told, noticing her master's tear-stained cheeks as he passed her on the way to the bed. "Oh, dear God. What has happened? Will she be all right?" Mrs. Werthers asked, her voice barely making a sound as she realized Emma hadn't opened her eyes nor made a sound.

"Dr. Talbot seems to think so," Thomas replied as he placed Emma on the bed. "Help me with her, will you? And whatever you do, don't touch her left arm. She has a gunshot wound."

The sound of Mrs. Werther's gasp woke up Emma. Alarmed by the comment, Humphrey, who stood on the threshold and was about to enter, stopped in mid-step. "Oh, dear," he said as he took in the sight of Emma's gown. Covered as it was in dried blood, it appeared as if she had been doused with rust-colored dye.

"Humphrey," Thomas said with a nod in the direction of the butler. "Please let Mr. Tanner know that Mrs. Wellingham will not be eating this evening, and that I'll be taking my dinner in here," he stated evenly. "And could you bring tea? A large pot, please. I know Emma will want some soon."

The butler bowed and said, "Right away, sir," before he rushed from the room.

Emma stirred and opened her eyes. "Very soon," she said with a wan smile. "And I'm quite sure I'll be hungry later," she murmured.

"Mrs. Wellingham!" The housekeeper said as her face brightened. "You must be in excruciating pain, you poor thing," she added as she reached out to push a lock of hair from her mistress' face.

Shaking her head, Emma replied calmly. "Not at all. I am just thirsty and tired," she whispered. Aware of the bloodstained gown and how she must look, she sighed. "Could you help me out of this gown, please?" she asked as she tried to sit up.

"Of course," Mrs. Werthers replied, hurrying to assist Emma. Removing the gown meant removing the sling first, and even with Thomas lifting Emma, it was some time before an exhausted Emma was dressed in a nightrail and settled on the bed under a light quilt.

Humphrey delivered a large tray with tea and biscuits and placed it on a side table. Once he completed the tea service, he bade Emma a quick recovery and took his leave.

When Thomas finally convinced Mrs. Werthers that he could take care of Emma without her help, she got up to leave and said, "The foreman requested a moment of Mrs. Wellingham's time. Something about the upholstery for one of the parlor chairs," she said with some hesitance.

Thomas stood up from the bed and stared at the housekeeper. "So soon?" he asked, his brows knitted together. He turned to look at Emma, who was watching the housekeeper with a wan smile.

"Perhaps you can answer his question," Emma said, her voice very quiet. "He probably just needs to confirm a color choice," she added as her eyes closed.

"Of course, my lady," Mrs. Werthers said as a worried look crossed her face and she turned her attention to her master. "I rather wish Mr. and Mrs. Grandby hadn't already left for Rome," she said in an apologetic tone.

"Me, neither," he replied. He gave a slight nod as the housekeeper curtsied and took her leave of the room.

Thomas bit his lip and regarded the master suite. For the next few months, he and Emma would have the entire estate to themselves. Contrary to what he had said to the housekeeper, he looked forward to the time they would have alone.

Blowing out all the candles but the one on the nightstand, he removed his clothes as he pondered the idea of a real honeymoon. He started to get into bed, realizing almost too late that he couldn't sleep on Emma's left side—he dared not get too close to her wound for fear he would press too hard against her and break the stitches or otherwise cause her pain.

Moving around to the other side of the bed, he pulled aside the covers and climbed in, careful to avoid touching her. His efforts were in vain, though, as Emma rolled onto her right side and molded her body to fit against his. Smiling, he wrapped an arm behind her shoulder and rested his hand just below her elbow.

"Does it hurt?" he whispered, aware that she hadn't yet fallen asleep. The rest of his body was also aware she was awake—his cock was hard, and he ached for her.

"Just a bit," she answered quietly, experimentally straightening her arm as her hands sought his manhood. When it didn't hurt any worse than it had, she flexed her fingers and then tightened them around him, making him gasp in surprise.

"No," he whispered, moving his hand to hers. "The doctor said no..." he started to say. He felt a pang when he realized this would be their first night without making love since the night of the Hornsby ball in July. Since the night he knew he would make her his wife.

For three months, they had made love every day, sometimes at bedtime, sometimes in the middle of the night, or in the early morning hours, or after returning from town, giddy from their horseback ride home and lustfully falling into bed. They had even made love during her monthly courses—she had begged him to—although he'd had to exercise restraint when he suckled her tender nipples.

A profound sense of loss consumed him as he realized how close she had come to dying. He nearly choked with grief as he remembered finding her bleeding on the floor in the company's vestibule. *Does Cavendish have other brothers ready to seek revenge? Or friends who would see to it?* His mind conjured any number of horrifying possibilities before he forced the worry away.

So he was quite startled when he opened his eyes to find Emma straddling him, lowering herself onto him and arching her back as she guided his manhood into the warm, wet cocoon between her thighs. The linen sling held her left arm protectively against the front of her body as she stroked the front of his with the long fingers of her right hand.

Inhaling sharply, Thomas grunted and grabbed her hips with his hands, instinctively pushing them down as he pushed into her. She lifted and lowered herself, slowly, teasing him until he pushed into her harder and quicker. He had never seen her like this, with her breasts above him, rhythmically rising and falling with each movement, their hardened nipples begging to be touched.

When she leaned back farther, he splayed his thumbs over the front of her hips and gently pressed against the space where he disappeared into her. She gasped and arched her back, and he pressed harder, watching her ecstasy by the dim light of the single candle lamp.

Her right arm disappeared behind her and she used the tips of her fingers to gently lift his sac against her, rubbing them playfully as he rubbed her. Thomas nearly cried out in surprise, the release so sudden he had to close his eyes and pull her body down onto his.

She allowed him to do so, careful to keep her bent arm at her side. His arms wrapped around her waist, his warm hands pulling her against him. Slowly, she lowered her head onto his shoulder, kissed his neck, and closed her eyes, the rise and fall of his chest putting her to sleep.

It was several minutes before Thomas' breathing returned to normal. Reaching out, he found the edge of the bed linens and pulled them over their bodies, careful to keep the coverlet from touching Emma's bandage. Pulling her pillow into the space above his shoulder, he rested his head against it and his chin onto the top of Emma's head. Exhausted but comforted by her body pressed against his, Thomas smiled when he realized he was still inside her. "I love you, you wicked woman," he whispered before he, too, fell asleep.

Humphrey regarded the white envelope that had just been delivered by a courier, rather surprised it was addressed to

Thomas rather than to Gregory. "Does the sender require an immediate response?" the butler asked.

The liveried courier shook his head. "Mr. Vandermeer said it is his response to Mr. Wellingham, in fact," the man answered. He gave a slight bow and remounted his horse for the ride back to London.

About to deliver the missive to the master suite, Humphrey thought better of it and instead took it to the library. He left it on Thomas' desk. The master of the house would find it in the morning, the butler decided.

CHAPTER 14

TODD VANDERMEER JOINS WELLINGHAM IMPORTS

October 5, 1802

"Are you nervous?" Deborah asked as she watched Winston help her husband dress for his first day at Wellingham Imports. Todd had twice attempted to tie his neckcloth and then pulled off the long strip of linen from around his neck, obviously frustrated. Although the butler, usually saw to tying his cravats, Todd was determined he do it himself on this auspicious occasion.

Todd regarded his wife with an embarrassed smile. "I have a fluttering in my stomach, to be sure," he answered before aligning himself with the mirror.

Deborah stepped up and stood in front of him, her silver morning gown shimmering in the early morning light from the east window. "Allow me," she said as she took the ends of the cloth and wrapped them evenly about her husband's neck. Folding the cloth into pleats, she wrapped and wound the cravat into a perfect mail coach knot and smiled when she realized Todd was watching her every move in the cheval mirror behind her.

Winston held out a dark blue waistcoat and Todd slipped his arms into it. "Thank you, both," Todd said with a nod, one hand wrapping around one of Deborah's so that he might kiss the back of it. "And what will my beautiful wife be doing while I am toiling away in my new position?" he teased while he pointed to one of the tailcoats his butler held out for him.

Deborah smiled and glanced away, her own nervousness apparent. "I am thinking I might go shopping on The Strand," she replied quietly, her body swaying slightly as she made the comment. "I'll take a footman with me, of course," she added.

Returning the broad smile, Todd gave his bride a look of disbelief. "Do you even know how to shop?" he queried, his grin betraying his amusement at her expense.

Still smiling, Deborah angled her head. "Not for what I was planning to buy today, no," she admitted.

The grin disappearing from his face, Todd asked, "What is it you want? Do you need me to replenish your purse?" His wrist flicked in Winston's direction, indicating he no longer required his services.

The butler bowed and left the bedchamber.

"No. My purse is still very full," Deborah replied. "But thank you. You are very generous to offer."

When she didn't answer his first question, Todd stepped back and eyed her. "So…?"

Deborah smiled then. "I believe I need to look for some items for the nursery," she said with a nod. "And perhaps some baby clothes, too," she added when Todd's expression did not immediately change.

Todd continued to stare at his wife. "Baby clothes?" he repeated, glancing away for a moment before returning his attention to her. "For whose baby?" he asked, his face screwed up in concentration. "Oh! For the Home, of course," he claimed with a nod, sure he had figured out what she was trying to tell him.

It was Deborah's turn to stare at her husband with a quizzical expression on her face. "No," she replied with a shake of her head. "For the nursery here at Grace Park."

His eyes widening, Todd stepped back and stared at his wife in disbelief. "You are… ?"

Deborah nodded as she placed a hand over her middle. "I am not far along, of course, but sometime in March..." The rest of her sentence was lost in the fabric of Todd's tailcoat as he pulled her into a hug.

"I cannot believe my good fortune!" he shouted, pulling her away from his body and kissing her on the lips. "That you would bless me with a baby so soon in our union! A *baby*!" he exclaimed happily, once again pulling into a hug. "Are you well, then?" he asked, concern replacing the elation he felt.

"I am very well, indeed," Deborah replied with a happy sigh. "I thought it best to tell you before you started your new position. In the event that I will not be in your company much these next few weeks," she added as she pressed her face against his shoulder.

Todd shook his head. "Why will you not be in my company?" he asked, his face showing disappointment. "Will you already be in confinement so soon?"

Shaking her head, Deborah replied, "You will be so immersed in your work for Mr. Wellingham that I rather doubt you will even come home for dinner."

Shaking his head, Todd regarded Deborah with a serious stare and said, "It's true I will spend a good deal of my time at the office, but I have every intention of being home in the evenings, especially for dinner and our walks in the garden," he assured her, kissing her forehead for good measure.

Deborah smiled then and stepped back. "Then I shall look forward to dinner with you every night," she said, adding, "Papa," over her shoulder as she was about to take her leave of the room. Todd was suddenly in front of her, though, blocking her exit. "I love you," he whispered. He captured her lips with his own.

Allowing a wan smile, Deborah said, "And I love you."

He moved a hand to her belly. "I love this babe." When he looked up again, Deborah recaptured his lips and kissed him thoroughly. When she finally stepped away, she gave him a playful shove. "Now, off with you, or you'll be late for your first day," she teased him.

Papa, Todd thought with a smirk. Me, a father! "I love you, Mrs. Vandermeer!" he called out, noticing he no longer felt a fluttering in his stomach due to his upcoming workday. Now a new one had taken its place.

I'm going to be a father!

CHAPTER 15

FIRST DAY AT THE OFFICE

An hour later at Wellingham Imports

Todd Vandermeer regarded the door to his office, a grin of embarrassment replacing the grin of recognition he had afforded Billy Overby only the moment before. The caddy had greeted him at the front doors to the establishment, offering his assistance in bringing up any boxes the broker might have brought with him.

Holding onto a flat package wrapped in brown paper, Todd shook his head and told the boy the painting was the only item he had for his office. "I may bring more on the morrow, though," Todd warned as he made his way up the stairs and to his office. He paused before opening the door, studying his reflection in the glass for a moment. Then his gaze dropped to his name.

Todd Vandermeer. Senior Broker.

The gold painted lettering matched that of the lettering on the door for the next office along the raised platform, where the words, Thomas Wellingham, Proprietor, graced the pebbled glass. He wondered how long ago Thomas had made the arrangements to have a sign painter do the lettering.

Once he had his painting hung on the wall adjacent to the door, he took a look around and considered what other accoutrements he might bring to decorate the room.

Settling into his desk chair, Todd grinned as he realized it was especially tall—the original legs had been replaced with longer spindles—and rather comfortable, given its deep-cushioned leather upholstery. To match the height of the chair, the desk was propped up with matching chunks of wood under each of its legs.

Leaning back in his chair, he continued to grin as he admired the painting he had just hung. A portrait of Deborah, the artwork featured his wife's long, bare back and a length of draped fabric barely covering her derrière. Given the scandalous pose, he wanted to be sure it was hung so that only he would see it directly.

When he finally tore his gaze from his Deborah, he examined the items on his desk. A small stack of papers lay on the left, an inkwell and pen were in front, and blank requisition forms were stacked on the right. A calendar detailing scheduled deliveries—both from ships as well as overland transports—covered nearly half the desktop.

Perusing the stack of papers on the left, he realized they were requisitions from various companies. One, from a draper in Oxford Street, was an order for several hundred bolts of silk while another, from a furniture maker, contained a list of various wood species and the lengths of lumber they required for their business. He continued reading the requests until he reached the bottom of the stack, where he found a handwritten note from Thomas Wellingham. The date at the top was several days in the past.

If you are reading this note, then thank you for accepting my offer of employment. I figured you would arrive well before the rest of the staff. If I am not yet in my office, then please take the time to get tea and breakfast.

Todd reread the note twice and smiled. Getting up from his chair, he heard the large warehouse doors and front doors opening, the sounds indicating several people were arriving for their workday. Most were dressed in dirty work clothes and were headed for the warehouse side of the building while a few wore tailcoats and climbed the stairs to head to offices located along the same wall as his office.

At the sound of Thomas Wellingham's voice, he hurried to his office door and found Emma Wellingham on the other side bidding adieu to her husband.

"Oh, good morning, Mr. Vandermeer!" she said brightly as she curtsied.

Todd grinned and bowed. "Indeed it is, Mrs. Wellingham," he said, catching himself when he realized he almost called her 'Emma'. "I am having a baby," he said excitedly, his grin broadening

Thomas poked his head around the corner from his office next door and gave his new colleague a sideways glance while Emma held a gloved hand over her mouth to hide her amusement. "Have you told your wife this unusual news?" Thomas asked as he gave a tardy bow.

Realizing he was being teased, Todd rolled his eyes. "I meant she is having the baby, of course," he said, his nervousness increasing. "In March, she says," he added as he took a deep breath.

"Congratulations, Mr. Vandermeer," Emma replied happily, doing her best to hide the shock she felt at learning Deborah had shared her news with her husband. She bobbed a quick curtsy. "Do have a good first day." She turned to walk toward the clerks' office. Once she had her face turned away from the new employee, she sobered. That Deborah had told her husband so soon in the pregnancy rather surprised her. *She cannot be more than two months along*, Emma thought at first. Then she remembered the two had wed in early July. *Three months, then*, she amended her guess. Perhaps it was time the man knew he was to be a father.

Careful to avoid bumping her wounded arm against the door jamb, Emma entered the accounting office and greeted the few who had arrived earlier, barely hearing her husband's response to Todd's announcement.

"You dog!" Thomas exclaimed as he reached out to shake

hands with the taller man. "Congratulations. By the way, do you find your office acceptable?" he asked as he joined Todd on the platform outside Todd's office. They both gave a glance into the sparsely furnished room.

"Indeed, it is. Thank you for the tall chair," Todd commented with a nod. "I was prepared to have one made."

Thomas shook his head. "It was the least I could do. I know this isn't as well appointed as your office at East India, but feel free to decorate it as you wish," he stated as he noticed the pile of papers in the middle of the desk. "I see you arrived early," he added as he stepped into the office.

Todd followed him and took his place behind the desk. "Yes. And, of course I have questions," Todd said lightly.

Noticing his note on the top of the pile, Thomas pointed to it and said, "No doubt, but let us get some tea and breakfast, shall we?" he suggested.

Nodding, Todd joined Thomas and the two headed down the street for the Crown and Anchor.

CHAPTER 16

A JEALOUS HUSBAND
REACTS POORLY

Later that day

"Master Billy!" Thomas called out from the platform outside his office.

The caddie came running from the warehouse. "Yes, sir?" he answered, his untidy appearance more apparent in the light from the windows below. The boy quickly climbed the stairs and stood before his employer, ready for instructions.

"Could you go to the clerks' office and ask Mrs. Wellingham to finish for the day? I wish to leave early," he said in a lowered voice. Rather unhappy after receiving a series of reports detailing delayed ships, short deliveries, and a news item in The Times about the shooting, Thomas was determined to simply take the rest of the day off.

Billy shook his head and pointed to the office next door. "Mrs. Wellingham isn't in the accomptants' office, Mr. Wellingham. She's still in Mr. Vandermeer's office," he explained, proud to be able to share the information.

"Still?" Thomas repeated, his brows furrowing. "How long has she been in there?" His mood, already rather sour, almost had him snapping at the boy.

The caddie shrugged. "Most of the day, sir. She's been taking those big books in there and showin' him stuff," Billy explained. Then he realized Mr. Wellingham wasn't very pleased to hear his news. "Mr. Vandermeer says he wants to learn everything he can about the business," he added with a shrug.

Thomas sighed and bit his lip. "Thank you, Master Billy. Have my carriage brought around," he stated, his demeanor more serious. Rapping on Todd's door, Thomas didn't wait for a reply before barging into the office. He found Emma pointing to something in a ledger book whilst Todd looked on from right next to her. Their chairs were impossibly close, although the two were not actually touching one another.

"Now, we keep track of inventory from each shipment... ," Emma looked up as Thomas entered and gave him a smile. "Mr. Wellingham," she said in greeting, nodding as she said it. Although they usually used their given names when in private, they were careful not to use them whilst at work.

"*Mrs.* Wellingham," Thomas replied, emphasizing the 'Mrs.' a bit too much. He didn't even try to hide his annoyance.

"Thomas, I cannot tell you how helpful it has been to have Mrs. Wellingham explain your books to me," Todd said as he stood to bow. "I fear I have monopolized her time today, however. Please forgive me," he stated, realizing too late that Thomas seemed displeased.

"Of course," Thomas answered abruptly. "Mrs. Wellingham and I need to leave early today, though. Please excuse us, and congratulations again on your impending fatherhood," he said curtly.

Surprised at hearing of their need to leave early, Emma stood up and curtsied to Todd before she moved to join Thomas. She dared a glance at the open ledger, wondering if she should return it to storage or leave it in the broker's possession. "Good evening, Mr. Vandermeer. Please give Mrs. Vandermeer my regards. And my congratulations," she added as she gave him a quizzical look over her shoulder. "I'll come for the book on the morrow."

When she and Thomas were outside the office, Thomas closed the door and led Emma down the steps. "My spencer and bonnet are in the accomptants' office," she said as she started to turn around.

"Leave them," Thomas stated as he continued down the stairs. "It is a warm enough day."

Sensing his bad mood, Emma thought better of protesting and quietly followed him down the steps and out the front door. Nearly running to keep up with her husband, she was finally able to stop when Billy Overby brought the curricle to a halt in front of them. The caddie gave Thomas the reins and the man climbed in, not stopping to assist Emma.

Billy held his hand out to Emma and she took it, giving her husband a curious glance as she climbed in and sat next to him. Thomas put the horse in motion even before Emma was completely seated, and her left arm was pressed hard against the side of the curricle before she could right herself. The searing pain forced her to grimace and gasp as she blinked back tears. Although she couldn't see the wound due to the bandage and the long sleeve of her gown, she was sure a stitch had torn. Thomas seemed to take no notice of her distress and simply drove the horses on the quickest exit he could maneuver toward the Great West Road.

"Whatever is wrong, Thomas?" she finally asked, her right hand pressed protectively over her wound.

"Nothing, my darling," he replied coldly, his eyes directed straight ahead. They rode in silence the entire way to Burlington Road, Thomas allowing the horses to run as fast as they wanted.

Even without hearing him speak a word, Emma could feel his rage increasing. "Did something go wrong? Thomas, you're scaring me," she said, knowing her words were mostly lost to the sound of the thundering hoofbeats and spinning wheels.

Once they were on the lane leading to Woodscastle, though, Thomas finally turned to Emma and asked rhetorically, "My God, Emma, did you have to spend the entire day with him?"

Shocked by the question and even more so by his curse, Emma shook her head. "You told him to ask for my help. For when he was ready to review the books," she stammered. "What wrong did I commit?"

Thomas ignored her question. "You are my wife," he said under his breath. Finally slowing down the horses in front of the house, Thomas turned to her and allowed his anger to show. "Not his," he spat out.

Mr. Larsen ran up to the curricle and took the reins, noticing almost immediately his master's dark mood. A quick look in Emma's direction had him paying witness to her distress. It was then he noticed a spot of blood on her sleeve and pointed toward it. "My lady, your arm is bleed—"

"That will be all, Mr. Larsen," Thomas stated before the groomsman had a chance to finish his comment. Stepping down from the carriage, Thomas strode around it and took Emma by the arm, pulling her out of the carriage so that she nearly fell.

Mr. Larsen frowned, but took the reins and led the horse to the stables at the west end of the house.

"My arm!" Emma wailed in pain as he pulled on it harder. "Thomas, you are *hurting* me!" she added in a hoarse whisper. When they reached the front door, Thomas' rage increased. "You are my *wife*!" he yelled again, gripping her left wrist hard enough that she cried out in pain again.

Having opened the front door, Humphrey was horrified to see his master practically dragging Emma by the very arm that had been wounded by a gunshot only the week before.

"Your wife's arm is bleeding, sir," the butler commented as he took Thomas' hat and helped to remove his tailcoat.

Thomas gave him a brief glare. "And she will probably bleed some more before I am done with her," he spat out.

Emma's eyes widened in shock. She gave the butler a look that begged for help. Thomas held onto her wrist, though, and pulled her up the stairs. Although she was able to say a step behind him for most of the way, she tripped and stumbled before they had reached the top landing. She felt—and heard— several stitches tear apart in her arm as well as in her gown. "Thomas, stop it," she screamed as the pain seared through her arm and nearly caused her to lose consciousness.

Her husband gave no reply and continued to pull her to the master suite. Once inside, he slammed the door and gave her a stare filled with rage. "You are my *wife*, not his!" Pulling her to the bed, he pushed her down onto it and removed his waistcoat, slinging it to the floor. "I am your *husband*, not him!" he whispered hoarsely, his outrage increasing with each breath. He fumbled with the button closures of his breeches, cursing as he did so.

"Thomas, please, do not do this," Emma pleaded, tears streaming down her face as she fought the pain from the wound as well as from his hate-filled remarks. Her vision going gray, she allowed her entire body to go limp when she realized they were no longer alone in the room. Concentrating on Thomas, she saw something change in his face—the features seemed to soften as if he had suddenly come to his senses and realized what he was doing. The curses he hurled were not intended for her but intended for him.

And then everything went black.

Unaware of the three men who stood behind him, Thomas reached down to cup Emma's face in one hand, to apologize to her for his ghastly behavior. The hand that gripped his arm and forced him to turn around wasn't nearly as strong as the large-knuckled fist that impacted his jaw and sent him tumbling to the floor, though. Grabbing onto a fold of Emma's dress as he was pulled from her, Thomas was vaguely aware of the sound of the tearing fabric fading as he stopped rolling and remained unconscious on the carpet.

The three men exchanged nervous glances with one another.

"I suppose I will be fired for that," Mr. Larsen said quietly, shaking out the fingers of his right hand as a grimace appeared on his face. "And Miss Dahlia just agreed to marry me, too," he added, referring to the house maid.

"We might all be relieved of our duty," Mr. Allen said with an arched brow, "But I bet she'll probably still cook for us," he added hopefully as he nodded toward Emma. "Any idea what got his goat?"

Humphrey gave the stableboy a quelling glance before he quickly moved to where Emma lay slumped on the bed. "Mrs. Wellingham," he whispered. When she didn't immediately respond, he hurried to the bath and came out with several linens. "Help me," he said to the two groomsmen. They rushed up to help Emma sit up as the butler wrapped a linen around her bleeding arm. "Get this wet, will you?" the butler said as he tossed a linen to Mr. Allen. "I cannot do much for her, I fear," he added as he realized Emma's arm was bleeding too much. The skirt of her gown was torn away from the bodice in several places, and the left sleeve was nearly free of the bodice. Humphrey tore it the rest of the way from the dress to expose the blood-soaked bandage.

"We need to get her to a doctor," Mr. Larsen said quietly as he averted his eyes. "She was already bleeding in the carriage."

Mr. Allen came running from the bath with a wet linen and gave it to Humphrey. "I say we take her to Grace Park," he said in a whisper. "Mrs. Vandermeer can take care of her there," he suggested when the other two gave him quizzical looks.

Humphrey nodded. "To Grace Park, then. Can you two take her? I fear someone must be here when he comes to," he said as he indicated the prone body of his master. "I... I will stall him as best I can, but at some point, I'll have to tell him where you've taken her."

"Yes, sir," the two replied as they nodded. Mr. Larsen lifted Emma into his arms and carried her out of the room while Mr. Allen followed with several linens and a quilt he took from the end of the bed.

"I'll get some tea," Humphrey offered as he followed them out the door, closing it once he was sure Thomas was breathing but still unconscious. "She's lost a good deal of blood due to this wound already, and Dr. Talbot said she was to drink tea," he explained as they descended the stairs.

In only a few minutes, the two groomsmen had Emma propped up in the curricle, a blanket around her and a large jug of tea on the seat. Mr. Allen agreed to drive while Mr. Larsen stayed behind to mind the stables.

As the groom set the horse on its way, Emma slowly awoke and glanced around. Surprised to find Mr. Allen sitting next to her, she stared at him open-mouthed. "What... what's happening?" she asked, almost immediately wincing at the throbbing in her left arm. She grimaced and then rearranged herself in the seat so her arm wouldn't hurt as much, noticing as she did so that her dress was torn and her sleeve was missing. "Oh, dear," she murmured, too embarrassed to make eye contact with the groom.

Mr. Allen shrugged and glanced nervously at his master's wife. "I am getting myself relieved of duty, ma'am," he answered, matter-of-factly.

Her eyes widening, Emma regarded the groomsman for a moment, about to ask what he meant when she remembered most of what had happened. "Where is Mr. Wellingham?" she asked, daring a look behind them as they turned onto Burlington Lane.

"In the master suite, ma'am," the groomsman replied, barely giving her a glance. "On the floor of the master suite, in fact," he said as an afterthought.

Emma relaxed back into the seat and sighed. "Oh, dear," she whispered again, her voice sounding drowsy.

"Ma'am," Mr. Allen spoke as he looked over at her, realizing she was in a great deal of pain. "I have been directed to take you to Grace Park so that Mrs. Vandermeer can fix you up," he explained evenly. "If it pleases you, of course."

Although tempted to roll her eyes at the irony of going to Grace Park, she found she could think of no place else where she might receive medical care and the shoulder of a best friend on which to cry. "It does," she replied simply. Noticing the jug on the seat, she helped herself to a few swallows of tea before allowing her eyes to close. She fell asleep and remained so until they reached Grace Park.

CHAPTER 17

DOCTOR DEBORAH TO THE RESCUE

Regarding the stack of baby gowns and blankets she had acquired during that day's shopping trip, Deborah allowed a satisfied grin. She lifted one particular gown to examine it by the light of the windows in the parlor, her smile widening as she noticed the tiny embroidered pattern in the smocking. Even if her first baby hadn't been lost to a miscarriage, she was quite sure it never would have enjoyed such finery as the items she had purchased on this day.

The sounds of a horse and carriage in the semi-circular drive of Grace Park had her moving to a window, angling her head in an attempt to see the equipage. Expecting to see her husband returning from his first day at Wellingham Imports, she gasped when she realized who sat at an awkward angle in the curricle.

Winston already had the front doors open and was staring out, open mouthed, as Deborah entered the vestibule. "Can you tell what's happened?" she asked, hurrying to join him on the threshold. When she realized Mr. Allen was carrying Emma Wellingham up the stairs, she gasped and rushed out the double doors. "What has happened?" she asked as she joined the groomsman.

Mr. Allen nodded to the mistress of Woodscastle. Struggling with his burden, he wasn't sure how much to tell the woman. "Mrs. Wellingham's gunshot wound is bad," he said as he maneuvered Emma through the open doors. "There's a jug of tea in the carriage," he added as he angled his head. "Humphrey said she would need it." He paused in the vestibule, awaiting directions. Not having been in the house before, he didn't know where he should take the patient.

Alarmed at the reference to a gunshot wound, Winston's eyes rounded. "I'll see to it. This way, please," he stated as he led the way to the stairs and a guest bedchamber just beyond the landing.

"What happened?" Deborah whispered, her concern growing as she pulled away a corner of the blanket and saw only blood, most of it dried.

"I dunno, ma'am," Mr. Allen claimed as he followed the butler. "Her arm was bleeding when she and Mr. Wellingham returned from town, but he was angry 'bout something and..." He stopped as he reached the bed and slowly lowered Emma onto it.

"Where is Mr. Wellingham?" Deborah asked then, surprised a groomsmen would be charged with bringing Emma to town without her husband coming along. She motioned to a nearby servant to join them.

Mr. Allen bit his lip and glanced about, his nervousness evident. "I would rather not say, ma'am," he replied uncertainly. "Mrs. Wellingham can explain it, I expect," he added. With that, he bowed and left the room, hurrying down the stairs and out the front doors before anyone else could ask him more questions.

"Anna, get me hot linens, please," Deborah ordered as she gave a glance in the maid's direction. She leaned over her patient and began removing the linen and blood-soaked bandage.

"Yes, ma'am," the maid replied as she hurried into the bath.

"You'll not find any hot water in there," Deborah called out as a reminder, gasping when she realized the extent of Emma's wound. "You'll need to fetch it from the mistress suite," she added, never looking up from her examination. Although a hot water heater had been plumbed into the mistress and master suites of Grace Park, none of the rest of the bathing chambers had yet been modernized.

"Of course, ma'am," Anna replied nervously, leaving the room in a near run.

Emma stirred as Deborah studied the wound. "Stay still, please," Deborah said dispassionately, her manner no different with Emma than with those she worked with at the Home for Unwed Mothers.

Returning with a stack of very wet, hot towels, Anna waited for instructions. Deborah nodded for her to leave them on the table next to the bed. "I require my sewing basket and the catgut in my bag," she said, taking a linen from the stack and using it to clean the area around the wound. Several stitches were torn, and although the skin had started to heal in several places along the original gunshot wound, the stitches had torn through uninjured areas. Most of the bleeding seemed to have occurred from where the stitches had torn through.

Deborah plucked the ruined stitches from the skin, relieved to see there was no sign of infection from the old wound. Aware she was being watched, she looked up to find Emma studying her every move.

"How bad is it?" Emma whispered. She struggled with forming the words, her mouth feeling as if it had been stuffed with cotton.

"Mmm," Deborah murmured as she nodded slightly. "You now have new wounds to go along with your old one," she acknowledged as Anna entered the room with a sewing basket and Deborah's medical bag.

The maid stood next to the bed for a moment before finally admitting in a nervous whisper, "Pardon me, Mrs. Vandermeer, but I do not know what catgut is."

Glancing up at Anna, Deborah held out a piece she had removed from Emma's arm. "It is this," she said as she handed the maid the small length of stitching material. "It's in the black bag. I will also need a match, and please bring Mrs. Wellingham some tea," she added, knowing Anna would need to be out of the bedchamber or she might faint at the sight of what Deborah was about to do.

Emma watched as Deborah threaded a rather large fish-hook-shaped needle with the wound up length of catgut Anna had found in the bag. Then she lit a match and held it under the end of the needle. "This is going to hurt, isn't it?" Emma whispered, remembering vaguely the pain she had felt when Dr. Talbot stitched her arm the week before. Back then, the pain had been dulled somewhat, the excitement of the gunshot masking it. Now, any excitement had passed, and Emma was well aware of what was about to happen.

"Some," Deborah acknowledged as she started to work taking tiny, even stitches across the wound. "But not as bad as it has hurt for the past hour or so." After a few stitches, she asked, "Are you at least going to tell me what happened?" she asked, her curiosity finally getting the better of her.

Grimacing with each poke of the needle, Emma regarded her best friend as tears appeared and dripped down her face. "Mr. Wellingham took extreme offense at my having spent several hours in the company of your husband today," she whispered, biting her lip as she used her right hand to scrub the tears from her face.

Deborah paused in her stitching, her eyes lifting to regard Emma. "And should I be taking extreme exception to you having spent several hours in his company?" she asked, one eyebrow cocking suggestively.

Rolling her eyes, Emma shook her head. "Of course not. I was merely familiarizing Mr. Vandermeer with the company's books. Mr. Wellingham told him that if he wished to know more about the company's books, I would show him the ledgers and explain how our accounting system works," she said in her own defense. "I was merely doing what I was told."

Satisfied with the explanation and sure she had nothing to be worried about with regard to her husband and her best friend—Emma had introduced her to Todd, after all—Deborah continued her work on the wound. "And what did Mr. Wellingham do?" she asked, occasionally glancing at

Emma as she pulled the length of catgut through her patient's flesh.

Emma's tears returned. "He was awful, Deborah. He kept saying, 'You are my wife'," mimicking the manner in which Thomas had said the words. "He pulled me out of the carriage by this arm, and dragged me to the house and up the stairs. He ripped my gown..." She paused to wince at how the skirt was half-torn from the bodice. "He was so very angry, Deborah. I think he was about to..." Before she could say more, Emma sobbed and covered her mouth with her free hand. Although she remembered the sudden change in his expression at the very end, the way he seemed to realize his madness had caused her great pain, she now wondered if she had merely imagined it.

Deborah gasped and stopped her sewing. "Oh, my," she breathed, aware of how upset her friend had become. "But he is your husband, Emma," she whispered. "You must obey him," she added when she saw Emma's look of doubt. "We must obey our husbands... is this not so?" she found herself asking, although not with the same conviction.

"Would you allow Mr. Vandermeer to treat you as I was treated?" Emma asked, her voice stronger.

Shaking her head, Deborah was about to answer that she didn't have a choice when Anna returned, breathless and proudly holding a match and a small cup of tea for Emma. Drinking the tea in just a couple of gulps, Emma gave the cup back to the maid. "More, please," she said, her thirst barely quenched. "Mr. Allen brought a jug, I think." she murmured, worried the stablehand would lose his position over what had occurred that afternoon.

"Use one of the large crystal goblets this time, Miss Anna," Deborah suggested as she took the match. The maid curtsied and left the room. Tossing the match into her medical bag to replace the one she had used, Deborah returned her attention to her sewing. "I cannot imagine my Todd treating me as you have been on this day," Deborah remarked in response to Emma's query.

Frowning, Emma found herself agreeing with Deborah.

"Neither can I," she agreed. "He worships you. You're a goddess to him. But Mr. Wellingham is used to having his own way, I suppose. He's a rather proud man. Too proud, sometimes."

Deborah huffed as she tied off the catgut and used the small scissors from her chatelaine to cut it. "He is a spoiled brat," she said, studying her handiwork and then allowing a wan smile when she found it to her satisfaction. "There. You are repaired," she said curtly. Pulling a looking glass off of the table next to the bed, she held it up to Emma's left arm so Emma could see.

"Very nice work," Emma said with a grimace, wondering for how long she would have the nasty scar. "Thank you," she added, the tears once again welling up in her eyes.

Deborah leaned over and kissed Emma on the temple. "You're welcome. I will fetch you one of my new nightrails. I order you to sleep for a very long time, and you are certainly welcome to do so right here," she added with a sad grin.

Anna returned with a large goblet of tea, and Emma took it with a nod. The maid then helped Emma out of her ruined gown and corset while Deborah arranged a stack of large pillows behind her patient. Once Emma was dressed in the crisp, white nightrail, Deborah tied one of Todd's silk cravats into a makeshift sling. Securing it around Emma's neck and bent arm, she allowed her patient to determine the least painful placement for her arm before tying it to the most comfortable length. Once it was in place, Emma collapsed into the pillows and was soon sound asleep.

CHAPTER 18

A PROUD MAN IS HUMBLED

Meanwhile, back at Woodscastle

"So, do I have you to thank for this?" Thomas asked as he sat up and gingerly rubbed his jaw. He was eyeing his butler from the floor of the master suite with a good deal of suspicion.

Humphrey shook his head. "I assure you that I did not strike you, sir. However..." the butler replied, his unfinished comment hanging in the air.

Thomas sighed. "Go on," he whispered hoarsely, remembering his awful behavior. He grimaced and ran a hand through his hair.

"I wish I had, sir," Humphrey stated, his own hands clasped behind his back and his chin firmly stuck out in defiance.

Thomas sighed again and scrubbed his face with one hand, wincing when he touched the tender spot where a fist—or something like it—had struck him. "I rather wish you had," Thomas said as he moved to stand up. "Or Mr. Allen. He should have decked me as soon as I was out of the carriage. Or Emma. I rather imagine she could form a decent fist... Oh, God," he murmured, remembering the rest of the details of the late afternoon. "Is she... ? *Where* is she?" he asked as he took in the sight of several bloodied linens and the mussed space on the bed where she had been.

Furrowing his brows, Humphrey watched his master as the

man's distress increased. Deciding it was safe to tell, he sighed. "I had Mr. Allen take her to Mrs. Vandermeer. She needed more medical assistance than I could provide, sir," the butler stated, hoping the mention of another Vandermeer would not upset his master.

Although Thomas had never come out and said who 'he' was when he was yelling at Emma, Humphrey figured it had to be Todd Vandermeer. The man was Emma's only other possible prospect for a husband before her marriage to Thomas— at least as far as the butler knew—and Humphrey remembered the man was to start work at Wellingham Imports sometime that week.

"Thank you," Thomas said with a worried nod. "Will she... will she be all right, do you suppose?" he asked, his guilty look enough for the butler to know Thomas was sincere in his concern.

"I expect she will recover from her reopened wound," Humphrey said with a nod. "I cannot say beyond that."

Thomas sat down on the bed and held his head in his hands. "I fear the green monster of jealousy has had its way with me," he murmured sadly. "I have been a jealous bastard. I cannot... I cannot *believe* how I reacted," he continued, his head shaking back and forth as he recalled his awful behavior. "It was as if a completely different person was inhabiting my body," he whispered. He sat quietly for a moment, his gaze aimed at the carpet. "The question now is, what do I do? What should I do now?" he asked, looking up to his butler for advice.

Humphrey angled his head first to one side and then to the other. "You ride off as fast as you can to Grace Park, and you beg for her forgiveness," he said evenly. After a long pause, he added, "Like mother, like son."

Thomas stared at the older man and swallowed hard. "Oh, drat. I have become my mother, haven't I?" he claimed in disgust, remembering all the nights that he had overheard his mother's cruel remarks to his father. By the following morning, she was all smiles again, her thorns having been somehow pruned by his father.

You must tend your garden...

His father had said those words to him a long time ago, as if he expected his son might one day marry a woman who was of a higher class or who had expectations of a life beyond his ability to provide.

The butler's eyebrows danced in surprise. "I would not have put it *quite* like that," he countered with an attempt at a grin. "I have seen to it that Mr. Larsen has your horse ready. If you have no chance of being granted forgiveness this evening, might I suggest you spend the night at the townhouse in Kingly Street and try again in the morning? If Mrs. Wellingham is in a forgiving mood, you will most likely spend the night at Grace Park." When he finished his response, he moved to pick up a valise from near the doorway. "Either way, here is a change of clothes for the morrow," he added with an arched eyebrow.

Appreciating his butler's foresight, Thomas nodded and grabbed his waistcoat from the floor. "I am off, then," he said with determination, pulling on the garment with Humphrey's help. He buttoned it as he left the room, accepting the valise from his butler as he did so.

Within minutes, Humphrey heard the sound of a galloping horse leaving the grounds of Woodscastle, its rider not wearing a tailcoat or even a hat.

CHAPTER 19

A FRIEND DISCOVERS
WHAT'S HAPPENED

Back in London

Todd Vandermeer finally left Wellingham Imports when his pocket watch displayed six o'clock. Most of the laborers in the warehouse had already departed, their workday having started at six or seven o'clock that morning. Only a few clerks remained in the accounting office.

Satisfied with his accomplishments for his first day and his head filled with the numbers he'd been shown in the company's ledgers, he stepped up onto his phaeton and set the horse on a trot. The route to Margaret Street was far easier and shorter than the one he'd had to follow from the East India Company to his home at No. 1 Chandos Street in Cavendish Square, but he was careful to keep a watchful eye for those who might wish him harm. He was also on the lookout for a coster selling flowers. He was sure his Deborah would be home waiting for him in the parlor, and he was heading home later than expected.

Once he turned into Oxford Street, he spotted a flower girl with a large basket. Slowing the horse to a walk, he leaned out and asked what she had.

"Just three red roses, sir," she replied as she started walking at the same speed as his phaeton. "Just a copper, good sir," she added hopefully. A small matted dog followed her as she hurried along the street.

"I will take them all," Todd said, stopping his horse and holding out a penny. She took the pence and handed him the roses. Although one was already wilting, the other two were newly bloomed.

"Thank you, kind sir," the flower girl said as she skipped away, the dog hurrying to keep up.

Armed with his roses, Todd pulled into the semicircular drive in front of Grace Park as Mr. Stevenson ran out from the carriage house. "Good evening, Mr. Vandermeer," he called out, running along side the phaeton. Pulling the horse to a halt, Todd stepped down from the phaeton and greeted the man as he gave him the reins.

At the same time, Thomas Wellingham, looking quite disheveled, rode up at a full gallop, dismounting his horse even before it came to a stop next to the phaeton. Mr. Stevenson grabbed the reins as Thomas tossed them aside and saw to removing the valise that seemed about to fall from behind the saddle.

Todd frowned as he took in the sight of his best friend. "Good God, Thomas, what has happened to you?" he asked, worry evident in his voice. "Were you... set upon by thieves? Highwaymen?" His eyes widened, certain Thomas had been robbed.

Thomas took a moment to catch his breath. "No," he replied quickly, shaking his head. "I must apologize for my appearance as well as my poor behavior toward you earlier today," he said, bowing his head when he realized he hadn't yet properly greeted his host. "I am so very sorry and hope you can forgive my atrocious behavior."

Bowing slightly, Todd nodded. "Apology accepted, of course," he replied, his face still showing concern. "You didn't come all this way to apologize to me, though, did you?"

Shaking his head again, Thomas put his hands on his hips and tried to decide how best to explain his appearance at Grace Park. "Are you just now getting home for the day?" he asked. They headed together for the steps leading up to the front door.

"Indeed. I left work at six of the clock," the taller man replied.

Thomas nodded. "An awfully long day for your first day," he remarked, rather impressed by his friend's commitment. He paused a moment as they reached the top step. "I have been a terribly jealous ass today, you see, and..." he began in explanation, still trying to catch his breath.

"Jealous of whom?" Todd interrupted, his face screwed into a quizzical stare.

Taken aback by the question, Thomas blinked. "Well, *you*, of course."

Todd stared at his best friend but said nothing at first. He leaned back on his heels as he regarded Thomas. "Whatever do I possess that would have you jealous of me?" he finally countered, his brows furrowed. "Is it because Deborah is giving me a child? Is that it?"

Thomas shook his head. "No, no," he insisted. "Not at all. I was just... I was angry when I found you and Emma in your office..."

Frowning, Todd shook his head. "But, you told me to ask her—"

"I know. And I reacted... badly. And..." Here, he sighed and rolled his eyes. "I have done something unforgivable," he admitted in a hushed voice, unable to make eye contact with Todd.

His breaths coming quicker, Todd regarded Thomas and leaned heavily on his cane. "What have you done?" he asked, his concern at first only curiosity. As he stared at Thomas, though, he grew suspicious. "Did you strike her?" he asked in disbelief, a hint of anger in the question.

"Never!" Thomas hissed, his own sudden anger matching his colleague's.

Leaning over the shorter man, Todd raised a finger and shook it in front of Thomas' face. "Did you hurt her?" he rasped.

Thomas closed his eyes for a moment and nodded. "Yes. Her arm... I pulled her by that arm... the wound on her arm has... it was bleeding when last I saw her," he stammered, tears coming to his eyes.

Todd stepped back, surprised by the admission of guilt. "Where is she?" he asked quietly.

"Here, I'm told," Thomas replied as he waved at the front doors. "Humphrey thought your wife could provide medical assistance."

Winston opened the front door, not too surprised to find Mr. Wellingham standing on the stoop with his master at his side. "Good evening, sir, Mr. Wellingham," the butler said in turn as he stepped aside. He regarded Todd and his rather disheveled guest as the two gentlemen entered the vestibule of Grace Park. "Mrs. Vandermeer was just tending to Mrs. Wellingham in the far north guest bedchamber," he stated formally. "I believe she is in the mistress suite now."

Todd exchanged a glance with Thomas. "Thank you, Winston."

"Would you care for some ice for your jaw, Mr. Wellingham?" the butler asked.

Thomas shook his head. "Thank you, no," he answered, very aware of Todd's sudden scrutiny.

"Did she do that?" Todd asked, just then noticing the blooming bruise on his friend's jaw.

"No. Someone else beat her to it," Thomas replied, running a hand along his jaw line and grimacing in pain as he did so.

The master of the house regarded his friend and new employer. "What will you do?" Todd asked as he gave his hat and cane to the butler. They entered the great hall and both paused.

"Beg her forgiveness, of course," Thomas answered simply, not sure what else he could do. "Like mother, like son," he added in a whisper.

Todd stared at Thomas, rather shocked at the comment.

The simple statement made many things clear to him as he remembered the Wellinghams from his youth—a doting husband who frequently had to—and could—placate his cruel, spoiled wife in a matter of minutes. "Here," he said as he handed Thomas the red roses. "I believe you need these more than I do."

Thomas gave a wan smile but took only one of the flowers. "Thank you," he said. "But you are very late and could probably benefit from one of these as well. With your permission?" he half-asked as he nodded his head toward the north.

"By all means," Todd replied. "And good luck." After a moment, he added, "There is another guest bedchamber should you find yourself in need of one," he offered in a whisper. "I am more than happy to provide hospitality."

Thomas gave a shake of his head before he hurried up the steps. He took most of them two at a time, and then nearly ran as he made his way to the guest bedchamber.

The door to the room was slightly ajar, and when he stepped in front of it, he listened intently. Not hearing any voices, he quietly slipped into the beautifully appointed room.

In the waning light from the room's only window, he nearly gasped at the sight of Emma. Looking ever so much like an angel, she lay sleeping on a huge white cloud of pillows. Some of her golden blond hair splayed out around her, but her left arm, held to the front of her body by a sling made from a white silk cravat, gave the impression of an angel with a broken wing.

He was immediately reminded of the night of the horrible rain storm, the night he had managed to make it to Woodscastle despite his growing fever and delirium. Of what he thought when he caught sight of Emma at the top of the stairs. Wearing only a nightrail and barely lit by the light from a candle lamp, she appeared as an angel to him that night. His saving grace at a time he desperately needed saving.

He had pulled her into his bed that night. Clung to her as if he believed he would die if he didn't have the benefit of her warmth.

I might have fallen in love with her that night, he thought in passing.

He might have, had he not already done so.

I was such a fool, he thought then, cursing over his missed opportunities. Over his behavior from earlier that afternoon.

I was such an ass!

Standing silent at the end of the bed, Thomas took a deep breath and willed himself not to say anything. After a few moments, he moved to the side of the bed and pulled up a chair as close as he could, determined to keep vigil as Emma slept.

He didn't know exactly what he would do when she awoke, but he allowed scenarios to play out in his head as he imagined the best and the worst of what might happen.

When Emma finally moaned and turned her head in his direction, he stood up with baited breath.

"Water," she whispered, her eyelids fluttering.

Thomas found the goblet by the side of the bed and immediately held it to her lips as he placed a hand behind her head to help her sit up. She drank several swallows before falling back into the pillows, her eyes closed.

Leaning over, Thomas kissed her on the forehead. Noticing that most of her hair was still twisted atop her head, he began carefully pulling the pins out of the messy bun. When he had taken out as many as he could find, he ran his fingers through her hair to loosen the curls. The blonde locks tumbled down around her head, but their movement didn't seem to disturb her sleep.

Returning to his seat, Thomas found he couldn't abide how far he was from Emma. He repositioned the chair so he could hold onto her right hand and gaze at her. He wanted to speak to her—apologize and beg forgiveness—but to wake her from the healing slumber would be a selfish act. So he simply sat and waited in the growing darkness.

CHAPTER 20

A ROSE BESTOWED IS STILL
JUST A ROSE

Meanwhile, in the mistress suite

Red rose in hand, Todd Vandermeer found his wife in her mistress suite, drying her hands in a bath linen. At the sight of him, Deborah rushed to him and wrapped her arms around his neck, the linen dropping to the floor as she did so. "You are home!" she exclaimed happily. "And yet the dinner bell has not yet rung," she added as she repeatedly kissed his cheek and neck.

Surprised by the happy greeting, Todd kissed his wife's hair and forehead, and when she turned to look up at him, he kissed her mouth, holding on to the kiss as long as he could. "My God, I will look forward to every return from work if they are always such a happy reunion," he whispered as he gave her a smile. "Are you feeling well?" he asked, his face taking on a more serious expression. "I have thought of you and the baby all day. I do hope your shopping trip was to your satisfaction."

"Very much so. Mostly baby gowns and a few blankets. I've put everything in the nursery," she said, wondering how she was going to tell him about Emma.

Todd held out the rose, secretly relieved when Deborah's smile widened.

"It's beautiful," she whispered, a blush coloring her cheeks as she took the bloom and raised it to her nose. She took a step back and remembered his other question. "I am very well, indeed," she added before she sighed. A look of distress took over her features. "My friend, Emma, is not, however."

Todd's brows furrowed, and he pursed his lips. "Thomas just told me what happened."

Deborah's eyes widened in shock. "He told you?" she repeated in disbelief. "But... when?"

Pulling her closer, Todd cupped her face in one hand. "A few moments ago," he replied, wondering what Emma might have said to Deborah. "He arrived here at the same time as I did."

Gasping, Deborah tried to step away from him, but Todd's arm around her waist held her in place. "I had to put fifteen stitches in her arm because of that *brute*," she was able to get out before Todd silenced her with a kiss.

"Thomas is not a brute," he countered quietly, pressing his forehead against hers. "He knows he did wrong, and I know why he was upset. It will not happen again, I assure you," he whispered hoarsely. "For if it does, I shall challenge him to a duel at Wimbledon Commons."

Deborah struggled in vain to break free of his grasp and then finally relaxed against his taller body. "You are quite sure he will not hurt her?" she whispered into the space between his neck and shoulder.

"I am most certain," Todd replied, letting go of his hold on her. "If you promise not to beat him with your fists, I will allow you to see for yourself," he suggested, thinking she would wish to check on her patient at some point.

Stepping back, Deborah curtsied and lowered her eyes. "I'm sorry I called Mr. Wellingham a brute," she said quietly.

Todd smiled then, not quite sure why he found her apology amusing just then. "Apology accepted, of course. Not that you really needed to apologize." He reached out with the palm of one hand toward her and held it near her belly. "May I... touch you?" he asked, a hint of wonder in his voice.

Deborah placed her hand over his and pressed it onto her belly. "It will be many months before you will feel anything," she said with a shrug, finding the warmth of his hand a comfort after such a traumatic afternoon.

Reaching over, he kissed her softly and grinned. "You must allow me to do this every day when I return from work," he insisted, kissing her again before removing his hand. "Now, I suppose I should change clothes for dinner."

"And I must, as well," Deborah said with a nod. "I will wait until after dinner before seeing to Emma," she added, sure her friend would be sound asleep for some time before requiring more water or a change of bandages. "While you drink your port."

Todd allowed a nod before he took his leave of the mistress suite, rather amused by her last comment.

He rarely drank port after dinner.

CHAPTER 21

A PHYSICIAN IS HEALED

Later that evening

Still dressed in her silk deNaples dinner gown and carrying a pitcher of water, Deborah crept to the guest bedchamber door and knocked quietly. When she heard a distant, "Come," she slowly opened the door and peeked around the edge of it.

Thomas stood up and bowed in her direction before motioning for her to enter. "Good evening, Mrs. Vandermeer," he said with a nod. "I wish to thank you for all you have done for my Emma," he said in a hoarse whisper. "I was so very worried."

Deborah regarded her husband's employer with uncertainty, finally noticing his tear-stained face in the light of the single candle that burned on the bedside table. "You're welcome, of course, Mr. Wellingham," she whispered in reply. "I would do anything for her." Moving to the nightstand, she was about to place the pitcher on the marble top when Thomas was suddenly there to take it from her. She couldn't stop the reflexive jerk of her body in response, nor the gasp that escaped her lips.

"I apologize. I only meant to help," Thomas murmured as he held up a hand. He lifted the crystal pitcher and refilled Emma's goblet.

Before she could stop herself, Deborah added, "She thinks

you might have raped her if she hadn't fainted. Is it true, Mr. Wellingham?"

Thomas winced in response to her question. He briefly wondered if Emma had truly thought him capable of such a thing, and then realized she must have thought he was about to do so—Deborah's query was proof.

He had come to his senses, though. Realized how he was hurting her—had hurt her. But before he could assure Emma she had nothing more to fear from him, he had been struck hard in the jaw and had passed out.

"No," Thomas replied, still stung that Emma thought it a possibility. "I recovered my sanity before it was too late. And was quite shocked at what I had done before..." He let the sentence trail off when he noticed Deborah had covered her mouth with an open hand.

"Please forgive me, sir," Deborah whispered, her other hand moving to her bosom. "It was not my place to ask such a thing of my friend's husband." Her embarrassment acute, she started to back up, her intent to take her leave of the bedchamber as quickly as possible.

Thomas regarded Deborah with a raised eyebrow. "But as you're her best friend, my wife appreciates and values your concern for her well-being. As do I," he added quickly, hoping to assuage some of Deborah's fear of him. "Apology accepted, of course, since none was required," he whispered.

Deborah nodded and swallowed hard. "Thank you," she replied, finding it rather interesting that twice that evening, an offer of an apology had come with a statement that it was unnecessary. "I came to see to her bandage," she said in a quiet voice, nodding toward Emma. "Has she opened her eyes?"

"Only once. She asked for water, which I gave her," he replied quietly, indicating the refilled goblet. "Otherwise, she has been sleeping the entire time. Is that... normal?"

Deborah placed a hand on Emma's forehead, concerned her friend might have developed a fever. "Of course," Deborah replied with a nod. "She will heal faster if she is allowed to rest," she added as she studied the bandage. Satisfied that her stitches had stopped the bleeding—the bandage had no evidence of blood on it—she rewrapped the wound. "The stitches have closed the wound. Now she just has to sleep and heal."

Thomas nodded his understanding. "Then, if you would be so kind as to allow me to stay with her, I shall see to it that she sleeps as much as possible," he promised, his voice tinged with pleading.

The midwife regarded Thomas for a moment, still not entirely sure of his motives. "Of course, you may stay, Mr. Wellingham," Deborah replied finally. "I will have your dinner brought up. You must be hungry—," she started to say as she moved to the door.

"No, thank you," Thomas replied. "I cannot eat a thing until I know my Emma will recover," he whispered, his head continuing to shake.

Deborah paused in her retreat from the bedchamber, her manner indicating uncertainty. She appeared ready to make a comment, but said nothing.

"What is it?" Thomas asked then, his brows furrowed in concern.

Swallowing hard, Deborah turned and said, "I do hope you understand why I was angry with you, Mr. Wellingham... when I thought you capable of such an act," she said quietly, her eyes not quite meeting his and her face flushed. One hand moved to cover her belly and she held it there protectively.

Thomas shook his head and moved closer to the woman, aware that she was shivering despite the room's warmth. "I don't... I don't understand," he stammered, not sure of the point she was trying to make.

Certain that Emma had taken her husband into her confidence regarding Deborah's rape by a madman, Deborah felt a flash of anger at the man who stood before her. "I did nothing, nothing, to make that man angry with me. I was just walking on a street after a visit to the market when I heard his awful voice yelling at me. 'Freak, you are a freak', he kept saying before he knocked me to the ground..." She stopped when she saw that Thomas was staring at her with a look of understanding on his face.

"Emma told me some of what happened," Thomas whispered as he moved closer to her. He recalled the Vandermeer's wedding day when Emma mentioned the rape. Then he remembered the phrase the guilty man had yelled at a rather tall woman before she removed a pistol from her reticule and shot him in the forehead. "I was at the Bank of England the day Mrs. Morton shot that man," he added as he stood before her, his eyes level with hers.

That man, he thought as he remembered how the vagrant had been shot. The very day Todd had purchased Deborah's wedding ring. Every time he and Todd exited a shop, they heard a man yelling the same phrase. 'Freak, freak. You are a freak!'

Deborah broke eye contact and reached behind her for something to hold onto. "She told you then, did she?" she half-asked, taking a step back when she found nothing to lean against.

Aware she needed assistance, Thomas took her hand and placed another on her shoulder, guiding her to a nearby chair. "Not exactly," he lied as he lowered himself to one knee beside the chair. "When... when did it happen?" he asked carefully.

Tears streamed down Deborah's face. "It's been over three years, Mr. Wellingham. I assure you—"

"Three years?" he repeated, somewhat surprised and then very concerned. "Did you ever tell Mr. Vandermeer?" he asked, his whisper fierce.

Deborah nodded as she used the back of her hand to wipe away the tears. "Emma told him when I could not. I... thought... I thought perhaps she had told you, as well," she stammered.

Thomas glanced over at Emma, relieved to find she was still asleep. "She told me some of it, back when I came to the wrong conclusion about you," he admitted in a whisper, now rather embarrassed he had at one time assumed Deborah to be a harlot based on where she worked. At the time, he had been concerned for his best friend, afraid Todd had fallen for a fallen woman.

Turning back to Deborah, he sighed. "Did you know the man?" When Deborah shook her head, he asked, "Have you seen him since?" When she continued to shake her head, he leaned toward her. "Did he wear a black cape coat, much like the old-fashioned coachmen used to wear?" When Deborah's eyes widened and she nodded, he added, "Was his hat badly crumpled?"

Deborah nodded again, "It was most certainly not from Fitzsimmons," she replied, her tears subsiding. "And he had a horrible odor about him, as if he had not bathed in a very long time." When Thomas didn't say anything but merely stared at her, she asked, "How... how do you know this man?"

Thomas shook his head as if to clear it. "I do not," he replied quickly. "Did not, rather. But the day that Todd and I shopped for jewelry in Ludgate Hill, there was an odd man yelling those very words every time we came out of a shop. I wondered then if they were directed at Todd."

Deborah's eyes widened and she swallowed. "Oh, dear," she whispered, quickly wiping a tear from her cheek. "He was yelling at Mr. Vandermeer, I am sure," she said quietly. "Because he is too tall. 'Tis why he yelled at me, why he..." She closed her eyes tightly as new tears formed.

"Justice has already been served, Mrs. Vandermeer," Thomas said quietly, taking her other hand in his so he held them both. "Mrs. Samuel Morton shot the man when he attacked her near the Bank of England. About three months ago now. She's a Tall Meg, as well..." He allowed his voice to trail off. "If she had not done so, I believe I would have seen to his death," he promised.

Opening her eyes, Deborah quickly shook her head. "It is not your place to seek vengeance on my behalf, Mr. Welling-ham," she stated very quietly. At his quizzical stare, she added, "That creature took something that should have belonged to my husband—"

"You may think the greatest gift you could give your husband was your maidenhood," Thomas interrupted quickly, remembering clearly the lectures he'd been given by both his sister and by Emma on the subject. "But I know that Todd values your heart and soul... and the babe you carry," he added as an afterthought, "Above all else."

Deborah stared at Thomas for several seconds, occasionally wiping away a tear with the back of her hand. "I could kiss you right now, Mr. Wellingham," she whispered as a wan smile came to her lips.

"Please, do not. I am already in enough trouble with my wife," he added with a nod in the direction of the bed. He moved to stand up. "And Todd lives to be kissed by you. His very life depends on you, in fact," he added with a sigh. He held out a hand and helped her to stand. "Since I believe he will make the best business partner I could ever have, I am counting on you to keep him happy and healthy."

Deborah's smile was broad as she moved toward the door. "I shall endeavor to do my best, Mr. Wellingham," she answered before dipping a curtsy and taking her leave of the bedchamber.

Thomas stared at the closed door for several moments before returning to the chair next to the bed. Sitting down hard, he reached out and took Emma's hand. Kissing the back of it, he studied the faded ink stains and delicate fingernails at her fingertips before finally allowing his head to rest on the edge of the bed. In a moment, he was sound asleep, unaware that Emma had been listening the entire time Deborah was in the room.

CHAPTER 22

A PATIENT AWAKENS

Later that night

At some point during the late evening, the movement of Emma's fingers woke Thomas, and he glanced up to find her staring at him with a quizzical expression. In the dim candlelight, she murmured, "I have just had the most awful nightmare."

Thomas gasped and stood up, realizing almost immediately that she was probably referring to the events of earlier that day. He offered her the goblet of water, and she drank what remained in it. When he removed the glass from her lips, he whispered, "Would you like more?" He turned to refill the goblet from the pitcher Deborah had brought.

Emma shook her head and opened her eyes completely. Wincing when she tried to move her left arm, she stared at Thomas. Recognition and recollection happened then, and Thomas saw fear in her eyes.

"I am so very sorry for what I have done to you," Thomas said very quietly. "I have come to beg for forgiveness. Forgiveness I know I do not deserve and can only hope to obtain after my death." After a brief pause, he added, "You look like an angel. An incandescent, beautiful angel with a broken wing. And I love you and cannot bear to live in this world should you banish me from your life." Tears streamed down the side of his face before he managed to brush them away with the sleeve of his shirt.

Continuing to stare at Thomas, Emma swallowed and asked very quietly. "Tell me, Mr. Wellingham. Of what impropriety did you believe me to be guilty?"

Startled by the question—and by the use of his formal name—Thomas sat down hard in the chair. "I didn't believe you to be guilty of any impropriety," he answered in a hoarse whisper as he tried to remember just why he had been so angry with her.

Jealousy, he remembered telling Todd. His anger was not aimed at her, but at his best friend, for an impropriety that hadn't existed. "I was... a fool. I was... angry with Todd. Angry about the amount of time you spent with him," he murmured.

Emma furrowed her brows and directed her gaze at the ceiling of the bedchamber, barely visible in the sphere of candlelight. "Then why were you so angry with me?" she questioned, tears coming unbidden at the corners of her eyes.

Moving to the edge of the bed, Thomas took her right hand in his, well aware of how she winced and turned her face away when he held it to his chest. "When Billy told me you had spent most of the afternoon with Vandermeer, I... I felt jealous. I was so jealous of him."

Turning her head back to look at Thomas, Emma gasped. "But... but, why?" she asked in surprise, not expecting a confession of jealousy.

"The time he spent with you is time I wish I could have spent with you," he answered, his voice cracking. "I know you are his first love. You will *always* be his first love. And knowing that you would have married him if there had been no Deborah White just makes me... angry, I suppose. Much like my mother used to be towards my father when she would imagine the worst."

Emma listened to Thomas and then closed her eyes. Taking a deep breath, she asked, "Does it not matter to you that you have been my only love?"

Thomas swallowed and stared at Emma, her words the most welcome he had heard in probably his entire life. "It matters like you cannot imagine," he answered. "Just as you have been my only love."

Squeezing his hand in return, Emma sighed. "He is your best friend, Thomas. You cannot be jealous of your best friend," Emma insisted as she tried to sit up. She stopped when she felt a stab of pain at the attempt to move her left arm.

Nodding, Thomas replied, "I know that now, of course, he said as he placed his hands beneath her arms and lifted her so she was sitting up. "I have apologized to Todd, and he has... forgiven me," he managed to get out, still hoping—praying— Emma would do the same.

"And now he is your partner in business," she continued, barely acknowledging his comment. "You cannot expect him to be successful unless he has learned everything about the company that he can, and if that means he has to spend some time with me, then he must, and if you cannot tolerate that he is spending time with me, time that you are not, then... then you must make yourself available to spend the time with us both, I suppose," she insisted quietly, her impatience barely kept in check.

"Agreed," Thomas replied with a quick nod of his head. "You have proposed the perfect solution, of course," he added as he lifted her right hand and kissed the back of it. "I should endeavor to think more like you when it comes to these situations," he stated, his tone almost patronizing. "Besides, if I do not, he'll challenge me to a duel, and I'd rather not suffer a gunshot wound..." He winced and blinked when he realized what he was saying.

Finally allowing a wan smile, Emma sighed heavily. "Then I suppose I must forgive you," she said quietly. "But there are consequences for your actions today, you must know," her tone of voice taking on a rather serious note.

Continuing to hold her hand, Thomas stood up straight and regarded her with an expression filled with doubt and worry. "I understand," he said uncertainly. "What... and what might they be?" he asked then, not sure what she had in mind.

Emma indicated her left arm. "Deborah informed me that I will be unable to work for several days."

Not surprised by the statement, Thomas allowed a shrug. "I would not expect you to, of course," he replied. He glanced around the bedchamber and then turned his attention back to her. "Would I be allowed to bring you to the townhouse for your recuperation? I can have Miss Dahlia see to your needs while I am at the warehouse," he suggested hopefully, referring to one of the maids at Woodscastle.

Shrugging her right shoulder, Emma considered the offer. "Perhaps," she said without too much conviction. She rather liked the comfortable bed and richer furnishings of the guest bedchamber compared to her own at the townhouse in Kingly Street. "Perhaps I will remain here with my best friend," she added, figuring she really didn't have to make a decision just then.

"Of course. You like her company. She's your... best friend," he acknowledged, remembering Christiana was gone and wouldn't be returning for several months. "What else?" Thomas asked uncertainly.

Emma angled her head to one side. "Deborah did beautiful needlework on my arm, but my scar will be larger than it would have been," she explained sadly. "I will no longer be able to wear any of my short-sleeved gowns."

"I shall take you shopping for new gowns as soon as you are recovered enough to try them on," Thomas agreed quickly. "Or... I will hire a modiste, and you can have her make whatever you wish," he offered. She had mentioned his salary. Of course he could afford to pay for a few gowns to be made if she were truly paying him what she claimed she was.

"And I rather like this nightrail of Deborah's—"

"As do I," Thomas said too quickly. He noticed Emma's slight frown when he interrupted her comment. "Although I actually prefer you in nothing at all, I believe I shall buy you one." At her arched eyebrow, he added, "One for every night of the week." When she didn't immediately respond, he asked, "What else?"

"I am terribly thirsty."

Thomas grabbed the goblet from the nightstand and held the glass while Emma drank nearly all the water. When she indicated she'd had enough, he said, "What else?" as he took her hand in his.

Emma regarded her husband and sighed. She pulled her hand from his and said, "Remove your clothing."

At the odd demand, Thomas' face took on a quizzical expression. "What?"

Emma angled her head as she regarded him. "If you expect to spend the rest of the night in this bed with me," she said as she patted the mattress to her right, "Then you need to remove your clothing. You smell like a horse," she accused.

Relieved at being forgiven, despite the consequences and maybe even because of them, Thomas dared a grin. He quickly complied with his wife's demands, shedding his clothing so it fell onto the chair. "I love you, you wicked woman," he whispered as he climbed onto the bed. He kissed her shoulder and neck and the back of her hand before molding his body against hers. Within minutes, he was sound asleep.

Emma, however, remained wide awake for a time, tears of relief streaming down her face.

CHAPTER 23

A WIFE IS MISSED AT WORK

A week later

After two days of recuperating under the careful watch of Deborah Vandermeer, Emma returned to Woodscastle and discovered a different form of attention.

That of the servants.

They seemed determined to dote on her at their every opportunity, as if they thought she was considering taking permanent leave of Woodscastle and of Thomas Wellingham.

Humphrey delivered coffee in the mornings and tea at midday, checked the level of ink in her ink well every day, and, if it seemed too cold or too hot, fussed about the temperature in the library.

Mrs. Werthers brought her luncheon and saw to clearing the dishes, despite Emma's assurances that she could see to them.

The grooms saddled her horse when she wanted a quick ride around the grounds, seeing to it she had an extra tall mounting block and an escort in the event her arm bothered her in the least.

At first rather embarrassed by all the attention, Emma supposed it was all just as well since she was determined to resume working as best she could from home. Just because her left arm was still healing didn't preclude her from continuing her work, she reasoned.

As he had done when she had first begun auditing for him, Thomas brought home ledgers every night for her to review in the library, and then returned to Wellingham Imports the following day with whatever she had completed the day before.

Elevated to lead accomptant in her absence, Benjamin Cunningham saw to it which ledgers to send with Thomas and took the completed ones from him in the mornings.

After a week, though, Emma found she missed the morning ride to town. Thomas seemed to grow more sullen with each passing day, although he always greeted her with a kiss and a careful hug upon his return. At night, he pleasured her until she could take no more but then refused any himself. He didn't seem to sleep as well, his face appeared drawn, and a touch of gray appeared at his temples.

Something was wrong, and yet Emma's queries as to what might be the cause brought looks of confusion or outright denials that there was anything amiss.

On the eighth morning, as Thomas was about to leave for London, Emma intercepted him in the vestibule and kissed him on the lips—despite Humphrey's presence not ten feet away.

"I should be home by four o'clock for tea," he offered when he pulled away from her.

"Whatever is wrong, Thomas? Please tell me," Emma pleaded quietly.

"'Tis nothing, really. I just... I just miss you when you're not in the office is all," he said lightly, unable to make eye contact with her.

"Then I'm coming with you," she stated before turning to Humphrey to ask for her redingote.

Thomas' eyes widened. "You... you are?" he asked, his entire manner changing. "You will?" He took the redingote from the butler.

"Of course. Perhaps we can take the curricle?" she suggested. "I have to go to town, after all. I'll have Master Billy take me to Dr. Talbot's office this afternoon." Movement behind Thomas had her directing her attention to Humphrey. Upon hearing her comment about the curricle, the butler was quick to summon Mr. Allen from where he stood with his master's horse.

Her husband frowned at the mention of Dr. Talbot. "Whatever is wrong?" he asked, the sound of his question identical to how she said the very words only moments before.

"Nothing, darling. He just needs to remove my stitches. 'Tis time, is all." She slipped her arms into the sleeves of her redingote as he held it for her.

Allowing a wan smile, Thomas nodded before turning to find Humphrey was already seeing to the curricle. "Let's get your ledger," he murmured as he left the vestibule. "It's a bit chilly today. Are you sure you wouldn't be more comfortable in the town coach?"

Emma followed him into the library and shut the door behind her. "I'll be fine. Now, tell me truly. What has you so...?" She sighed, not quite knowing how to describe his behavior of the past week. "*Sad?*" Half-expecting him to deny there was anything bothering him, she was surprised when he moved to lift the ledger from the library table and instead lowered himself into the chair. His shoulders sagged.

"They hate me, Emma," he murmured as his gaze moved to where the grooms were hitching the horse to the curricle.

Her brows furrowing, Emma stepped closer to the table and regarded her husband for a moment. "Who hates you?"

Thomas rolled his eyes. "My employees. My grooms. My butler, for God's sake. And I cannot blame them." At her look of confusion, he added, "They saw how I treated you. They think me a blackguard. A brute," he whispered. "If I could go back to that day and... and do it all over again, I would. I think of how different things would be if I hadn't overreacted."

Angling her head to one side, Emma nodded her understanding. "Your grooms do not hate you, and neither does Humphrey," she said quietly. "I have assured them you have apologized, and that I have forgiven you. As for your employees—"

"A few paid witness to my... treatment of you," he murmured.

The comment had Emma straightening. "Oh," she managed. Did the entire workforce in the warehouse know what had happened? "I'm not sure how we can change their opinion, but I should think time will help in that regard."

"You just being there will help," Thomas countered, finally coming to his feet. He took her into his arms and kissed her thoroughly, completely unaware they were being watched by the two grooms.

Having just finished hitching a Cleveland Bay to the curricle, Mr. Allen and Mr. Larsen stood gawking in the direction of the library windows. That is, until Humphrey moved to join them. He was about to admonish them for staring when his attention was captured by the image of the master and mistress of the house as they engaged in a rather long and languorous kiss.

"This is a relief, if you were wondering," Mr. Allen commented.

"Indeed," Mr. Larsen agreed. After another moment of staring, he added, "I do believe I'll ask Miss Dahlia if we might try that tonight."

Mr. Allen gave him a quelling glance. "You mean, you haven't yet?"

The other groom snorted. "She hasn't yet married me."

The butler cleared his throat. "You would be wise to return to your horses, or you'll both find yourselves unemployed and unable to take wives," he warned.

Pulled from their stupor, the two nodded in agreement and took off for the stables. About to return to the house, Humphrey realized what had their attention. For a moment, he too, stared while Thomas held his wife in his arms and kissed her. Sighing, he returned to the vestibule.

Meanwhile, in the library, Thomas finally ended the kiss but left his forehead resting against Emma's. He watched as her eyelashes fluttered and a grin appeared.

"Now that we have convinced the employees here all is well, we should do the same with all the others," Emma suggested, one eyebrow arching up. When she noticed his furrowed brow, she added, "We had an audience," a finger pointed toward the window.

"I do love how you think, you wicked woman," Thomas murmured. Retrieving the ledger from the library table, he offered his other arm and the two were off for Wellingham Imports.

CHAPTER 24

DINNER AS AN ADVENTUROUS AFFAIR

December 20, 1802

The scent of pine assaulted Thomas' nostrils as he entered the library. He paused and inhaled deeply, a memory from younger years bringing a grin to his face. A moment later, and he was frowning. "This will be my first Christmas without Christiana. Well, the first since she was born," he commented as he watched Emma tie evergreen boughs into a large wreath. At Emma's insistence, he had bought them at one of the nearby nurseries on his way home from town. Most of the trees on the Woodscastle land were live oaks, and the few evergreens on the property didn't suit for making Christmas sprays and wreaths.

"Do you miss her?" Emma asked, using a pruning shears to remove a wayward twig from her creation.

Thomas angled his head. "Not yet. I might on Christmas Day, though," he replied. "Which reminds me." He pulled a small envelope from his waistcoat pocket. "A footman from the Simpson residence stopped by the office today. Seems we're to be their guests for Christmas dinner. That is, if you—"

"How splendid!" Emma cried out, her wreath-making forgotten as she reached for the envelope. "I haven't seen the Simpsons in weeks," she murmured. "Nor their new town-house," she added with an arched eyebrow. "I wonder how many others are invited?"

Thomas watched as she pulled the handwritten note from the snowy white envelope and read the beautiful script. "I've no idea. It might just be us." At Emma's look of doubt, he allowed a shrug. "We could stay at the townhouse that night if you'd like," he offered, thinking they could have a quiet night together after the dinner party.

"That would be lovely. I'll send Mrs. Simpson a note letting her know we'll be there." She turned to regard her other handiwork—a few sprays as well as a series of branches strung together for the top of the mantel in the parlor. The remodeling in that room had been finished for nearly a week, although the new furniture hadn't yet arrived. She hoped the existing furnishings didn't appear too shabby against the new carpet and wall coverings. "A few more ribbons on these, and they'll be ready to hang," she said brightly. "When do we expect the Vandermeers?"

Thomas pulled his chronometer from his waistcoat pocket and frowned. "Any moment, I should think. Are we having dinner at eight?"

Emma shook her head. "Seven, actually. Deborah said she cannot stay awake much past eleven these days, especially since Todd is such an early riser. I really thought he would adopt later hours once he started working for you," she commented as she finished tying a large ribbon bow at the base of the wreath. "I told them they could spend the night here if they were so inclined. I'd rather not have them heading back to London when there's barely a moon." She regarded her latest creation. "There. This one is ready for the front door," she said, her attention going to the butler.

"Very nice," Thomas murmured as Humphrey took the wreath from Emma and made his way to the vestibule. "As for Todd's early hours, it goes back to our days of being caddies, I suppose. Hard habit to break." He lifted the long series of boughs intended for the parlor mantel. "And I suppose Mrs. Vandermeer's position as a midwife doesn't help in that regard." After a moment, he added, "Where does this go?"

"Parlor mantel," Emma replied. "Just be sure it doesn't hang down so as to catch fire," she warned as Thomas moved toward the door.

"Yes, milady," he replied. A moment later, he reappeared with news that the town coach bearing their guests had just pulled into the drive off Burlington Lane.

Emma's eyes widened. "Oh, I've not yet dressed for dinner!" she said as she hurried out of the library.

Allowing Humphrey to see to welcoming the Vandermeers, Thomas followed his wife to the master suite, intending to make a quick change into a different waistcoat and topcoat. Instead, he helped with Emma's gown, a new velvet and satin dinner gown in emerald green. The long sleeves puffed up near the shoulders and then tapered to points at her wrists.

Staring at his wife in wonder at the transformation that had taken place with just the change in her gown, Thomas remembered his mother had a gown in a similar color.

"What is it? You look as if you've seen a ghost," Emma accused.

Thomas shook his head and then glanced about the bedchamber. "Have you seen my mother's jewel box?"

Emma finished pinning up her hair in a bun atop her head, rather surprised by his query. "I think it's in her wardrobe. At least, if that's what the box at the bottom is." Despite having moved into the master suite on the occasion of their marriage, Emma had yet to remove any of Christina Wellingham's gowns or accessories from the wardrobe. She simply hung hers on the hooks in the dressing room. *I don't believe it's my place to do so, but rather your sister's,* she remembered telling Thomas.

After a moment, Thomas had the box out of the wardrobe and was rummaging through it, the baubles and gemstones reflecting the light from a nearby candle lamp in a cascade of colors. "Here they are," he said with a good deal of satisfaction. He lifted a set of earbobs from the velvet lining, holding up a set of emerald drops from his thumb and forefingers.

Emma gasped. "Oh, they're beautiful," she murmured, leaning over to examine them.

Thomas moved to put them on her ears, but Emma stepped away before he could do so. "What's wrong?" he asked.

"I couldn't," she replied with a shake of her head. "Those were your mother's. They should go to Christiana."

Frowning, Thomas shook his head. "As my wife, you have just as much right to them, and probably half of what's in this box," he countered. "Besides, Christiana has already taken what she wanted," he added as he threaded the rings through her piercings and tightened the screws on the back of each earlobe. "If she wants anything else, Gregory can buy them for her," he added softly.

Admiring the emeralds in the cheval mirror, Emma sighed. "They're perfect with this gown. Are they real, do you suppose?"

"The emeralds? Yes, I believe so. And actually, they're perfect with your eyes."

Emma grinned and then, hearing the faint sounds of voices downstairs, she sobered. "We have guests," she reminded him.

Thomas quickly undid his buttons and shed his topcoat and waistcoat in favor of more elegant choices. Emma had to grin when he pulled on an emerald green waistcoat. "I don't suppose you have an emerald cravat pin?" she teased.

His own grin widening, Thomas held up a finger, opened up his own jewel box, and extracted a rather ornate emerald pin set in gold. "I haven't had an occasion to wear this in years," he murmured as he stabbed it into the silk around his neck. He took a moment to admire the jewel in the mirror, wondering on what occasion his father might have worn it. Graham Wellingham never struck him as a man who might have worn anything more formal than dinner clothes, but he knew there had to have been a time when he did. He was an earl's son, after all.

"You don't need the looking glass to know you're hand-some," Emma whispered, her lips close to his ears. "I thought my assurances were quite enough."

"You minx!" Thomas countered, turning to give her a quick kiss on the lips. "Careful, or I'll have our guests waiting another half-hour."

Emma giggled as the two headed out the master suite. They reached the top of the stairs just as Deborah was making her way up the steps. The drape of her dark red gown gave the barest hint of her condition.

"I thought perhaps you needed some help dressing," she said as she stopped halfway up the stairs. "Still no lady's maid?" she teased.

Emma gave her friend a wide smile as Thomas offered Deborah his other arm. "Why, he's right here," she replied.

Thomas grinned. "She keeps threatening to replace me, if you can imagine," he said as they made their way into the parlor.

And stopped short.

For the room was half-filled with billowing smoke, the pine boughs on the mantel having caught fire only moments before. Coughing and waving one hand in front of his face, Todd was doing his best to pull the branches down and push them into the firebox.

"Jesus! Humphrey!" Thomas shouted as he grabbed the fireplace poker and moved to help Todd. Meanwhile, Emma rushed back toward the kitchens as Deborah hurried to open a window. Waving a hand in front of her face, she was about to open another when Todd shouted for her to leave the room. She was about to do so when she noticed an ember had started a small fire in the Axminster carpet. Moving to the sideboard, she opened the only decanter holding clear liquid and gave it a quick sniff.

"Is this water?" she asked of Thomas. "Or... or rum?" Given the odor of smoke was all she could smell just then, she didn't want to risk making the fire worse.

Stuffing the last of the pine branches into the firebox, Thomas realized what had Deborah asking about the decanter and his eyes widened in fright. "Water," he replied with a nod.

Deborah poured what little water was in the crystal decanter over the flames, which extinguished the fire but left a black scorch mark. She used her slipped feet to crush out several other burning embers that had scattered about the carpet, holding her skirts up well above her ankles as she did so.

By the time Emma and Humphrey returned with pails of water, the small fires were all out, but smoke permeated the entire parlor. His soot-covered face nearly black, Todd stepped away from the fireplace and the raging fire within, nearly stumbling as he struggled to catch his breath in the smoky air. He was soon bent over and coughing.

Sensing his distress, Emma grabbed onto one of his arms and pulled him out of the parlor. Deborah was right behind, tugging on Thomas' sleeve. Humphrey followed, having managed to open another window. "I'll open the back doors," he shouted as he hurried off down the main hall.

"Are you hurt?" Emma asked as she surveyed her guests. "Are you?" she added as she turned to regard Thomas, her gaze quickly going to his hands. Although they were stained with soot, as was his face and his cravat, he didn't appear to have been burned. She couldn't help but notice how his emerald cravat pin winked from the grayed fabric.

"I'm fine, I think," Thomas managed to get out, wheezing. "A few years older perhaps." He turned and gave Todd a thorough look. "My God, you look like that day we shot off the fireworks," he accused, a slight grin touching his lips.

Todd chuckled, his white teeth and eyes appearing in high contrast to the rest of his face. "I believe this was far more exciting," he murmured, daring a glance down the front of his dinner wear.

"When you said we would have a grand adventure tonight, I thought perhaps you were referring to *charades*," Deborah remarked as she removed a hanky from the pocket of her gown and began wiping soot from the front of Todd's topcoat. The white linen was soon black.

"I owe you a new suit of clothes," Thomas stated when he realized how ruined Todd's clothing was from the smoke.

"Nonsense," Todd countered. "My waistcoat is untouched. But I do believe we need to make ourselves a bit more...

presentable." With a quick nod from Thomas and bows to their ladies, the two made their way up the stairs.

A slight breeze ruffled the hairs on the back of Emma's neck, an indication that the back doors had been opened. She moved to open the other parlor door, her expression turning to disappointment when she paid witness to the carnage in the newly-remodeled room. She allowed a sad sigh.

"This was all new, wasn't it?" Deborah asked as she stepped up next to Emma. Although the smoke was slowly clearing from the room—some had been pulled out of the room with the blazing fire and some moved out by the slight breeze—a layer of soot had already begun to settle over the furnishings in the room. The fire was dying down in the firebox, its fuel having been gobbled up in just a few minutes.

"At least the new furniture hasn't yet arrived," Emma replied. "We thought to surprise the Grandbys when they returned from Italy."

Deborah shook out her skirts and dared a glance down the front of her gown, rather surprised to find the dark red silk hadn't suffered any damage. "Well, they will be surprised if they show up in the next week or so," she replied. "I smell like smoke," she added, giving Emma a pleading look.

"Let's get some fresh air," Emma suggested, leading her friend to the front door. "Air out our gowns a bit. I know it's chilly, but it should help. Then we can use Christiana's bathing chamber," she suggested, remembering the plumbing had been upgraded on that end of the house.

Arm-in-arm, the two stepped out the front door and stopped before they had a chance to take another step—or before Emma had closed the door behind them.

Two pairs of eyes pinned them in place, their whites illuminated by a lantern held in a beefy hand along with the little bit of light from the vestibule. Emma heard as well as felt Deborah's gasp of surprise, and her first thought was of the housebreakers who had attempted to rob the house in June.

The housebreakers who had ended up dead because she and Humphrey had shot them.

Her pulse pounding in her ears, and the area around her gunshot wound causing discomfort, Emma barely heard the word when one of the men said, "Evening." He gave a slight bow, the movement putting him into the light enough so that Emma could see he wore a cape coat.

The other man, cast mostly in the shadow of the first, seemed to give a slight bow before saying, "Good evening, ladies." His voice sounded breathless as the other raised the lantern. The pool of light illuminated the side of his clean-shaven face as well the front of Deborah and Emma. "We saw the smoke. Thought you might need some help."

The sound of footsteps and a distant shout came from the direction of the stables, and Emma dared a quick glance to her left, hoping it was one of the grooms. In the dark, and despite the lantern that bobbed about from that man's hands, she couldn't be sure who it was. Neither man who stood before her seemed to take notice of the shout from the stables.

"That's very kind of you, sir. Her husband was able to get the fire out, though," Emma said with a nod to Deborah.

"Just some pine boughs caught fire is all," Deborah managed.

"I do hope you didn't have to come far," Emma added lightly, praying her voice didn't betray her nervousness. She heard no evidence of horses in the drive, and it was too dark to tell if a gig or cart was parked nearby. Although she didn't recognize either of the men, she hadn't exactly met many of the neighbors since moving into Woodscastle. "Do you live nearby?"

The two men traded glances. "We were just passing and saw the smoke," one said. Neither made an immediate move to leave, as if they were trying to make up their minds about something.

Emma felt the pull of Deborah's arm in the crook of hers. She thought perhaps the two of them could step back and shut and lock the door before the two men could advance the five or six steps necessary to get into the house.

She didn't have to decide, though. Deborah did it for her.

All at once, Emma was back in the vestibule and the front door was closing as she was whirled around, Deborah's arm still hooked through hers. She was suddenly released, though, when Deborah used both hands and all her weight to push against the front door. Just as it was about to shut completely, a boot appeared on the threshold, effectively stopping the door's closure.

A blood-curdling scream rent the relative quiet of Woodscastle. Momentarily frozen in place, it took a second for Emma to realize it had come from Deborah. The midwife appeared far too calm to have screamed, though, her profile displaying her fierce determination to get the door closed and locked.

The deafening crack of a pistol shot had Emma's right hand going up to her ear as she spun around to find Humphrey lifting the second dueling pistol to aim it through the opening in the doorway. He didn't have a chance to pull the trigger, though, for the boot keeping the door open disappeared and the door slammed shut under Deborah's weight.

Shouts and what sounded like thunder and all matter of commotion followed in the next few seconds.

As if in slow motion, Emma watched as Deborah drove home the bolt on the lock and turned around, leaning heavily against the door as she struggled to catch her breath. The thought of the open windows in the parlor had Emma scrambling to get into that room, every step seeming to take far more time than it should. A gun shot sounded from somewhere outside, and Emma instinctively ducked down as she hurried across the ruined carpet. Just as she reached for the edge of one of the windows to pull it in, a hand grabbed it from the outside.

Too stunned to scream, Emma let go of the window frame and stumbled backwards. Sure she was about to fall to the floor, she was startled when a bare arm wrapped around her waist and pulled her against a naked chest. She watched in wonder as the right hand holding a dueling pistol took aim and fired at the silhouette of a man's upper torso. The *thunk* of a body hitting the ground outside the parlor followed a moment later. No other sound came through the windows after that.

"Are you all right?"

Emma blinked, stunned to hear Thomas' voice next to her ear. "I think so," she whispered, allowing herself to relax.

"How many were there?"

She blinked again. "Two at the front door. I'm not sure if there were others, though," she managed to get out as she regained her footing and turned to regard her husband. Obviously in the middle of changing clothes when Deborah screamed, or perhaps aware there was something wrong even before then, he had grabbed the second pistol from Humphrey when he realized where Emma was headed. "Did the gunshot bring you downstairs?"

He shook his head. "Todd was in my old bedchamber getting cleaned up. He saw the lamps of the men when they approached and asked if we were expecting anyone else for dinner," Thomas replied. "Said he thought they might have been following their carriage once it passed Merriweather Manor. When I heard the shot, I was already at the top of the stairs. I slid down the bannister," he added sheepishly.

Emma was about to smile at his comment, but her eyes widened in horror, and she tensed as if she were about to run. "The back door!" she cried. "It's open!"

Thomas held onto her, though, preventing her from taking a step away. "Humphrey is seeing to it." He moved them to a lit candle lamp and blew it out.

Emma hurried to the other and shortened the wick until the flame was nearly out. With the room entirely dark, it would be easier to see if anyone was still outside. "What of the stables? Someone was coming from there, but I couldn't see if it was one of our grooms or...," she stopped, frightened that the gunshot she had heard might have been one of them losing his life.

Thomas didn't reply, his head cocked as if listening. After a moment, he took a deep breath and then gave a start when the sound of a bell broke the silence.

The dinner bell.

"As usual, Mr. Tanner is unaware of what's been happening," Emma murmured.

"That's because he's nearly deaf," Thomas whispered. He sighed. "But Miss Dahlia and Mrs. Werthers are probably back in the dining room, so they should be safe."

Emma nodded. "Good. That's everyone in the house, right?"

"In the house, yes. I daresay I'm rather concerned for our grooms."

"And Mr. Stevenson. He drove the Vandermeers here and took the carriage to the stables for the night." She expected the man had brought their valises into the house, although she couldn't remember seeing them in the vestibule. "Was Todd with you?"

Thomas nodded. "He was on his way to see to Deborah when I came in here," he answered as he pulled one of the other parlor windows shut. He drove home the latch before moving to the other, pausing to risk a sideways glance just beyond the opening. Given the darkness—the moon was barely a crescent —he couldn't make out any figures in the half-circle drive nor see any signs of horses. Closing the window, he was about to latch it when he caught sight of a man with a lantern. Given how the light bobbed about in his hand, Thomas was sure the man was limping.

Thomas gave a start when Emma's whispered, "Who is he?" sounded next to his ear.

"Jesus, Emma, you scared me," he scolded just as light flooded the drive and another gunshot rang out. The lantern— and the man holding it—fell to the crushed granite. Then the light faded. In the brief moment of illumination, Emma could see the man wore a cape coat.

"I think that was one of them," she whispered.

"He was shot by someone in the vestibule," Thomas said as he finished latching the window. He was about to hurry to the vestibule when he dared a glance down the front of his body. "I suppose I best get dressed first."

Emma gave him a peck on the cheek before she passed him on her way to the vestibule, her concern for Deborah. She found her best friend pressed against her husband as Todd stood with his back against the front door, the other dueling pistol held in both hands and aimed straight up. He wore britches and a shirt, although he'd obviously been interrupted in dressing just as Thomas had, the tails of his shirt still out. His face was clean, though, as if he'd just had enough time to wash it before Deborah's scream.

"How do, Emma," he said as one of his arms moved to wrap around Deborah's shoulders. "May I be the first to say that your dinner parties are rather adventurous affairs?" he asked rhetorically.

A quick glance at the hall table had Emma realizing how he had managed to reload the pistol. The wooden box that held the dueling pistols, emblazoned with the Wogdon & Barton logo, was open to reveal the gunpowder flask and rod while musket balls were scattered about the marble top. "Well, I shouldn't want you thinking dinner at Woodscastle is dull," she countered. "Have you any news of our groomsmen?" she asked, worry evident on her face.

"Mr. Stevenson is armed," Todd remarked. At Emma's look of shock, he added, "Our particular part of London is prone to visits by footpads. I rather think the man who was limping—the one I just shot—was shot first by him."

"Is there a servants' entrance in the back?" Deborah asked, her face betraying her worry.

Emma shook her head. "West side, facing the stables."

"Show me," Todd ordered, giving up his hold on Deborah as he pushed away from the door. He pocketed a few of the bullets from the hall table as he passed it.

Nearly running to the west side of the house, Emma remembered Thomas' comment about Merriweather Manor. "Do you suppose these men paid a visit to Merriweather Manor before they came here?" she asked, nearly breathless. "Thomas said you thought they may have followed you here."

They ran past the statuary filling the west hall and through the dark music room, Emma nearly missing the door in the corner that led to the servants' entrance and to the back stairs. "Here," she said as she moved to open the door.

Todd placed a hand over hers, preventing her from lowering

the handle. He held a finger to his lips and placed an ear against the door.

Emma nodded, although she wasn't sure if he could even see her in the dark. She dared a glance toward the windows. One set faced west, its vantage toward the stables while the other set faced the front of the house. The drapes had been pulled shut—with Christiana out of residence, no one used the music room—so the lamps from the stables weren't visible.

Pulling her hand from Todd's, Emma crept toward the west windows. Using a single finger, she slowly pushed aside one of the drapery panels until a bit of light showed. Daring a glance through the slight opening, she was able to make out the outline of the stables. The Vandermeer carriage was parked on the north side of the building, the horses having been unhitched and moved to stalls somewhere inside. There wasn't any sign of the grooms. She angled her head in time to see movement closer to the house, though. "Someone's just run to the house," she whispered. "I couldn't tell who, though."

Todd opened the door and took aim so that when the outer door opened, he was ready with a warning. "Identify yourself or prepare to be shot," he said in a calm voice.

The figure paused on the threshold. "Lars Larsen, sir. Who... who are *you?*"

"That's one of our grooms," Emma said, her relief palpable as she quickly joined Todd at the door.

Lowering the gun slightly, Todd waved the man into the corridor. "Do you have a match?" he asked in a quiet voice.

"Yes, sir." A moment later, and the hall was lit by the small flame. Emma retrieved a candle lamp from atop the piano-forté and soon the hall was bathed in light.

"So good to see you're well, Mr. Larsen," she said.

"And you," the groom nodded. "Mr. Allen may have broken his hand. Punched one of them. Knocked his lights out. He took a horse and headed out to fetch the sheriff. Your Stevenson has a gun on him right now," he said as he turned his attention to Todd.

"Do you have any idea how many there are?"

"Four, milady. We saw them ride in from Burlington Road. I just came over to be sure none of 'em got into the house. They were at Merriweather afore, down the road. Apparently only a few servants are there this time of the year. The ruffians thought to rob the place. Thought you was gone to the country for Christmas, too, so they thought they would make off with the silver."

Todd and Emma exchanged nervous glances. "Four?" she repeated. "If Mr. Stevenson has one in the stables and two have been shot out front, then—"

"There's another one out there," Todd whispered.

"Or in here," Mr. Larsen warned. "We've been watching the house ever since we saw them ride in and heard the first gunshot, and we haven't seen the fourth. I don't mind tellin' ya that I am worried sick about Miss Dahlia."

Todd and Emma stared at the groom before they turned to regard one another. "I rather wish we had more guns," Emma whispered. "And a way to get to the east wing without being seen." She thought of Thomas, upstairs dressing, probably unaware of a fourth gang member.

Mr. Larsen cleared his throat. "Beggin' your pardon, Mrs. Wellingham, but I can get you to the kitchens from here if that will help. Then you can use the other back stairs to get up to the east wing."

Emma blinked, rather surprised by the man's claim. "How?"

The groom pointed towards the servants' stairs. "There's a door at the top of the stairs that leads into Mr. Grandby's study. The south wall has a... secret panel," he claimed as he lowered his voice to a whisper. "Behind it is a stairwell that leads down to the kitchens. Been there since the house was built."

Intrigued, Todd regarded the groom for a moment. "I rather like that idea," he murmured. When he saw Emma's quelling glance, he added, "I admit to being a bit hungry."

"I don't know how you can think of food at a time like this," she complained. She turned her attention back to Mr. Allen. "Lead the way," she said, and was about to follow when Todd held out his arm to stop her.

"I must see to my beloved," he stated. "I left her back in the vestibule," he added, his nervousness apparent. Leaving Emma and the groom in the servants' hall, Todd hurried back through the music room and west hall. He was just past the entrance to the library when Deborah appeared from the vestibule.

About to call out to her, Todd stopped when he realized she wasn't alone. A man had his arm wrapped around her neck, and because he was several inches shorter than Deborah, she was forced to bend backwards. Her condition was readily apparent, a condition the cur was just realizing as he lifted a muff pistol to her head. "Why, what have we here?" he asked in an oily voice, just the moment before Todd lifted the dueling pistol and took aim.

"Let her go," Todd ordered.

The man swung Deborah around so she was directly between him and Todd. "I don't think so. In fact, you're going to drop the gun. You're going to drop the gun and give me all the gold in this place. The gold and the silver," he stated, as if he was just then deciding he was going to rob the house. "Make it quick, or your Tall Meg will take a bullet." He moved the gun from Deborah's temple so it pointed to her distended belly. "Do it, or your heir will be stillborn."

Although he was aware of a sudden movement somewhere beyond the thief—a body making a quick descent from the top of the stairs—Todd kept his attention on Deborah. "Actually, I am not about to drop this gun," he replied. "And in fact, you will wish you were stillborn."

Shocked at her husband's words, Deborah gasped and was about to shove her elbow into the man's ribs when she heard the click of a gun being cocked somewhere behind her head.

Thomas pointed his dueling pistol at the back of the man's head. "Drop it, or you're dead."

The man's eyes widened in surprise. As if he could see his options disappearing, he quickly moved the gun up to Deborah's head. Sure he was about to pull the trigger, Deborah squeezed her eyes shut, lifted a knee, and kicked backwards against the front of his knee at the same time she poked a bent elbow into his ribs.

Wrenched to the side by her actions, the man howled and shouted a curse. Released from his hold around her neck and completely off-balance, Deborah stumbled sideways. The muff pistol went off, the bullet sent at an odd angle that missed her by mere inches and ended up embedded in the side of the west wing stairs.

A pair of loud cracks split the air then, eliciting another howl from the would-be thief. Two bullets penetrated his body, one from the front and one from the back. He dropped to the marble floor, a hollow *thonk* sounding when his head hit.

Gasping, Deborah went down as well, but Humphrey was there to catch her, his arms sliding beneath her arms as she fell. He quickly put her to rights, lifting the tall woman as best he could until her feet were beneath her. His continued hold was unnecessary, though, as Todd was suddenly there, gathering her into his arms and pulling her hard against the front of his body.

Emma rushed down the east wing stairs. She'd been able to reach Thomas and warn him about the fourth man just as he was about to leave the master suite. Now she was colliding into Thomas' arms as Mr. Larsen hurried from the kitchens. The groom stopped short to survey the situation. The maid, Dahlia, wasn't far behind, her hands covering her mouth until the groom had her pulled into his arms. Mr. Tanner and Mrs. Werthers appeared behind the maid, their widened eyes a testament to their ignorance of what had been happening for the last half-hour.

"Well, it's no wonder none of ye' came in for dinner," the cook announced, his hands going to his hips. "And here I was thinking you was playing charades in the parlor."

Thomas closed his eyes as he held onto his wife. "If I'd had any idea there was a fourth—"

"I know," she replied with a nod. She dared a glance at the dead man, quite sure he wasn't a relative of Cavendish or the other two housebreakers that had attempted to invade Wood-scastle the June prior. "Mr. Allen is on his way to get the sheriff," she murmured. "And Mr. Stevenson has another at gunpoint out in the stables."

"Christ," Thomas whispered in reply. "Let's get the thief tied up so Mr. Stevenson can have some dinner," he suggested.

Humphrey gave a nod. "I'll see to it, Mr. Wellingham."

Thomas turned to his other guests. "My apologies," he said as gave up his hold on Emma and moved to join them. "We don't usually have such eventful evenings here at Woodscastle," he added.

Todd exchanged a glance with Deborah. "Your choice of parlor games is most imaginative," he agreed. "But I am starving. Where can I get a bite to eat, do you suppose?"

Deborah gasped. "But you're hardly dressed appropriately," she murmured.

"I am declaring dinner an informal affair this evening," Thomas stated, despite the fact that he was wearing formal dinner clothes. He waved a hand toward the dining room, offering Emma his arm. She took it, and soon the four of them were seated around the dining table, enjoying dinner despite the drama of the evening.

Later, whilst they drank brandy in the library, and after a short visit from Sheriff Morgan, and while the women took baths in the Grandby's bathing chamber in the west wing, Thomas regarded Todd for a moment. "Killing is not any easier the second time, is it?" he murmured.

Todd regarded him a moment before allowing a nod. "I suppose not. I just never thought..." He swallowed before giving his head a shake. "I never thought of the possibility of losing my Deborah to a ruffian. I think this time I shall not forget killing a man so easily," he murmured. He downed the rest of his brandy in a single gulp.

"And now you know how I felt when I learned Emma had shot a man to protect my property," Thomas countered. "Rather humbling, isn't it? That our women might be braver than we are?"

Nodding his agreement, Todd stood up from the leather sofa he had sunk into after dinner and gave his host a slight bow. "Which is why I am beholden to my Deborah. I am going to make love to her until dawn and perhaps beyond," he stated. "I expect I'll be late for breakfast." He moved to take his leave of the library.

Thomas blinked. "I don't believe you, but it will be served when you are ready," he replied with a grin. "Thank you for all you did this evening." He paused a moment, angling his head to one side. "Some of this is my fault."

Todd stopped on the threshold and gave his host a quelling glance. "Whatever do you mean?"

Shaking his head, Thomas remembered how he had placed the pine boughs across the top of the mantel in the parlor. Although there were several knick-knacks he might have used to keep them in their place, he had simply draped the boughs haphazardly and left the parlor to dress, never once checking to be sure the ends weren't hanging down in front of the firebox. "I was careless in how I placed the pine boughs on top of the mantel," he admitted. "The ends were obviously too close to the fire."

Todd shrugged. "And I should have warned you that I thought we were being followed by highwaymen," he said quietly.

"You were? I mean, you actually thought that?" Thomas countered.

Angling his head to one side, Todd considered how to answer. "We did. We even joked about it in the carriage," he admitted. "Thought it would make for an entertaining game of charades."

Thomas shook his head. "I never want to play charades with you," he stated. With that, he downed the rest of his brandy and joined his friend for the trip up to their bedchambers. There were wives to love, after all.

CHAPTER 25

CHRISTMAS DAY TIDINGS OF GOOD AND BAD CHEER

December 25, 1802

The morning of Christmas Day, Thomas took the reins from Mr. Larsen and bid a happy Christmas to the groom. He knew the man and his intended, Miss Dahlia, would be spending the day together since the groom had told him he planned to propose marriage. "After what happened earlier this week, I have decided I can no longer wait to make her my wife," the groom had said upon receiving his Christmas bonus. "And this is exactly what I require to purchase a ring."

Meanwhile, Mr. Allen, nursing a broken hand, was scheduled to speak with a reporter from *The Morning Chronicle* about the events of the evening of December 20. Not willing to speak with the press on the matter, Thomas was happy to have one of his employees relay the news, and told him so as he gave the man his Christmas bonus.

Rather reserved that morning, Humphrey walked with Thomas and Emma to the curricle and gave a curt bow. "Happy Christmas," the butler said with a seriousness that had Thomas almost asking what might be wrong.

"And to you," Thomas replied, pulling a white envelope with the man's Christmas bonus from his waistcoat pocket. "Do take some time off, won't you?" Thomas encouraged.

Frowning, Humphrey shook his head. "Not just yet, Mr. Wellingham," he replied.

"Well, at least invite her to your bed," Thomas suggested with an arched brow.

The usually unflappable butler regarded his master with a look of shock. "Sir?"

Thomas gave the man a quelling glance. "I've seen how you look at Mrs. Werthers. She's a widow going on ten years now. Probably been waiting for you to make your move for the past two. Get on with it already." Having never seen the butler blush, he gave the man a brilliant smile. "Happy Christmas!" And with that, Thomas had the horse in motion.

"You're incorrigible!" Emma scolded as they made their way to Burlington Lane.

"I'm in love, is all," he countered, giving her a sideways glance.

The past four days had been a blur of activity and worry, anticipation and excitement. The news from Italy was good— Christiana loved visiting the cathedrals and ancient sites while Gregory seemed determined she see everything.

There are not enough hours in the day to accomplish what my husband wishes to do, she wrote in her latest missive. *I keep reminding him we shall return. As for when we'll return to London, it won't be before the end of February.*

Sheriff Morgan had paid them not just one visit, but two. He insisted on hearing statements from everyone who was in the household or the stables at the time of the attack. *That you would be set upon by housebreakers not once, but twice in seven months suggests you are either the target of a vast network of such men, or extremely unlucky*, he complained. *I have to believe it is the latter, for if it is the former, then my job will prove to be the death of me.*

Thomas wasn't about to remind the man that Cavendish's brother had shot Emma in between the events, but he did suggest the estate homes in Chiswick were an easy mark for such ruffians. *There aren't enough lawmen to prevent them from doing so*, he countered. At least no charges were filed against his friends or servants—he rather expected to have to play the 'grandson of an earl' card when it came to the sheriff.

The one housebreaker who had been kept at gunpoint by Mr. Stevenson was most cooperative with Sheriff Morgan when the lawman finally arrived to remove him from the premises—especially when he was threatened with transport. Seems the housebreaker was allergic to horsehair.

With the colder temperatures, fewer ships were making the treks across the Atlantic, but goods from all over England and Scotland arrived on a daily basis in the overland transports operated by Wellingham Imports. Todd had contracted with a domestic silk manufacturer to receive all of his product, making the import house a favorite for drapers throughout London and cities in southern England. Products from countries not already under contract to the East India Company made for interesting acquisitions, even if not all of them found a retailer in London.

As for transparent gowns, well, one only needed to attend a *ton* ball to determine just how prized they had become.

"I rather wish we had taken the town coach," Thomas said as the cold bit his cheeks.

Emma, her head topped with a fur hat and her hands stuffed into a fur muff, almost agreed. There wouldn't have been enough space in the mews behind the townhouse for the equipage and extra horses the town coach would have required. "It's a fine day for a drive," she replied. "I'm glad we're going early, though. Gives us a chance to warm up at the townhouse before we descend on the Simpsons."

She hoped their gifts of European chocolates and French brandy would be appropriate for the older couple. Despite having hosted the Simpsons for dinner in her townhouse, and having them as landlords, Emma didn't feel as if she knew them very well. Given their familial status as Christiana's in-laws, she was curious as to why they hadn't been to visit Gregory and Christiana at Woodscastle.

Emma knew enough about them, at least, once she and Thomas had figured out Sophia Simpson was Gregory's mother.

Once Gregory announced he intended to marry Christiana,

the secret was out for anyone in London who cared to know. By then, though, it had been so long since Sophia Burroughs Grandby had disappeared from Merriweather Manor, she was hardly mentioned in Mayfair parlors.

Even though it was Christmas, Master Churchill manned the stables, his bright red cheeks a testament to the cold. "Happy Christmas, Miss Emma," he said as he gave a bow so deep he nearly toppled over. He gave Thomas a slight nod. "Sir," he said before he saw to removing their valises from the curricle.

The stable boy had never warmed to Thomas. Once Emma had moved out to Woodscastle, the boy's steady supply of biscuits had been reduced to an occasional two or three when the couple spent a night or two at the townhouse.

On this day, Emma made sure Thomas was the one to give the boy a basket nearly overflowing with biscuits. "Happy Christmas," Thomas said as he handed over the basket. He followed it with a shiny sovereign.

The boy's eyes boggled. "Happy Christmas, Mr. Wellingham!" Master Churchill responded, his mouth left hanging open in awe.

"We'll be spending the night here and leaving tomorrow," Emma said as she hooked her arm through Thomas'. "Don't eat all the biscuits at once," she added in a whisper.

Master Churchill nodded and gave her another bow. "I won't, Miss Emma." With that, he saw to unhitching the bay from the curricle and leading it into the mews.

Entering their townhouse through the back door, the two took a few minutes to light the stove and the parlor fireplace. "It's nearly as cold in here as it is out there," Thomas complained before taking the valises upstairs. When Emma didn't follow him right away, he paused on the steps. "Anything wrong?" he asked as he watched her unfold and read one of the posts that had been shoved under the front door.

Emma held up a twenty pound note. "Seems Mr. Smith has done rather well with the hat shop," she said with a wan smile. Her father's shop, now known as *Fitzsimmons and Smith*, had not only survived her father's death, but the man's hat designs continued to be made under the new ownership. The royalties for the use of his name and designs were proving rather lucrative.

"Indeed," Thomas replied. "You can take me to dinner tomorrow."

Emma allowed a giggle as she continued to peruse the mail. Halfway up the stairs, she paused and opened a bright white envelope.

Dear Emma,

Happy Christmas! I hope this day finds you in Good Health and Happiness. Your uncle, Matthew, is relieved to learn you have taken a husband of such high regard, as am I. A Wellingham, no less! Although marriage can be difficult, I cannot imagine life as a spinster and consider myself lucky to be married to your uncle.

I write today to beg your forgiveness as well as request your continued discretion. I am in receipt of your letter regarding those you found in your desk. I can only imagine how upset you must have been to learn of me and your half-sister. Please, please know that I loved your father with all my heart. I would have happily married him had it been an option. My father and brothers had other plans for me, though, and so I married your uncle instead.

My dear George must have known he was not long for this Earth back then, for despite my willingness to defy my father, he would not hear of it. He thought me too young for a man of his years. I don't mind admitting, I was heartbroken.

As for my dear Sam, I must ask that you keep our secret safe. Matthew does not know the truth, and given his position with the Foreign Office and as Viscount Chamberlain, I dare not make public (nor even tell him) what could be a scandal for such an important man. At some point in the future, perhaps when Samantha is ready for her come-out, I shall be brave enough to broach the subject with him. I am a coward now, though, a condition I must abide given I am married to a viscount. I will contact you should the situation change.

Congratulations again on your marriage. Please know that

should you ever wish to pay a call at Fitzsimmons Manor, you will be welcome.

Sincerely yours, Caro.

Emma blinked back the tears that collected in the corners of her eyes. To learn she would not be able to acknowledge Samantha Fitzsimmons as her own sister was as disappointing as it was heartbreaking. *How could Caroline withhold the information from her own daughter?*

"Emma?"

Emma glanced up from the parchment, stunned to find Thomas standing on the step just above her. "It's from Caroline Fitzsimmons," she whispered, the tears finally dribbling down her cheeks. "Viscountess Chamberlain, although you would not know it from her informal salutation," she added, showing him how the woman had signed the letter.

Frowning, Thomas moved to gather Emma into his arms, the move made awkward given they were on two levels. "I take it she won't allow you to meet your sister?" he half-asked.

Shaking her head, Emma sniffled. "She didn't forbid me from meeting her, though," she replied, rather relieved Caroline had at least left that option open. "Only from acknowledging her as my sister. And telling her, of course. At least until she is brave enough to tell Viscount Chamberlain about the *affaire*."

Thomas angled his head. "That's something then." He continued to hold her, rather liking how she seemed to melt into his arms. And how she helped to warm his chilled body. "We know the truth, and that is all that matters."

Nodding, Emma let go her hold on him. "I'll get changed now. Will you play lady's maid?"

A wicked eyebrow was his only reply until he reached the top of the stairs. "If you'll help me with my buttons."

CHAPTER 26

CHRISTMAS DINNER DELIGHTS

An hour later

Thomas regarded the brass elephant's trunk for a moment, not sure if he should use the door knocker or simply rap his knuckles on the brightly painted door.

As it happened, he didn't need to do either. The door opened, revealing their host, James Simpson.

"Happy Christmas!" he said as he waved them into the vestibule. His former profession as a butler always in evidence, he was quick to take their coats.

"Happy Christmas to you," Emma replied happily, her gaze taking in the decor. "You've managed quite the elegant remodel with this one," she murmured in appreciation. Besides a mariner's compass in the middle of the marble floor, there were cherubs painted on the vestibule's ceiling, and a deep green silk covered the walls in between.

"Good of you to say so. I believe my wife finally has the house she deserves," James said proudly. He turned and led them into the grand hall, which lived up to its name given not only its elaborate design, but the greenery that graced the stairway's bannister and the papered walls. "I understand Woodscastle is undergoing the same?"

Thomas allowed a 'huff '. "The west end, certainly. Your

stepson spared no expense. It's going to be some time before the east side is up to snuff."

James angled his head. "One word when you do. Plumbing," he stated with a hint of a grin. "Best decision I ever made." He paused a moment, as if to think. "Well, second best, really. Marrying my Sophia was the best decision."

From a room somewhere nearby, Sophia's voice sounded. "Oh, do spare our guests your banter, you bounder!"

Grinning, Emma realized their hostess was in the parlor. As they made their way, she continued to gaze at their surroundings. Would she ever feel comfortable living in such a magnificent house, with plenty of servants at her beck and call? The lifestyle was completely foreign to her, although her father had grown up in such an environment.

"Now that you've completed the remodels on all the properties, when will you sell?" Thomas asked as they entered the parlor. He stopped short upon seeing Lady Sophia Simpson.

Seated in the middle of a velvet settee, she looked as if she ruled all of England. She wore a deep red velvet gown, its satin overlay skirt spread open enough to reveal her pregnancy. Her hair was piled into a mass of curls atop her head and secured with ruby-tipped pins. Rubies hung from her plump earlobes. A passing thought that her ruby necklace might have cost more than he made in a year had Thomas remembering she was an heiress.

Thomas quickly gave a leg and hurried to stand before her. She had already lifted her hand, and he brushed his lips over the back of it, pretending to ignore her diamond and ruby ring. "My lady, you look stunning!" he said, trying his best not to stare at her middle. She was obviously well on her way to motherhood.

"Did he pay you to say that?" she teased, nodding her head toward her husband.

Thomas chuckled. "He didn't need to, milady. You look... happy, too," he added. He remembered a time when he couldn't say that about the daughter of a duke. Although Gregory had been born during her short marriage to Roger Grandby—the man had died of pneumonia before Gregory was in his fourth year—Sophia never seemed particularly comfortable at Merriweather Manor. She was certainly living a different life than the one she would have had she remained a widow of the aristocracy.

"I am happy, actually," she admitted. Sophia indicated the chair adjacent to the settee. "Oh, do have a seat, Emma. Your gown is perfect for the season," she gushed, referring to the gown Emma had worn the night the thieves invaded Woodscastle. Emma had no other gown appropriate for Christmas, and decided it would be better to replace the bad memories of the last time she wore it with the good ones she expected to make this day. "And it's so good to see you wearing Christina's emeralds," Sophia continued as Emma gathered her green velvet skirts and took a seat in a floral-patterned upholstered chair. "I rather wondered what might have happened to them," Sophia murmured.

Emma blinked. She knew Sophia and Christina Wellingham had been friends back before Sophia married James. Before Christina died in childbirth. "Thomas found them in her jewel box a few nights ago and insisted I wear them," Emma replied. "I thought they should go to Christiana..." She dared a glance in the direction of her husband, rather relieved to see the men were already seated and engaged in a conversation of their own. A footman entered the parlor with a silver tray, no doubt laden with coffee and walnuts, and made his way to the ladies.

"Nonsense. My son will see to buying her every jewel she could ever want. Short of the Crown Jewels, of course," Sophia countered with a wave of her hand. She accepted a cup of coffee from the footman right after he gave Emma a cup of the steaming brew. "He could probably afford those as well, and goodness knows Prinny could use the money, but I don't think her tastes lean in that direction," she amended.

Having a hard time deciding if Sophia was being serious or flippant, Emma shook her head. "Not in the least," she responded, deciding it was the safest reply. She paused a moment. "I must say, impending motherhood certainly seems to agree with you. You look... radiant. May I be so bold as to ask when you expect to deliver your baby?" The woman seemed far larger around the middle than she should if her son's comments could be believed.

Sophia beamed. "Why it's so kind of you to say so. I do love being pregnant. James dotes on me even more than usual," she said in a whisper. "As for a date, I was thinking sometime in late March, but Dr. Talbot insists it will be earlier. My age and all," she added with a roll of her eyes. "And it's not as if I can pin it down to a particular date of conception." An impish grin appeared at the same time one of her eyebrows arched.

Emma did her best not to blush. "He's a good physician," she replied, thinking she agreed with Dr. Talbot's assessment. Either the woman would deliver the first week in March or she was bearing more than just one child.

Or perhaps she was merely eating too many cakes at tea time.

"Mrs. Dawes sends for Dr. Talbot whenever she knows something isn't going right during a delivery."

Sophia's eyes widened. "I am relieved to hear you say it. Now, you must tell me all of what you know about midwives. I fear my sisters will be of no help since it's been years since their last babes were born. I'll be in need of one in a couple of months, after all," she said as she rested a hand on her belly. "And I remembered you have some experience in that regard."

Angling her head to one side, Emma thought of Deborah. The woman was due to deliver her own child sometime in late March. "Todd Vandermeer's wife, Deborah, is a very experienced midwife. She's been under Mrs. Dawes' tutelage for several years," Emma explained. "And she lives not far. In Cavendish Square, in fact."

Sophia leaned in Emma's direction, her eyebrow waggling. "Is she familiar with the latest... *recommendations* when it comes to childbirth?"

Emma could no longer hide the blush she had felt coming on since their discussion began.

"Oh, my, I've made you blush, which means she does!"

Sophia said in a voice loud enough to have the men ceasing their conversation to give her a glance.

"My sweeting, have you already scandalized our guest? We haven't yet made it to the dining room!" James scolded in a teasing voice.

"My apologies," Sophia said quickly. "I didn't..."

Emma waved a hand. "Please don't. Yes. She's quite... *modern* when it comes to childbirth. Why, I've known her to call upon the services of a young man to perform nipple chewing and sexual intercourse when a labor requires it," she whispered.

Sophia's eyes widened, and it was her turn to display a pink face. "Oh, do tell," she demanded, leaning towards Emma. "Nipple chewing?" she prompted.

Clearing her throat and realizing she would have to tell the matron what she knew, Emma said, "It's important to have your husband..." She sighed before continuing. "Suckle your nipples, from now until you deliver, to help draw down the milk."

When she didn't offer any more information, Sophia shook her head. "And?" she prompted.

Emma ducked her head. "You're to have... marital relations... with your husband as often as possible until such time as you go into labor."

Her eyes widening in delight, Sophia actually clapped her hands together. "I knew it! Grandby wouldn't come near me once I started to show—I think he preferred the company of his mistress back then—but I wanted him—or someone— in my bed. Why, had I any idea James had a *tendré* for me, I might have invited him to my bedchamber those many months before I gave birth to Gregory," she claimed with an elegantly arched brow.

Emma did her best to keep an impassive expression on her face. She still couldn't decide if the woman was telling the truth or merely trying to scandalize her. "Well, should you have need of his... services, then perhaps you can persuade him of your... need... for him," she managed to get out. "Make your labor go a bit easier."

Giggling, Sophia glanced over at her husband and gave him a brilliant smile when she had his attention.

"You're embarrassing me again, aren't you, my sweeting?" James asked from the other side of the room. He turned to Thomas. "She does that on occasion. Shares some juicy gossip about me," he complained.

"Oh, but for the very best reasons," Sophia called out.

James allowed a grin before returning his attention to Thomas. "You must know it's not my decision to make. If it were up to me, I would sell every property on this street." At Thomas' look of surprise, he added, "I've been seeing to maintenance and remodeling since the day my wife purchased these townhouses," he explained in a quiet voice. "But now I wish to see to my family." He paused and then allowed a shrug. "I shall put in a good word for you. Encourage her to sell you the townhouse. I've already heard from other tenants with the same mind as you. Once the babe is born, I rather think being a landlady will not hold the appeal it does now."

Thomas regarded the former butler with a raised brow. "I believe you have more influence over her ladyship than you know," he teased.

James dared a glance in the direction of his wife and allowed a nod. "Sometimes I do. Like any man, I suppose, when you have them in the throes of pleasure."

Resisting the urge to blush—Thomas knew exactly what the man meant—he allowed a nod before saying, "Every morning and every night."

Allowing a slow smile, James regarded Thomas with an arched brow. "Every morning?" he murmured happily. "I shall have to try that."

He might have said more except the dinner gong sounded. "Dinner is served," a footman announced.

In mixed company, the conversation wasn't nearly as diverting. By the time the Wellinghams took their leave of the Simpson townhouse—James had dubbed it Kingly Place given its location—the clock was well past twelve and Sophia was ready for bed. "Happy Christmas, you two," she said before making her way up the beautiful staircase.

"And to you," Emma replied. A few minutes later, she and Thomas were back in their own townhouse. By one, they were snug in a bed warmed by a hot brick and engaged in an activity that would keep them warm for the rest of the night.

And the following morning.

CHAPTER 27

CHANGES IN LIFE BEGIN
WITH A HOUSE

Early January, 1803, Bank of England, Threadneedle Street

"Are you absolutely sure about this?" Sir William asked as he regarded his youngest sister. One of his pudgy hands held onto a parchment so it didn't quite touch the top of his massive mahogany desk, as if allowing it to do so would somehow pollute everything else that lay scattered over the polished surface.

Lady Sophia Simpson angled her head in the same manner their mother was fond of doing when asked a similar question. "Of course. Why aren't you?"

The banker regarded his sister with an arched eyebrow. "Because you've been rather successful as a landlady of this particular very valuable property, and all the others in your street," he countered. He didn't add that he'd had to employ a good deal of subterfuge to keep the original purchase of said properties under wraps when Sophia Grandby first took her leave of Merriweather Manor with the intent of marrying the butler. That was one-and-twenty years ago.

"It's just one house, brother. The end one, closest to Oxford Street, in fact," she argued. She didn't add that James had been hearing requests from other tenants regarding ownership of their units, including the Wellinghams. "The current occupants rather like what James did with the remodel, and they wish to own it outright," she explained. "I stand to make a tidy profit, and since you'll receive a cut of that, why, I think it's in your best interest to assist me with seeing to it the sale goes forward. Now do be a good brother and see to the necessary paperwork, won't you?"

Sir William blinked. His sister had a point when it came to the futility of arguing with her. She was her—and his—mother's daughter. "As you wish," he replied with a sigh, allowing the parchment to drop to the desk. "Do tell me this doesn't have anything to do with your husband's ridiculous notion of raising a family at this stage of his life. And yours," he added as he leaned forward. His round belly prevented him from leaning too far forward, though, which kept him a safe distance away from his sister's reach should she decide he deserved a slap across the face for his impertinence.

Sophia's eyes not only widened, but they darkened in color. As did her cheeks, which were a shade of pink beyond her normal shade. "You would do well to accept the fact that you are to be an uncle again, dear brother," she replied in clipped tones.

Sir William leaned back as far as his desk chair would allow without dumping him backwards onto the carpeted floor. "Indeed?" he ventured, caution evident in his voice.

Angling her head to the other side—another clear sign she was Sarah Pendleton Burrough's daughter—Sophia waited a moment before giving him the dagger stare he was quite sure his mother had invented. "Sometime in March, in fact," she said, her chin rising with the statement.

His mouth dropping open in astonishment, his gaze drifted down her front, although the edge of the desk prevented him from seeing any evidence of a pregnancy. "*This* March?"

Sophia gave him a quelling glance. "Of course, this March." She sighed. "I was... well, how should I say this? One step ahead of James when he spoke with me about his desire to sire an heir," she managed with a prim smile. "Almost as if we were of a similar mind at exactly the same time, which is the way it's been for the two of us our entire marriage," she said with a great deal of satisfaction. She watched as her brother covered his face with both hands, which put his enormous onyx and gold ring on display.

"I'm so happy to see you wearing father's ring," Sophia remarked. She figured her oldest brother, the current duke, probably couldn't keep such a large ring on any of his slimmer fingers.

Ignoring her attempt to change the subject, the man sighed heavily before finally removing his hands and placing them rather gingerly on his desktop. "Does your son know?" Sir William asked, wondering if his nephew might have escaped London before learning he was destined to become an older brother.

"Of course. I told him the day after I told James," Sophia answered happily. "I think he's rather excited. Why, his baby will have an uncle or an aunt just about his same age!"

The banker wasn't about to argue that the scenario wasn't exactly optimal. "And you? You do realize you're going to have a grandchild the same age as your child?" he countered.

Allowing a teasing grin, Sophia nodded. "I do," she replied, one eyebrow arching up. "Which is why I'm rather open to the idea of selling the townhouses. Not all at once, of course. But if our tenants wish to become property owners, and they have the funds, then I shall sell their homes to them for fair market value, and we shall invest the funds in one of Gregory's concerns."

This last had Sir William balking. "You won't put the money in the bank?" he asked, rather disappointed to hear her plans.

"You're welcome to put your share in the bank," Sophia answered with a shrug. "I just think my returns will be greater should I invest it with my son. Why, if I'm to believe the *on-dit*, my brother-in-law, Milton, has already done so." With that, Sophia stood up, albeit slowly given her expanded girth, and gave her brother a slight curtsy.

Her brother managed to get out of his chair, just about as slowly, to give his sister a bow. "Sister, you're a vexing woman, you must know," he accused, the gleam in his eye suggesting he was merely teasing her.

Sophia grinned as she turned sideways and smoothed her gloved hands over her gown, revealing the rounding silhouette of pregnancy. Her condition readily apparent, Sophia delighted in seeing her brother's rounding eyes. "I do know. Now do have a good day, and let your sweet wife know she'll be an aunt soon, won't you?"

With that, Sophia Simpson made her way out of her brother's office. She took her leave of the Bank of England, a grin of satisfaction firmly in place.

CHAPTER 28

A NEW YEAR BRINGS
SAD NEWS

Late January

The change in Thomas occurred over the course of just a few days. Those closest to him sensed it almost immediately, but even those he only occasionally came in contact with at work knew something wasn't quite right.

Suffering from a head cold, Emma elected to stay home from work one Friday in late January. The news seemed to disappoint Thomas more than usual, his melancholy displayed in what had become a permanent look of sadness.

"I don't believe I've seen you so much as grin for nearly a week," Emma accused that morning over chocolate and toast.

Her husband gave a shrug. "I'm fine. Just... preoccupied is all," he answered, even though his attention never returned to the newly-ironed copy of *The Times* next to his plate.

Not sure of what to say, Emma finished her chocolate and waited until Thomas finally announced he was leaving for London. She joined him in the vestibule as he pulled on his redingote. "I'm sure Mr. Cunningham can see to the office," she murmured, hoping he didn't think the accounting would suffer in her absence. "I love you," she added as he took his leave of the house. She hurried to the library and watched through the window as her husband mounted his horse and took off down the road toward Burlington Lane. Despite his assurances that nothing was wrong, she couldn't shake the feeling that there was something wrong.

Very wrong.

Had something untoward happened at Wellingham Imports? Something she was obviously unaware of. Going by the numbers she'd been recording, she knew it couldn't be anything related to the business itself. All was well there. Despite his short tenure, Todd's presence had already had an effect on the bottom line. The company was growing more profitable by the week.

About to consider other options, Emma remembered she had work to do, and decided it was time to get lost in the numbers or she would go mad with worry.

By the time Thomas returned at four o'clock in the afternoon, Emma had managed to complete her work on a ledger as well as plan menus for a fortnight of dinners. When she was aware of him riding up the lane, she ran to the vestibule and greeted him at the front door. Hugging him hard, she whispered, "I am so pleased you are home. How was your day?" she asked, kissing him on the cheek. Almost immediately, she realized her fears of something being wrong did indeed have merit. She released her hold on him and stepped back. "Oh, dear," she breathed as she studied his face. He was nearly in tears and trying hard to maintain his composure.

"Did you... receive bad news from Christiana? Or Gregory?" she asked in a whisper, fear replacing her concern.

Thomas shook his head. "Nothing like that. We need... we need to have a talk," he finally said with a nod.

Sighing, Emma took his arm. "Of course," she murmured. They climbed the stairs to the master suite in silence. A mix of fright and sadness filled Emma as she tried to imagine whatever could have her husband so close to tears.

Thomas took a seat on the bench at the end of the bed. After another moment trying to decide if she should sit or remain standing for his news, Emma joined him. He took one of her hands in his.

Not quite sure how to tell her his news, Thomas allowed a

sigh. "I saw the doctor today," he finally began. He took a deep breath. "Dr. Talbot." Emma's eyes widened as she imagined the worst. "It is nothing life threatening, I assure you," he said quietly. "It's just that... we have been together now for..." He was about to say 'a year' when he realized they hadn't been married the entire time he had known her. They had only met not quite a year ago at Warwick's Grammar and Finishing School.

"Six months," Emma whispered.

Thomas nodded, the news still not making his confession any easier. "You have your monthly courses, we have intercourse nearly every night, and although I know we have been... careful to some degree, we haven't been as much lately..." He paused, allowing a sigh. "I just figured... there would have been a baby on the way by now," he whispered as he took her hands in his and kissed them one after the other. "I remember the way you talked about Christiana when you knew she was with child. The way you gazed at Deborah when you were at Grace Park last week. I remember the excitement you showed at learning Gregory's mother was expecting. I saw the way you admired her as we had Christmas dinner. It pains me that you do not have a baby of your own on the way," he said sadly.

Emma gave a 'huff' and allowed a sigh of relief. "But, I look at all babies like that, Thomas," she said with a wan smile as she lifted a hand to the side of his face. "That's how I was even back when I worked at 'Mrs. Dawes' Home for Unwed Mothers'," she added.

Although she wanted desperately to tell him she didn't yet wish to have a child of her own, she now wondered if he did. Had he changed *his* mind already? They had discussed this only a couple of months ago!

Perhaps the news of the other impending births had changed his mind on the matter.

Thomas held a finger to her lips. "I cannot father a child, Emma," he said, tears filling his eyes. "Dr. Talbot says I do not have... sperm," he said in a whisper, as if he struggled with saying the word. "He thinks because of an illness. A high fever, for example," he said as he arched an eyebrow. He turned away from her. "I could only think of that night last June. When I was so sick," he whispered as he squeezed her hand. That night he had attempted to ride home from London in a blinding rainstorm. The night he had been so sick with a fever, he was delirious by the time he reached Woodscastle. The night he had paid witness to Emma at the top of the stairs and thought her an angel. The night he had pulled her into his bed because he needed her warmth to survive.

Needed her.

Needed her in his life.

Emma pulled his head to her chest and hugged him hard. "I suppose I was not such a good nursemaid, after all," she murmured, a wan smile appearing in spite of her welling tears.

Thomas wept for a moment, and Emma felt his body rock with a sob. "I love you, Thomas. Please know this does not change how I feel about you," she insisted as she held him.

"I will divorce you, of course," Thomas said as he straightened. "It would be most unfair—"

Emma's head jerked up as she stared at him. "You will do no such thing!" she gasped, coming to her feet and whirling about to face him. She had to still her hand, for she realized she was about to slap him across his face for putting voice to such a scandalous word. *Divorce?* Never!

Still angry that he could suggest such a thing, though, and hurt that he would think she would consider such a fate, she planted her fists on her hips and stared at him. "Please believe me when I tell you that the idea of having a baby of my own scares me nearly to death," she stated vehemently. "I have paid witness to too many births that did not go well. Should you want children, Thomas Edward Wellingham, I assure you, I would welcome a..." She was about to say 'street urchin' but decided against it. "An adopted baby," she finally finished.

Stunned, Thomas furrowed his brows and realized she spoke the truth. In their half-year of marriage, she had never raised her voice nor seemed quite so upset with him. And the fact that she used his formal name suggested she was particularly cross with him.

He took a handkerchief out of his pocket and wiped his face dry. "You are quite sure about this?" he replied quietly.

"I am *very* sure," she responded, taking his hands in hers. "You are my husband. I meant my marriage vows, Thomas. I love you."

Thomas sighed as a sob shook his body. "All right," he finally said with a nod. After a few moments of silence, he added, "Thank you," before he sighed again. "I should have realized... I take so much for granted."

Emma lowered herself to the bench and leaned against him. She allowed him to hold her hands, his larger fingers stroking her longer, slimmer fingers. "So... just how many children do you want?" she asked, kissing his cheek and then nibbling on his earlobe.

It was a few seconds before he replied. "This may sound selfish, but at the moment, I really don't want any," he replied as he enjoyed the sensation of Emma's lips on his skin. His fingers moved to undo the buttons down his waistcoat.

Emma relaxed in his arms, content to stay there as long as he was willing to hold her. A thought struck her, though, and she moved her head to look at him. "Tell me something. How could the doctor tell you have no sperm?" she asked with a furrowed brow.

Thomas angled his head to one side. "Well, he looked at my semen through some sort of instrument, some kind of magnifying device," he explained with a shrug. "I didn't look for myself, of course." He shrugged his waistcoat off and began undoing the ties of his cravat.

Raising an eyebrow, Emma asked, "How did he get the semen?"

Thomas' ears reddened. "I had to ejaculate, if you will, onto a piece of glass," he said very quietly. He surreptitiously unbuttoned the placket of his breeches.

Emma raised her other eyebrow. "Who *helped* you in that regard?" she asked, her heart beating faster as she felt panicked.

"You did, actually," Thomas admitted, his ears still bright red. He pulled his boots off. "I just had to think of you. What you were doing to me that first day of our honeymoon, and, well..." He pushed his breeches and smalls down in one swift motion before using his arms to sit her upright on the bench. He indicated his hardening manhood. "Well, I did have to rub it while I imagined you... your lips. Your mouth."

Emma wasted no time in grabbing a pillow from the bed and dropping it on the floor in front of the bench. Lowering herself to her knees, she lifted his shirt and shoved her face into his belly, sucking the skin fervently while wrapping her fingers around his manhood.

"Oh, God," Thomas breathed as he leaned back against the bed, helpless.

Working her lips down to his manhood, she took him in her mouth and began the rhythmic sucking and stroking that would send him into euphoria. Cupping his balls with the pads of her fingertips, she gently lifted them as she stroked him with her tongue. She could sense his oncoming release several seconds before his body was gripped by the contraction, and she relaxed her mouth's hold on him as his pleasure peaked.

Wracked by the sudden pleasure her ministrations set off, Thomas yelled out and gasped, trying hard to breathe despite the spasms that were just on the verge of claiming his sanity. He sensed the moment when she allowed his manhood to escape her hold, and knew she would recapture it and draw it back into her mouth with her tongue and teeth at least one more time.

The pleasurable sensation was so sharp, so intense, Thomas thought of it as an exquisite torture that would have him giving Emma anything she wanted—she merely had to ask. When his manhood was once again in her hold, the movement of her lips and tongue at once slow and then quick, his hands cupped the sides of her head to still her movements. She gently let go of him and once again buried her face into his belly, wiggling her nose across the whorls of dark hair that covered the front of his body.

"Stop it, you minx," he pleaded in a hoarse whisper, his body jerking in response to the ticklish sensation.

Emma stilled her movements and rested her head on his thigh for a moment. When his breathing was no longer audible, she climbed onto the bench next to him, leaning against him and the end of the bed.

"You are a wicked woman," Thomas whispered, his eyes closed but a look of contentment settling on his face.

Emma closed her eyes. "Would you have me any other way, Mr. Wellingham?" she murmured happily.

Opening one eye, Thomas regarded his wife. "Yes. Yes, I would, actually," he admitted, closing the eye and sighing loudly. "But this way is best."

CHAPTER 29

NEWS FROM ABROAD LEADS
TO A DISCUSSION

February 28, 1803

Thomas nearly missed the envelope Humphrey had left at the edge of his desk, one that had clearly seen better days given it was so crumpled and discolored. Examining the writing, he realized almost immediately who had sent it—Christiana.

From the date she had penned in her perfect script, he realized it had been sent from Italy nearly two weeks ago.

Dear Brother,

I write this as I gaze out from our third-story apartment in Rome. The sun is setting, there is a slight breeze, and I find myself almost wishing I could live here all the time. My maid has said she would stay as well, but, alas, in another week it will be time for us to board a ship bound for British shores. Gregory has introduced me to so many people, I hardly know how I will remember their names. We have visited churches and museums, sites of wondrous antiquities, and walked more miles than I thought possible. His business is nearly complete, so we are left to tour some villages south of Rome before we depart. Our ship, the Fairweather, is due to arrive in London around March the ninth.

Until then, I hope this letter finds you happy and healthy. Please give my greetings to Emma and let her know I will come bearing a surprise upon our return. Yours very truly, Christiana.

Thomas allowed a grin to form, wondering if her surprise would indeed be the news that she was expecting a baby. He was also curious as to Gregory's business. He hadn't been aware the man intended the trip to include any business dealings, although given the man's penchant for investing, he supposed he shouldn't have been surprised by the news.

Setting aside the missive, he remembered the date and gave a start. "Humphrey!" he called out. The butler appeared within seconds, suggesting he had been just outside the library.

"Sir?"

"It seems our wayward travelers are to return on March ninth," Thomas stated. "Could you be sure Mrs. Werthers has their bedchambers ready?"

The butler nodded. "Indeed, sir. I'll see to it right away." He paused a moment. "The foreman insists they will have the last of the rooms complete in a few days."

Timing is everything, Thomas nearly replied before giving the servant a nod. "It's about time. After what this house has been through these past six months, I can hardly bring myself to have them start on the east side."

"Understood, sir," Humphrey said with a nod. He gave a short bow and disappeared from the library.

Sighing, Thomas gave a passing thought to how nice it would be to have the carpenters continue their work on the east end of the house. The parlor, refurbished since its smoke damage and fully furnished, was complete. There weren't nearly as many bedchambers in the east wing, but there was the kitchen and the dining room. A quick glance around the library had him deciding he rather liked it just the way it was.

"Are you ready?" Emma asked from the threshold. She had a redingote pulled on over her gown and a fur hat and muff clutched in her gloved hands.

Her husband grinned and quickly joined her. "I am, and I have news."

Emma's eyes widened. "Do tell," she encouraged. She walked with him to the vestibule, where he helped himself to his own redingote and hat.

"The Grandbys are due to arrive on the ninth. Seems if Christiana had her choice, they would be staying in Rome," he explained. They hurried out to the town coach just as Mr. Larsen took the reins.

"From what I've read of Rome, it doesn't seem very appealing," Emma countered as she stepped up into the coach. The groomsmen had seen to adding a hot coal to the brazier. Given the rain that threatened, Emma was happy to have the warmth.

"Not to me, either, but Gregory sees these ancient cities in a different light. It's the scientist in him, I think," he said as he joined her in the coach. Once he was seated, he asked, "Do you think we should have the workman redo the dining room while they're still about the house? Humphrey said they are due to be finished in a few days."

Emma stared at her husband and then blinked. "Where is my husband, and what have you done with him?" she asked in mock shock.

Thomas allowed a shrug. "The dining room is a bit on the shabby side, especially now that the parlor is finished."

"How you know that, I have no idea. You never go in there," Emma countered. Although it was on the opposite side of the vestibule from the library and featured a matching bank of windows facing north, the room was rarely used by anyone in the household. The library had been their gathering place for the entire time Emma had been in residence.

"Christiana admitted she'll return bearing a surprise. I just can't think it's anything other than news that she's about to give Gregory an heir—"

"Or a daughter," Emma interrupted.

"Or a daughter," Thomas acknowledged with a nod.

"Why did we redo the parlor? They have a nursery, children's bedchambers—"

"Christiana and I played in that parlor when we were growing up," Thomas countered. "It's where we went after dinner. It's where we played hide-n-seek—"

"Aren't you ten years older than she is?" Emma interrupted,

rather surprised at learning her husband and his sister had played together as youth.

"Nine years, actually," Thomas corrected her. "But we were the only children in the house. Which is part of why I spent a good deal of time down the way at Merriweather Manor," he added. "Getting into trouble with Gregory and his cousins."

Emma angled her head as she considered his comments. "Are you thinking that's where the Grandby children will play after dinner?" Emma asked in a quiet voice, rather liking Thomas' foray into nostalgia. "The parlor, I mean?" She could practically see him color up despite the high collar of his redingote.

"I suppose... I hope so," he finally agreed. He took a breath and leaned forward. "Which reminds me. I learned that the Simpsons are accepting offers on the townhouses in Kingly Street."

"Offers?" Emma repeated, her brows furrowing. "Are they looking to sell all of them?" she asked in alarm.

"To those who currently occupy them," Thomas clarified. "Since they're completely moved into Kingly Place, Mr. Simpson is seeing to the renovation of their old townhouse. When he's finished with it, he'll be done remodeling, or so he claims. The townhouse at the opposite end of the street—the one closest to Oxford Street—has already been sold."

Emma considered how fortunate she had been to lease one of the Simpson townhouses. James had already seen to renovating hers long before she took up residence. Although she hadn't lived there very long before marrying Thomas, they had agreed to continue leasing the unit so they would have a London residence in the event they didn't wish to make the trip back to Woodscastle. "Are you thinking we should make an offer?" she asked, a hint of hope in her voice. "We can afford it, I think," she added.

Thomas grinned. "You have read my mind. I'll write the Simpsons and ask as to what they think might be a fair offer," he promised. After a moment, he added, "Mrs. Simpson is probably in confinement by now, though."

Emma's eyes widened. "I haven't seen her since Christmastime. I wonder if she's accepting visitors?" she replied. "Poor woman."

At Thomas' look of surprise and, "Whatever do you mean?" Emma angled her head to one side.

"She's in her forties, Thomas. It's been so long since she had Gregory, it will be like giving birth to her first babe all over again. I do hope she has a good midwife. I haven't heard if Deborah has been arranged or not," she murmured.

The familiar clatter of cobbles beneath the wheels had Thomas glancing out the window. "If Gregory hasn't already recommended Mrs. Vandermeer, then I suppose you should," he replied.

"I already did. When we were there at Christmas."

After another moment, Thomas said, "We're nearly there."

Indeed, a minute later, and Mr. Larsen had the town coach pulled up in front of Wellingham Imports. "Do have a good day, Mr. Wellingham," Emma commented as he helped her down from the equipage.

"And you as well, my sweeting."

CHAPTER 30
THE OVERBY KIDS

Earlier that morning

As was his custom, Stephen Bingham arrived at Wellingham Imports by five-thirty in the morning. He left his horse in the capable hands of one of the stable boys who cared for the company's horses as well as those of employees who rode to work. And, as the warehouse manager, he usually unlocked the front doors of the establishment upon his arrival.

He found them unlocked on this particular morning.

Cautious and on alert, he entered the premises and listened intently, trying to determine if Thomas Wellingham had uncharacteristically arrived early or if someone else had already entered the warehouse. Not hearing anything other than the ordinary sounds of the riverfront, he made his way to the stairs leading to his office. At the sound of quiet weeping, he stopped and cocked his head. Sure it was coming from within the building, he changed direction and walked into the warehouse, quietly following the sounds of sniffling and weeping until he found their source huddled in a blanket behind a crate.

"Please, Mr. Bingham, don't be angry," Billy Overby pleaded as he looked up to find the warehouse manager staring down at him. The boy had his arm wrapped around the shoulders of a small girl, and it was her quiet sobs that broke the early morning silence.

Mr. Bingham stared at the two children for a moment before replying, "I am not angry. But who is she?" he asked as he indicated the filthy toddler the boy held in a protective hug.

"This is my sister, Miss Katie, sir," Billy replied quietly. "I didn't know where else to bring her," he added as he fought back tears of his own.

His brows furrowing, Mr. Bingham regarded the caddie. "Shouldn't she be with her mother, boy?" he asked, surprised that Billy even had a sister. The caddie never talked about his family life nor mentioned where he lived.

"Yes, sir," the boy replied, his tears finally appearing in the corners of his eyes. "But she went to sleep two nights ago and hasn't woke up," he added. "I think she's dead."

Failing to suppress a hiss, the warehouse manager took a deep breath and nodded once. "When was the last time you ate something?" He noted the boy's deep set eyes and pale complexion. The toddler's condition was worse. Her hair hadn't been combed in at least a week, and her tear-stained face and the hand that showed over the top of the blanket were so dirty, he wasn't sure if she was indeed a little girl.

"I... I don't know, Mr. Bingham," the boy replied, his tears finally letting loose in a sob that shook his entire body.

The warehouse manager nodded his understanding. "Stay here while I find ye something to eat. We'll figure out something for you when Mr. Wellingham gets here," he said as he scratched his head.

When the Wellinghams arrived for work at nine o'clock that morning, Stephen Bingham hurried to intercept them before they could make their way up to their offices. Even before he could finish telling them about the Overby children, Emma left his side and hurried to where he indicated the children were nestled. She bent down and took in the sight of the caddie and his small sister. "Master Billy, are you all right?" she asked as she reached out to place her open palm on his forehead. The boy tried to back away from her touch but could not, and the little girl gave a cry of fright at her sudden appearance.

"Oh, you poor creatures," Emma breathed as she determined that neither seemed to have fevers. "You must be freezing in here," she added as she realized she could see her breath in the chill morning air of the warehouse. "Come. Let us get you upstairs near the fire." When neither child seemed to move, she looked over her shoulder to find her husband staring down at them. "Thomas, it is too cold for them down here," she said as she noted his stern look.

Thomas nodded his head quickly. "Indeed. Come, Master Billy. Up the stairs you go," he ordered with a nod in the direction of his office. The caddie started to get up, but his sister clutched his arm and whimpered with fright.

"Get up, Katie," he said impatiently. The toddler hung on to her brother as he stood up and kept the blanket wrapped around his sister. Neither child wore shoes, and both were filthy.

"Oh, dear," Emma sighed as she reached out and picked up the girl with her right arm. Her left still gave her pain when she put too much pressure on it. "When was the last time you had anything to eat?" she asked softly as she pushed the girl's blonde hair away from her face.

"I gave them my supper when I got in this morning," Mr. Bingham said as he joined them. "And they ate it faster than I would have," he added.

Thomas watched as Emma held and comforted the girl. Perhaps mothering came naturally to a woman, he considered, but it appeared to him as if Emma had been doing it for years. "I'll get Master Billy into some warmer clothes and have him take me to his mother," he said quietly. "I would go without him, but he's never divulged where he lives," he added with a sigh.

Emma nodded her understanding. "If it is all right with you, I will borrow one of the water buckets from the stables and give her a proper bath," she offered, not sure what else she could do with the tyke until a caretaker could be found.

Thomas smiled and kissed his wife on the cheek. "Be careful not to wash her too much. I fear there won't be much left when you get that layer of dirt off of her," he teased gently.

Relieved he wasn't angered by the situation, Emma reached

out with her free hand and squeezed one of his. Then she hoisted her bundle onto one shoulder and climbed the stairs to her husband's office. Mr. Bingham followed a few minutes later with a large metal water trough. Several warehouse workers followed him carrying buckets of water. Once they were set next to the fireplace in the back room of the office, the men filed out and wished her luck with the youngster. "Mr. Bingham," Emma called out before the warehouse manager could leave the office.

"Yes, Mrs. Wellingham?" he replied as he poked his head back around the corner.

"Is that crate of French milled soap still on the warehouse floor?" Emma asked, remembering she'd seen an entry about it on the ledgers the week before.

The warehouse manager thought for a moment and caught her meaning. "Why, yes, I think I can find it easily enough. How many bars of the stuff should I pull out?" he asked, half-teasing as he nodded in the filthy girl's direction.

Emma smiled at his inference. "Just one bar should do," she replied. "And see if you can pilfer some linens and little girl clothes while you're at it," she added in a loud whisper.

When Emma began undressing the toddler for her much-needed bath, the girl protested loudly at first, finally quieting down when she realized the water was warm and Emma wasn't out to hurt her. It took several minutes of washing and playing before Emma dared to try washing the girl's hair, but once done, the struggle was well worth the results. With her large blue eyes and pink cheeks, blonde curly hair, and two front teeth, the toddler was simply adorable. And her disposition improved even more when she was dried and dressed in a long, white gown and nappies, squealing in delight as Emma poked and teased her. Kneeling on the floor of the office, Emma held the girl in front of her while she struggled to get socks on her tiny feet.

"Mama," she said as she patted Emma's back. "Mama, mama. Dada."

Emma inhaled as she pulled away from the child and looked up to find her husband watching the two of them on the floor of his back office. His weary look took on a hint of amusement.

"I believe I have come to the wrong place. I was looking for a filthy little girl named Katie," he said quietly.

Katie toddled up to him and wrapped her arms around his legs. "Dada dada," she murmured, the bath having washed away her fear of Thomas along with the layers of filth.

Trying desperately to hide her smile, Emma watched her husband's reaction to the little girl. He stood quite still and regarded the toddler for a moment before reaching down and lifting her up to his shoulder. The girl squealed happily when she noticed her brother standing next to the man that held her.

"Katie?" the boy asked, incredulous at the change in his sister. "Is that you?" he asked as he stared at the girl. He wore a pair of boots and a jacket at least two sizes too big for him.

"Bill, Bill, Bill," she said as she squirmed in Thomas' arms. Emma watched, trying hard to suppress a grin. She finally gave up. "She is an adorable child," she said in a quiet voice. After a moment, though, her face took on a serious expression. "And what of their mother?" she asked in a whisper. Although Emma had briefly met the woman when she was pregnant with the girl, Emma couldn't recall what she looked like or how old she was. If it hadn't been for Billy recognizing Emma, she wouldn't even know she was at one time acquainted with him through her charity work at the Home for Unwed Mothers.

"We found her. She let a room in a house in the Seven Dials," he said grimly, referring to the particularly poor part of the city. "She passed sometime yesterday. Probably died of hunger if not pneumonia. The undertaker is seeing to her right now," Thomas said quietly, absently bouncing Katie as he shared the sad news. "Master William knows of no immediate family, so I'm afraid we have a decision to make," he added as he moved to sit in one of the chairs in the back corner. He propped Katie on his knee as he leaned back in the chair and regarded the toddler.

Emma nodded and caught Billy Overby's reaction to Thomas' last statement. "Please, sir," the boy said quietly. "I can look after myself, but Katie cannot go to an orphanage," he said, tears once again welling up in his eyes. "They'll send her to a workhouse, and I'll never see her again," he whispered before he started to sob.

Gasping, Emma shook her head. "Oh, no, she cannot go to an orphanage, Mr. Wellingham," she concurred as she continued to shake her head. "We must know someone who would care for her," she added as she watched her husband interact with the toddler. He seemed to know what to do to keep the child entertained. He had raised his sister, she considered.

"Agreed," Thomas stated emphatically. "So we could ask the Grandbys, but they won't be back from Rome for over a week, and we can ask the Vandermeers," he suggested with a nod as he allowed Katie to grip one of his fingers and attempt to shake it loose from his hand.

Emma's mouth opened in surprise, but she shut it quickly as she realized her husband was serious. "What about… us?" she asked, her brow furrowing. Although she wasn't yet ready to start a family, she was at least willing to make the offer to care for the orphans.

Uncomfortable, Thomas looked away and chewed on his free thumb before replying. "We haven't a nursery here," he replied simply, "And we are here most of the day. If we take them, then who is to care for them while we're working?" he reasoned with a shrug. The thought of hiring a nanny didn't cross his mind.

Understanding his meaning, Emma bit her lip. "So if the Grandby's take them, they'll still live at Woodscastle with us," she said.

"There is that," Thomas agreed. "And if Gregory isn't up for it, I think we could probably convince Todd to take them," he suggested.

Billy Overby continued to stand in the doorway between the front and back office. "Mr. Vandermeer likes me," he said as he puffed out his chest. "He'll take care of her. I'm sure of it," he said, his voice making it sound as if he were trying to convince himself more than the Wellinghams.

Emma pressed her lips together, not sure what to think of

the situation. Would Deborah want to take on two children before her first was even born? At least she knew the boy, Emma considered.

Emma was still lost in thought when she realized there was someone else in the office.

"Pardon me, Mr. Wellingham," Stephen Bingham said as he poked his head around the wall that separated the front and back offices. "Could I have a word with you?" When he noticed Emma sitting on the floor next to the washtub, he gasped and moved in her direction. "The floor is no place for a lady," he stated with a frown as he reached down to lend his hand.

"Thank you, Mr. Bingham," Emma replied as she allowed him to help her up by her right arm. "I was playing with the baby," she said by way of explanation. Once on her feet, she moved to take Katie from her husband so he could stand up. The toddler squirmed, and Emma let the girl stand on her own. At the sight of the warehouse manager, Katie smiled brightly and pointed in his direction. "Papa, papa," she said loudly and toddled toward the large man.

Startled by the title bestowed on him, Stephen Bingham smiled broadly. Bending down, he took her in his arms and lifted her to his shoulder. "My wife and I will take care of these two, if it's all right with you," the manager said as he allowed Katie to pound a fist against his chest.

Gasping, Emma stared at the man and then looked at her husband. His rather stunned attention was on his warehouse manager. "Are you sure your wife will agree to such an arrangement?" Thomas countered, surprised and rather relieved by the offer.

"Oh, aye," Mr. Bingham assured them as he kissed Katie's forehead and motioned for Billy to join him. He placed a large hand on the boy's shoulder. "Mrs. Bingham's been wanting bairns for years. And her mother's been asking about grandchildren for even longer," he said with a shrug.

Turning his attention to the window, Thomas stood in silence for a moment. "Will your wife allow Master Billy to continue his position, do you suppose?" he asked as he turned to regard his warehouse manager.

Stephen Bingham smiled broadly. "I think that can be arranged," he replied as he looked down on the caddie. "He'll be a lot cleaner, to be sure," he added with a wink in his boss's direction.

Billy gasped and seemed to back away from his new father. "Cleaner?" he repeated, his disgust apparent. "You mean, I have to take a *bath?*"

The Wellinghams both laughed and nodded their heads at the boy. "I was just about to have you get in the tub," Emma stated as she pointed in the direction of the watering trough.

"I don't think that would be such a good idea, dear heart," Thomas countered as he looked over at his wife. "I do believe that that water is more filthy than he already is," he teased playfully.

Mr. Bingham reached down and took Billy Overby's hand. "If I could, sir, I would like to take them home now. I won't be gone long, I assure you," he added as he realized Thomas Wellingham was regarding him with a curious stare.

After a moment, Thomas leaned against the chair and nodded. "Of course, Mr. Bingham. Take as long as you need," he said with a sigh, his face finally showing a grin.

Emma nodded to the warehouse manager. "'Tis very kind of you, Mr. Bingham," she said with a sigh, her mixed feelings apparent. But she noticed Katie's head pressed against Mr. Bingham's shoulder and realized the toddler was sound asleep.

"Just like an angel, isn't she?" Mr. Bingham whispered as he noticed the subject of Emma's attention.

"They are when they sleep," Emma agreed with a nod. Reaching over, she took her husband's hand and squeezed it gently.

Thomas glanced at Billy Overby and gave him a nod. "You can take the rest of the day off to go meet your new mother," he offered in a business-like tone, "But I expect you back here in the morning."

Billy's face lit up, and his eyes widened. "Yes, sir, Mr.

Wellingham," the boy replied happily. With that, the new Bingham family left the building.

Thomas sat back down, pulling on Emma's hand until she lost her balance and had to sit on his lap. Wrapping an arm around her waist, he pulled her close and kissed her on the cheek. "I'm not sure what to think," he whispered as Emma relaxed against him and rested her head on his shoulder.

"Likewise, I am sure," Emma replied quietly. She smiled finally and kissed Thomas on the cheek. "It is for the best, I suppose. And you still have your caddie," she reasoned.

Nodding, Thomas smiled in return. "That I do," he agreed. "Because, if Todd Vandermeer had his way, that kid would be *his* caddie," he added with a sigh.

Emma laughed, and at Thomas' quizzical expression, she said, "Now that Todd Vandermeer is working here, that kid is his caddie."

Thomas rolled his eyes and shook his head.

Damn, he murmured under his breath.

CHAPTER 31

THE HONEYMOONERS
RETURN

March 9, 1803

When a post chaise pulled into the half-circle drive in front of Woodscastle in the late afternoon, several new footmen accompanied Humphrey to meet it. They formed a line adjacent to the front door until such time as the coach driver opened the doors.

Mrs. Gregory Grandby was the first to step down, although she did so rather slowly, gripping the driver's hand until both her feet were on solid ground. She quickly stepped aside to allow her husband to follow, his height requiring him to bend down nearly in half to keep from hitting his head. Once Gregory had unfolded his body and took a deep breath, Humphrey motioned for the footmen to begin their work.

"Good afternoon, Humphrey," Christiana said as she hurried as best she could to the front door.

"It is indeed, my lady," Humphrey agreed as he gave her a deep bow. Given the amount of rain that had fallen in the past several days, it was refreshing to have a day with clear skies.

"Are the Wellinghams in residence?"

The butler shook his head. "Not as yet, but they are due shortly. I'm to inform you that the work on your apartments and the parlor is complete. However, the work on the dining room is just getting started."

"The parlor?" Christiana repeated, her mouth opening in shock. She hurried into the house, her skirts bunched into one hand just below her swollen belly and the pelisse she wore. She stood on the parlor threshold and stared in wonder.

"The workman were instructed to make it look as much the same as possible. They just had to replace the broken moldings, install new wall coverings, and replace the furnishings," Humphrey explained when he noted her expression. "Oh, and there is a new carpet, as well." He didn't add that it was actually the second new carpet. The first had suffered too many visible burns.

The news seemed to provide some solace. "It looks lovely," she murmured just as Gregory joined her.

"You mean Thomas hasn't had enough of the renovations on our side?" he teased as he wrapped an arm around her shoulders. He gave a nod of approval at seeing the updates in the parlor.

Humphrey resisted the urge to roll his eyes. "He... was *reluctant*," he dared. "But Mrs. Wellingham thought it best it be done now so there would be a place for the women and children to congregate after dinner."

This comment had Christiana's eyes opening wider. She gazed up at her husband. "Do you suppose she already knows I'm expecting?" she whispered.

Gregory pretended to consider the question before giving her a nod. "I rather think Emma was wise to your condition before we took our leave of London." His eyes widened, as if he expected her to admonish him for telling his sister-in-law. "But it wasn't because I said anything, I assure you. Now, shall we go see what's been done in the west wing? I rather imagine you'd like a bath. I know I would," he murmured.

Christiana allowed a grin. "Yes. But first, I really must use the facilities," she whispered as she hurried off toward the refurbished end of the house.

Watching his wife as she made her way down the hall to the west wing stairs, Gregory couldn't keep a grin from forming. Although she still had a month or more to go before she would deliver his first babe, Christiana was already displaying all the signs of a woman with child. He had expected her to complain of her discomfort whilst they toured the ruins and sights around Rome, but she had let out nary a peep of protest. Well, except for the night she had discovered her swollen ankles, mostly because the dance slippers she planned to wear to a count's ball wouldn't slip onto her feet.

At the sound of familiar voices in the vestibule, Gregory moved to the edge of the wall and poked his head around the opening. "Welcome home," he said happily.

Emma and Thomas gave him matching expressions of surprise. "We thought we would make it home before you," Emma said as she moved to kiss him on the cheek.

"Ten minutes faster, and you would have," he countered, giving Thomas a quick handshake.

"What have you done with my sister?" Thomas asked when he realized Christiana wasn't with her husband.

Gregory wondered if the question should be his opening to tell them of his wife's condition. She would probably berate him for not allowing her to be in on sharing the news, so he motioned toward the west wing. "She's already reviewing her new rooms," he answered. "Anything else going on here besides a new parlor?"

Giving up her pelisse to Humphrey, Emma shook her head. "They're working on the dining room now. Then they'll move to some of the east wing bedchambers," she warned with an arched eyebrow. Lowering her voice, she asked, "Is she well?"

Understanding her meaning, Gregory nodded. "She is. Plump and more beautiful than the day I married her," he replied. "But I would be careful about mentioning the freckles. I rather adore them, but she's quite incensed about how they appeared despite her using a parasol everywhere we went."

Emma grinned. "Poor thing."

"What of my mother? Have you heard any news from the Simpsons?" he asked, his concern evident.

"They're completely moved into their new home," Emma

replied. "We had Christmas dinner with them. Mrs. Simpson looked... radiant when I last saw her," she added when it was apparent Gregory wanted for information.

"She hasn't lost the babe?" he whispered.

Emma gave a start. "Not that I'm aware," she replied, wondering why he would ask such a thing.

At that moment, Christiana appeared at the top of the stairs and carefully made her way down, her pregnancy very much in evidence as she gripped the bannister.

"So you did get her knocked up," Thomas murmured well before Christiana was close enough to hear him. She was hurrying toward them, though, her condition made apparent at how snug her gown fit around her middle.

Gregory frowned. "I take it Emma must have figured it out before our departure," he replied in a hoarse whisper. "Do try to act surprised. She's been looking forward to this for weeks."

"Emma! Thomas!" Christiana cried out, her arms wide so that she gave first Emma and then her brother a hug.

"Oof!" Thomas grunted, barely managing to keep his feet under him as his sister collided with him. "I see you come bearing a future niece or nephew," he teased.

Christiana beamed. "I do, and I can hardly wait to deliver whatever it is to be," she replied. "I do so want to be able to wear my good slippers again."

Emma blinked, rather surprised to hear the young lady's comment. She rather expected a tirade about how uncomfortable she was, how nothing fit, and how her feet were sore. "When do you suppose you'll give birth?" Emma asked, hoping Gregory's mother would do so before Christiana. It was awkward enough that Gregory's child would be the same age as his younger brother or sister. He had no other siblings, after all.

"About two months, I believe," Christiana replied. "I shall be the last of the three, I should think." She sobered. "Has anyone else given birth yet?"

Emma shook her head. "It won't be long. A week or two, perhaps," she replied. "Have you given a thought as to whom you would like as your midwife?"

Christiana seemed to take a half-step back. "But... I thought you would be my midwife."

Taking a breath to reply, Emma held it a moment and finally allowed a shrug. "I suppose I could. But I shall hope that another is available to help. I haven't the experience of Mrs. Vandermeer or Mrs. Dawes," she warned.

Seemingly disappointed, Christiana merely nodded. "Well, I find I really must take a bath before dinner. Do excuse me," she said as she bobbed an awkward curtsy.

Before she could head for the stairs again, though, Gregory gave a nod to them both and joined her. "If you think you're getting into that tub without any help, young lady, think again," he said with mock menace.

Just as the two started to climb the stairs, Christiana gave Emma a pointed glance and rolled her eyes.

Coloring up when she realized what Gregory had planned, Emma moved a hand up to cover her grin of embarrassment. Thomas scratched the back of his head before guiding Emma toward the east wing stairs. "I do believe that man has a very good idea," he whispered. Turning to find Humphrey near the library, he called out, "Have some bath water brought up, won't you?"

The butler gave a nod and hurried off to the kitchen.

Emma had to suppress a giggle. "Too bad they're home. I rather liked drawing a hot bath using their new plumbing," she sighed.

Thomas gave her a buss on the cheek. "Then let's forget about the other bedchambers for now. I'll have the workmen start on our bathing chamber next," he promised.

Giving him a look of surprise, Emma nearly stopped in her tracks. "Does that mean a larger tub, too?" she asked hopefully.

Frowning, Thomas considered the query. "I thought we fit in ours just fine," he countered, disappointment evident in his voice.

Emma blinked. "Not even for more knee room?" she hinted with an arched brow.

It was Thomas' turn to blink. "Oh, well, when you put it

like that, then, yes, I suppose we could do with a larger tub," he agreed as his face took on a reddish cast. "Capital idea."

CHAPTER 32

BABY BLUES

March 15, 1803

"She hates me," Todd stated as he led Emma into his house and through the vestibule. Todd's groom, Mr. Stevenson, had arrived at Wellingham Imports in the middle of a late Friday afternoon requesting that Emma return to Grace Park with him. His master was most upset and asked if she could come to help restore Mrs. Vandermeer's good spirits.

As was his practice, the broker had already spent most of the day at Wellingham Imports, his work day beginning around six in the morning and ending around three o'clock in the after-noon. Todd made it clear after a few months in his position that he intended to put his family before his work, a concept that surprised everyone who heard it.

"And I do not know what I have done to incite such a feeling in her," Todd added sadly. "I have done all that she has asked of me—"

Emma rolled her eyes and shook her head. "She does not hate you, Todd," she replied reassuringly, patting the arm she held onto as they climbed the stairs. "She is nearly nine months with child," she continued in explanation. "She probably has not slept well in weeks, she is behaving irrationally, her ankles are no doubt swollen, her back is probably very sore. And she's carrying an extra stone, so her knees are aching even more so than usual," she added for good measure.

Todd paused at the top of the stairs. "'Tis true. All of it. But how did *you* know?" he asked in surprise.

Emma tried hard to suppress a smile. "I worked at the Home for Unwed Mothers as my charity, remember?" she replied, as if mentioning the place where half the women were pregnant and the other half were mothers of small children was enough of an explanation.

"Oh. Of course," the tall man replied with a nod. "Well, I do hope you can be of assistance to her," he said sadly. "I do miss my Deborah." He bowed as they stood outside the door to the mistress suite.

As he started to take his leave, Emma reached for his hand. "Stay close, will you?" she suggested, hoping she would be able to smooth things over between the lovers and leave them both in good spirits. "'Tis all right if you want to listen, I should think," she added with a shrug. Curtsying, Emma gave him a wan smile and knocked on the door. "Deborah?" she called out, finally opening the door when she didn't hear a response.

Worried she might awaken Deborah from a much-needed nap, she entered the room quietly and instead found Deborah leaning in a chaise lounge, tears streaming down her pale face. Even in tears, she was a beauty to behold, her dark hair styled so a lock fell onto one shoulder and the rest swirled into a large bun atop her head. Her satin dressing gown draped over her long legs and barely hinted at her advanced pregnancy.

Hurrying to her side, Emma knelt next to the lounge and placed a hand on the side of Deborah's face. "Whatever is wrong?" she asked quietly. "Why are you crying?"

Deborah sniffled and finally turned to face Emma. The surprise on her face made it apparent she hadn't been aware of her friend's arrival. "Oh, Emma, I have been so cruel," she sobbed as she reached out to hug her visitor.

Emma returned the hug and patted Deborah on the back. "Whatever are you talking about?" she whispered. "Cruel to whom?"

Wiping the tears from her face, Deborah struggled to turn her body so that she could sit on the edge of the chaise. "My beloved Todd, of course," she said between sobs. "He has done everything I have asked of him, and yet I cannot help but say cruel things to him."

Emma sighed and took one of Deborah's bare feet between her hands. *Thorns*, she thought with a frown. *Poor Todd.* Massaging the ankle she held, she said, "I think he understands that you are most uncomfortable," Emma finally replied. "Has he been putting salve on your knees?" she asked, noticing Deborah's wince when she moved her legs.

"No," Deborah replied, sniffling. "I was concerned the medicine might harm the baby, so I have not used it in several months," she explained, finally feeling relief as Emma worked on her swollen ankle.

Emma regarded her friend for a moment. "What good are you to your baby if you are in pain all the time, Deborah?" she asked with a sigh.

Deborah sat up straighter and stared at Emma. "What are you saying?" she asked, her voice taking on an edge.

Closing her eyes for a moment, Emma considered her words before replying, "I shouldn't think the salve contains anything that would hurt your baby, but it helps you, and at this point, you need to be concerned about your well-being."

Dropping her shoulders in resignation, Deborah sighed. "All right, I will have Todd put some on this evening," she replied with a nod, sniffling as she did so.

Shaking her head, Emma said, "No. I will put some on you now. You need to get out and walk around your garden. 'Tis not that cold, and the fresh air will do you good. Where is it?"

Tears began flowing down Deborah's face again. "I... I don't know. I've not been able to put it on Todd..."

Emma let go of Deborah's ankle and got up from the floor. "What is it? Deborah?"

The pregnant woman sobbed quietly against the side of the chaise lounge. "Oh, Emma, I just cannot do this any longer," she struggled to say between gasps for air.

Sitting down hard next to Deborah, Emma took the woman in her arms and tried to comfort her. "Shh. What can't you do?" she whispered, rubbing Deborah's back with one hand.

When her body had stopped shaking from the sobs, Deborah took a deep breath and said, "I don't wish to be... *pregnant* any longer. It is making me behave so poorly. I have become as irrational as any of the girls I used to care for at the Home, and I hate it. I hate what I've become."

Shaking her head, Emma continued to rub Deborah's back as she listened to her cry. She was reminded of comments Deborah used to say about the girls who were near their due dates. Deborah was always surprised that advanced pregnancy could make a woman seem almost irrational.

How can they say such things? she would ask when Emma showed up on Saturday mornings. *I do not understand their constant complaints of discomfort. They should be grateful they have a place to sleep and a hot meal.*

Well, Deborah certainly understood now, Emma considered. "When... when was the last time you... slept with your husband?" Emma whispered in Deborah's ear, thinking that Todd would be just outside the open door.

A new round of tears started as Deborah leaned against Emma. "I... I haven't let him touch me these past... I love him, I do, and I want him so badly... but I am suddenly so... large, so... *ugly*," she struggled to say between sobs, her arms held out around her swollen belly.

Indeed, she was quite large, Emma realized. And as she watched the bump pressed against Deborah's lounging gown, she could see movement there. The baby was no doubt responding to its mother's distress, and Deborah moved a hand to the place where she had just been kicked. "Oh!" Deborah gasped and struggled to smile in spite of her tears.

Grinning, Emma said, "Deborah, you must know, there are things Todd can do now that will help you when the baby comes."

Deborah nodded and took a deep breath. "Oh, my, I forgot about that," she replied, leaning her head back against the top of the chaise and taking another breath, her eyes closed. "My nipples..."

She stopped in mid-sentence, and Emma looked up to find Todd leaning over to kiss Deborah. She had not even been aware of his presence in the bedchamber, but he held a jar of salve in one hand and Deborah's chin in the other. When he finally ended the kiss and pulled away from Deborah, he knelt on the floor and motioned for Emma to lift Deborah's gown.

Startled by his take-charge manner and self-confidence, Emma folded up Deborah's lounging gown over her knees. Deborah's ankles were swollen, and the slippers she wore barely covered her feet.

"You must tell me these things that I can do for my love," Todd stated as he began rubbing salve into one of Deborah's knees. His practiced hands massaged the salve deep into the joint, and Deborah moaned with relief as the medicine began its work.

Blushing bright red, Emma stole a quick glance at Deborah. The woman was smiling and wiping tears from her face. "Well, there is... nipple chewing... ," Emma started to say, obviously uncomfortable with the topic of discussion.

"To draw down the milk," Todd finished for her. "Yes, I know about that," he said with an amused expression. "What else?"

Swallowing, Emma continued to blush. "Frequent intercourse," she blurted, glancing nervously at Deborah as she said it.

Todd looked up from his ministrations on Deborah's knee. "How frequent?" he asked, his demeanor becoming serious again.

Emma exchanged glances with Deborah. "That's up to Deborah, but there are some girls—"

"As often as you can," Deborah interrupted. "Whenever you want, if... if you can stand to love me in the state I am in," she added, losing her composure. Tears threatened again, but the baby kicked and she gasped in surprise.

Todd's eyes widened. "Did you see that?" he asked, referring to the movement he had witnessed in Deborah's belly.

Emma couldn't suppress a grin as Deborah regarded her husband. "I felt it. The baby has been kicking me all afternoon," she complained, but a smile broke out on her face. Lifting one of Todd's hands from her knee, she placed it on her abdomen. It was only a moment before the baby kicked again. Awed, Todd placed an ear against her belly and listened intently. He jerked away when another kick impacted the side of his face. Deborah laughed and Todd began chuckling as he held a hand against her belly.

Emma continued grinning as she watched the two of them interact. How might Thomas behave in the same situation? Todd was certainly playful and loving, not at all what she expected considering the first time she had met the man during a business meeting in the library at Woodscastle. *That was only nine months ago*, Emma thought to herself. *If I had never introduced them, I would be the one sitting in the chaise lounge, nine months pregnant, married to a doting man who wanted only the best for his wife.*

Wrapped up in her own thoughts, she didn't notice that Todd was once again kissing Deborah, murmuring to her about how beautiful she was and insisting that she sleep with him in the master suite for the rest of her life. Even as he helped her up from the chaise lounge to take her for a walk in the garden, Emma was oblivious to the couple.

Would Thomas be this loving? Would he put up with the irrational behavior brought on by pregnancy? Would he still make love to her when her body was so misshapen?

Even when Thomas was being romantic, he did so in a controlled and intentional manner. He bought gifts, he devised plans, he left nothing to chance, she realized. But it was also a trait she found endearing in him. Because he was so good at planning, he had built a successful business and raised his sister. And at the first sign the business might be threatened by embezzlement, he recognized the signs and hired her months before she could even start the work of auditing for him.

His one unplanned life event had been their wedding, she realized. He intended to ask her for her hand, and he did so on the day he planned to, but the wedding—it was as if he hadn't looked beyond the betrothal.

Coming up with the excuse that Gregory might try to take over the business if he didn't marry her immediately was the only case of spontaneity she could recall him exhibiting. And although he hadn't been able to plan their wedding and honeymoon quite the way one would expect, he had still managed to arrange a week of entertainment and romance in London while making sure they were with Christiana on her seventeenth birthday and for her betrothal to Gregory. *Yes, he is a remarkable man,* she thought with a smile. *I did end up with the right man.*

"Emma?" Deborah said for at least the third time. "Are you well?"

Startled, Emma looked up to find the couple staring down at her. "What is it?" she replied. How many times had she been addressed before realizing she was being spoken to?

"Are you well?" Todd asked as he leaned down to take a closer look at Emma. "You looked as if you were in another world," he commented with a mischievous grin.

"I am fine," Emma replied with a wan smile. "I was just... woolgathering," she said, her face turning pink with embarrassment. When she noticed their look of expectation, she stood up. "Oh, I should be getting back to work," she said then. "You two have much to... to do," she added lamely as she curtsied and hurried out the door.

CHAPTER 33

A PRODIGAL SON RETURNS

Meanwhile, in Kingly Street

Hat in hand, Gregory stood in the rather large vestibule of his mother's new home and gazed at the ceiling. His attention drifted down the walls and to the marble floor beneath. He boggled at the mariner's compass pattern made up of contrasting tiles, at the statuary lining the walls, at the largest bouquet of roses he had ever seen in his life, and at his mother as she slowly descended the staircase directly ahead. If there was another woman who looked as if she should be the queen of England, he certainly hadn't seen her.

"Am I allowed to say you are the most beautiful woman in the world, or would your husband give voice to a protest?" he asked, hurrying to offer her a hand as she managed the last few steps.

"It wouldn't matter if he did. I rather adore hearing your compliments. Just don't tell your wife," she warned with an impish grin. "How is she, by the way?" she added as she took the last step down.

"Surprisingly... calm. Rather unexpected, really. I was led to believe she would spend these days in a constant state of... *complaint*."

"Like me?" Sophia asked, a self-deprecating grin appearing.

"How was your trip, darling? And why have you waited so long to pay a visit?"

Gregory sighed. "I have tried. Twice, in fact, but it seems you were either not at home or you were napping," he replied with an arched brow. "I thought to try tea time instead, and here you are."

"You were always smarter than your father," she said as she led them to the breakfast parlor.

Rather surprised they weren't headed to the regular parlor, Gregory paused as he allowed her to step into the room ahead of him. "I don't remember Father," he murmured as his gaze swept the breakfast parlor. "Wouldn't you be more comfortable in an upholstered chair?"

Sophia patted his hand as she slowly took a seat in one of the dining chairs, a hand landing on her protruding belly once she was settled. It was then Gregory realized all six chairs at the breakfast table sported upholstered seats in a butter yellow fabric, and the tall backs, carved in a simple concave design, seemed to accommodate a person's back perfectly. He didn't know how comfortable they were for his mother, but she seemed to be doing just fine in hers.

"I rather adore this room," she replied as she glanced around at the rosewood furnishing and yellow decor. "There are days I think I could sit here until it was time to move to the dining room for dinner." She allowed a satisfied sigh. "The sun lights the room just perfectly. Your stepfather certainly knew what he was doing when he redesigned this house." A servant appeared in the doorway to the butler's pantry and she turned her attention to the woman. "Tea, please. And do be sure to include cakes," Sophia added happily.

Gregory took the chair opposite hers. "Enjoying cakes now, are you?" he teased. His mother's figure had always been trimmer than was fashionable, but then it was a trait she shared with her sisters and her mother.

Sophia blinked. "Oh, they're not for me," she replied. "They're for you."

Grinning, Gregory dipped his head. "Where is my stepfather, by the way? I expected he would have met me at the front door."

Sophia gave a shrug. "Across the street. He's overseeing the work on our old townhouse. Getting it ready to sell," she said, one of her eyebrows arching up suggestively.

Gregory frowned. "Sell?" he repeated in shock. "Not... *let?*"

Inhaling deeply, Sophia shook her head. "If you ever expected to inherit these properties, Gregory, please know that there may not be many of them left by the time we're gone. We've been accepting offers for purchase. Shoring up our accounts in anticipation of the next stage of our lives. James has nearly finished his life's work and wants to be available for his next project."

His eyes widening in surprise, Gregory stared at his mother a moment before he asked, "And what might that be?" as if he feared her response.

Sophia allowed a huge smile just as a maid delivered the tea tray. "Why, your sibling, silly," she replied. "I have never seen a man more excited about a baby in my entire life. And I used to live at Merriweather Manor where there were all manner of babies all the time."

"Which is why you never saw a man excited over the prospect," Gregory said under his breath.

"I think he's more excited than I am," she said as she attempted to lean forward and found she couldn't. "Do be a good son and serve, won't you?" she asked. "Why, I find my arms have grown shorter," she claimed.

Chuckling, Gregory poured the tea and stirred in cream in both cups before handing one to Sophia. "Are you... doing well?" he asked carefully. "I worried about you the entire time I was in Italy. I shouldn't want this baby to cause you... harm."

"Why, Gregory, I do think you're jealous," she accused, although there was humor in her words.

Gregory's head jerked up, and he stared at his mother. "I am not," he countered, annoyance sounding in his voice. He just as quickly sighed, as if he thought better of his response. "Concerned, of course, more than anything."

Sophia angled her head. "Because you think I'm too old to have this baby? Goodness. How old do you think I am?"

Her son shook his head. "Your age has nothing to do with it, Mother. It's just... Mr. Simpson says you don't intend to hire a nurse, so a babe will require all of your time and attention. What happens when you decide you don't want the responsibility? It's not as if you're going to be able to just leave it behind and go off..." He clamped his mouth shut, aware of his mother's changing expression.

"How dare you?" she whispered hoarsely. Sophia appeared as if she were about to stand up but thought better of it. "If I could move as quickly as I could a mere month ago, why, I would be up and out of this chair in an instant so that I might slap your arrogant face," she hissed.

"Mother—"

"Is that truly what you believe? That I decided I didn't wish to raise you, so I ran off with the butler?" she went on, ignoring his attempt to interrupt her. "I'll have you know, I saw far more of you once I *left* Merriweather Manor than I would have had I stayed," she continued. "Do I need to remind you that as Roger Grandby's son, you weren't mine to raise?" she asked. "Mary Margaret insisted that only the nurses and nannies needed to feed and dress you, that you had to eat with your other cousins in the schoolroom, and spend your days with tutors. When it was made quite clear you would be attending a boarding school in London until it was time for you to go off to Eton, then I knew I had to leave. I would never see you unless I went to that school every day and watched for you. Which is what I did." Tears streamed down her face as sobs robbed her of breath.

Rather alarmed by her outburst, Gregory shook his head. "I apologize," he murmured, already out of his chair and moving to her side of the table as he pulled a handkerchief from his waistcoat pocket.

"Don't touch me," she warned, her arms moving to cover her swollen belly.

"Mother," he murmured, reaching down to wrap his arms around her shoulders. He lifted her from her chair, aware she had gone limp once he did so. "I do so apologize. I didn't mean it. Not truly," he whispered, his head angling down to rest against hers. When he realized she was still lifeless in his arms, he pulled his head away. "Mother?" He pulled away to discover her eyes closed. "Jesus, Mother, wake up," he whispered. He managed to get one arm beneath her legs and lift her into his arms just as James Simpson appeared on the threshold.

"Sophia?" He stared at Gregory for a full second before waving him forward. "There's a chaise lounge in the parlor next door," he said as he pointed down the hall. "What the hell happened?"

Gregory ignored his stepfather's question as he moved his mother into the parlor and placed her on the lounge. "She's breathing, at least," he whispered as he glanced up to find James opening a vinaigrette. The sour odor had Gregory leaning back as James waved it under her nose. "I take it this has happened before?" he asked in a whisper.

James gave him a quick glance and a nod as he gently patted Sophia's cheek. "Wake up, my sweeting," he whispered. "Please, Sophia, you're frightening me." He pulled his hand away and regarded the tears that moistened his fingers. "Was she crying?" he asked. "She was the last time she fainted, as well."

"Has she seen a doctor?" Gregory asked in alarm.

Her eyelashes fluttering, Sophia finally inhaled and opened her eyes. A sob caused her to hiccup before James landed a kiss on her cheek. "Are you all right, my sweeting?"

Sophia took another breath and allowed a nod. Her attention went to her son, who gave her his best look of contrition.

"I apologize for being an ass," he said before she could say anything. When James turned his attention onto him, Gregory added, "I fear I've been a rather bad son today." Even as he said the words, he could see that tears once again streamed from his mother's eyes. "Do get the corset off of her." When he noted how his mother was about to put voice to a protest, he raised a staying hand. "If she insists on an undergarment, she can wear stays. Christiana... she had similar issues in Rome," he added with an arched brow.

James frowned as he continued to stare at Gregory, wondering just what had happened between the mother and her son before his arrival. "I'll take her to John Arpthorp's when she's feeling better," he said, referring to the corset maker in High Holborn Street.

"You needn't speak of me as if I'm not even in the room," Sophia complained as she moved to sit up. James placed a hand on her shoulder and gently pushed her back down. "And I'll be the one to decide if I wear a corset or not," she added. Her head seemed to wobble before she allowed it to settle back onto the lounge.

"The 'or not' has won out, my sweeting," James warned her gently.

Gregory sighed. "I'll take my leave. I don't wish to cause further distress. My apologies." He gave a bow and made his way to the door, pausing a moment before he turned to regard his stepfather. "Take care of her, won't you?"

James stood up and gave Gregory a quelling glance. "Don't I always?"

A moment later, and James heard the front door open and close. Turning his attention back to his wife, he allowed a long sigh. "I'm not sure I want to know what happened between the two of you, but I do hope whatever it was can be mended," he murmured.

Sophia hiccuped from a sob and fresh tears streamed down her face. "He thinks I abandoned him all those years ago, and that..." She paused as another sob caught her breath. "I'll do it again with this child." Sniffling, she let out a quiet wail as James lifted her into his arms.

"Nonsense," he countered. "He thinks nothing of the sort." But as he carried her up the stairs to the mistress suite, James knew very well just why Gregory would think such a thing. And he couldn't blame the young man. "Besides, he knows I'll be the one seeing to this babe," he added, a grin appearing on his face as he placed her on the bed. He covered her with a blanket and kissed her on the forehead. "Do have a good nap, and try not to cry. You know how it upsets the babe."

Sophia nodded, sniffled one more time, and was asleep within moments.

James was halfway down the stairs before he realized Gregory hadn't left the premises. The man was standing next to the hall table, staring at the roses. "I thought you'd gone," James said with an arched eyebrow.

Gregory shook his head. "I merely wanted her to think so. May we talk?"

About to deny his stepson out of spite, James instead led the way to the study, shutting the door once Gregory was over the threshold. He motioned to a set of overstuffed chairs near the fireplace as he moved to the credenza behind his desk. He didn't ask but rather poured brandy for them both and made his way to join Gregory. Holding out one of the crystal balloons to the taller man, he said, "I have no idea what you actually said to your mother, but I had half a mind to pop you in your perfect Grandby nose."

Gregory took the brandy with a nod. "It's actually a Merriweather nose, but I wouldn't blame you if you had. In fact, I'm rather surprised you didn't when you had the chance," he countered with a sigh. He took a sip of the brandy and savored the flavor before finally swallowing. "My compliments to your smuggler," he murmured, an arched brow daring the older man to counter his implied accusation.

James allowed a chuckle. "It's actually domestic, but I refuse to divulge my sources," he replied as he held his brandy balloon up so that the light from the window showed through the glass. "Now, young man, you're going to tell me whatever it was you said that had my wife so upset with you."

Angling his head to one side, Gregory considered how to respond. "The entire time I was in Italy, I watched my own wife —who is exactly the same age Mother was when she was last with child—"

"With you?" James clarified.

Gregory blinked. "Yes. Anyway, I have spent the past four months in a constant state of worry. I can't help but think something will go wrong. That Mother will—"

"Die in childbirth?"

Gregory blinked again, rather startled to hear the words spoken so plainly. "Yes," he admitted. "Or that the babe will be stillborn, or that they'll both perish—"

"As have I," James interrupted. He allowed a sigh. "Or that I will die before I see my progeny learn how to walk or talk, or take his first drink, or dance her first dance," he said in a quiet voice.

Gregory gave him a look of alarm. "Are you... ?"

"No, no, I'm fine. Never been better, in fact," James claimed quickly. "But life can be very cruel when you least expect it. And it can be wonderful, as well. You're young enough—and rich enough—that you shouldn't have to always think the worst."

Sighing, Gregory took another sip of brandy. "Whilst we were in Rome, Christiana managed to keep up with me nearly everywhere we went. But I know it cost her. She was exhausted every night. Her ankles were swollen. Her back ached. But she never complained..." He rolled his eyes when he saw the look of surprise cross his stepfather's face. "And when she should have, she couldn't because she had just fainted," he finished with a nod.

James gave a slow nod, beginning to understand some of what Gregory was trying to express. "This is only the second time your mother has fainted, and I do believe it's merely because her corset is too tight. I'll see to it she's not so laced up when I speak with her lady's maid later this afternoon."

"I didn't mean what I said earlier," Gregory said in a hoarse whisper. "That I thought she would leave the babe. It was awful of me. I don't even know why I said it," he claimed, his expression indicating his dismay.

"It's good of you to say so," James replied with a sigh. "Of course, you know she would have had to leave Merriweather Manor even if she hadn't done so to marry me."

Gregory stared at his stepfather, stunned by his words. "Whatever do you mean?"

Rather surprised by the question, James gave a shrug. "Well, that whole business about Mary Margaret expecting her to marry your Uncle Harold, of course," he said, as if everyone in London had been privy to the machinations of the late matriarch of Merriweather Manor.

"Uncle Harold?!" Gregory replied, leaning forward in his chair. Harold had been one of his father's older brothers, a twit of a man who could best be described as a 'momma's boy'. The thought had Gregory shaking his head in disbelief. "I don't recall anything about Mother marrying *Harold*. Besides, was it even legal for him to marry his late brother's wife?" A look of disgust crossed his face, and he downed his remaining brandy in a single gulp.

"Contrary to popular belief, it's actually not illegal. Just... frowned upon," James replied carefully. "So you can imagine I was rather glad when she opted for me instead," he added with an impish grin. "Still, it made for a rather awkward departure for her. At least Sir William was of a mind to help—he certainly had no good opinion of Harold Grandby, either," he explained.

"I had no idea," Gregory murmured in sudden understanding. He closed his eyes a moment, the only sounds in the study those of the crackles coming from what little was left of a fire that warmed the room. When he finally inhaled sharply, he gave his stepfather a pointed glance. "Should something happen—"

"Don't. Don't say it. Don't even think it," James ordered, as if he'd had to give the same order to someone else. "I know you think she's a petite piffle of a thing, but she's a damn strong woman, and she's determined, and she's never looked more radiant in her entire life," he whispered. "Allow her... allow *me* this next chapter in our lives, won't you?" he asked rhetorically.

Gregory considered the man's words and finally nodded. "Agreed." He allowed a sigh. "Don't you suppose you could at least hire one nurse. Someone to look after the babe should you wish to attend the theatre or go shopping?" he asked hopefully.

"You mean you weren't planning to make yourself available for nursing duty?" James chided playfully. He sobered quickly, though, and whispered, "I expect I'll have her talked into one before the auspicious day."

Gregory grinned and nodded, rather happy to hear that his

stepfather understood his concerns. After a pause, he added, "Do you think she'll ever let me see the babe, given how I've made such a cake of it today?"

James rolled his eyes. "Knowing your mother as I do, I rather imagine she'll expect you to be just outside the bedchamber when she gives birth."

His eyes rather wide, Gregory considered just such a scenario. "Perhaps we could go to White's that night," he suggested hopefully.

Shaking his head from side to side, James pointed to the study door. "*Out* with you. And don't come back until you're summoned to do so," he chided.

This time, Gregory left the Simpsons' townhouse entirely, determined to find his wife and see to making her more comfortable.

CHAPTER 34

A MIDWIFE IS SUMMONED

On the evening of March 26, 1803, an unexpected rider arrived at Woodscastle, quickly dismounting his horse and hobbling it in a most expert fashion.

From their vantage point in the library, Gregory and Thomas could see the man was probably unarmed and, in fact, was dressed in livery.

Humphrey glanced at his master, waiting for the signal that it was acceptable to open the front door. Ever since the day the housebreakers had shown up on the front steps of Woodscastle and been shot by Emma and Humphrey, Thomas required the butler to take special care when opening the door to strangers.

Thomas nodded to Humphrey while Gregory turned and said, "It's all right. I recognize him. He's one of Vandermeer's grooms."

Thomas turned his attention back to the window, but the man was already at the front door. "He's in a hurry."

Humphrey returned to the library only a moment later. "Sir, it's Mr. Stevenson, the coachman from Grace Park. He is requesting that Mrs. Wellingham return with him post-haste. He says it's most urgent, sir," he added rather nervously.

Thomas and Gregory exchanged curious looks before their eyebrows rose simultaneously. "The baby," they said in unison.

Emma, who had been on her way down the stairs to join

Thomas for drinks in the library, found the coachman in the vestibule and recognized him immediately. "Mr. Stevenson, whatever is wrong?" she asked as she beckoned him to come further into the house.

"'Tis Mrs. Vandermeer, ma'am. She is having a baby, and Mr. Vandermeer has requested you come as soon as you can," he said, still breathless from his ride from town.

Emma furrowed her brows. She had expected Mrs. Dawes would be Deborah's midwife. Even Deborah had mentioned that Todd wanted the woman to deliver his child. *Like father, like son. Or daughter*, he had said with a happy grin, almost as if the man remembered Mrs. Dawes delivering him six-and-twenty years ago.

If Todd had sent for Emma, it was only because Mrs. Dawes was unavailable or otherwise unable to help with the birth.

So what of Dr. Talbot? He was usually the back-up if Mrs. Dawes couldn't handle a delivery. "Oh, dear," Emma replied as her eyes widened. "I haven't delivered a baby in a... in a *year*," she said, her heart in her throat. "Have her waters broken?"

Mortified by the question, the coachman took a step back. "Pardon me, ma'am?" he replied, his expression making it clear he knew nothing about impending birth.

"Is she having contractions?" she asked, relieved to see Humphrey coming out of the library.

"I... think so," the coachman replied. "I've been asked to bring you back with me, if that is agreeable with madam," he said, hoping the woman would agree, but worried that she was obviously dressed for dinner and might refuse him.

Emma turned to the butler. "Humphrey, I need my horse. Please tell Mr. Wellingham where I've gone," she added as she grabbed the bottom of her gown, lifted it well above her ankles, and hurried up the steps to the master suite. "I'll be but a moment. I just have to change my gown," she yelled from the top of the stairs.

Thomas and Gregory emerged from the library and stopped at the vestibule. They glanced at one another and smiled. "Shall we give Todd some moral support?" Thomas asked with a sly grin in Gregory's direction.

"I do believe you have the right idea," he answered, clinking the edge of his glass against the one Thomas held. "Todd will have the best cheroots for this occasion," he added mischievously. "Humphrey," he said as he turned to the butler. "Could you have Mr. Allen bring the town coach 'round? We're going to town. Oh, and let Mr. Tanner know we won't be home for dinner this evening," he added, heading back to the west wing. "The servants are welcome to have it all. I'm off to fetch Christiana."

Thomas finished off his drink and set the glass on the round table, wondering if it was such a good idea for Gregory to bring Christiana along. She was probably eight months along herself, and although the doctor had said it would be good for her to get out and breathe some fresh air, he didn't know if attending the birth of a baby was quite what the doctor had in mind. At least it wasn't too cold on what could have been a wintry evening.

"And how is Mr. Vandermeer holding up?" he asked of the coachman, noticing how impatient the man had become as he waited just inside the vestibule.

Mr. Stevenson swallowed and carefully considered his response. "I believe he has worn a hole in the carpet outside Mrs. Vandermeer's room," he replied as he bit his lip.

Thomas laughed and shook his head. "Poor man," he commented, wondering how he would react to the impending birth of his own child.

Emma appeared at the top of the stairs in a simple, unadorned muslin gown just as Humphrey appeared in the vestibule with her redingote and hat. Thomas moved to the bottom of the banister and beckoned her to slide down. She grinned and sat on the banister, balancing herself as she slid down and into his arms.

Humphrey stood open-mouthed as he watched the mistress of the house slide down the polished bannister, her practiced dismount proving she had done it at least once before. Tempted to put voice to a comment, he instead cleared his throat and stood waiting with her coat and hat.

"I must go," Emma said as she wrapped her arms around Thomas and kissed him on the cheek.

"I heard," Thomas replied, kissing her on the forehead as he allowed her to get her feet under her. "Do be careful. No racing at this time of the night, even if there is a full moon. And we'll be along shortly," he added. "Gregory went to get Christiana, and someone is seeing to the town coach," he said with a nod in the direction of the west wing.

Humphrey held her redingote and she slid her arms into it. "Is there a moon tonight?" she asked as she allowed him to put the hat on her head while she wrapped the coat around herself.

"Yes, ma'am," Mr. Stevenson replied with a nod, relieved that she had appeared so quickly and was ready to leave. "Waning, though, but not yet quarter."

"Mr. Allen has your horse ready," the butler added as he opened the door.

"Thank you, Humphrey," Emma said as she hurried out the door and hopped onto her horse with the help of Mr. Allen's interlocked hands beneath her half-boot. She didn't give the coachman a chance to prepare his mount before she was off at a full gallop toward Burlington Lane.

Humphrey closed the door and, turning around, eyed his master and shook his head.

"What is it, Humphrey?" Thomas asked, wondering what he had done wrong.

"If I might inquire, sir, why would Mr. Vandermeer request Mrs. Wellingham's presence at such a late hour?" he asked, apparently unaware Deborah was in labor.

"Because Mrs. Vandermeer is about to have a baby," Thomas replied with a grin. "Mrs. Wellingham has delivered four that I know of," he explained as he recalled her telling him how frightened she had been on all four occasions. How frightened and then how relieved she had been when the babies were born alive and with all ten fingers and ten toes. "And she's about to make it five."

"Oh," the butler replied, his eyebrows indicating his surprise. "Oh, my!"

Thomas smiled as he watched Gregory lead his sister down the hall from the west wing. His brother-in-law was a full foot taller than his younger sister, but Christiana was a vision. Her strawberry blond hair was swept up in a beautiful chignon, and ringlets framed her still-freckled face. The dark green velvet gown she wore was adorned with ribbons around the empire waist and at the top of the long sleeves. She was definitely with child—her swollen belly pushed against the fabric of her dinner gown when she stood up straight. Her redingote, though, helped to hide her condition.

She reached up and kissed Thomas' cheek when she entered the vestibule. "Good evening, Thomas," she said as she closed her coat and regarded her brother.

"And to you, sister. You're looking well," he added as he took her hand and squeezed it. "And how is the little one?" he asked as he waved to her belly.

"'Tis fine, although he's rather good at being wide awake in the middle of the night," she complained with an embarrassed grin. "I suffered being kicked from within for hours, and now my back is sore."

"He?" Thomas repeated, rather surprised to hear her assign a sex to the baby.

Christiana gave him a quelling glance. "If this is a girl, why, she'll be a hoyden!"

"Your coat, sir," Humphrey said as he held out Thomas' redingote for him.

"Thank you, Humphrey. I've no idea how long we'll be, but please don't wait up," he said. "In fact, have a quiet dinner with Mrs. Werthers—"

"Thank you, sir," the butler interrupted him as he opened the door. Outside, Mr. Allen, wrapped in his cape coat and a woolen blanket, had the town coach pulled up to the front steps. When they were all seated, he cracked his whip and the two horses set off at a quick trot down the road to Burlington Lane.

Emma found concentrating on the road a good way to keep her mind off of Deborah and the reason she was being summoned. Her horse did this run nearly every day when she raced Thomas home from work, but she knew once they arrived in the West End, the cobblestone streets to Cavendish Square would slow him down. Aware Mr. Stevenson had caught up to her, she slowed down her mount to a trot and called out, "How long ago did you leave Grace Park?"

Despite riding a horse, Mr. Stevenson managed to pull his pocket watch from his waistcoat pocket. It was a moment before he could make out the position of the hands by the light of the moon. "About an hour and fifteen minutes ago," he shouted, careful to replace the watch in his waistcoat.

"And why aren't you wearing a coat?"

The groom gave her a grin. "I am warm enough, my lady."

Her mind now back on Deborah, Emma was relieved as they made the turn onto Picadilly and then north to Cavendish Square. She slowed her mount to a trot as they approached the circle drive to the Grace Park mansion, and she quickly dismounted as Mr. Stevenson reached for her reins. "I'll see to it that he is brushed and fed," the coachman said with a nod.

"Thank you, Mr. Stevenson," she replied. When she turned to climb the steps to the front door, she nearly collided with Todd Vandermeer.

"Thank God, you've come," he said as he pulled her into a hug usually reserved for family members.

"Well, of course... ," she started to say, but he was already leading her up the steps and into the house. Surprised Winston wasn't in the vestibule, and sensing Todd's distress, she quickly slipped out of her coat and hat and simply left them on the hall table. Todd took the steps two at a time, but Emma kept up as they made their way to Deborah's bedchamber.

Emma burst into the room to find Deborah lounging against a stack of pillows and calmly reading a book. Dressed in a thin, voluminous nightrail with her hair in a loose bun atop her head, she looked like a Madonna.

"Emma!" she greeted her visitor happily. "Whatever are you

doing here?" she asked. Then she noticed the worried expression on her husband's face.

Emma curtsied and made her way to the edge of the bed. "Are you in labor, by chance?" she asked carefully.

Deborah lowered her book and nodded her head. "I had back pains all night last night and most of today. And my waters broke about an hour ago," she admitted with a nod. "But I haven't had many contractions, and they are still too far apart," she explained with a wave of her hand. "So I'm not about to give birth."

"Then I am not too late," Emma said with a sigh of relief. "Thomas and the Grandbys are on their way in the town coach. They wanted to provide moral support for Todd," she said before she turned to find Todd still standing on the threshold, as if he didn't think he would be welcome in his wife's bedchamber. She gave the tall man a smile. "I guess Mrs. Dawes is not to be found?"

Todd shook his head. "Mrs. Dawes is now Mrs. Howell, and she is on her honeymoon in Scotland with Mr. Howell," he explained as he bit his lip, trying to hide his nervousness. "Had I any idea my dear Deborah was this close to childbirth, I never would have allowed the two of them to take their leave of the city."

At the news of Mrs. Dawes' marriage, Emma gasped and smiled broadly. "I have it on good authority that butlers make excellent husbands," she said as she took the older girl's hand in hers. "And what of Dr. Talbot? Is he also otherwise engaged?"

"Dr. Talbot seems to be out, as well," Deborah answered with a shrug. "Dinner at the Clarendon Hotel followed by an evening at the theatre." She said this last in an exaggerated manner, suggesting she was imitating a stuffy butler.

Emma grinned at her best friend's antics. "Are you agreeable with me doing the delivery?" she asked quietly. "I am here and will do so if you want me to," she offered, not sure she really wanted to be responsible for delivering the Vandermeer baby.

"I would like that very much," Deborah said with a sigh of relief. "Miss Anna has been seeing to me and should be arriving with some bath linens," she explained. "I've tried to keep her busy, but she'll only be in the way later, I'm afraid."

Nodding, Emma stood up and walked over to Todd. "This may take awhile. Thomas and Gregory are on their way. They wanted to be here for you—to help you celebrate," she said, hoping to calm him.

"Of course," Todd replied, his nervousness apparent. "I'll let the cook know we'll have... six for dinner," he said with a nod. "Is there anything else I can do?" he asked, not wanting to leave his post at the door.

Emma considered her next words before asking them. "Have you... have you been doing your ministrations on your wife?" she asked quietly, her ears turning bright pink as she asked the rather personal question.

"You mean the nipple chewing?" Todd countered, his head held low so he could hear Emma. He showed not the least bit of embarrassment at admitting his duty. "Oh, yes. Several times a day. Deborah has been quite insistent," he added with an enthusiastic nod.

Rolling her eyes, Emma regarded the father-to-be. "Well, then, I guess it's best for you to wait in the study until I send for you," she said with a wan smile.

"Well, if you're sure," he said doubtfully. Before he left the threshold, though, he hurried to Deborah's side, kissed her on the lips, and held her head to his chest. "I love you, my sweet. Be well," he said simply, his large hand cradling her belly in a protective gesture. And then he bowed and left the room.

CHAPTER 35

LABOR IS WORK

Deborah sighed and lay back on the pillows. "I feel so fat," she said in disgust. "I have been so rude to that poor man the past few days. And he has been so... *attentive*," she added, her voice filled with sadness.

Emma tried hard to suppress a grin as she imagined Todd's recent behavior. "At least he is being... attentive. Supportive. 'Tis much more than some men would be at a time like this," she said with a raised eyebrow, imagining most would be at their clubs. Some would probably even visit a brothel.

What would Thomas do?

Sighing, Deborah nodded. "He is, at that," she agreed and then gritted her teeth as a contraction took hold. When it passed, she relaxed back into the pillows and sighed again.

"He's also very different from when I first met him," Emma commented, daring a glance at a clock on the only dresser in the bedchamber. She was about to make a comment about the time, but decided it was better to keep Deborah's mind off her labor.

Her best friend inhaled sharply, whether from the contraction or from hearing the words, Emma didn't know. "Whatever you do you mean?"

Emma shrugged. "The day I met him, Thomas was hosting several businessmen at Woodscastle. I..." She started to admit she had been tasked with taking notes for Thomas— spying, as it were—but thought better of it. Having been able to eavesdrop and record the conversations of the attendees allowed Thomas to determine whom he could count on for support and learn which ones might try to block his expanding business. "Todd was quite well regarded among those in attendance, I suppose because they knew he worked for the East India Company. He seemed... *confident* among them. Even with me when he insisted I join them for luncheon," she went on. "But after that, I never had the impression he spent much time in a female's company."

"Probably because he hadn't," Deborah replied with a grin. "He was always rather timid with me. Almost as if he..." She paused and frowned.

"What is it?" Emma asked, alarmed when Deborah seemed to stare off into space. She relaxed when her friend gave her a quick wave.

"Our first night together, I'm quite sure he admitted to never having bedded a woman before," she whispered, her attention still on something far away. "I really had no way of knowing, of course. But when I thought he was asleep, I went into the bathing chamber to wash, and he followed me. He was... a completely different man from earlier in the evening."

Emma stared at Deborah for a moment. "How do you mean?"

"It was as if he finally realized I was his... *wife*, I suppose. That I wasn't going to leave him. He was so... confident." She turned her gaze onto Emma. "Not the least bit timid."

"Confident?" Emma repeated. "But not... *arrogant*, I hope?" she half-asked. She couldn't imagine Todd ever changing his personality so much that he would behave in an entirely different manner.

"No, not arrogant, surely," Deborah agreed. She hissed and was about to put voice to a complaint from a contraction when instead she merely sighed. She didn't notice how Emma glanced at the clock. "He didn't accept your husband's renewed offer of employment right away because he wanted to discuss it with me. Do you find that odd?"

Emma blinked, rather surprised at the change of subject. "It's certainly unexpected for any man to consider a woman's opinion, unless of course it's about a color, or a particular fabric, or how he looks," she replied in agreement. "But I suppose Todd values your input. There are ways in which you are far more worldly than him."

Deborah scoffed. "He has been to India. Twice. And to—"

"True, but your life experiences are far different. You grew up in a middle class household and then lived among pregnant harlots. He should have grown up in a middle class home, but instead... if not for Mrs. Dawes..." Emma shook her head. "Mrs. Howell, rather," she corrected herself. "He would have been a street urchin. He never would have had his position as a caddy and later as a broker with the John Company." In fact, Emma often wondered what might have happened to Todd Vandermeer if he hadn't had Mrs. Dawes in his life.

Inhaling sharply, Deborah nodded. "In a way, we changed places in Society," she struggled to get out before the pain passed.

"And now you've met in the middle," Emma said quietly.

Deborah stared at Emma for a moment before finally allowing a nod. "It's true. Although I do believe Todd was better regarded by Society at his old position. He used to be invited to soirées and balls and such. Now, we rarely receive invitations. I cannot help but think..." She stopped speaking, but it wasn't because a contraction interrupted her.

"What is it?" Emma asked, glancing toward the clock.

"I think that by marrying me, Society has given him the cut indirect," she whispered.

Emma's eyes widened. "That's not true, Deborah. Aristocrats merely leave London for their country estates during the winter months. They'll return later this spring, and the invitations will resume. You'll see," she claimed, hoping she was right.

Deborah had never aspired to marry higher than her class— a good thing given she might well have remained a spinster the rest of her life given she worked as a midwife. Had Emma not introduced her to Todd, Deborah would still be living at the Home for Unwed Mothers.

"His father was William Vandermeer, an army officer," Deborah countered.

"Yes, I know."

"His mother was a cousin to the Earl of Everly, so he is a second cousin to the heir!"

"The very same is true for Thomas," Emma stated with a nod. "And Thomas is the grandson of the Earl of Torrington. You have an uncle who is married to the daughter of an earl —"

"Aunt Lucy is a bit eccentric, though," Deborah interrupted, as if she didn't think that particular relationship counted.

"I have an uncle who is a viscount," Emma went on, ignoring the interruption. "We are all related to someone in the peerage if you look back far enough," she added with a grin. She sobered, reminded that her uncle's wife had at one time been her father's secret lover. Caroline Fitzsimmons had even borne a child from that union—a sister Emma hadn't been allowed to acknowledge as such given the viscountess' edict that she remain quiet on the subject.

Emma only knew about Samantha Fitzsimmons because of the letters she had discovered tucked away in an old desk. At some point in the future, she hoped Caroline would allow her to meet the young girl and admit the familial relationship. *I am a coward,* she remembered reading in the letter Caroline had sent at Christmas.

Truer words were never written, Emma thought.

"What is it?" Deborah asked. "You look as if you're the one in labor."

Emma lifted her head and regarded her best friend for a moment. "I have a sister," she said quietly.

Deborah blinked before giving her head a shake. "What?" was all she could think to say at first. She squeezed her eyes shut and then took a deep breath. "Since when?"

"You cannot tell anyone," Emma warned, turning to the clock. "I should not have said anything. It's just... I really wish the girl's mother would allow me to acknowledge her as such.

But she's keeping the girl a secret. Has a plausible story for how she came to be in her care. And because the woman is a viscountess, and she had the girl out of wedlock, I'm to remain mum on the subject."

Frowning, Deborah shook her head. "Damnation, Emma! How long have you known?"

Emma ignored the curse. "Since the day I moved into the townhouse," she whispered. "I found love letters in my mother's old desk. From the viscountess to my father. She wasn't yet a viscountess when she was with my father, of course, but she married shortly thereafter. She's raising the daughter as her niece, claiming her eccentric sister..." She arched an eyebrow as she used the same word as Deborah had used to describe her aunt. "And her even more mad brother-in-law were the parents."

Deborah considered Emma's words for a moment. "The truth will come out someday," she whispered. "If not before, then when the mother dies. You will show the letters to your sister, and she will be ever so grateful to know you."

Tears collected in the corners of Emma's eyes. "I do hope so," she whispered. "Oh, now look at me. I'm not even the one in pain," she said as she shook her hands in front of her face. She sighed. "Would you like to take a walk? Perhaps a bit of exercise would help?" she offered, deciding she had to change the subject or she would turn into a watering pot.

"No," Deborah replied with a shake of her head. "I walked for nearly an hour earlier this afternoon, and now my knees are aching," she said sadly.

*O*ver the course of the next half-hour, Deborah's contractions were never more than three minutes apart, and she was getting anxious.

And cross.

The maid knocked and entered, her arms stacked high with white nappies, linens, and baby blankets. Emma stood up and introduced herself as the midwife. Miss Anna curtsied, her expression changing to show her extreme relief. "I am so glad you have come, my lady," she said with a nod. "Will you require anything else?"

Emma moved to stand next to Deborah, one hand held to the woman's forehead. "A cold compress would be good," she replied, noting a slight fever.

Miss Anna disappeared for a few moments. When she returned, Emma pulled her aside. "Could you please ask Mr. Vandermeer to join us?" she asked of the maid. Emma took the compress from her and placed it on Deborah's forehead.

"Mr. Vandermeer?" the maid replied. "Already?" she asked quietly, her brows furrowed in confusion.

"Yes, if you would, please," Emma assured her. Turning her attention to Deborah, she sat on the edge of the bed and smiled at her patient. "You're doing very well. But I think we need to speed things along," she said with a nod. "Is it agreeable if I have Todd... help you along?" she asked with a raised eyebrow.

Deborah nodded and tried to sit up. "I am not progressing, am I?" she asked, annoyance evident in her voice. "My contractions have been three minutes apart for the last half-hour. At this point, I do not just want my nipples suckled, Emma. I want a bed-breaking, mattress rending orgasm, and I want it *now!*" she stated in a hoarse whisper between clenched teeth.

Not having seen her best friend in such a state before, nor having heard her use such colorful language, Emma felt her face pink up. "I understand," she said before she swallowed. "Did you... *warn* him that he might be required to perform such a... service... at this stage of labor?" she asked carefully, afraid she was going to have to explain things to Todd when he arrived.

"Oh, he knows," Deborah said with a nod. "I told him everything. And he seemed most... amenable to doing whatever it took to get this baby out of me," she said, her patience wearing thin. Another contraction gripped her and Emma checked to see if she was dilated anymore than she had been a few moments ago.

A knock at the door announced Todd's arrival. Apparently in the middle of changing for dinner when he was summoned, he wore only a shirt, breeches, and his boots. He rushed to

Deborah's side. "God, you are beautiful," he said as he took Deborah's hand in his.

Deborah took a deep breath and regarded him for a moment, deciding he wasn't just putting voice to the compliment to make her feel better. "I need you," she whispered as she loosened the ties on the front of her nightrail.

"And I want you," he replied, leaning over her and kissing her fully on the mouth as one hand disappeared under her nightrail and pressed up on her swollen belly.

Emma watched Todd kiss Deborah and felt her own body respond to the way he held her, to the way his large hands moved over her body, the way his fingers stroked her skin. She could practically feel skitters of pleasure dance under her own skin, and she inhaled sharply.

Emma forced herself to look away when Deborah pulled his shirt off his body. They had barely finished their kiss—how had Deborah had managed to get the shirt off of him so quickly?

Deborah's nightrail was tossed aside as Todd moved his mouth and hand to a nipple. From the way he massaged the breast with his hand, it was obvious he had done it many times before in preparation for this very moment. Deborah undid the buttons on his breeches whilst he managed to remove his boots with his available hand. When she struggled to reposition herself on the bed so that she could wrap her legs around him, he reached out, moved his hands under her bottom and swung her body around on the bed. And he did it all the while keeping his lips gripped to a nipple.

From the sure way in which he handled Deborah's swollen body, Emma realized Todd had performed that particular maneuver several times. When Deborah cried out, due to a contraction or an orgasm, Emma did not know, he let go of the breast and moved his attention to the other one. Emma watched as his tongue circled the nipple and then his lips sucked it into his mouth.

Mesmerized—of course she had never paid witness to two people making love before—Emma stood transfixed. She understood exactly what Deborah had meant when she said Todd was confident. His manner was most sure, his moves practiced, his manhood most certainly about to spring forth from his breeches. Gasping, Emma forced herself to look away, but felt her own nipples respond as if his lips had captured hers instead.

With his boots off, Todd deftly removed his breeches and was about to remove his drawers when Emma realized they would have intercourse right in front of her if she didn't leave the bedchamber that very instant. "I'll be downstairs," she whispered nervously as she backed up to the door, her nipples hard and her breaths coming quicker as her own sexual desire increased. Once she was on the other side of the door, she leaned against it. She couldn't help but overhear the sounds of slow, passionate lovemaking. The moans and murmurs of two lovers lost in each other. Feel the pulse of their movements through the floor beneath her feet.

Pushing herself away from the door, she hurried downstairs to find Thomas, Gregory, and Christiana in the study enjoying walnuts and coffee.

And brandy.

Breathless, she entered and stopped short when the two men and Christiana looked up at her in surprise. "Are you... well?" Thomas asked as he quickly stood up and took in the sight of her. Gregory also stood, of course, but soon resumed his seat when he realized Emma had come for Thomas.

"Could you... come out here in the corridor for a moment?" she asked as she stepped back into the grand hall. She looked both ways to ensure no one was in the hall, so when Thomas came out of the study, she led him to a nearby alcove. Before he had even tucked his body into the small space, Emma reached up and kissed him hard on the lips. Grabbing his hand, she placed the palm squarely on her swollen breast.

After a moment, Thomas returned her kiss, but gently pulled his lips away and left his forehead pressed against hers. "Does childbirth usually result in this much... passion?" he whispered as he regarded her with a curious smile.

Emma rolled her eyes and tried to think of a suitable response. "Well, not usually, I suppose. But this is the Vandermeers having a baby," she said between gasps for air. When she noticed he still held a glass of brandy in his other hand, she took it and helped herself to a gulp. Nearly choking as the fluid burned her throat, she gave the glass back to Thomas.

"What... what are they *doing?*" Thomas asked as he realized his hand was still pressed against her breast and the nipple under it was begging for attention. He absently rubbed it with the side of his thumb while keeping an eye out for wandering servants.

"They're having... *sexual intercourse*," she said in a whisper. She kissed him again. "I had to leave," she added in her own defense, "But if I hadn't, they would be doing it right before my very eyes," she claimed in a hoarse whisper.

"Indeed?" Thomas replied as he took a quick glance around. "Is Mrs. Vandermeer... well?" he asked as he did his best to suppress a smile, rather liking the effect the events of the evening were having on his wife.

"She's doing... fine. Her waters broke a few hours ago, but her contractions have been the same for a long time. She was getting... restless," she explained, "So, I—"

"Called in the troops, eh?" Thomas teased as his grin grew. "Tell me this isn't going to happen with my sister. Because I just don't think I could..." He shook his head, not wanting to imagine Gregory having intercourse with his sister at all, let alone in her ninth month of pregnancy.

"That depends on Christiana," Emma countered. "And be careful what you say. Someday you may have to do it to me," she warned with a raised brow.

The expression on Thomas' face changed. "Promise?" he countered, angling his head to one side as he waited for her reaction.

"You... you would do that?" Emma asked in a whisper, her eyes widening in surprise.

Thomas blinked. "Make love to you? Why, of course," he replied quickly. Before Emma could respond, he kissed her on the lips. "I rather imagine I would have to be rather *inventive* in my approach, of course," he whispered in a teasing voice, "But I am most sure I could manage. Perhaps we could practice later tonight. We could stay at the townhouse instead of heading back to Woodscastle," he suggested as he kissed her jaw and the space in front of one ear. "Tomorrow is Sunday."

A slow smile spread over Emma's lips, and she reached up to kiss her husband on the lips. "What a capital idea," she murmured, kissing him again. Before they finished, though, a loud moan came from upstairs and Todd shouted, "Emma!" At the top of his lungs.

"Hold that thought," she said and then kissed Thomas once more. She was up the stairs and into the mistress suite in just a few seconds.

CHAPTER 36

A BABY MAKES AN
APPEARANCE

"I think… I think it worked," Todd said as Emma made a timid entrance in the mistress suite. At least the man had had the wherewithal to pull on his long shirt, but his breeches and drawers still lay where he had tossed them. Deborah gasped as a contraction took hold, and she clenched her teeth to suppress a scream.

"Breathe, Deborah. 'Tis all right to yell and curse, if you must," Emma said as she washed her hands in the basin. She rushed to the edge of the bed where Deborah tried to hold her legs spread out. "Can you move her back on the bed?" Emma asked of Todd.

Todd immediately moved to the other side of the bed, gently lifting Deborah with his hands beneath her shoulders. He pulled her body farther back on the bed until her feet were supported on the edge of the bed. Then he moved around to the side she faced and kissed her naked belly, rubbing his large hand over the surface of it. Pressing up against it, he felt a sharp kick and backed away suddenly. The stunned look on his face had Deborah giggling, but before she could finish, another contraction gripped her.

"You're crowning, Deborah," Emma said in awe, placing a linen beneath her and another in Todd's hands. "Shake this out," she ordered, wishing she had brought Christiana with her. "When the next contraction…"

But the next contraction had already started. "Push!" Emma said as she moved to support the baby's head in her hand. "Help her sit up," she ordered when she realized Todd wasn't about to take his leave of the room—or to faint.

Todd jumped onto the bed and knelt behind Deborah, using his arms to lift her as she struggled to push.

"You can stop pushing," Emma said as she pulled the baby gently out and held it in the linen. *Ten fingers, ten toes, good color, a full head of dark hair, and a penis.* "You have a boy," she said with a relieved smile as she held it up for Deborah and Todd to see. Using the corner of the linen, she cleaned off its face and the inside of its mouth. Then she gently blew on the baby's face until he let out a wail that surprised both his parents.

From the look on Todd's face, Emma thought he might yet faint, but instead, he moved off the bed to take the messy bundle into his arms. "A boy?" he repeated. He turned to show the baby to Deborah. She reached for it but he placed it on her still-swollen belly. *He has been taught well*, Emma realized with a smile.

"Can you cut the cord?" Emma asked as she tended to Deborah. Todd looked at her and then at Deborah. "Me?" he asked, startled.

"I'll show you how," Deborah said in a whisper as she took the knife from Emma.

Once she was assured that Deborah wasn't bleeding and that she had cleaned her up as best she could, Emma nodded to Todd. "She is all yours, Mr. Vandermeer," she said with a satisfied smile. "I still think it would be a good idea for Dr. Talbot to take a look, though. I need to get this little one cleaned up," she said as she reached for the baby.

"May I take her to my room now?" Todd asked, tears streaming from his eyes.

"Of course, but you'll have to carry her," Emma warned as she took the baby into the bathing chamber. "Her knees are giving her pain." Elated at the sight of hot and cold faucets— the bathing chamber really did have modern amenities—she filled the basin with warm water. She spent several minutes bathing the baby, cooing and nudging him gently as she wiped away the evidence of birth. Although he was awake through most of the bath, the baby fell asleep once he was swaddled in a fresh linen. Emma cradled him in her arms and took him to his father's bedchamber.

Todd was already dressed in fresh clothes when she knocked on the half-open door to the master suite. A huge room, it took a moment for Emma to see that Deborah was already sound asleep in the middle of a very long bed. Emma smiled when she noticed the new mother's serene expression. The deep sleep she managed now would be her last in a long time, Emma considered.

"She is a beautiful woman," Todd murmured as he took his son from Emma. "As are you," he added as he kissed her forehead. "I do not know what I would have done if you hadn't come when you did," he said in a quiet voice. "He arrived early, you see. Mrs. Dawes... I mean, Mrs. Howell, is on her honeymoon, and I arranged for Dr. Talbot to be the physician at the Home for Unwed Mothers until she returns." He sniffled. "I didn't know who else to send for," he added as a few tears continued to slide down his face.

"You would have managed," Emma said with a wan smile, sure that Todd could have delivered the baby with Deborah's instructions.

She placed a hand on Deborah's forehead, reassured when there wasn't evidence of a fever. "He is a beautiful baby. What will you name him?" she asked quietly as she moved to stand next to him.

Todd considered her question and glanced over at Deborah. "William, for a first name, but we are still deciding on his other names," he said with an embarrassed grin.

Emma smiled at that. *Todd's father's name.* "You must be starving," she said as she realized she was rather hungry. The clock on the dresser showed only eight o'clock, but it felt much later. A chime sounded somewhere in the house.

"Now that you mention it," Todd replied, "Yes, I am hungry," he said, his attention on his son, "But what about William?"

Emma shook her head. "Not for awhile yet, but he will let you know, I assure you. Has her milk started to flow?" she asked as she angled her head in Deborah's direction.

Todd's ears turned bright red as he nodded. "Indeed. 'Tis quite good," he said with a mischievous grin. He regarded Emma for a moment and nodded toward the door. They left the bedchamber, but before Todd headed down the corridor, he stopped. "Tell me something, Emma. If... if I had never met Deborah, is it true you would have married... ?" he started to ask before the expression on his face turned to one of uncertainty.

Emma nodded. "Yes, I believe I would have," she replied with a sigh. She placed a hand on his free arm and allowed him to escort her toward the stairs.

"I ask only because... now, I cannot imagine a life without my Deborah," he explained. "Without him," he added as he held up the baby and kissed its forehead. "But, at one time, I imagined an entire life with you," he murmured as he again stopped walking and regarded her.

Noting his worried expression and furrowed brows, Emma was afraid that Todd regretted his decision to marry Deborah. And yet the woman had just borne him a healthy baby boy. "Why are you telling me this?" Emma asked as she swallowed hard, not sure she wanted to hear what he had to say.

"I just thought you should know that... you... *you* were my first love, I suppose," he said, biting his lip. "Emma, if anything should ever happen to Thomas... if you should ever need anything, you come to me," he whispered hoarsely. "You come to me, do you understand?" he asked, taking her hand in his and kissing the back of it.

Emma stared open-mouthed at Todd, a tear drop escaping the corner of her eye. She nodded, at first not quite sure what to say. "Thank you. You cannot know what that means to me," she finally replied. And why she kissed him, she didn't know, but she was as surprised as he was when she did so. Especially after what had happened after Todd's first day on the job—just a few months ago.

Sighing loudly, she turned her attention to the baby still sleeping in Todd's arms. "Now, I believe it's time to introduce the newest Vandermeer to your friends."

Todd grinned, offered her his arm, and they continued on their way to the study. When they entered, Christiana, Gregory, and Thomas all stood in unison, surprised to see Todd holding the baby. "It is a boy!" he announced happily, supporting the bundle in the crook of his arm.

"That was fast," Gregory commented as he downed the last of his brandy and moved to join Christiana, who was already taking the baby from Todd.

"Have you named him?" Christiana whispered, her finger gently stroking the baby's forehead and cheeks.

Todd nodded. "William. He'll have other names, of course," he replied with a grin as he watched the sleeping baby.

"And how is Mrs. Vandermeer?" Thomas asked, concern in his voice.

Emma was about to answer, but Todd replied, "She is beautiful, Thomas. Simply gorgeous. She is in the master suite getting some much deserved sleep." Todd took the baby back from Christiana. "And I do not know about all of you, but I am starving," he said with a big grin. "And this little one will probably need to eat soon, too," he added as he lifted the baby and held it out in front of him.

Thomas watched Emma as she kept her eyes on the baby, her face revealing wonderment and adoration. If only someday she could give birth to his baby. *And that look of wonderment and adoration would be for our child,* he considered sadly. *But that won't be happening.*

When he was jolted from his reverie, he found Emma with her arm in his and her head resting against his shoulder. Her face glowed as if lit from within.

"Are you coming?" she asked as she gazed up at him.

Thomas realized everyone else had left the study in favor of the dining room and dinner. "Did everything go as expected? With the delivery, I mean?" he asked, concern in his voice.

Emma regarded him for a moment before allowing a shrug. "Yes," she replied with a nod. "It was the best delivery yet, as a matter of fact," she added with a smile. "No complications, although I told Todd he should have Dr. Talbot pay a visit just to be sure."

Nodding, Thomas led her out of the study and through the great hall to the dining room. "And you are well?" he asked, stopping before they entered the dining room.

Emma angled her head as she looked up at Thomas. "Yes, I am fine. A bit euphoric, I suppose, but otherwise, I am fine," she answered happily.

Finding her grin infectious, Thomas smiled and kissed her. "If I wasn't so hungry, I would take you to the townhouse right now," he whispered mischievously.

"And if I wasn't so hungry, I would let you," Emma replied with just as much mischief.

CHAPTER 37

ANOTHER MIDWIFE IS SUMMONED

Deborah awoke slowly. Feeling empty and alone, she moved her head toward the candlelight on the bedside table and finally realized where she was. *Master suite*, she thought as she sniffed the pillow next to hers. *Todd*. Her hand instinctively moved to her belly, and the memory of childbirth came flooding back. *You have a boy*, Emma had said.

Gingerly sitting up in the huge bed, she looked around and realized she was alone. Naked and alone. "Todd?" she called out, thinking he might be in the bathing chamber. When she didn't hear him respond, she listened for the sounds of the household. From somewhere came the voices of conversation and laughter. *The dining room, perhaps?* Reaching for the bell pull, she hesitantly jerked on it. She disliked summoning a servant, but at the moment, she was feeling panicked and desperately wanted her baby with her.

There was a quiet knock at the door and Anna curtsied. "Yes, ma'am?" she greeted her mistress, her hands twisted together.

"Where is my baby?" Deborah asked quietly, tears beginning to well up in her eyes.

"With Mr. Vandermeer, ma'am. Would you like me to bring him to you?" the maid asked politely. "That is, if I can get the wee one away from the master," she added. "He has not put the babe down since he went in for dinner."

Deborah grinned in spite of her sudden discomfort. Her breasts felt engorged, and she desperately needed to start feeding William. "Please, Anna. Hurry," she pleaded.

The maid curtsied and gave a quick, "Yes, ma'am," before backing out of the room. It was less than a minute later when Todd came striding in, a huge grin on his face and their baby tucked in the crook of his arm. Leaning over the bed, he kissed her forehead. "Are you well?" he asked, breathless from his run up the stairs.

Deborah nodded, but tears had begun to make tracks down her cheeks. "I woke up alone," she whispered as she reached out for the swaddled baby.

"I... I am so sorry," Todd replied, the grin replaced with a look of consternation. "I wanted to allow you some time to sleep," he said as he sat on the edge of the bed and relinquished his hold on their son. As Deborah took the baby from him, she gave him a small smile and lifted him to a breast for feeding.

"He slept through the soup course," Todd whispered as he watched Deborah try to position the baby. The baby's lips began the sucking motion, but they didn't latch onto the nipple. Sighing, Deborah relaxed back into the pillows and began weeping.

Alarmed, Todd placed his hand along the side of her face. "What is it?" he asked quietly. "Tell me what I can do to help." He noticed that William was now wide awake, but the eyes seemed unfocused, and there was a good deal of squirming going on inside the linen he was wrapped in.

"My breasts hurt," Deborah moaned, sniffling as more tears fell down her cheeks.

Todd leaned forward, taking the baby from the one breast to suckle it. When he tasted milk, he let go and put William's face against the wet breast. Instinct took over as the baby's lips latched onto his mother's nipple, and he began sucking furiously. Finally free of the linen, one of his fists rested on the top of Deborah's breast.

Mesmerized by what he was seeing, Todd sat quietly for

several minutes, the only sound in the room the slurp-sucking sound coming from his son.

Deborah watched her husband as the man watched their son. Reaching out a hand to stroke his arm, she whispered, "Thank you."

Todd tore his attention from the babe and gazed at Deborah. "Are you... well? I know you were in a great deal of pain," he whispered, worry replacing the look of adoration.

"I'll be fine," Deborah replied as she lifted William away from the one breast and moved him to the other side. Before she had him in position, Todd leaned forward and took the nipple, sucking it gently. Once the milk was flowing, he moved away, feeling a pang of jealousy as he watched William take over. "Could you... could you rub some salve on my knees?" Deborah asked quietly. "And then I will do yours," she added when she saw his look of surprise.

"Of course!" Todd replied as he reached for the jar on the nightstand. Happy to have a job to do, he pulled the covers away from her legs and began his ministrations.

"Did you give cheroots to your friends?" she asked as she watched him rub the salve into her knees.

Todd's quick intake of breath answered the question for her. "No... and I have left them all in the dining room without a host," he answered with an embarrassed grin. "The next course was about to be served when your maid appeared."

"I am sure they've excused you," Deborah murmured with a grin. Realizing her son was sound asleep, she moved him to her shoulder and began patting him on the back.

Watching her every move, Todd sat up straighter on the bed. "What... what are you doing?" he asked, his brows furrowing as a look of concern came over his face.

"Burping him," Deborah replied matter-of-factly, at which point a rather loud belch could be heard coming from the baby. "Oh, I bet you feel better now," Deborah whispered as Todd stared at his son in shock. "I think he must have taken in as much air as he did milk," she murmured.

"Even I feel better after that burp," Todd whispered in awe.

Grinning, Deborah leaned back into the pillows and moved William to the space next to her on the bed. "I am so very tired," she whispered before closing her eyes.

Todd leaned over and kissed her forehead and then William's. He wanted desperately to stay with his family but decided he best return to his guests. On his way down the stairs, he met Emma on her way up.

"How is she?" she asked quietly, concern evident in her voice.

"Sleeping, as is William. He just finished his first meal," Todd replied happily.

Emma let out the breath she'd been holding. "I am so relieved to hear it," she said as she placed a hand over her chest.

"I am surprised you did not. William burped louder than most men at my club," Todd stated proudly as he offered his arm to her.

Nodding her head, Emma did her best to suppress her laughter. She took his arm and the two returned to the dining room.

At least, they were on their way to do so when a commotion in the vestibule caught their attention.

With Howell away on his wedding trip with the former Mrs. Dawes, a footman was seeing to the butler's duties. He stood at the door arguing with a rather young boy.

"What is it, Thompkins?" Todd asked as he strode into the vestibule.

The footman straightened and turned to address his master. "It's a caddy, sir. Says he's been dispatched to collect your wife."

Frowning, Todd motioned for Emma to remain where she was as he moved to speak with the boy. "Who sent you?" he asked, noting the caddy couldn't have been more than six or seven. He was fairly clean, though, and his clothes were in good repair. A faint odor of hay and horse hung about him.

"Mr. Simpson, sir. Said his wife is going to have a babe and to fetch Mrs. Vandermeer to do the mid..." The boy paused, his brows furrowing until he seemed to remember the word. "Midwifing, sir. Said I'm not to leave here until I have her in my company."

Todd blinked as he stared at the caddy a moment and then finally turned to find Emma at his side. "Mr. Simpson?" he repeated. "As in… ?"

"James Simpson. Gregory's father-in-law," Emma clarified. "His mother must be in labor." She looked down at the boy and realized it was Master Churchill, the stableboy from the mews behind her townhouse. "How long ago did you leave Mr. Simpson?" she asked.

"How do, Miss Emma," he said, his face breaking into a grin. He sobered, though. "Don't know how long it's been, seein' as how I can't tell time, milady," he answered.

"Oh, dear," she whispered. She tore her attention from the boy to give Todd a worried glance. "I can go, but… can you have someone collect Dr. Talbot from the Clarendon? Or perhaps he's already at the theatre? I don't dare attempt this by myself," she whispered. She thought of Christiana, but thought it best the girl not see her mother-in-law in labor. Poor thing would probably go into labor herself, and the very last thing Emma wanted to do was deliver yet another baby.

"Thompkins, see to it Mrs. Wellingham's horse is saddled," Todd ordered. "It'll take too long to get a carriage readied," he said in an apologetic tone.

"Yes, sir." The footman was out the front door and down the steps before Todd could give him additional instructions. He turned back to the boy. "How did you get here?"

"Walked, sir. It's not far to Kingly Street."

"My groom will give you a ride back," Todd said before turning to Emma. "I'm afraid Dr. Talbot isn't out this evening," he explained quietly. At Emma's quizzical expression, he added, "I told Deborah a white lie because I had arranged for him to do the deliveries at the Home for Unwed Mothers tonight. In place of Mrs. Holmes, given I allowed my butler to take her to Scotland."

Emma sighed. "And I suppose he's busy delivering other babies this evening," she guessed.

Todd nodded. "I apologize. I've put you in this position—"

"No need to apologize," Emma interrupted. "It's rather good of you to have allowed the Holmes their wedding trip."

Todd noticed another footman in the vestibule and pointed to him. "Have another groomsman ready the carriage the Grandbys arrived in. I'm sure they'll wish to go as well." He turned to Emma and angled his head. "Have I forgotten anything?"

Emma blinked. "Did you manage to get much to eat this evening?"

Grinning, Todd shrugged. "Soup, same as you. I'll see to it the cook puts something together for you to take along."

Her eyes wide, Emma nodded her thanks. "I'll let the others know I'm leaving," she said as she hurried off to the dining room.

She found the dining room empty, the dishes already cleared away except for her place setting. Turning, she listened for the tell-tale sound of voices as she walked as quickly as she could first to the library and then to the study.

She found the men enjoying cheroots as they lounged on leather sofas, their brandy balloons already drained. "Where's Christiana?" she asked, attempting to catch her breath and not feel too much annoyance at how drunk the two men seemed. Faith! How long had she been upstairs?

Thomas managed to stand up, although he wavered on his feet. "Ladies lounge," he answered with a nod towards the door.

Having used the facilities in that very room the first time she visited Grace Park with Deborah not even ten months ago, Emma realized Christiana was probably finding it just as appealing as she had. "I have to go," Emma managed to get out between gasps for air.

"To the lounge?"

Emma blinked. "No," she replied with a shake of her head. "To deliver another baby." Noting the men were apparently too drunk to be of any help, she took her leave of the study and nearly ran back to the vestibule.

"Stevenson will ride with you," Todd said as he joined her, a cloth covered basket gripped in one hand. "Dinner," he added as he handed her the basket.

"Bless you. The men are hopelessly drunk in your study. Now, go spend some time with your family, won't you? I'll come by on the morrow to check on Deborah."

Todd grinned. "Indeed, I will. Give Mrs. Simpson my very best. And I do hope for Mr. Simpson's sake that it's a boy. I believe that man is in need of an heir."

Emma gave a nod and took her leave of Grace Park on horseback, Mr. Stevenson once again her riding companion. In front of him on the saddle sat Master Churchill, the stableboy obviously enjoying the opportunity to actually ride a horse. Feeling guilty at not having any biscuits for the boy, she decided she would give him whatever sweets might be in her dinner basket.

Emma found the fear she felt for Mrs. Simpson had replaced any sense of hunger she might have felt only moments ago.

CHAPTER 38

A PROUD PAPA IS FLOORED

At the end of the portion of Kingly Street owned by the Simpsons, Emma aimed a longing glance at her townhouse. She rather wished she had the key so that she might change into a different gown before going to the Simpson's.

She gave Master Churchill the reins to her horse. "I apologize. I don't have any coins for you, Master Churchill," she said as she tested her pockets. She checked the basket of food strung over one arm. "But here are some Dutch biscuits," she said as she passed him the two she found.

"'Tis all right, my lady," the boy said as he took her horse's reins. "Mr. Vandermeer gave me some."

Emma sighed. When had Todd managed to do that? She turned her attention to the groom. "Thank you for the escort."

"Of course, milady," he replied. "I'll wait 'til you're safely inside before I take my leave."

Turning to the front doors of the newly refurbished townhouse, its windows lit so the entire street seemed illuminated, Emma sighed. Located directly across the street from her own townhouse, it was far larger both in height as well as width. With its petite yard out front lined with a wrought iron fence, it appeared charming in the daylight.

Emma was about to knock when she realized James would

probably be with his wife. Testing the handle, she found it unlocked and opened the door a fraction. "Mr. Simpson!" she called out.

Despite having been in the townhouse on Christmas Day, she again marveled at how new everything appeared. New and yet *old*. Classical Greek was mixed with Italian marble. Paintings in the style of Old World masters hung on new silk-covered walls. Dark-stained baseboards were shiny. Brass lamps gave off brilliant light from wicks kept trimmed. Emma was tempted to simply stand in the middle of the vestibule and stare at everything and then move into the hall and do the same.

A maid appeared from one of the ground floor rooms and regarded her with wide eyes before she relaxed. "You must be the midwife," she said with a slight Cockney accent. She seemed about to scold Emma for not having come to the servants' entrance at the back when her eyes narrowed. "Mrs. Wellingham?"

"Yes, to both, I'm afraid," Emma replied. "Might there be an apron I can borrow?" Although she'd worn one when attending to Deborah, she had left it behind when she went down for dinner.

"'Course, milady. I can bring it to you." She led Emma up the marble staircase, unaware of how the visitor stared at everything around them as she climbed each step.

"How is she?" Emma thought to ask.

"Can't say as I know, milady."

Rather surprised by the maid's response, Emma simply followed the young woman until they reached an ornate set of double doors near the end of the corridor on the left.

"This is the mistress suite, milady."

Emma knocked when she realized the maid wasn't going to open the door. "Has someone brought up linens? Water?"

"There's a bathing chamber with running water, milady, and linens, as well. The nursery is across the hall," she turned and pointed to the door opposite. "Nappies are in there."

Nodding her understanding, Emma was about to knock again when she realized one of the doors was slightly ajar.

"Lady Simpson?" she called out, pushing on the door so it opened only a few more inches.

The scene that greeted her was far different from the one she had found at Grace Park. Lady Sophia Simpson had obviously given birth to a baby—she was holding one that looked as if it could be no more than a minute old—but no one else seemed to be in the bedchamber with her. The warmth she felt upon entering was a testament to the large flames in the fireplace where fresh logs must have been added within the past hour.

"Oh, dear, I really must have screamed louder than I thought if I've brought you here from all the way across the street," the older woman said as she seemed to struggle to catch her breath. She visibly winced. "But I am so glad that you did. I could use..." She winced again and gasped. "A bit of assistance."

Emma hurried into the room and stopped short when she noticed someone else *was* there.

He just wasn't conscious.

"Oh, my," Emma murmured in shock, her attention on the man who lay crumpled on the Aubusson carpet at the end of the bed. "Whatever happened to Mr. Simpson?" she asked, not sure where to start. A quick glance at Sophia assured her the woman was alert but still in pain.

"He fainted, poor dear. Did an admiral job up until he had this one out, and then his eyes..." She squeezed her own eyes shut and a rather indecorous curse sounded from between her clenched teeth. "Rolled up and..." She waved a dainty hand in the air as if that explained the rest of what she was about to say.

Emma took a quick look beneath the linen that covered Sophia's upraised knees and realized just why the woman was in pain.

"I didn't know you were due to have *twins*," she said in alarm. Her eyes widened.

"I should have suspected as much," Sophia replied. "I've grown enormously large in the past two months, but I certainly couldn't attribute it to too many cakes at tea time. Twins do run in the Pendleton family."

Emma frowned at this news, finally realizing the woman

referred to her mother's side of the family. She remembered just then that there were twins in the Grandby family as well, and she had a passing thought that Christiana might be carrying twins. "Has that one cried yet?" she asked as she turned to regard the baby held in the crook of Sophia's arm. The baby seemed far too quiet for one just born.

"Oh, he's managed a wail or two," Sophia assured her. "He is quite alive. Thank the gods, but a bit difficult to hold onto. Sleeping now, bless him."

"Put him aside then…" Emma glanced about and grabbed a linen from a stack on one of the dressers. Moving quickly, she took the babe from the crook of Sophia's arm and quickly wrapped it in the cloth, swaddling it even as she wished she could have cleaned him better before doing so.

"Mr. Simpson sent a caddy for Mrs. Vandermeer at least an hour ago—"

"She's not coming, my lady," Emma said with a shake of her head. "I just came from helping her deliver her son." Daring a glance toward the door, she found the maid hovering just outside, a folded apron on one arm.

"Oh, dear. Well, I have done this before. Not five minutes ago, in fact, but —"

"Where's your lady's maid?" Emma asked as she retrieved the apron from the maid and put it on. Before she could ask the girl for help, the maid was gone again.

"At the theatre. With her husband. It's her day off," Sophia explained with a shrug. "And that one wouldn't be of much help, I'm afraid," she added in a hushed voice, indicating the maid who had just left. Sophia sighed, her head falling back onto the mountain of pillows behind her back. "My son was right. I am too old for this."

"Nonsense." At the mention of a husband, Emma moved to check on James Simpson. Patting him on the side of his cheek, she said, "Mr. Simpson. Wake up." She glanced about. "Are there any smelling salts about?"

Sophia once again grimaced but pointed to an elaborate

vinaigrette on the dressing table. "I rather doubt there's time to..." She let out a howl, and Emma realized why.

"Push!" Emma urged her patient. "Breathe, too, my lady," she added, realizing just how tired the poor woman must be.

A moan from the floor below had Emma daring a quick glance at James. His eyelids fluttered as she turned her attention back onto the newest baby. "One more push. You can do this, my lady."

But Sophia's exhaustion had her settling back into the pillows, her body seeming to go limp all at once.

Emma struggled with the infant, determined to pull it out. Before she could, though, James was up on his feet, his look of confusion quickly replaced with concern. "Sophia!" he bellowed.

His wife's eyes flew open and she attempted to sit up, the last bit of a push all that was necessary for Emma to grab hold. The baby, far smaller than the first, appeared lifeless as Emma moved to wipe away what she could of the mess surrounding it. The cord appeared to have been wrapped around its neck. "No, no, no," she whispered, using a finger to open its mouth. She blew on it, rubbed its cheek with another finger, and blew on it again, but to no avail. The baby didn't move or cry out.

"It was a girl," she whispered, her tear-filled eyes meeting those of James. "I need the knife," she added, not sure what else she could do for the baby but cut its umbilical cord.

James regarded her with a frown and stepped next to her. Pale and looking as if he might faint again, he used a scissors to cut through the cord—closer than she would have, but given the circumstances, Emma decided it probably didn't matter.

"I'm so sorry," she whispered as she used the corner of a linen to clean off the babe's face and the inside of its tiny mouth.

"Why are you sorry?" James asked as he lifted the baby girl by her feet and gave her a swift swat on her tiny behind. A strangled cry followed by a healthy wail broke the silence. "It's rather kind of you to be gentle with her, but in this instance..."

Not sure what to do next, he offered the upside-down baby to Emma. "Take her, will you?"

"Oh!" Emma managed as she reached for another linen and quickly wrapped up the babe. "How did you know to do that?"

James gave a one-shouldered shrug. "Although I've never actually done this before, I paid witness to a few births during my tenure as butler at Merriweather Manor. Not this close, of course," he added as he gave a nod toward his wife.

Emma regarded the tiny bundle, concerned by just how small she was. *Warmth is most important*, she remembered Deborah saying. *The wee ones will succumb to the cold the quickest.* She placed the babe on Sophia's swollen belly, quickly adding another linen and then a layer of blanket over that. Unaware of the tears that streamed down her face, she regarded Sophia with a wan smile. "You have a daughter," she whispered before she realized she hadn't even counted its fingers and toes. A sob nearly robbed her of breath as exhaustion took hold. She was about to allow her legs to go out from under her when she remembered she still had to see to Sophia. The poor woman had given birth to two babies and had barely put voice to a complaint.

"Do you have a footman available?" Emma asked of James. "Or another caddy, perhaps? I really do believe Dr. Talbot should see to your wife," she said as she did a quick inventory. Everything she expected to find after a birth was present, and Sophia didn't seem to be in distress or bleeding, but given the woman's age, she thought it best the physician be summoned.

"Where can he be found?" James asked, all business again.

Emma was about to answer with the address for the Home for Unwed Mothers. Remembering what Todd had said, though, she realized he would be seeing to the babies being born there. "He's probably at the old Cooper Hotel. In Oxford Street," she answered. "The Home for Unwed Mothers. Their midwife is on her wedding trip to Scotland."

James angled his head to one side. "The poor dear," he murmured under his breath. He straightened and stepped outside the bedchamber door. "Pentworth!" he called out.

A commotion ensued beyond the door as Emma checked on her patient. "My lady?"

"I'll be fine. Really," Sophia murmured. "I'm just tired, is all."

Nodding, Emma hurried into the bathing chamber for water. She had been impressed with the bathing chamber attached to Deborah's bedchamber, but this one had her staring in wonderment. She knew how to operate the faucets, of course, but even before she reached them, she noticed the odd collection of pipes bent up and over a tub.

"It's a shower bath," James stated from behind her. "A quick way to bathe, and an even quicker means to wash hair," he added. "Although her ladyship still prefers a regular bath."

"It's... amazing," Emma murmured as she moved to wet some bath linens. "I need to clean your wife and see to the babies."

"I can take care of my sweeting if you'll see to them," he offered as he took some of the linens from her. "I'm embarrassed to say, I'm not even sure what the sex of the first baby is," he added in a whisper. "I passed out before I could check."

Emma chuckled, the first bit of humor she had felt that entire evening. "It's a boy," she said. "As was the Vandermeer baby. He arrived a few hours ago."

James' eyes widened in understanding. "Which is why *you* came instead of Mrs. Vandermeer."

"Yes," she replied as she handed him the warm, wet linens and hurried out to get the first-born. "This was not the best night for babies to be born, I'm afraid."

"Oh, but it 'twas," James replied with a grin. "I am the rather proud father of twins." He paused a moment and moved to wash his wife. "I do apologize for having fainted, my sweeting. Don't recall ever having done that before."

"I might have found it amusing if it wasn't so ill-timed," Sophia murmured, a wan smile touching her lips. "I know this wasn't how you expected to spend your evening," she added in a whisper, her eyes closed as if she were napping.

"I don't even recall how I expected to spend the evening," he replied, his gentle pressure with the warm linens against one of her thighs eliciting slight gasps from Sophia. He kissed the inside of her knee before he started on the other thigh.

"I believe you intended to go to your club," she replied, the words nearly lost to sleep.

"Huh. I'd quite forgotten," he whispered as he had the distinct impression he was being watched. Completely pulling away the linen that covered his wife's raised knees, he found his daughter where Emma had left her, perfectly placed so the babe was slightly angled on her mother's belly, swaddled in a linen, and almost entirely covered in a blanket. Red-faced and wide-eyed, she was apparently staring at him. "Well, good evening little darling. What shall we call you?" he asked in a quiet voice. "So many choices, but only one will do, don't you suppose?"

Emma, repeating what she had done for William Vandermeer just a couple of hours ago, listened intently at the quiet conversation going on in the mistress suite. She was relieved to find this boy more alert than William had been. Perhaps it was merely because he was a few minutes older than the Vandermeer baby had been at the time of his bath, but his arms moved about and his legs kicked in various directions in the water.

"What will you name him?" she asked as she brought the swaddled boy back to his mother. She moved the other baby onto the bed, breaking the spell that had been cast between father and daughter, so she could settle the boy onto his mother's distended belly. When she picked up the tiny girl, she found James staring at her. "What is it?" she asked in alarm.

"I've absolutely no idea," he murmured, a grin finally breaking out. "We've discussed it, of course, but..." He gave a shrug. "We have time."

Emma grinned as she helped herself to another linen and set about washing the baby girl. Although the babe wasn't nearly as old and was way too small, her wide-open eyes seemed to take in everything around her. "You have a much older brother whom I rather imagine will be quite charmed by you," she said as she washed the baby. Her grin changed to consternation.

"Which has me wondering why *he* isn't here yet," she murmured. Of course Todd would have let Thomas and Gregory know where she had gone—and why.

So where are they? She remembered Todd's orders that their carriage be brought around to the front of Grace Park. Mr. Stevenson, the groom who had seen to her safe arrival at the Simpsons' townhouse, should have already made it back there—she'd been gone for nearly an hour!

Aware the baby still stared at her, Emma smiled. "Why, aren't you just the most adorable little princess?" she whispered.

The babe stared at her as her tiny legs kicked in the water, her eyelids slowly settling over her eyes.

Emma hated to remove the babe from the warm water, knowing it probably reminded her of where she had just been only moments earlier. "Let's get you back to your mother, shall we?" she whispered, gently lifting the girl onto a linen. Drying her off as quickly as she could, Emma placed her into another dry linen and quickly wrapped her up, ensuring her arms were captured in the fabric so that her tiny fingernails couldn't scratch her delicate skin.

Making her way back into the mistress suite, Emma found James still whispering to his wife while she held her son to her breast. "He's already hungry?" she asked in surprise.

"The boys always are. Gregory certainly was, the greedy little bastard," Sophia replied with a sigh.

"Language, my sweet," James murmured.

Sophia managed to look suitably chagrined before adding, "Where *is* my older son this evening?"

Blushing at Sophia's comment, Emma blinked. "He was in the study at Grace Park when I left there."

"Deep in his cups?" Sophia asked with an elegantly arched eyebrow.

Emma winced. "He and Thomas were celebrating the birth of Todd's son, it's true," she agreed. "But I thought they would be here by—" She stopped when she realized there was someone outside the mistress suite.

Several someones.

The maid from earlier appeared and curtsied. "I apologize, but there's a gentleman here requesting an audience with Mrs. Wellingham. He says it's a matter of utmost importance."

Emma frowned. Had Thomas come, three sheets to the wind, expecting her to join him at the townhouse? Well, despite how she had felt earlier that evening, she wasn't about to be joining him in the bed across the street anytime soon. But she had barely finished the thought when Gregory Grandby appeared at the door.

"Mother, James," he said in turn, his breath catching when he took in the sight of his mother nursing a baby and another resting on her belly. James had finished his ministrations and helped to straighten Sophia's legs so she no longer looked as if she was about to give birth.

"Good evening, darling," Sophia said happily. "Have you come to meet your new brother and sister?"

Gregory blinked, his breaths coming in pants as if he had run all the way from Grace Park. "Not exactly," he managed as he staggered slightly. "I've... I've come for Emma," he managed to get out between attempts to catch his breath. "Christiana needs her," he added as he slowly entered the bedchamber.

"What's wrong with Christiana?" Emma asked in alarm.

"She's going to have a baby," Gregory whispered as he stared at the babies and then slowly turned his attention to Emma. "And Deborah is sound asleep."

"As she should be," Emma replied, just then realizing what he had said. "She's in labor?" she asked in alarm. "But... but it's far too *soon*," she said in a whisper. "Oh, dear."

Gregory furrowed his brows and angled his head, as if he were trying to decide how to best answer the comment. Then he regarded his younger siblings. "Twins? Or am I seeing double?" he asked as he seemed unsteady on his feet. He turned his attention to his stepfather. "I must have had far more champagne than I thought."

"You were drinking brandy," Emma whispered.

"That, too," he replied.

"You have a sister and a brother," James stated proudly, pretending not to overhear Emma's comment. "And it sounds as if they're about to have a niece or a nephew," he added with an arched brow. "Where did you leave your wife, Mr. Grandby?"

The tall man blinked. "In the ladies lounge. Her waters broke..."

Emma gasped. "How long ago?"

Gregory shook his head. "I've absolutely no idea. A maid discovered her in there—weeping, bless her heart—and came to find Thomas and me in the study. He's with her now." When he noticed Emma's look of confusion, he added, "He's not nearly as... drunk as I am." This last was said under his breath, as if he didn't want his mother overhearing the remark.

"However did you get here?" Sophia asked, thinking her son might have fallen off a horse if he rode one.

"Stevenson drove me. Said it's his third trip here tonight." He turned back to his mother. "One would think he should be offered his own room. I think he might be having an *affaire* with one of your servants!"

His mother gave him a quelling glance. "Nonsense, dear. Now you were telling us about your wife, who is about to give birth. Where exactly is she?" she prompted.

Gregory straightened at the reminder of Christiana. "At Grace Park. Thomas was carrying her into one of the guest bedchambers just as I left to come find Emma."

"Forgive me, my lady, but I really must take my leave," Emma said as she gave the tiny baby girl one last frantic look. "Do keep her as warm as possible," she whispered to James before she curtsied and left the mistress suite.

"Me, too, Mother," Gregory managed. He gave a nod to James. "I'll introduce myself to them—properly—the next time I'm here." He leaned against the door frame. "You appear to have things in good order," he added in his stepfather's direction.

James grinned. "I always do. Now off with you. And give our regards to Christiana," he added as Gregory finally bowed and took his leave of the bedchamber.

James allowed a chuckle as he turned his attention onto his wife. "Poor man," he murmured.

Sophia gave him a look of shock. "You do mean 'poor Christiana,' I hope," she replied with a quelling glance.

James blinked. "Yes. Yes, of course I do, my sweeting."

He may or may not have been lying.

CHAPTER 39

A CARRIAGE RIDE PROVES
ILLUMINATING

Emma held onto the side of the carriage as if her very life depended on it, the dinner basket she hadn't yet had a chance to open strung over one arm and her redingote half pulled onto the other. She was about to grill Gregory on Christiana's condition when he leaned over and helped her into the coat.

"How drunk are you?" she asked as she dug into the basket and extracted an apple.

"Truth be told, I am not," Gregory replied simply, the manner in which his torso waved about on the seat at odds with his claim. "I am rather light-headed, though, which I'm sure makes me appear foxed. Can't seem to breathe properly."

Emma stared open-mouthed at her brother-in-law. Now that she studied him by the dim light of the gas lamps they passed, she realized he appeared frightened near to death. "You need to slow your breathing, Gregory, or you're going to faint," she warned with a good deal of authority. She remembered quite well how she had felt when she had arrived at the Simpson's townhouse. Light-headed, and not just because she was scared. She had been hungry. And still was. Although she had a chance to finish the soup course, she had excused herself to see to Deborah before any of the meat courses were served.

She bit into the apple and chewed as she watched Gregory attempt to control his breathing.

"I have a confession to make," he stated.

Having heard those words before from him, Emma stilled herself. "Oh?" She might have disabused him of putting voice to a confession, but curiosity had her wondering why he would say such a thing just then.

"I don't believe this baby is arriving earlier than... than it should," he went on. "I have to admit, I am rather glad Mother has given birth to my brother—"

"And sister."

"—Before Christiana provides her with a grandchild."

"As is she," Emma put in with a wan smile, returning her attention to her apple. She blinked and turned to stare at him. "Are you saying Christiana was with child when you two *wed?*" she asked in a hoarse whisper. She wasn't sure how much of their conversation Mr. Stevenson could hear from his perch on the bench, but she certainly didn't want anyone hearing this particular question.

Had there been more light, Emma might have seen the rush of color that suffused Gregory's neck and cheeks. "Possibly," he replied, his head remaining straight as his eyes darted in her direction.

Emma sighed her disappointment. Christiana had already given the older man her virtue over a year ago and suffered a miscarriage when she was still sixteen. Gregory hadn't become aware of what had happened until he was at Woodscastle for an extended stay two weeks after it happened.

"Despite my... words to the contrary, she was rather... insistent... we lie together again," he stammered. "She was determined to be with child as soon as possible."

"You're older and far larger than she is," Emma admonished him. "I'm sure you could have denied her had you wanted to," she scolded in disgust.

Gregory stared at Emma, rather surprised by her outburst. "I did want to. Dissuade her, I mean. But I have no intention of ever denying her anything she wants," he countered. "She's my wife. She was going to *be* my wife, and if she wanted me to bed her, then..." He allowed the comment to trail off when he realized he wasn't going to convince Emma of his side of the situation.

"You do spoil her," Emma said before taking another bite of her apple.

Grinning, Gregory nodded. "I do. I love her. And I can afford to indulge her. Especially in matters of—"

"Don't say it," Emma interrupted just as the carriage pulled into the half-circle drive in front of Grace Park.

"Babies," Gregory finished with a nod. He stepped out of the carriage and held the door, offering a hand when Emma moved to step down.

"I do hope we're not too late," she said as she leaned on his arm.

"I'm sure Thomas has the situation well in hand," Gregory managed hopefully.

The front door opened even before they climbed the steps, the tall figure of Todd Vandermeer holding his son silhouetted by the light from the vestibule. "So glad you could join us again, Emma," he said with a sigh of relief.

Weary and still rather hungry, Emma merely nodded and made her way into the house.

CHAPTER 40

BABY MAKES THREE

Thomas sat in the same chair he had been in just a few months ago, in the same room his wife lay prone whilst she recovered from her reopened wound and forgiven him his uncharacteristic behavior. Instead of Emma lying in the room's only bed, his sister wept quietly between whimpers and hisses.

A maid had helped her into one of Deborah's nightrails, the gown entirely too long for Christiana. She looked liked an angel, though, her strawberry blonde curls spread out over the pile of pillows behind her back.

"How long has it been?" Christiana whispered.

Thomas frowned before pulling his pocket watch from his waistcoat pocket. "Not even an hour," he replied. "He'll get here." *He has to*, Thomas nearly added. He had no idea how he would be of any assistance if the baby made an appearance before Emma arrived.

"After a stop at his club?" Christiana asked, a hint of derision in her voice. "For more drinks and to place a bet? What are the odds of me having a boy, do you suppose?"

His brows furrowing at the implication of her words, Thomas shook his head. Gregory hadn't been to White's very often since his wedding day, and when he was, it was usually during the afternoon hours. Once he was back at Woodscastle for dinner, the man tended to remain there, either indoors or in the back gardens when he took Christiana for walks.

As for bets, well, the man wasn't a gambler.

What had Christiana thinking Gregory would pay a visit to his club on this night of all nights? She was about to give birth to his first child!

"I would say the odds are fifty-fifty for you having a boy, but I have it on good authority he's hoping for a girl," Thomas said sternly. "As for if he's paying a visit to White's, I would put those odds at zero. Whatever has you thinking such an awful thought, sister?"

Christiana sniffled as she tried to sit up. "I have absolutely no idea."

The sound of voices drifted up from the main floor, and Thomas heaved a sigh of relief. He could almost feel the vibrations of someone running up the stairs. Someone tall and large and married to his sister...

Emma rushed into the bedchamber and stopped short at finding Christiana and Thomas looking as if nothing was amiss. "Good evening," she managed between gasps for air. She was about to struggle to get out of her redingote when Thomas moved to assist her.

"I cannot tell you how relieved I am now that you're here," Thomas whispered. "She's become a bit *irrational*." He said the words as his eyebrows lifted nearly to his hairline.

Emma gave him a quelling glance before turning a wan smile onto Christiana. "Congratulations are in order. You are an aunt, twice over," she said. At Christiana's expression of shock, she added. "Twins. A boy and a girl."

Christiana blinked and then winced for a moment. "That's where you've been?" she asked, her brows furrowing. "Delivering Mrs. Simpson's babies?" She grimaced again and took several breaths before turning her attention onto her brother. "Why didn't you tell me?"

Thomas blinked, not sure of what he had done to earn his sister's sudden wrath. "I'm quite sure I mentioned it," he whispered, intending for only Emma to hear his words.

Angling her head to one side, Emma regarded her husband a moment. He seemed sober. "Todd told me Deborah is still sleeping, but if I require any assistance, we're to have him wake her."

"Understood," Thomas replied. "How is Mrs. Simpson?"

Emma grinned. "Rather calm, actually. Happy, I think, since her husband has an heir. But then, she's done this before. Both babies are rather small, though. The girl is so tiny," she murmured, worry evident in her voice. "I don't know that she'll make it."

Christiana suddenly let out a howl that had Thomas and Emma turning to stare at her. Tossing her coat onto a chair and hurrying to the edge of the bed, Emma pulled the coverlet off of her sister-in-law. "How long have you been having contractions?" she asked as she rearranged the pillows behind her patient.

Struggling to answer, Christiana gasped and turned her attention onto her brother. "Ask him. He's got the timepiece."

Even before Emma could turn to Thomas, he shook his head. "I haven't been keeping track," he managed to get out. "I... I didn't know I was supposed to be *timing* anything."

Emma pointed to the door. "Out!" she ordered before she took a look around. "Wait! I need... cloths. Bath linens. A basin of hot water. A knife. Have a maid bring them, if you would."

Thomas rushed to the door. Before he took his leave, though, he hurried back to Emma and kissed her on the cheek. "I love you. I love you more because I know my sister is in capable hands. And I'll know better for next time. About the keeping track of time. I promise."

With that, he disappeared just as Gregory ducked his head into the room.

"Next time?" Christiana repeated, just before Thomas was out of earshot. "I am never doing this again," she shouted just as she squeezed her eyes shut.

About to chide her, Emma looked up as Gregory strode into the bedchamber, his long legs moving him to his wife's side in just a few steps. "I apologize for having been gone so long. My mother—"

"Had twins," Christiana finished for him. "You didn't tell me she was expecting *twins*," she accused, sounding ever so cross.

Gregory was about to respond one way but gave it a second thought. "She didn't tell me, either," he remarked, just as Christiana's face screwed up into an expression of pain. "What is it, my petunia?" he asked, placing a hand on the side of her cheek.

Christiana didn't answer with words, but with a rather long, drawn-out yell that included sounds in several octaves and finished with a high-pitched scream.

"If you don't wish to pay witness to this, you'll want to leave the room right now," Emma said as she leaned over the bed. "Push, Christiana," she urged. "It's time."

A maid appeared at the door, her arms filled with bath linens while another maid followed with a basin of water. Neither said a word, but rather hurried into the room, placed their items on the room's only dresser, and immediately took their leave with quick curtsies.

"Hand me some of those linens, if you would," Emma said as she shoved the long nightrail farther up Christiana's legs and over her knees.

Momentarily frozen in place, Gregory simply stared at her. Then he quickly doffed his topcoat and began undoing the buttons down his waistcoat at the same time he grabbed several linens and handed them to Emma. "If my stepfather can do this, then so shall I," he announced, although most of his words were drowned out by Christiana's loud complaints.

Emma sighed as she rolled her eyes. "Might I remind you that your stepfather fainted?" she countered, her attention on Christiana's nether region. She supposed if the man intended to father ten children, he could find out first-hand what his wife would be suffering in order to bring them into the world. "Climb up onto the bed and get behind her. Help her sit up straighter the next time I say..."

The howl sounded again, and Emma said, "Push!"

Gregory recognized his cue and did as he was told.

"I cannot do this any longer," Christiana whispered.

"Oh, yes you can, my buttercup. Remember our second day in Rome?"

Whatever had happened during their second day in Rome had Christiana revived.

"You can relax now," Emma said as she managed a sigh.

"Is anything wrong?" Gregory asked, his face a testament of worry. "I love you, my daffodil," he added in a whisper.

Emma shook her head. "No. Your progeny is just taking its time. I'd have Christiana stand up and walk some, but I think she's too far along."

"I walked earlier," the mother-to-be whispered. "In the gardens, after dinner." When her face screwed up again, Emma gave a nod to Gregory. "This time, you're going to push very hard."

"Remember our first night on the ship, my beautiful rose?" Gregory murmured.

Blinking, Emma was about to ask what happened on the ship when Christiana let out a growl and squeezed her eyes shut. "Push. Push. That's it." There was a brief moment when Emma was sure it would be the last, but she sighed her disappointment.

Exhausted, Christiana rested against the front of Gregory's body. "You do it now," she said between her pants for air.

Gregory managed a chuckle. "All right, my daisy, but you're going to have to help. Just think of our five-month anniversary night."

Quite sure she didn't want to know what had happened on their five-month anniversary night, Emma paid witness to the tell-tale signs of another contraction. She wasn't sure if it was because she said, "Push," so loudly or because Gregory seemed extra determined, but Christiana managed a rather loud scream —as did the baby who emerged. "You can stop pushing," Emma said as she guided the crying baby onto a linen. "You have a girl. Goodness, but she has a head of dark hair," she added, as she lifted the baby for the parents to see. "And a set of lungs." She studied the baby before reaching for the knife. "Ten fingers, ten toes."

Tears streaming down her face, Christiana's smile replaced the strain of childbirth as Gregory looked as if he would be sick. "I am so glad that's over," she said as she fell back onto Gregory. "I was afraid you would call me every flower in the garden."

Emma moved to the basin and tested the water before dunking the baby into it. The howling baby immediately quieted as the water surrounded most of her body. "She's much larger than your sister," Emma commented as she washed the baby. A shadow fell over her as Gregory moved to watch.

"Christiana has either fainted or she's sleeping," he whispered. "Is that... normal?"

Allowing a wan smile, Emma nodded. "Of course. She's probably exhausted. But this one won't require a feeding for some time. Would you like to hold her?" She lifted the baby from the water and quickly wrapped it in a linen, moving to the fireplace for the added warmth.

Gregory took the bundle from her, settling his daughter into the crook of his arm as if he had done it a hundred times before.

"You've done this before," Emma murmured.

Her brother-in-law nodded. "Of course, but never with a newborn," he acknowledged. "She's not having twins, right?" he added as he lifted his head toward Christiana.

"No," Emma replied as she shook her head. "I need to see to a few details. She should be dry enough to wrap in a new linen. Do you think you can manage?"

Gregory didn't reply but merely took the chair nearest the fire and set about swaddling the baby with a dry linen. "No nappy?" he asked.

"Not yet," Emma replied as she finished cleaning Christiana. "But the need for those will come soon enough," she added as she pulled the nightrail down over Christiana's legs. The young lady looked like an angel once again, and Emma briefly wondered how the generally good-natured girl could emit such awful sounds.

"She never cursed me once," Gregory said, as if he could

read Emma's mind. "I was told I would hear my name spoken in vain. I expected a litany of 'you're never touching me again' and 'don't you come near me' and 'I hate you', and yet, the only complaint was that I called her the names of flowers."

Emma sighed. "Yes, well. That was a bit much. Had you called her 'sweet pea', I would have had you bodily removed from the room myself," she teased.

Looking suitably chastised, Gregory didn't admit that he was about to use that particular endearment when the situation next required it. "My stepfather calls my mother 'sweeting'. What should I call Christiana, do you suppose?" he asked, his attention on his daughter despite the topic of conversation.

"I suppose it depends on what you plan to call her," Emma replied as she indicated the baby.

"I'm thinking Ariel."

Emma jerked her head up from her post-birth chores and regarded her brother-in-law. "'Tis a beautiful name. Is it a family name?"

Gregory shook his head. "No, which is why I'm thinking to use it," he murmured. "I certainly don't wish to name her for my paternal grandmother, and my maternal grandmother's name is Sarah."

Angling her head in his direction, Emma said, "A duchess, isn't she?" Her eyes widened as she realized just which duchess. *Sarah Pendleton.* "The Duchess of Ariley," she murmured.

"Dowager duchess now, but yes. She lives in a rather majestic cottage in Derbyshire. Her brother, John, was the Duke of Pendleton," Gregory explained. He paused as he studied the tiny hand that had escaped from the linen surrounding his squirming daughter. "Ariel," he whispered, using his forefinger to give her fingers something to wrap around. The baby's eyes opened for a moment but soon drifted shut again. "Ariel it is," he said with a grin.

"Is it safe to come in?" Thomas asked from the threshold. "I heard... crying," he said carefully, deciding it was safer not to mention his sister's howls.

"I'm sure you heard far more than that," Emma said in a

whisper, one eyebrow arching up as she wrapped up several ruined linens in a ball.

"Come meet your niece. I've decided to name her Ariel," Gregory said as he motioned for Thomas to join him.

The baby's uncle joined his brother-in-law to stare down at the sleeping form in Gregory's arms. "She's not ugly," he said in surprise.

Both Emma and Gregory jerked their heads to regard Thomas in surprise. "Who said she was?" Gregory demanded to know.

Looking suitably chastised, Thomas gave a shrug. "I was told all babies were ugly." He lowered his voice. "Todd's boy certainly is."

Emma gave him a quelling glance. "He'll look entirely different in a day or two. Speaking of Todd, is he still up and about?" Emma asked. "We should introduce him to this one, and I should probably see how Deborah is faring."

"He's out in the hall. Been walking all about while telling his son the entire Vandermeer family history," Thomas said with an arched brow as he moved to peek out the bedchamber door. When he spotted their host at the end of the corridor, he whispered hoarsely, "Do join us. Your son's distant cousin is finally accepting visitors."

Todd appeared on the threshold a moment later, his sleeping son resting in the crook of his arm. A grin split Todd's face as he moved to the fireplace. "This is quite an auspicious evening," he said as he moved to regard Ariel. "Why, she's not ugly in the least!"

Gregory rolled his eyes. "Of course, she isn't. Not like..." he paused, thinking twice about what he intended to say. "Most babies." He nodded to Todd's boy. "Have you finished naming him yet?"

The taller man shook his head. "William, I'm quite sure. But... we'll wait. And to whom do we have the pleasure of meeting this beautiful night?"

"Ariel Christina Grandby," Gregory stated, thinking that including her maternal grandmother's name was appropriate for this baby—he would save his mother's name for the next girl. "I rather wish my mother could be here, but, alas, she's quite busy with her own two."

"I wish my mother were here. She would be... thrilled," Thomas added. "I cannot tell you how relieved I am that Christiana survived this. I don't mind admitting that I feared she would suffer Mother's fate."

There were murmurs of agreement among the men, none of whom were aware that Christiana was awake and listening intently. Although she displayed a rather serene expression of contentment for most of their banter, her brother's last comment had her frowning. Frowning and feeling a slight bit of panic.

Mum's fate?

CHAPTER 41

A BRIEF RESPITE WITH A FRIEND

Emma made her way to the master suite in Grace Park and dared a glance through the slightly open door.

"I'm awake," Deborah said from where she seemed to be sleeping in the large bed.

"You fooled me," Emma replied as she moved into the bedchamber. "How are you?"

Deborah took a deep breath and let it out slowly. "I'm not sure. Relieved, certainly. A bit... lonely, I suppose, although I know I should relish this time by myself." She paused a moment. "How is Christiana?"

"Sleeping, thank the gods. I was worried, of course. Her mother died giving birth to her, and she's so small," she added. "And yet her daughter is larger than both of Mrs. Simpson's babies."

Deborah grinned. "I heard you were summoned," she murmured. "Some young caddy? I wonder how much Mr. Simpson paid for him to find you."

"I've absolutely no idea, but Master Churchill was sent for *you*," Emma corrected her. "I'm quite sure my appearance at the Simpson townhouse was completely unexpected."

Sighing, Deborah rested her arms on her still swollen belly. "Four babies in one night. You have delivered as many as I have on my busiest night at the Home," she claimed.

Emma shook her head. "You still have me beat. I only delivered three. Mr. Simpson managed to help in delivering his son. Before he fainted," she added when she noticed Deborah's quizzical look.

The new mother giggled. "Poor man!" she replied happily. She sobered. "He wasn't holding the... ?"

"No, thank the gods. Her ladyship had him in hand when I arrived. Mr. Simpson was out cold. Had to revive him with a vinaigrette before the baby girl arrived," Emma explained. "So tiny, she was. I worry that she won't make it through the night."

"Did you tell them to keep her close to the fire?"

"I told Mr. Simpson. He was holding her when I left, and the boy was already nursing."

Rather surprised at this bit of news, Deborah straightened on the pillows. "How is Mrs. Simpson?"

Emma gave a shrug. "She was so calm and well-behaved. Not at all what I would expect from the daughter of a duchess. But then, she's done this before."

"At least five-and-twenty years ago," Deborah countered.

Nodding, Emma sat down on the edge of the bed. "Is it wrong for me to feel relieved that I am not among those giving birth this evening?" she asked in a hoarse whisper.

"I should hope not. Who would have played midwife if you hadn't been available?" she asked rhetorically. "Besides, your babe would be... far too premature." She frowned. "Which makes me wonder how it is that Christiana went into labor so soon... ?"

Emma swallowed, not sure how much to admit. "I'm quite sure her babe arrived right on time," she said with an arched brow.

Deborah shrugged. "As did mine," she countered with a guilty grin. She sighed. "Could you let my husband know I need my son now? I rather hate to take the boy from him—he's been so attentive—but I really need to nurse him."

"Of course," Emma replied as she stood up. She started to leave but stopped and turned around. "I am relieved, and I am not ashamed to admit it. I may not have a babe in the next year. Maybe two—" *Probably never.*

"And that is your choice," Deborah finished for her. "As long as your husband agrees?" she half-asked.

Emma nodded. "He does," she whispered. "Thank the gods." And with that, she took her leave of the master suite in search of Todd and his baby boy.

CHAPTER 42

AN EXPLANATION IS IN ORDER

"Is it time?" Todd asked as Emma returned to the guest bedchamber.

About to ask him what he meant, Emma gave a wan smile when she realized he knew very well it was time to give up his son to his wife for a feeding. "It is. She certainly appreciates your seeing to the babe for so long. She's managed to get some sleep and is doing well, but she's ready to give him his midnight feeding."

Todd returned the smile. "I am so glad. My son has increased his weight ten-fold since his birth! My arm is about to fall off," he claimed as he gave a slight bow and made his way out the door. He turned around. "I will take my leave of all of you, and see you, Thomas, tomorrow at the office."

"You will not, for tomorrow is Sunday, and I forbid you to come to the office," Thomas countered. He held up a hand at Todd's attempt at a protest. "I don't intend to go there again until Monday morning," he added as he arched an eyebrow in Emma's direction.

"As will I, since I usually arrive with my husband," Emma added.

Todd considered the edict and angled his head. "Then I shall see you the day *after* tomorrow," he replied. He gave a bow and took his leave of the guest suite.

Emma sank onto the edge of the bed, an overwhelming sense of exhaustion finally claiming her. "If you do not take me to a bed this very moment, Thomas, I shall share this one with Christiana for the entire night," she warned in a whisper.

Thomas straightened and stood. "I wonder if Mr. Allen is still up and about?"

Still holding his newborn, Gregory didn't seem to be paying attention to anyone else in the room. "You can have Mr. Allen drive you to the townhouse. I am spending the night holding my dear wife with our daughter tucked in between us," he announced. As if he meant to prove his point, he stood, placed the baby on the bed next to Christiana, and began unwinding his cravat.

"And that is our cue to take our leave," Thomas said as he took Emma's hand and pulled her out of the bedchamber with him.

Mr. Allen was, indeed, still up and about. "The carriage is ready, sir," he said as Thomas and Emma made their way into the vestibule. The poor groom had obviously been waiting there for some time. "Where would you like me to drive you?" Since he expected them to say, 'Woodscastle,' he was rather surprised when Emma said, "The townhouse directly across the street from the Simpson's."

Rather relieved he wouldn't be spending the remainder of the night driving the six miles to and from Chiswick, Mr. Allen gave a nod. "Right away, my lady."

*H*aving stripped down to his smalls, Gregory climbed into the bed next to his wife and gave her a kiss on the cheek. "Thank you for my daughter, my... goddess," he murmured, deciding to try out a new endearment on her.

Christiana managed a wan smile before she turned over on her side to face him. She regarded him a moment. "What did Thomas mean when he said, 'Mum's fate'?" she asked as a tear slid down her cheek. "Did she die... ?"

Gregory frowned, lifting onto an elbow as he regarded her. "You heard that?" he asked, immediately regretting the question.

"I was awake for most of the conversation," Christiana replied with an arched eyebrow. "Did she truly die giving birth to me?"

Sighing again, Gregory dropped a kiss on her forehead. She would know if he didn't tell her the truth. He was sure of it. "No. At least, not right away," he finally said. "Later that night. She was holding you, I think," he whispered. "She wasn't well for a long time, Christiana. I remember she was pale. Sickly. My mother remarked on it many times when she visited me in London," he added when he noticed her look of disbelief. "Said she was not long for this earth and wondered how she could even *be* with child." He kissed her again, this time on one of her eyelids.

"I killed my mother," Christiana whispered as more tears streamed down her face.

Gregory blinked. "You did no such thing," he countered, wondering how he could pull her into a hug with the baby right there. He lifted Ariel and placed the babe onto her mother's middle before he lifted his body over Christiana and the babe. "You actually kept her alive far longer than she would have lived," he murmured, sprinkling her face with kisses.

As if sensing her mother's distress, Ariel began to fuss, her quiet crying forcing Gregory to give up his hold on his wife. "I think Ariel is ready for her first dinner," he said in a whisper.

Christiana blinked. "Ariel?" she repeated in surprise. "It's a beautiful name."

"I thought you'd like it."

"You remembered," she whispered, sniffling between sobs.

"I could never forget your favorite doll," he replied. "You took such great care of her. Took her with you everywhere you went. So it only seemed appropriate we name our first daughter after her."

Still weeping, Christiana managed to kiss him. "Thank you," she whispered.

"For what? You did all the work," he replied before he kissed her again on the other eyelid. When Ariel's whimpering increased to a wail, he added, "And it sounds as if you have more to do, mother of my daughter."

Christiana gave him a wan smile. "Undo the buttons on my nightrail, would you?" she asked as she repositioned herself against the pillows and pulled Ariel into her arms.

Rather surprised by the request, it took Gregory a moment to realize she only meant for him to help her expose a breast for feeding. "Of course, my goddess."

Within moments, but not without a struggle, Ariel was nursing.

CHAPTER 43

AN EVENING ALONE

Two o'clock in the morning

Thomas unlocked the townhouse door and gave a wave to Mr. Allen. The groom, obviously tired, waved back before setting the horses on a course back to Grace Park. There he would spend the night. When the Grandbys were ready to return to Woodscastle, he would take them in the carriage while Thomas and Emma would ride her horse to Wellingham Imports.

"It's rather kind of Todd to offer a room in his servants' quarters for him," Emma remarked as she entered the townhouse.

"Grace Park has plenty of them," Thomas replied. "As well as servants. I rather wish I had borrowed one of them. I could use a bath."

"As could I," Emma countered as she gazed down at her ruined gown and sighed. Her eyes widened. "I wonder..." She gave a sideways glance at Thomas before reopening the front door. The Simpson townhouse was still lit up. "I'm quite sure Lady Simpson will want to know about Ariel," she said with an arched eyebrow.

Thomas frowned. "At this time of the night?"

Emma shrugged. "She just gave birth to twins not three hours ago. I rather doubt the household is abed," she countered.

"And?" Thomas prompted.

Sighing, her tiredness evident in how her shoulders sagged, Emma replied, "They have bathing chambers. With hot and cold running water and shower baths."

Thomas blinked. "I'll escort you," he said as he ushered her out the door and locked it behind them.

Although she had simply slipped into the house earlier that evening, Emma allowed Thomas to use the brass knocker to announce their arrival. Much to their surprise, James Simpson opened the door after only a few moments, a blanket-wrapped babe resting against one of his shoulders.

"I rather hoped you might stop by tonight," he said by way of a greeting. "Dr. Talbot just took his leave a few minutes ago. He has pronounced my wife in good health," he added as he stepped aside and waved them in. "Could hardly believe she'd given birth to twins, although he did say it was fortunate they were on the small side." He led them through the vestibule and into the hall beyond. "I do hope you come bearing good news about our grandchild."

Emma angled her head in an attempt to determine which baby he held. Given how tiny the bundle seemed, she guessed the girl. "We do. You have a granddaughter," she whispered as she reached out and took the sleeping baby from him.

"Sophia will be thrilled," James stated. "As am I, actually. Gregory must be over the moon."

Thomas nodded. "He wanted a girl first, which rather surprised me, but given how many cousins he has, I suppose he knows what's best."

"And how is everyone faring at Grace Park?" James asked as he led them to the study.

"Christiana was sleeping when we left. Gregory named the girl Ariel," Emma explained. "And the Vandermeers seem fine. Todd was actually doing what you've been doing, it seems," she added as she angled her head towards the bundle she carried.

"Which means his arm probably feels as if it's about to fall off," James remarked in a whisper.

Despite his weariness, Thomas took note of his surroundings, his eyes widening in surprise. "Your study is a masterpiece. You must have a favorite carpenter?" he half-asked, determined to discover who had done the carpentry work. The detailing was exquisite, and the plasterwork and mouldings precise.

James gave a nod as he waited for them to be seated. "Thank you for saying so. I took my time with this remodel. I figured it would be our final home, so I wanted it to be the very best it could be. And appropriate for the family of a duke's daughter," he added.

"How is your son doing?" Emma asked, shifting the baby to her other shoulder as she settled into a wingback chair.

James sighed. "He's with his mother. They were both sleeping when Dr. Talbot left."

"And why aren't you?"

The older man gave a shrug. "Besides the doctor's late visit, like you, I am determined that my daughter make it through the night. We named her Hannah, by the way. After Sophia's favorite aunt. And the boy is Henry, after one of her brothers—the current Duke of Ariley—and my father," he said proudly.

"Has Hannah had her first meal?" She could feel through the blanket that the babe wore a nappy.

James nodded. "Took a bit to get her situated, but my wife knew what to do, bless her heart." He sighed. "Why, you must be more exhausted than me," he said. "Four babies in one night?"

Emma allowed a wan smile. "I am, and although I look forward to sleeping, I am more in need of a bath. I wonder... might I prevail upon you for the use of one of your bathing chambers? In exchange, I would be happy to hold your daughter until she requires her mother, of course," she offered. "Give you a chance to get some sleep."

His expression one of profound relief, James nodded. "Why, you're more than welcome to the entire guest suite," he replied happily. "Truth be told, I wondered how I might prevail upon you to stay the night. Had there just been the one babe, I'm sure we could have managed, but with two, well, I believe I'll be hiring a nurse to help out."

"Probably for the best," Emma agreed.

"I'll escort you to the guest bedchambers," James said as he stood up.

"I can hold Miss Simpson while my wife bathes," Thomas suggested as James led them up the steps. "Give me some practice, seeing as how there will be a babe at Woodscastle now."

"Now there's the spirit," James replied happily. He opened the double doors to reveal an apartment suitable for the master and mistress of the house.

"Surely you don't mean for us to take *your* rooms for the night?" Thomas commented in awe. The room was decorated in the finest fabrics, its peach and rose-hued color scheme extending from the sitting area to the bedchamber. The furnishings were new—the faint scent of wood and oils were still evident in the air, and thick carpet covered the entire floor.

James gave his head a quick shake. "This is the guest suite, actually. Our apartment is on the opposite hall," he added. He turned to Emma. "You'll find nightclothes in the dresser and linens in the bath. Do make yourself at home." He leaned over and gave his daughter a kiss on the side of her head. "When she fusses, I suppose it will be time for her to go to Mrs. Simpson."

Emma smiled. "Thank you. Do get some sleep, Mr. Simpson, and congratulations."

The older man nodded and took his leave of the room, his manner not much different from that of a butler.

Gazing at their surroundings, Thomas put his hands on his hips and allowed a sigh. "I do believe I will have the carpenters work on the master suite," he murmured, just then realizing Emma was no longer beside him. He made his way into the bathing chamber and watched as Emma turned on the bath water. Despite the odd collection of piping and handles, she seemed to know what to do. With Hannah still held to one shoulder, she tested the streams of water coming from what Thomas realized were hot and cold water pipes. "And I do believe I'll hire some plumbers to modernize the bathing chamber, as well," he whispered hoarsely as he regarded the furnishings included in the bath. An upholstered chaise lounge and a side table were situated so whoever sat there would have a clear view of the tub. "I suppose anyone bathing in here should expect an audience?" he half-asked.

Emma grinned as she lifted Hannah from her shoulder and gave her to Thomas. "I rather imagine there are some women who enjoy enticing their lovers whilst they bathe," she whispered, an impish grin appearing. "Do you remember how to do this?" she asked quietly.

Thomas nodded as he allowed an uncertain grin. "Some things you never forget how to do," he replied, settling onto the chaise lounge and then moving Hannah into the crook of his arm. He regarded her a moment, his brows furrowing when he realized how truly tiny she was. When he looked up, he found his wife divesting herself of her gown and stays and stockings. "And some sights you hope you will never forget having seen."

Wearing only a translucent chemise, Emma regarded him a moment, a pleasant frisson passing through her entire body at seeing him play a doting father. She lowered herself into the warm water and allowed a sigh. "There's enough room for you, too," she remarked with an arched brow, helping herself to a bar of soap and a bath linen.

Tempted to join her, Thomas regarded the babe he held. "I'm so tired, I may not be able to get *out* of the tub," he replied as he undid the buttons of his waistcoat. "Besides, I'm on duty."

"I can hold her while you undress," she offered. "She liked the water when I bathed her earlier. As long as we keep her warm, she should be fine."

Thomas leaned over the tub and gently moved Hannah into Emma's arms. The babe's eyes opened once she was on Emma's shoulder, but she remained quiet as Thomas stripped his clothing and stepped into the tub behind Emma. "Now this is a bit of heaven," he murmured as he gripped the edges of the tub and slowly descended into the water.

Once he was seated, he bent his knees on either side of Emma and wrapped an arm around her midriff while he used his other hand to locate the bar of soap. "Would you like me to wash you?" The hand around her middle moved to cup a breast as he slid the soap over her smooth skin. Her nipples pebbled despite being covered by the warm water. At her soft sighs, he moved his attention to the other breast, to her arms and hips and to what he could reach beyond.

Emma knew even before his hands reached the apex of her thighs that his simple ministrations had her aroused. When his fingers brushed over her engorged womanhood, the perfect pressure and sudsy water set off a series of frissons that had her inhaling sharply. Resisting the urge to cry out lest she wake the baby, Emma had to place her hand over his to still his movements. "No more, Thomas, or this baby will end up under the water," she warned.

She felt his lips nip the back of her neck as he pulled her body back into his hold. "Can it be that all these babies have me wanting to bed you? Even when we're both so exhausted?" he whispered.

Emma allowed a giggle. "As I recall, you wanted to bed me even before the first one was born tonight," she reminded him.

"Was that tonight? Seems like days ago," he murmured, his voice drifting off in a sigh.

Emma relaxed back against him. "When I finally get into that beautiful bed, I may sleep for an entire day," she warned. She felt his grunt of a response against her back and allowed a smile. "Have you given any more thought to..." She stopped and swallowed, reminding herself how inconvenient it would be to have another child in Woodscastle so soon after Ariel's birth.

"Adopting a child?" Thomas whispered. From the tone of his voice, Emma couldn't tell if he welcomed the question or was bothered by it.

"I was thinking we should wait about a year or so," Emma whispered. "By then, I would have Mr. Cunningham trained to do my position. Then I could be away from the company for a time," she went on. She felt Thomas' chest rise and fall behind her, and was curious as to what he thought of her plan. When he didn't offer a response, she angled her head to look back at him and found him sound asleep.

Although she, too, was tempted to simply fall asleep in the

tub, there was the baby to consider. Emma hurried her ablutions as she held Hannah to her shoulder. Deciding she should get out of the tub, she nudged Thomas awake. "Take her, please. Once I'm in a linen, I'll get her into another," she explained as she carefully stepped out of the tub and wrapped a linen around her body. The absorbent looped fabric was unlike anything she had used before. "When our bathing chamber is updated, I shall look forward to adding these," she murmured as she indicated the linens. "Perhaps we could acquire some even before then."

Thomas regarded the baby he held. "A year would be about right," he whispered, marveling at her tiny fingers and the even tinier fingernails that appeared above the edge of the linen in which she was wrapped.

Emma leaned over and took Hannah from his arms, the tiny baby fussing when she was removed from the warmth of Thomas' bare chest. Emma paused a moment as she openly admired his naked body. Barely covered by the bathwater, he looked like a model for a Greek statue. "So, you heard that, did you?" she whispered.

Rising from the tub, Thomas allowed the water to sluice from his body before he accepted her offer of a dry linen. "Every word," he acknowledged. His eyes darkening, he nodded to the baby. "Let's get this one to her mother, shall we? It's time I have you to myself."

Gasping at his words, Emma finally nodded. "I'll put on a gown and take her to Mrs. Simpson right away," she replied.

She found the nightclothes in the top drawer and pulled on a nightrail before moving to rewrap the baby in a dry linen. With Hannah's tiny mouth already making the movements to suckle a nipple, Emma knew it wouldn't be long before the babe would be fussing for its mother. She almost managed to make it to the mistress suite when the first cries erupted.

Once Hannah was settled into her mother's arms—Sophia was wide awake from having just fed the other twin—Emma asked how she was faring.

"Oh, I'm fine, really. James has finally gone to bed. He took the boy with him to his bedchamber." She gave a sigh of relief when the baby girl finally suckled a nipple. "I do hope he's left some for her," the new mother added in a worried whisper.

"You can hire a wet nurse if need be," Emma suggested, hoping the Simpsons would consider the extra help. She still wasn't convinced the older couple realized what was ahead of them with two babies in the household.

"If need be," Sophia replied. "I'll keep her in my bed tonight. You go on to bed," she whispered.

Emma said, "Good night," and made her way back to the guest bedchamber. Anxious for what Thomas might have in mind for her in the large, luxurious bed, she slipped out of the nightrail and climbed onto the mattress.

And found Thomas sound asleep.

CHAPTER 44

DAY OLD BABIES

The morning after

The heavenly scent of chocolate had Sophia Simpson slowly opening her eyes. That and the quiet whispers of her husband speaking to someone. Quiet whispers he might have at one time bestowed on her. Whispers about smooth skin, delicate beauty, and silken hair.

Why, he had said those very sentiments to her not even a full day ago!

Wondering if she should feign jealousy, she turned her head to find James holding their daughter in the crook of his arm. Not wanting to interrupt—she decided she was curious as to how long he could hold the infant's attention—Sophia merely watched and listened. Movement somewhere else on the bed followed by the unmistakable sounds of a baby about to cry reminded her there was another baby in their midst.

Twins.

"Your brother Henry is about to wake your mother. Again," James whispered softly. "Something tells me you're going to be the quiet, well-behaved one in this family."

No sooner had he said the words than the girl's face changed, her angelic visage screwing up until a wail erupted from her tiny mouth.

"You do realize your mistake, I hope," Sophia said with a

grin as she straightened on the pillows. She took the babe from him and settled her against one breast, the babe fussing until she finally discovered a source of nourishment and struggled to latch onto it.

James gave Sophia a look of shock and then angled his head to one side. "I suppose I was pushing my luck," he admitted. "She's just so... *sweet*," he murmured. "I found her wide awake a few moments ago, tucked up against you, quiet as could be." He didn't add that she was there because he had put her there after seeing to it her nappy had been changed. Reaching over Sophia, he lifted the cup of chocolate from the nightstand and offered it to her. "Good morning, my beautiful."

Sophia leaned over and kissed him on the cheek. "Good morning, handsome. How is the new father of twins this morning?" she asked before she took a long draught of the chocolate. Although she expected she would feel exhausted after the eventful night, she found she felt rather light. At least a stone lighter, in fact.

"Happy. Exhausted. A bit overwhelmed, I suppose," James replied as he took their son into his arms in an attempt to settle the boy. "I've sent a footman to the agency to ask about the availability of a nurse," he added, his manner most conciliatory.

Sophia dared a glance at him before returning her attention to the bundle she held. Hannah's eyes were already closed, and her suckling was slowly subsiding. "Well, that didn't take long," Sophia said, her brows furrowing. "Although I suppose it doesn't take much to fill a tiny tummy," she whispered then, hoping that's all it was. She turned to James. "Has her nappy been changed?"

James nodded. "One of the maids helped me. About an hour ago or so," he added. "We had to cut a few nappies in half or there would have been far too much fabric to wrap about their bums," he explained when he noticed her initial reaction to his news.

Grinning as she pulled her daughter from her breast, Sophia said, "It won't take but a few weeks before they grow into them," she warned.

"That may have been true for Gregory, but he's a rather tall man," her husband replied.

Sophia blinked. "He didn't start out that way. Why, I don't remember him being any larger than Henry when he was born."

"But Hannah is far smaller than her brother," James countered as he gave her Henry. He took the girl and lifted her to his shoulder, his free hand gently patting her on the back.

Sophia regarded him in surprise. "You've done this before," she accused.

Her husband's eyes widened at her tone of voice. "Well, I admit I've held a babe or two," he acknowledged. "Do you have any idea how many were born during my tenure at Merriweather Manor?"

Henry settled into the crook of his mother's arm and immediately found the source of his breakfast. "Including Gregory?" She mentally attempted to count how many babies had been born while she had lived at the manor.

"Two-and-twenty," James claimed. "I was only on staff for seven years. That's three babies a year for every year I was there."

Sophia grinned at his words, remembering all too well what life had been like at the manor house in Chiswick with five families at various stages of their lives. "Do you miss it?" she asked, her question coming at the same time a soft burp erupted from Hannah.

"Ah, there it is," James whispered with a grin. "I haven't lost my touch, now have I?" he asked rhetorically. "And no, I don't miss that madhouse," he added with a sigh as he lowered Hannah into the crook of his arm. Quiet for a moment, he simply stared at his sleeping daughter.

Glancing at him after a time, Sophia wondered what he might be thinking. She rather hoped he didn't regret getting a child—nay, twins—on her at this stage in their lives. "A penny for your thoughts," she whispered.

James jerked his head up and regarded his wife for a moment. "I do hope she lives," he said as tears collected in the corners of his eyes. "For I fear I have fallen truly, madly, deeply in love with her," he murmured before the tears spilled freely down the planes of his face.

"Oh, James! Oh, my," Sophia whispered, stunned at her husband's comment. And his tears.

"I want to hear her call me 'dada,' and see her take her first steps, and teach her how to dance, and... and fight off her unscrupulous suitors, and give her away at her wedding." He sniffled and then shook his head. "Scratch that last. I won't want to give her away. Why, there isn't a man on this planet worthy of her," he went on, a sob interrupting his words.

Sophia blinked, not quite sure what she could say except, "Well, it's possible he's not been born yet, and I'm not about to send her away to a *nunnery*."

James seemed to consider her comment before sniffling again. "Perhaps the Wellinghams will have a son," he hedged.

Suppressing the sudden urge she felt to giggle–James Simpson had never put voice to these sorts of sentiments the entire time she was expecting—Sophia found tears falling from her own eyes. "Oh, now look what you've gone and made me do," she whispered as a teardrop fell onto Henry's cheek.

James was about to go in search of a handkerchief when a soft knock sounded. "Come!" he called out in a hoarse whisper.

One of the bedchamber doors opened, revealing Emma and, behind her, Thomas. Upon seeing the Simpsons in Sophia's bed with tears streaming down their faces, Emma's eyes widened and she let out a strangled cry. "No!" she wailed as her hands went to her mouth.

Thomas had his arms around her in an instant, pulling her close as soon as he realized what had his wife so upset. "We're ever so sorry," he managed to get out.

James stepped from the bed, giving their guests a bow as he continued to hold Hannah in his arms. "Whatever is wrong?" he asked, giving his wife a quick glance. When he realized how bereft she looked, with tears streaming down her face and her golden blonde and gray locks not yet combed, he understood.

"I was so sure she would make it," Thomas said sadly,

holding Emma's head against his shoulder as she sobbed uncontrollably. "Please accept our—"

"She's not... dead," Sophia interrupted, the words coming out between two sobs that robbed her of breath.

"The boy then?" Thomas countered, his brows furrowing in confusion. "But... he was so much larger—"

"He's not dead, either," James said. He hurried to the door, holding his daughter out so Emma could see for herself.

Tears streaming down her cheeks, Emma regarded the tiny bundle and finally reached for it. "Oh," she managed to get out before sniffling. She brought the babe into her arms and stared down, her face lighting up in delight as Hannah opened her eyes and stared at her. "Oh, look at you," she whispered. When Hannah's eyes drifted shut again, Emma looked up and regarded the Simpsons with concern. "If not the babies, then whatever has you two *weeping*?" she asked in concern.

Sophia and James exchanged embarrassed glances. "We were... we were just contemplating Hannah's future," James finally said. "It was more than I could bear all at once, it seems. Especially the part where I'm to give her away at her wedding..." He sent his eyes up to the ceiling as a new set of tears threatened.

Thomas blinked. "She's not even a day old, and you've already arranged a marriage for her?" he asked in disbelief.

Angling her head to one side, Sophia said, "Why, we were actually wondering if perhaps you two were planning to have a son, for we cannot think of another suitable suitor for her," she replied, the hint of a grin suggesting she was merely teasing.

Emma and Thomas exchanged quick glances. "That all depends, I suppose," Emma replied, trying hard to keep the sadness from her voice. "But I for one rather adore the idea," she added with a nod. She settled Hannah into the crook of her arm and grinned at how angelic the baby appeared in slumber.

"Or there's William Vandermeer. I rather think he'll be raised to become a fine, young man," Thomas offered with a shrug.

James finally allowed a chuckle. "We're being foolish, aren't we?" he murmured as he took Henry from his wife's arms—the boy had long since finished his breakfast and was sound asleep —and saw to it her chest was covered with her nightrail. He still wasn't sure what he thought of having his son see his wife's breasts, but he definitely didn't want Thomas to see them.

"Indeed," Sophia agreed. "I'm rather famished, and I rather imagine you two are as well," she said as she pulled her dressing gown around her to finish what her husband had started. "Shall we go down for breakfast? James arranged for me to have a breakfast parlor when he did the remodeling. It's my favorite room," she added as she moved to get out of the bed.

James was by her side in an instant. "You're not yet dressed, my sweeting," he whispered as he held out an arm for her.

Stepping farther into the bedchamber, Hannah now held to her shoulder, Emma said, "Since our children might one day be married, I wouldn't be the least bit offended if you came to breakfast dressed exactly as you are."

Sophia beamed. "You see, darling?" she murmured. "Our daughter is already set for life."

Daring a glance at the baby boy he held, James decided he had better not ask about *his* future as he led his wife to her favorite room.

For besides his sister, the only girl that had been born the night before was his niece!

"Any chance you'll be having a girl?" he asked of Thomas as they made their way down the stairs.

Thomas traded glances with Emma and finally allowed a chuckle. "Time will tell," he whispered in reply.

CHAPTER 45

MAMA'S MILK IN A VACUUM

March 28, back at Woodscastle

Sometime in the middle of the night—two nights later—Emma was awakened by the urgent sounds of someone coming up the stairs. Someone who was large.

Someone who was tall.

Someone who was in a hurry.

She was halfway out of bed when the knock came at the door. Wrapping a dressing gown around her naked body, she rushed to the door. She opened it to find Gregory leaning against the door frame. Breathless and frightened given his expression, he gasped, "Please, Emma, Christiana is in great pain, and I don't know what to do!"

Daring a glance back at the bed—Thomas appeared to be sleeping—Emma rushed from the room. "What kind of pain?" she whispered as she flew down the steps and through the long hall to the west wing stairs. A distraught Gregory followed closely behind. "What did she say?" Emma asked as they made the turn to climb the steps.

"Something about Ariel not taking her right breast. She's very upset. She's been in tears all night, as has the baby," he panted as they reached the top of the west stairs.

Emma burst into their master suite to find Christiana bawling uncontrollably while holding her squalling newborn.

"Shhh," Emma whispered as she sat down on the edge of the bed.

The entire room was lit with candle lamps, and it only took a moment to see what was wrong. Christiana's right breast was considerably more swollen then her left. "Have you been able to get her to feed off your right breast at all?" Emma asked quietly, wanting to instill some calm into the room. She stroked the baby's head as she regarded her sister-in-law.

Ariel quieted as Christiana's cries died down. "No. She won't take it," Christiana sobbed. "She only ever nurses on the left." With that, the new mother started crying again.

Emma turned to Gregory, who was at least as exhausted as Christiana. "For two whole *days?*" she asked him, a look of realization appearing on her face.

Gregory nodded, a motion she could see cost him dearly as he seemed to be dead on his feet.

Turning back to Christiana, she explained, "Your breast is engorged. It's full of milk, and that's what is causing you so much pain." She stood up. "Come, we're going to the kitchens," Emma ordered as she took the baby into her arms. She reached out a hand to Christiana and helped her out of bed. "Gregory, please bring a lamp," she added as she hurried past him.

"This way. It will be faster," Gregory said as he ducked into the study and pulled open the door to the secret stairway. He held up a candle lamp as he motioned Emma and Christiana to join him.

Emma allowed a wan smile as she remembered going to the kitchens via the study back when the thieves had paid a visit before Christmas.

"What's this?" Christiana asked as she regarded the opening in the study's wall, her hand still gripping her sister-in-law's.

"A shortcut to the kitchens," Gregory and Emma stated in unison, the two giving each other a glance of surprise. Gregory ducked into the inky blackness. The lamp he carried illuminated the steps below, although it was still rather dark as Emma crept behind him with Ariel against her shoulder. "The workmen discovered it when they were doing the renovations.

I've only used it a few times myself," he added as he turned on the landing and headed down another short flight of stairs.

"Whatever for?" Christiana whispered, her free hand pressed against the walls as they made their quick descent.

"Midnight snacks," her husband admitted, just as he opened the door at the bottom of the stairs. He pushed aside the table that blocked the way.

Having quieted down as Emma carried her to the kitchens, Ariel was returned to her mother's arms when Emma had Christiana sit in the room's only chair—Mr. Tanner's wicker seat chair. Gregory lit another candle lamp and a torch. Locating a stock pot, Emma pumped water into it and set it on the stove. Although a small fire still burned, she added more wood and set the pot to boiling.

"We need a milk bottle or..." Emma struggled to think of another vessel that might suit their needs. "Something with a large bottom but an opening about this big," she described as she circled her thumbs and forefingers together and held them up. Nodding, Gregory disappeared from the kitchens but returned moments later with a crystal carafe from the butler's pantry.

"Oh, my," Emma said with a grin as she rinsed it out with water from the pump. "Nothing's too good for your wife."

"'Tis true," Gregory replied defensively, too tired to wonder if he should be offended by Emma's remark. After their discussion the night of Ariel's birth, he still wasn't sure of what she thought of him and his penchant for indulging his wife.

Dipping a ladle into the boiling water, Emma allowed just a few tablespoons into its bowl before transferring the steaming water into the carafe. Then she plunked the carafe into the water in the stock pot. "This should just take a few moments," she said as she turned back to Christiana. "Now we need something... sticky," she said as she looked around the kitchen.

"There's apple jelly here somewhere," Gregory commented quickly. "We had it at breakfast this morning."

Smiling, Emma started the search for the jar of jelly. "I can never understand how Mr. Tanner organizes his pantry," she complained as she studied the various jars on the pantry shelves.

"Here 'tis," Gregory said as he held up the jar.

"Oh, good. Now, Christiana, pull down your gown, and Gregory," she said as she noted he had the jelly jar opened, "You smear some jelly around her breast. Liberally," Emma ordered as she checked on the steaming water.

When she turned back around, she found Gregory and Christiana, who still had tears streaming down her face, staring at her.

"You want me to do *what?*" Gregory replied, a look of disgust on his face.

"Smear it on her," Emma repeated, her free hand motioning in circles. "Not on the nipple, of course. Just around the outside of it. And be gentle about it. She's in a great deal of pain. It just needs to provide an airtight seal," she added as if that was enough information to explain what she was trying to accomplish.

Gregory threw up his arms and smiled triumphantly. "Now I understand what it is you're trying to do!" He dug his finger into the jelly jar and placed a glob on Christiana's breast. Kneeling down on the floor, he regarded his wife. "I remember this from my science classes," he commented as he gently rubbed the jelly around Christiana's areola.

"Indeed?" Christiana whispered as she watched her husband's hand. Had she not been so uncomfortable, she might have enjoyed what he was doing with his sticky fingers.

"We're creating a vacuum," he stated happily.

"Is that what it is?" Emma asked as she helped herself to a finger full of the jelly and coated the top of the wine carafe. The water inside it was steaming.

"Indeed," Gregory replied with a nod. "We used one to vaporize aluminum onto a piece of ground glass to make a mirror for a telescope," he explained as he gently pushed the jelly around until he was sure there was an even coating surrounding the nipple.

"Indeed?" Christiana whispered again, her tears drying on

her face. Although quiet, Ariel was wide awake and seemed to be watching her father with great interest.

"Ready?" Emma asked as she checked on Gregory's progress.

"Yes," he said, his anticipation growing.

Her wet eyes wide with fright, Christiana straightened on the chair. She handed the baby to Gregory as Emma removed the carafe from the boiling water, poured out the little bit of water still in the carafe, and shoved the top of the carafe onto Christiana's jellied breast. The new mother jerked and let out a squeak of surprise as the seal took hold.

All three watched with fascination when, after only a few seconds, a stream of milk shot into the carafe.

"Fire away!" Gregory breathed in delight.

Both Christiana and Emma gave him withering stares. "If you'd like, we can pour this into one of those glass baby bottles you bought, and you can feed Ariel," Emma suggested to Gregory as they watched the contents of the carafe get higher. She had another thought of who might benefit from the milk, but thought better of mentioning Hannah just then.

"Indeed?" Gregory replied, already the doting father. "I think I would rather like that. Not all the time, of course," he added, suspicion creeping into his voice. "Those bottles are in here somewhere. I was told they would be good for water. Between feedings. Mr. Tanner said he would sterilize them for me." He stepped aside and went in search of the bottles.

Finally feeling relief, Christiana sighed and allowed a wan smile. When, at last her breast was emptied, Emma carefully twisted the carafe until air rushed into the bottle.

Gregory found the collection of bottles with their odd tops lying on a linen. He helped himself to one and returned to stand next to Emma. "Now what?" he asked, eagerly awaiting orders from Emma as he stood holding a bottle and a top.

"Well, in a few hours, Ariel should start to take that breast, and Christiana will be fine," she answered. "I'll pour this into that bottle for you," she offered as she straightened up and took it from him. "And you, sir, can clean up your wife."

Gregory did a double-take and stared at her. "How... what should I use... ?"

Emma rolled her eyes and whispered, "Might I recommend that you use your *tongue?*"

The normally unflappable Gregory Grandby was awestruck. "Oh. Of course," he replied, emboldened.

"Thank you, Emma," Christiana said as she allowed a smile. "I am so relieved you knew what to do."

Emma gave a nod and then filled the bottle. Although she hadn't spent that many Saturdays working at 'Mrs. Dawes' Home for Unwed Mothers', she had certainly learned a great deal about new mothers and babies.

Sealing the bottle with its nipple top, she gave it a shake before she took it to Gregory. "Good night, you two... three," she amended as she noticed Ariel sound asleep in her father's arms. "I'll see you at breakfast." With that, Emma turned to leave the kitchens by way of the regular door and found Thomas standing on the threshold. Wrapped in his woolen robe, he opened one side and pulled her into a hug.

"You must know that I absolutely adore you," he whispered as he held her.

Emma grinned. "I do," she replied in a whisper as she wrapped her arms around his waist and rested her head against his bare chest. "How long have you been standing here?"

Thomas grunted and kissed her forehead. "I arrived just as Gregory found the jelly," he whispered hoarsely. "I fear I shall never think of apple jelly the same way again," he added with a frown. "And it was my favorite."

The sounds of a throat being cleared had Thomas and Emma turning. Gregory stood regarding them as he carried Christiana in his arms. Christiana held Ariel in hers. On top of Ariel rested the baby bottle, its nipple having disappeared between her tiny lips. "I am taking my goddesses to bed now," he said as he marched past them. "That stairwell is a bit tight to use after a midnight snack," he added with an arched eyebrow aimed at Emma. "Good night, and thank you again, sister." He disappeared down the hall and up the west wing stairs.

"You're welcome," Emma sighed as she once again relaxed against Thomas. "I suppose I would have learned of Christiana's discomfort had I not gone into work today," she murmured.

"She could have told you when we returned from town this afternoon," Thomas countered.

Emma decided not to remind him that his sister had been asleep at the time. The thought of sleep had her asking, "Bedtime or tea time?" as she kissed his neck.

Thomas didn't answer right away but ran a hand down the side of her body and around her bottom. "That all depends, I suppose. Are you... *naked* under that dressing gown?" he whispered as he moved his hand up to her breast and cupped it, pressing his thumb against her hardening nipple.

"I am," she whispered between slight gasps as Thomas continued his gentle fondling. His other hand slipped beneath the satin and cupped her other breast, eliciting a much louder gasp from Emma. She was vaguely aware of the dressing gown's ties coming undone and the front of her robe falling away.

"Then 'tis jelly time," he answered with a mischievous grin. He stutter-stepped her back into the kitchen, managing to keep a hand on her bare breast while guiding her body with the other.

Once he was near enough, he grabbed the jar of apple jelly and then sat down on the chair. His robe fell open, revealing his own nakedness. With his free hand, he pulled a rather startled Emma down onto him, her legs having to spread apart to straddle his.

"You naughty boy," she whispered, well aware of his hardened manhood attempting to impale her.

"Guilty as charged," he replied, nibbling her neck and the line along one collarbone.

Emma used the balls of her feet to lift herself up and over his manhood, gently rubbing her wetness against its tip. She reveled in the sensation a moment, teasing him until he captured one of her nipples with his lips. His free arm wrapped around her waist and pulled her down so that he finally entered her. He shoved aside the edges of her gown as he continued to kiss a nipple, suckling it until it was hard and red. Scooping out some of the apple jelly, he rubbed it around the nipple and licked it off nearly as fast as he smeared it on.

Delightful skitters of pleasure danced beneath her skin and set off waves of pleasure through her entire torso. Emma had to bite her lip to keep from making too much noise. Thomas smeared the last of the jelly on her other nipple and bit it playfully before using his tongue to send her on another wave of pleasure.

Leaning back in the chair, Thomas moved his hands to her hips and pushed further into her. Arching her back in response, Emma gasped. He pushed into her again, his thrust more powerful, forcing her to grip his shoulders for support. On the next thrust, he allowed his release, burying his face into the space below her breasts to suppress his groans of pleasure.

Just as his climax abated, he leaned back and gazed up at Emma. She reached down and drew a finger gently along the base of his manhood. Thomas tried but failed to suppress the shout brought on by the renewed pleasure, burying his face into the top of her breast. When she cupped him with her fingers and gently lifted his sac, he jerked beneath her as he experienced the last of his release.

Emma giggled at the sensation of his open mouth against her skin, and she joyfully kissed his head and temples.

When he at last leaned back again, his breathing becoming more even, he whispered, "Promise me we can do that again sometime."

Emma lifted the empty jelly jar. "Well, I'm afraid we won't be able to tonight, but, yes, I promise," she nodded with a happy sigh. Carefully stepping onto the floor and pulling herself off of him, she reached for her gown and pulled him out of the chair. "Bedtime?" she suggested as she realized just how tired she'd become.

"Bedtime," Thomas replied, not sure he could even make it to the east wing and up the steps. As they made their way, he opened up one side of his robe and pulled her next to him, his arm draped around her waist. "However did you get to be such a good lover?"he asked in a whisper.

Emma turned to regard him with widened eyes, rather surprised by the question. "I learned everything I know from you," she replied quietly. "Well, and that book," she added with an arched brow. After a moment, she dared a glance in his direction. "Have you ever looked through it?"

Ah, yes. The book from India, Thomas remembered. A copy was on a top shelf somewhere in the library. Although he had never read the book—the text was written entirely in Sanskrit—he had certainly paged through it. Fully illustrated, it had been as instructive as it had been frightening when he last gave it a glance. "I have," he admitted. "When I was twelve, I think," he added with an arched brow.

Emma tittered as the two settled into bed. "I hope you've forgotten most of it," she whispered. "For there are some things I shall never agree to do in our marriage bed."

Thomas was about to ask but decided against it. She had already shocked him quite enough with what they had done, after all.

CHAPTER 46

POST PARTUM MELANCHOLY

Late April

When he was sure Thomas had left his office and was somewhere down in the warehouse, Todd Vandermeer sneaked into Thomas' office and appeared before Emma.

"Hullo," she said in surprise, not expecting a visit from the broker. From his strained features and bloodshot eyes, she realized he probably hadn't slept well in a long time. "Is the baby keeping you awake?"

Todd blinked. "I rather wish he were," he said in a quiet voice.

Emma's eyes widened. "What's happened?" she asked in alarm.

The broker shook his head. "William is fine. Growing like a weed and..." He paused. "Endearing himself to me at every opportunity." He sighed. "Is it supposed to be like this?"

Allowing a wan smile, Emma nodded. "If you mean he has you completely and irrevocably wrapped around his pinky, then yes," she replied with an arched brow.

"I wasn't referring to William."

Blinking, Emma quickly sobered. "What's wrong with Deborah?"

"I... I don't know. She won't answer my simplest queries as to her health. She won't allow me in her bedchamber, and when

I pay a visit just because I find I must at least give her a kiss good night, she's most... distant."

Emma waved to the other chair in her part of the office, an upholstered chair she sometimes used when taking tea in the mid afternoon. "Have you... invited her to your bed?" she asked carefully.

"Every night," he answered quickly. "I tell her of her beauty, and how much I adore her, and how appreciative I am of her giving me an heir, but it's as if she wants nothing to do with me," he whispered, his face taking on an expression of pain. "What's happened to my Deborah?"

Emma sighed and dared a glance at the clock. "How is she with William?"

It was Todd's turn to blink. "Happy. Doting. She's an excellent mother, but then I knew she would be," he claimed.

Well, at least she isn't suffering from the despondency some mothers do after childbirth, Emma considered. "I was about to take my luncheon. I'll ride up to Grace Park and pay her a visit," she offered as she moved to stand up.

"I'll escort you," Todd offered.

Emma regarded the broker for a moment and shook her head. "No, you won't. I'll have Master Billy join me," she replied. "She's more likely to tell me what's amiss if you're not there," she added when she paid witness to his look of surprise.

Or was that hurt?

"If you think that's best," Todd finally replied before giving her a leg and taking his leave of the office.

A few minutes later, Emma was on her way to Grace Park.

"Emma!" Deborah cried out in surprise as her best friend appeared on the threshold of the parlor.

"Good afternoon." Emma moved to join her friend. Held in Deborah's arms, William was busy availing himself of one of his mother's breasts, his noisy suckling bringing a grin to Emma's lips. "He seems like a happy baby," she remarked.

Deborah grinned. "Oh, he is. The very best baby I could hope for," she enthused. "I share my bed with him at night so I don't have to get up when he's hungry. He rarely cries," she went on before she stopped and stared at Emma. "What is it? You look as if—"

"As if your husband has paid me a visit and put voice to his concern over how distant you've become since William was born," Emma said in a quiet voice.

Deborah allowed a long sigh. "I have been rather distant with him," she admitted sadly. "I don't mean to be."

Frowning, Emma realized right then something was bothering her friend. "What is it? What has you sending him away?"

Instead of replying, Deborah unbuttoned the front of her nursing gown, exposing her now-flat belly. She spread the edges of the gown apart and pointed to a series of white lines on her abdomen.

"Oh, those?" Emma countered, having seen the odd skin discoloration on a few of the women at the Home for Unwed Mothers. "They're merely—"

"Stretch marks," Deborah murmured. "Aren't they awful?"

Emma frowned. "They're not awful," she replied quickly. "They're merely the evidence that you carried a child." Her eyes widened. "Are *they* the reason you've been keeping your husband at a distance?" she asked in alarm.

Deborah sighed. "I cannot believe he told you," she replied. William must have sensed her distress, for he let go of his hold on her nipple and began to fuss. Deborah rocked him for a time and then moved him to the other side.

"He's merely worried. He thinks something is wrong. That he has somehow offended you—"

"But he hasn't," Deborah said with a shake of her head. "I just cannot abide him seeing me like this. With these awful white lines—"

"Deborah!" Emma interrupted. "He's your husband. He loves you. He won't even *see* those tiny lines in the dark," she claimed.

Blinking back tears, Deborah ignored how William's face seemed to screw up in anticipation of a good cry. Emma reached over and took the babe from Deborah's arms, lifting the boy onto her shoulder. She began patting him on the back.

"I love him, I do," Deborah claimed as tears dripped down her cheeks. "But he likes it when we leave a candle lit." She sobbed. "He likes to... watch me," she managed to get out before another sob robbed her of breath. "To see me when I'm pleasured. What will he think when he sees how different I am? When he sees those awful marks?"

"I will be reminded that you are my tigress, of course," Todd announced from the threshold.

Emma and Deborah both gasped as they turned to stare at the extremely tall man who had been standing in the doorway for some time. He gave a bow before he made his way into the parlor, his eyes dark and his stride purposeful.

"I will be humbled that you bore me a worthy cub," he added as he stood before Deborah. "And I will be more determined than ever to make love to you in every possible way."

His wife stared up at him, her bare chest rising and falling as her quickened breaths gave away the excitement she felt. "You will?" she whispered.

Todd's answer was to reach down and lift his wife into his arms. He gave a nod to Emma. "Thank you," he mouthed before he carried Deborah out of the parlor and up the stairs.

A rather loud burp broke the silence in the parlor, and Emma was forced to allow a burble of laughter to escape. "Well, now that you feel better, I rather imagine you'll want to take a nap," she whispered, wondering if the boy had ever slept in the nursery.

William gazed at her with an expression that suggested he might disagree with her at any moment, but soon his eyelids grew heavy, and he fell asleep. She was about to take him to the nursery when Thomas appeared on the threshold. "Well, hullo," she whispered. "If you've come to see William, he's just fallen asleep," she added as she joined her husband.

Thomas regarded the sleeping babe for a moment before daring a glance at his wife. "Should I ask why you're here? Or is this something I'm just supposed to know?" he asked carefully.

Emma gave him a shake of her head. "My best friend was just having a bad day, is all, so I thought to spend my luncheon time here. But now her husband has come to make it all better." Her expression changed. "How did you know where to find me?"

Thomas gave her a quelling glance. "My caddie informed me where he had taken you, of course," he replied. "I've come to take his place as your escort."

Emma's eyes widened. "I didn't realize he had left," she said, about to say something to admonish Billy.

"He claimed you would be here for the rest of the *night*," Thomas added with an arched eyebrow. "Which made me think that perhaps we should simply spend the night at the townhouse."

Grinning, Emma leaned over and kissed her husband. "I adore you," she murmured.

Thomas grinned before turning his attention to William. "But not with him," he clarified.

Emma grinned. "To the nursery then," she replied.

They were back at the townhouse within fifteen minutes and enjoying an afternoon delight a few moments later.

CHAPTER 47

JEALOUS OF A BABY

Four months later

"Will you be coming with me to the office today?" Thomas asked as he found Emma in the library with Ariel cradled in one arm while she held a pen poised over a piece of ledger paper. Another ledger was spread out on the library table and hundreds of receipts were stacked neatly to one side.

She gave him a look of disappointment. "I would dearly love to join you, Thomas, but Christiana is sick again, and Gregory has already left for town, so I'm afraid I am the one to look after Ariel." The five-month old, now sleeping quite soundly in her aunt's arm, had started crawling the week before and required a good deal more attention.

Thomas bent down and kissed the sleeping Ariel on the head. Then he kissed Emma on the temple. "Is Christiania with child again?" he asked, a mixture of worry and annoyance lining his face.

Emma blinked. "She is not," she replied, surprised he would ask such a thing when Ariel was still nursing. "Her monthly courses haven't begun again."

Thomas managed a sigh of relief.

"Thomas, what's this about?" Emma asked as she moved to place the sleeping babe on one of the large sofas.

Thomas followed her so he stood in front of the other sofa,

regarding her as she tended to Ariel. "Jealousy, I suppose," he said quietly. At Emma's look of confusion, he added, "In fact, I admit I am rather jealous of Ariel when you are holding her," he stated as he reached out and started pulling the pins out of Emma's hair. At Emma's amused reaction to his admission, he added, "And I won't even begin to tell you what I thought when I saw you changing William's nappies at the Vandermeer's last Saturday."

About to capture one of his earlobes with her tongue and teeth, Emma's eyes widened. Despite an attempt to suppress her amusement, she giggled. "Indeed?" she whispered. "Oh, you must tell," she teased as she kissed his neck and began to unwind his cravat.

When Thomas had removed all the pins from her hair, he said, "When you were cleaning his bottom, you were touching his balls with your finger. I could see the little bastard grinning. And then, when you were leaning over him to kiss his forehead, the little bugger's cock was in your cleavage!"

Gasping in feigned shock, Emma lowered herself onto her knees in front of him and started to undo the buttons on his waistcoat. "It was not!" she replied with a grin of embarrassment, her cheeks turning bright pink.

"I know what I saw," Thomas countered as he took off his topcoat and waistcoat and allowed Emma to undo the buttons of his breeches.

"Well, then, I suppose I had better give you the same consideration," she said with a raised eyebrow.

Pulling down his breeches and drawers in one swift motion, Thomas lost his balance and fell onto the divan behind him. Left wearing only his shirt, with his breeches down around the tops of his boots, Thomas watched as Emma pulled her arms out of the sleeves of her gown and pushed the garment down around her waist. Still on her knees, she leaned forward, presenting her corseted décolletage.

"I cannot fit in there," Thomas protested happily. "I am far larger than William," he stated confidently.

"Indeed," Emma agreed, rolling her eyes in amusement. She

turned sideways so that he could reach the bowtie that held the back of her corset secure. He pulled the bow and the ties began loosening, allowing her breasts to spread apart. Turning back around, Emma leaned forward as Thomas pushed toward her. His hardened manhood slipped down between her breasts and behind the busk of the corset, which had him emitting an audible groan. He slid his hands down the sides of her breasts and pressed them together, pinning his cock between the white orbs and sending delightful frissons through her body as he used his thumbs to brush the sides and tops of her hardened nipples.

"I do believe the little bugger had the right idea," Thomas whispered as Emma raised and lowered herself slightly, feeling his wet manhood thrusting between and against her breasts. As the rhythm of his thrusts increased, his breaths came in shallow gasps, and Emma raised her eyes to watch him. She smiled slyly as Thomas sat up straighter and allowed his release, a deep growl finally escaping his throat as his head fell back.

"And I promise never to change his nappies again," Emma said between gasps for air, breaking into a fit of giggles as she tumbled to the floor and lay on her back, her dress still down around her waist and her breasts barely contained in her corset. Her long hair splayed out around her head in a mass of golden waves.

Thomas fell back into the sofa to catch his breath and laughed. "Actually, I rather like the idea that for every time you do, we get to do this," he countered between labored breaths.

Still giggling, Emma nodded. "Agreed, but only if I can put pillows under my knees."

"Done," Thomas replied, leaning over the edge of the sofa to admire his wife. "You realize, of course, that we are never going to be able to look at William again without thinking of this," he commented with a grin. "For the rest of the little bugger's life."

"Indeed," Emma replied as she smiled, rather content and happy that she had restored her husband's good humor.

"You are a beautiful sight, Mrs. Wellingham," he stated as he reached for her hand. She took it, and he helped to pull her up and onto the sofa next to him. Cradling her in his arms, he kissed her neck and the tops of her breasts and finally her mouth, his lips pausing over each as he did so. "I love you, Emma," he murmured and continued to hold her for several minutes. "I suppose I had better put some clothes on, or we'll scandalize Humphrey when he comes with your breakfast."

Emma giggled as she pulled her gown back into place. "Aren't you going to have any?" When she noticed how his gaze drifted to her bosom, she added, "Breakfast, I mean."

He gave the question some thought. "I am," he replied, his mind obviously still in a muddle. "And when I return from town, I should like to join you for tea and..." He allowed the sentence to trail off. "Perhaps we can take dinner in our bedchamber tonight?" he murmured hopefully.

Managing a shrug despite how she was being held, Emma regarded her husband for a moment. "Gregory will be home by then, surely. He went to pay a call on the twins," she whispered. "Oh, and his mother, I suppose."

Thomas frowned. "Is everything all right?"

Emma shrugged again. "He seemed fine when he left."

"So Hannah is doing well?" For some reason—perhaps because he had held the babe for so long the first night of her life—Thomas had taken a shine to the tiny baby and always seemed more concerned for her welfare than he did for Ariel's. Although Henry was thriving, Hannah was far smaller in size and not yet crawling.

"I am quite sure I would have heard something if she was not," Emma countered.

Thomas sighed. "Will you help with my cravat?" he asked as he moved to stand up. Emma twisted off of his lap and landed next to him on the sofa. "Of course. But you had better hurry. I just heard the kitchen door," she whispered, deciding her hair would have to remain down for the time being. Her hairpins were scattered all over the Aubusson carpet.

Thomas redressed as fast as he could manage, although several buttons remained undone as Humphrey entered the library carrying a salver loaded with dishes.

"Good morning, Humphrey. You can just leave it on the

table. I'll see to serving Mr. Wellingham," Emma said as she stood between the butler and Thomas.

"Very good, milady," Humphrey replied before he set down the tray and took his leave of the library.

Once he was gone, Thomas murmured, "I don't suppose he knew what we'd been doing."

Emma glanced down at the front of her gown, still askew from their earlier play, and then back at Thomas, a lock of her golden hair falling down over one eye. "Only if he's blind and lacks imagination," she replied with an arched brow. After another moment, she added, "You're blushing."

"Are you hungry?" Thomas asked, rising from the sofa to finish buttoning his waistcoat before kissing her temple.

Emma angled her head. "I was starving," she whispered, curious if his question had anything to do with food. "As a result, now I need to change my corset."

"Well, I am hungry. Let's have some breakfast, shall we?"

Daring a glance at the still-sleeping babe on the other sofa, Emma nodded. "And dessert later tonight?"

Thomas blinked and waggled his eyebrows. "I rather like the way you think, you wicked woman."

CHAPTER 48

A MAN ON A MISSION

When Thomas returned to Woodscastle later that afternoon, he found Emma in the parlor. On the floor, in fact, entertaining Ariel.

"Did Gregory ever get home?" he asked as he entered the room.

"Oh, it's you!" Emma replied in surprise. "When I heard the horse outside, I thought it was him," she said as she allowed Thomas to help her to her feet. Ariel remained sitting on the thick carpet, her huge grin at her uncle's appearance putting two bottom teeth on display. "I do hope nothing is amiss. He's been gone since before eight this morning," she whispered.

Thomas was about to accuse his brother-in-law of spending time at his club or in the company of his uncle, Sir William, at the Bank of England, but the man rarely spent an entire day in town. "How is Christiana?" he asked as he bent over and picked up his niece. The girl giggled as he tossed her up and over his head. "She hasn't just been fed recently, I hope," he murmured as she ended up with her bottom in the crook of his arm and her head resting on his shoulder.

Emma suppressed a giggle. "I was hoping to take her to her mother just as you arrived. I didn't realize how late it is," she added as she dared a glance at the mantel clock. "How was it at the office?" she asked as she moved to the door.

Thomas kissed Ariel's forehead and turned to join Emma. "Sad. Lonely. Boring as hell—"

"Language, darling," Emma whispered.

"—But profitable."

Emma arched an eyebrow. "I take it Mr. Cunningham gave you the numbers for last month," she said as they made their way to the west stairs.

"You say that as if you already knew what they were," Thomas accused.

"That's because I did," she replied. "What kind of lead accomptant would I be if I didn't know the state of the company at all times?"

Thomas blinked. "Well, you might have shared your good news with me so I didn't look so damned—"

"Language, darling."

"—Darned surprised and ignorant in front of my second lead accomptant," he complained. "My God—"

"Language, darling."

"—*Goodness*, Todd has made us more profitable so far this year than we were for all of last year," he remarked.

"I know," Emma replied, her self-satisfied grin giving way to an outright smile.

"I've a mind to punish you for your impertinence," Thomas warned as they reached the top of the west stairs.

"I'm rather counting on it."

Thomas blinked. "Oh, you wicked—"

"*Language*, darling."

Thomas clamped his mouth shut, mostly to hide his amusement, as they made their way to the mistress suite.

"Mama," Ariel said as they approached Christiana's bedchamber.

"Very good, Ariel," Thomas replied just before he knocked on the door. "She speaks rather well for one so young." At a murmured, 'come in', he opened the door and stepped into his sister's bedchamber. He blinked and then turned to Emma. He was about to say something before he turned back again. "You rake!"

"Language, darling," Emma scolded him, although her curiosity had her pushing the door open wider. There, in Christiana's bed with Christiana, was Gregory. Although he appeared to have been sleeping only the moment before, he was awake now, and it was quite apparent he was naked beneath the covers.

"Afternoon," he said sleepily. "Somethin' wrong?" he asked when he noticed Thomas was scowling at him.

"How long have you been home?" Thomas asked as he moved to place Ariel on the bed. The baby was immediately in motion, crawling until she ended up between her mother and father.

"Dada," she announced happily.

"Dada has some explaining to do," Thomas replied.

Gregory sighed. "I arrived while Emma and Ariel were having luncheon in the dining room," he said with a shrug. "So I took the opportunity to spend some time with my beautiful wife."

Thomas crossed his arms over his chest and regarded his brother-in-law with a frown. "Denying me the opportunity to spend time with my own," he countered, annoyance evident in his voice. "No more, brother. 'Tis past time you hired a nanny."

"Already done," Gregory replied as he sat up in the bed, forgetting he was naked beneath the covers. When the counterpane slid down the front of his torso, exposing his rather generous chest and bare shoulders, Christiana gave a squeak. She had to reach over and quickly lift up a corner of the bed linens in an attempt to hide him.

Gregory ignored her efforts. "'Tis the reason I went to town this morning. Mrs. Tompkins will start work on the morrow and live in one of the servants' quarters upstairs."

The fight going out of him in an instant, Thomas regarded his sister for a moment. "Feeling better, are you?"

Christiana sighed as she lifted Ariel into her arms. "I am. Thank you for asking."

"How are the twins?" Emma asked, hoping Thomas wasn't too terribly angry with Gregory. She rather liked spending a day at Woodscastle once in a while.

At the question, Gregory seemed to slump down, one hand moving to the back of his head as if to scratch the nape of his neck. "Henry is... great. Large and in charge in that household, I would say. Happy and spoiled. Crawling everywhere, including down the stairs."

Emma gasped. "Does no one go with him to be sure he doesn't tumble down?" she asked in alarm.

Gregory grinned. "Oh, there's always someone with him," he assured her. He sobered. "But Hannah..." He shook his head. "She's still so small. She wheezes in her sleep. Loves watching her brother play, but since she can't yet crawl, she can't join him on his adventures..." He shook his head again. "I rather doubt she'll see her first birthday."

The words were like a dead weight dropping into Emma's stomach. "No," she whispered. "Has Dr. Talbot seen to her?"

"He pays a visit nearly every day. Mr. Simpson has even taken her to his office if the man cannot make the house call," Gregory explained in defense of his stepfather.

Near tears, Emma excused herself and hurried down the stairs and through the hall. She was nearly to the master suite in the east wing when Thomas caught up to her.

"We'll pay a call on them tomorrow," he said as he pulled Emma into his arms. "Perhaps—"

"Promise?" Emma murmured into his topcoat, the tears spilling forth onto the superfine.

"I do," Thomas replied. He held her for a few minutes more before pulling away. "Then you can see for yourself. Come. I realized I left this morning without helping you with your corset." At Emma's furrowed brows, he raised his own and pulled the front of her bodice forward with a crooked finger. "As I recall, I was a bit naughty before I took my leave of you," he hinted.

Emma allowed a wan smile. "Oh, that," she managed.

Thomas allowed a grunt. "That 'oh, that' made my day far more tolerable than it would have been otherwise," he said, giving her a kiss on the forehead. Noticing Mrs. Werthers down the hall, he called out, "Mrs. Wellingham would like a bath, Mrs. Werthers. Could you please see to the water?"

The housekeeper immediately ceased her dusting, bobbed a curtsy, and said, "Right away, Mr. Wellingham."

Noting Emma's arched brow and hearing her whispered, "I do?", Thomas gave a shrug. "If I had said I wanted to take a bath, she wouldn't have been nearly as quick about it," he reasoned.

Emma shook her head. Well, the servants did seem to like her better.

CHAPTER 49

AFTERNOON DELIGHT

"Now, where were we this morning when we were so rudely interrupted by breakfast?" Thomas asked as he led his wife into their bedchamber. He unbuttoned his topcoat and shrugged out of it.

Emma gave him a quelling glance. "With your breeches down around your ankles and your..." She stopped when Thomas whirled around to regard her with an arched brow. His fingers were already deftly undoing the buttons down the front of his waistcoat.

"Exactly. And I never had the chance to return the favor," he stated as he tossed off the waistcoat and moved to stand behind her.

Despite her recent bout of tears, Emma couldn't help the frisson that shot through her body just then. About to ask what he was doing, she instead stood still when she realized he was undoing the buttons down the back of her gown. No sooner did he have them undone when he once again pulled the ties of her corset. She could feel the garment loosening as his fingers plucked at the crossed strings, one after the other.

"Do you enjoy playing lady's maid?" she asked in a whisper.

"Oh, I do," Thomas murmured. He bent down as he pulled her gown down to the floor and then got to work on rolling down her stockings.

"Perhaps you could hand me my dressing gown. Someone will be coming with water at any moment." She didn't have to pull it on—Thomas had the sleeves held out for her only a second later and quickly wrapped it about her middle.

"I do so enjoy doing your bidding, my lady," he said as he knelt once again and removed her slippers and stockings.

"If only I'd known," Emma responded with a grin. "I might have bid you to stay home today."

Thomas gazed up at her and blinked. "I would have," he said in a whisper, his eyes glazing over as his expression darkened. "Maybe not on your first request, but probably on your second. Most certainly on your third," he amended quickly as he got to his feet. He was about to kiss her when he felt footsteps through the flooring. Instead, he took a seat on the bench at the end of the bed and removed his boots.

There was a knock at the door and Mr. Tanner appeared with two pails of steaming water. Behind him, Mrs. Werthers carried another. The two disappeared into the bathing chamber for a moment and then reappeared, their pails emptied. They took their leave of the room with a bow and a curtsy.

Emma moved from behind the door where she'd been hiding when the servants arrived. "I need to clean up, and then I will be right out," she said in a seductive whisper.

Although he gave her a nod, he followed her to the bath. "I will help," he said as he stood in front of her and lifted and lowered her so that she was left standing in the tub.

"Whatever are you doing?" Emma asked happily as he slid the palms of his hands down the front of her dressing gown, finally pushing the edges open. He kissed her nipples, one after the other.

"I am helping," he said as he removed her gown. He slowly plucked at all the corset ties until he could remove the offending garment from around her torso.

Giving her a nod to indicate she should take a seat in the tub, Emma swallowed and watched him with suspicion as she did so She wondered what had him so aroused. So determined to seduce her.

Taking a linen from the stack next to the tub, Thomas knelt down and dipped it into the hot water and then rubbed it on a bar of milled soap. The scents of rose and lemon drifted in the damp air surrounding the tub.

Very gently, he wiped down the front of Emma's body, spending as much time kissing her as he did cleaning her. He reached over and pulled a few pins from her hair, his brow arching when it fell from the top of her head. "Will you leave your hair down for the rest of the day?" he asked, stroking a finger down the side of her body.

Emma arched her back at the ticklish sensation. "I will do whatever you wish," she answered in a murmur.

"Even if I want you to come to bed with me for the rest of the afternoon? Maybe the entire night?"

Emma allowed a demure smile and wrapped her arms around his neck. "Is that all you want?" she asked as she stroked her fingernails down his back. She was tempted to pull him into the tub with her, but it was far smaller than the one in the Simpson bathing chamber, and Thomas seemed more interested in what was to come in the bedchamber. In the bed.

"Very much," he replied, kissing her deeply. Emma slowly leaned back in the tub, forcing Thomas lower to keep her lips captured with his. He soon moved his lips down her jaw, along her neck, over her collarbones, stopping occasionally to nibble and nip at her heated skin.

Emma arched her back as his lips took purchase on a hardened nipple, whimpering when he let go to quickly capture the other one. Whimpering again when a frisson shot through her body, she allowed her head to drop back. Reaching over his back, she gripped the fabric of his shirt until she could pull it over his head and off of his arms. When he finally let go of her nipple, she removed the shirt completely.

Her eyelids lowered as she drew the edge of a fingernail down the front of his chest. She took delight in hearing his slight inhalations of breath, in paying witness to how his barely contained lust was about to overpower him. About to overpower her.

"As much as I know you enjoy a bath, I fear we must end this one right now," he whispered, his eyes darkening as he put voice to the warning. He was up on his feet and leaning over the tub to help her out in one smooth movement.

Emma stepped out and into the linen he held for her. Pressing the front of her body against her husband, she wasn't at all surprised to discover his manhood was hard and ready to take her. Shivering when he removed the linen from her body, she was about to use her arms to cover her breasts when Thomas lifted her into his arms and took her to the bed. When she made to remove the counterpane from beneath her, Thomas said, "Leave it."

Emma leaned back on her bent arms, wondering what he might do first. Her entire body seemed to throb with anticipation, although she couldn't understand her heightened response to him. They enjoyed the marriage bed nearly every night, although they rarely engaged in lengthy foreplay.

Shedding his breeches and smalls, Thomas stood naked before the bed and regarded his wife for a moment. When he didn't move to cover her body with his own, Emma arched an eyebrow. "We're not going to have intercourse right now, are we?" she asked in a breathy whisper.

Thomas shook his head as he climbed onto the end of the bed. "As I said earlier, I am going to return the favor you granted me earlier." Crawling towards her on his hands and knees, he took great satisfaction in watching as Emma settled back onto the bed and slowly opened herself to him. He took even greater satisfaction in hearing her slight inhalations of breaths, in hearing her whimpers and moans and pleas as his tongue and lips teased and tasted her. The greatest satisfaction, though, was hearing her demand that he take her. Take her right then and there.

He had no intention of denying her anything.

CHAPTER 50

GOING UNDERCOVER

Mid-September, 1803

Demands at work had kept Emma and Thomas at Wellingham Imports later than usual. They rarely arrived home before six and were only home for afternoon tea on the Sundays. With Emma away so much, Mrs. Tompkins, the nanny, saw to Ariel. And when he informed Mrs. Werthers—or rather, the future Mrs. Humphrey—that another housekeeper had been hired to handle the west wing, the news thrilled the aging woman to the point that she nearly cried when Gregory gave her the news.

On one quiet Sunday, with Thomas in the back chopping wood and Ariel napping, Emma sought out Gregory and found him in his study writing a letter. When she determined he had finished, she approached him and stood at his desk until he looked up in surprise and acknowledged her.

"What is it?" he asked as he noticed her look of consternation.

"Might I take a moment of your time to request a favor?" Emma asked, hoping he would agree to a talk.

Gregory regarded her for a moment before motioning her to sit in a nearby chair. "Of course. What is it?" His brows furrowed as he stood from his desk and moved to sit with her on the room's new leather sofa.

"I was wondering if you might know how one would acquire a... a *microscope*, I believe they are called," she whispered, glancing nervously at the study door to be sure no one else was about to come into the room.

Raising his eyebrows, Gregory sat up straight and considered her question. "I... I don't know exactly, but I'm quite sure I can find one," he replied with a shrug. He was tempted to ask why she wouldn't have Thomas find one for her—certainly an importer would know from where such scientific instruments could be procured—but curiosity had him curious as to her motives. "Why ever do you require one, may I ask?"

Emma bit her lip and took a deep breath.

"Is this about Thomas?" Gregory asked quietly. "About his... sterility, perhaps?"

Emma gasped as she regarded her brother-in-law, her mouth forming an 'o'. "You *know?*" she whispered, surprised that Thomas would admit such a thing, even to his best friend.

"Well, yes," Gregory hedged. "I'm rather sorry. He... he told me, although it was only after a few too many drinks, I believe," Gregory replied as he scratched the side of his face. "On the one hand, he seemed... upset about the situation, but on the other hand, he seemed relieved. I don't think he considered himself a family man at the time, at least," he added quickly as he watched Emma's reaction.

"I am aware of his mixed feelings on the subject," Emma admitted with a nod. "And I shared them, actually," she added as she bit her lip. "But then Deborah... and your mother, and Christiana—"

"So, why would you require a microscope?" Gregory asked.

Emma swallowed hard and rested her elbows on her knees. "You cannot say anything to Christiana or to Thomas," she whispered fiercely. "You must promise me you won't divulge this conversation to anyone," she insisted in hushed tones.

Gregory nodded, his brows furrowing again. "I promise to keep your secret," he agreed.

Glancing at the doorway again, Emma leaned closer to Gregory. "I... I am either with child, or I have become...

barren," she said quietly. "And since I have never been with another man, then it can only be that either I am barren or that Thomas is no longer... sterile. But I must have the means to prove it—"

"Oh, my God," Gregory interrupted her, shaking his head from side to side. "You cannot think that he would accuse you of being with another man?" he asked, shocked at her supposition. "When would you ever have the time for an *affaire?* You two are together almost all the time, for God's sake," he whispered, continuing to shake his head in disbelief.

Tears welled up in Emma's eyes, and she struggled to keep them from spilling over. "I must know, Gregory. Before he realizes that I have not had my monthly courses for over two months," she insisted, the tears now flowing freely down her cheeks.

Sighing loudly, Gregory considered the situation. "I will endeavor to find such an instrument for you, Emma. But how do I... how do I explain why I would purchase such an unusual item?" he asked as he pursed his lips.

Shrugging, Emma replied, "You have always had an interest in the natural sciences. Perhaps you can explain it as a... as a teaching tool for the children?" she suggested. "Or a... novelty for your own scientific interests?"

Gregory grinned at that. "It would be rather interesting to own such a device," he considered. "I do believe you have a rather novel idea, sister," he said as he realized he rather liked the idea of owning a microscope. "I will go to town on the morrow and make inquiries," he promised. "And Emma," he added as he allowed a small smile. "May I be the first to congratulate you?"

Emma sighed and gave a shrug in return. "If you insist," she replied. She still wasn't sure she would welcome impending motherhood.

But the alternative was just as frightening.

CHAPTER 51

A RATHER DAINTY
SURVIVOR

The next day

As was his custom on most mornings, James Simpson finally left his wife's bed to do what had become his second favorite activity in life—spending time with his children. His first was pleasuring his wife, of course, a task he found seemed more welcome in the mornings these days.

Fresh from a good night's sleep and a round of nursing the twins whilst enjoying a cup of chocolate, Sophia had looked rather radiant that morning. With her blonde locks down past her shoulders, the creamy white skin left bare from her having lowered her nightrail, she appeared years younger than her three-and-forty years.

"Happy birthday," James had whispered after the nurse and a maid took the babies back to the nursery.

"Oh, it's not really, is it?" Sophia countered, her eyes losing focus for a moment.

"I will not allow you to deny it, for otherwise how am I to explain my rapid ascension to fifty?" he replied in a teasing voice. He gave her a kiss on the cheek. "I have something for you, of course," he started to say, and when he saw her impish grin and the way her cheeks pinked up, he added, "Besides that." He reached over to the nightstand and pulled a tiny box from the top drawer. Covered in blue velvet and topped with a satin bow, the box could only hold one piece of jewelry.

"Oh, James," Sophia breathed as she removed the lid to reveal a ring. Two diamonds were mounted side-by-side and set in yellow gold. Tiny filaments of gold surrounded the diamonds.

"For having given me twins," he said quietly. "And for believing in Hannah's survival."

Sophia regarded her husband with a wan smile as he removed the ring from its velvet perch and slid it on one of her fingers. "She's still so tiny," she murmured. "But she's made it this long. As long as she doesn't come down with some awful disease, she will grow up to be a truly beautiful young lady," she said in a whisper.

James nodded. "Just like you," he agreed before he kissed her again. He made love to her then, slowly, carefully, until her soft mewling and insistent pleas required he speed things up. The sound of her release was swallowed up in his deep kiss, and his own had him burying his face in the space between her neck and shoulder lest he be heard by everyone else in the household.

Now that he was dressed and sitting cross-legged on the floor of the nursery, James allowed a grin of satisfaction as he regarded his children. His oldest, still dressed in a gown suitable for a babe his age, was quite adept at making a mess of the nursery. Toys were scattered about the Aubusson carpeting, at least those that Henry wasn't trying to stuff into his mouth. When he was displeased, he made sure everyone around him was well aware of it.

Hannah, on the other hand, was garbed in a short dress her mother had found whilst shopping in The Strand. Layers of soft, white lace made her appear as if she had been baked into the middle of a layer cake covered in sugar frosting and topped with a satin bow. Tiny white booties in the same soft lace covered her feet. The girl rarely fussed and seemed satisfied playing with rattles and small pillows.

Although Henry had been crawling for well over a month, Hannah merely watched him from where she sat in the middle of the nursery floor, her miniature brows furrowed and her eyes wide, as if she were studying how he managed such a feat. She was still watching her brother when Sophia appeared on the threshold. Wearing a day gown in yellow muslin sprigged with tiny blossoms, her hair gathered into a large bun atop her head, Sophia allowed a brilliant smile as she watched her family.

"Mama," Hannah said as a grin replaced her frown.

James and Henry both turned their attention to Sophia. "Ah, here's your mother," James said, as if Sophia had been missing from the house. "Now you two must be on your very best behavior because it's your mother's birthday," he warned with an arched brow. He managed to get up from the floor to give his wife a bow and to kiss the back of her hand. He led her to a rocking chair in one corner. "Is it time for breakfast?" he asked.

"In a moment," Sophia replied as she settled into the rocker. "I thought I would pay a call whilst they were both still clean," she added, giving her son an arched brow. "He's going to play with tadpoles and such, isn't he?" she asked with some distaste, her gaze going back up to her husband.

James blinked. "Well, not around here," he countered. "Oh, I suppose he will when we spend time at Cherrywood," he added, excitement in his voice. "The pond there is full of them."

When Sophia felt a tug on her skirts, she looked down to find Hannah with her arms lifted above her head. Sophia reached down and lifted the girl onto her lap, and Hannah immediately nestled into her mother's arms. "How is my dainty little daughter?"

Furrowing his brows, James looked over to where Hannah had been sitting when Sophia entered the room and then turned his attention back to her. He looked over to where Henry was busy trying to take apart a wooden toy and glanced back at Sophia.

"What is it?" she asked, noting how confused James appeared just then.

"How... ?" He pointed to Hannah.

"Darling, it's rather impolite to point at your daughter," Sophia admonished him.

James ignored the comment. He pointed back to where Hannah had been sitting on the nursery floor. "How did she get from there to you?" he asked, obviously flustered. His gaze settled on his daughter, who looked up at him with a huge grin on her face. Her fists captured some of the flounce that surrounded her body and she dipped her head, making it appear as if she was curtsying from where she was sitting.

Sophia giggled. "Why, I do believe she scooted here, my darling," she replied.

"Scooted?" James repeated, his brows furrowed so they joined together in the middle.

"On her bottom."

"On her bottom?" he repeated, sounding ever so much like a parrot.

It was Hannah's turn to giggle, the musical sound soon joined by Henry's giggle. Dipping her head to one side, Sophia regarded her husband with a shake of her head. "She's a dainty little girl, darling. She's not about to scuff her knees when she can get to where she needs to go on her bottom," she explained.

Hannah watched her mother as the woman made the comment, one of her own brows arching up as if to copy the expression.

Blinking in disbelief, James chuckled. "Like mother, like daughter," he murmured. "I suppose you were about to tell me that's how you got about when you were that age."

Sophia shrugged. "I've really no idea. I don't remember that far back. It was nearly three-and-forty years ago, after all."

James turned to his son, who was in the process of attempting to eat a rather large wooden block. "And here I thought you were the more advanced one," he lightly admonished his son.

Not about to remind him that girls matured faster than boys, Sophia handed him their daughter and stood up. "On that note, let's retire to my favorite room and have some breakfast, shall we?"

CHAPTER 52

MICROSCOPIC SIGHTINGS

A month later

The arrival of anything in a crate was always cause for excitement at Woodscastle. In the past, it meant new furnishings or accessories for the recently renovated east wing or an elaborate toy for Ariel.

The wooden crate that rested on a table in the library had just been delivered in the back of a dray cart. Gregory had managed to pry open the lid and was removing the straw-like padding from around his recent acquisition when his wife joined him.

"Whatever is it?" Christiana asked as Gregory proudly pulled the instrument out of its protective packaging. He set the small crate to one side and removed the bits of shredded straw and paper that clung to the sides of the object.

"This, my dear, is a microscope," he announced as he peered through a hole in the top and looked straight down. "Somewhere, there should be small glass slides," he muttered as he turned his attention back to the crate and rummaged around inside. "Ah! Here," he said excitedly as he pulled out a package and began undoing the wrapping.

"What is this for?" Christiana asked as she looked through the hole she had seen Gregory look through. Not seeing anything but a blurry image, she stepped back so that Ariel's groping hands couldn't reach the instrument.

"It allows you to look at very small things and see them in fine detail," Gregory explained as he held a rectangular glass slide up to the window. Picking a piece of lint off of his vest, he carefully placed it on the slide and then put another slide on top of it, sealing the lint between the two slides. Placing it under the tube and securing it in place with two movable arms attached to the base of the instrument, he positioned his eye over the tube and began turning a geared knob on the tube. "Amazing," he breathed as he stood up and indicated that Christiana should take a look.

Handing the baby to Gregory, she leaned over and looked through the lens. Startled at what she saw, she let out a small shriek and jumped back and into Gregory, who wrapped an arm around her waist and laughed.

"What did you see?" he asked as he leaned over and looked again. His reaction was nearly the same, but he gingerly approached the instrument and noticed the source of the frightening sight. A gnat had dropped onto the slide and was skittering across it. "This is capital!" he exclaimed as he watched the bug through the microscope, careful to keep Ariel's busy fist from hitting it.

"What is it?" Christiana asked, not sure she wanted to know.

"A gnat!" he said proudly, finally pulling away so that she could take his place.

Christiana eyed him doubtfully and peered through the tube again. "Eew!" she said as she forced herself to watch the magnified movement of the insect. Once she recovered from her initial revulsion, she continued to watch the bug with more interest. "Are those the *eyes?*" she asked, awestruck.

"Let me see," Gregory insisted as Christiana stepped aside and let him take her place. "Indeed," he said. "What an odd shape," he whispered, absently giving Ariel back to Christiana. Offering a forefinger for the baby to grab onto, Christiana gave her a quick kiss when she did so. The toddler grinned, her two front teeth gleaming. At the sound of horses, though, Ariel's attention turned to the windows and she pointed. "Orse!" she cried out excitedly.

Christiana looked out the window to see Thomas and Emma dismount and give their reins to Mr. Larsen, who had run out to meet them. They were having an animated discussion, and when Christiana heard Humphrey open the front door, their conversation continued over in the vestibule.

"Have you asked him recently?" Emma was saying as she removed her riding cloak. "He may be waiting for you to ask him."

"No, not since... not since he's been working there," Thomas answered. Their voices got louder as they approached the library.

"I should probably not say this," Emma mentioned in a quiet voice, "But Deborah said he is less pleased with his work these days. She doesn't know if something has changed or if Todd is just... bored, but she feels it would be good for him to travel. And soon," she added as they headed down the corridor to the library. "He used to travel all the time for the John Company," she added. "And since he is experienced in traveling, and since you do not wish to make the trips to the Continent, it only makes sense that he be the one to go."

Thomas thought for a moment. "And Deborah won't mind if he is gone for a fortnight now and then?"

Emma considered the question. "Not if she's with him," she answered with a gleam in her eye.

He sighed audibly while he rolled his eyes at his wife's logic. "Then I will speak with him on the morrow," Thomas countered as he and Emma entered the library. They both stopped short when they took in the sight of Gregory and his family standing next to the microscope.

"Good heavens, is that what I think it is?" Thomas asked as he approached.

"'Tis a microscope," Christiana replied as she reached up to kiss her brother on the cheek. Ariel's fist pounded on her uncle's shoulder and Thomas took it absently.

"Indeed?" Thomas answered, his interest piqued.

Emma reached over for Ariel, who had let go of her mother in favor of her aunt's arms. "What is it for?" she asked as she walked around to the other side of the library table and studied the instrument.

"It allows you to look at very small things and see them in very great detail," Gregory explained again, glad he would not have to explain it again now that they were all in the library. "I bought it for me, of course," he added. "But I'm hoping our children will take an interest in the sciences. I must admit, I think I will get more enjoyment out of it than they will for a few years at least."

Thomas raised an eyebrow and glanced over at Emma. "Well, as long as you don't allow your kids to experiment with gunpowder....," he said with a wry grin.

"Oh, dear," Emma whispered, looking from Gregory to Thomas and back. "Which one of you did that?" she asked in a louder voice.

"He did," they both said in unison as they pointed to one another, and then turned to look at each other in amusement.

Christiana stared open-mouthed at her husband and brother. "And what did you destroy in the process?" she asked, mortified.

"He launched a glass bottle into the sky," Thomas said as he indicated Gregory. "The thing flew up at least thirty feet."

"After he blew up the dog house," Gregory accused as he nodded in Thomas' direction. At Emma's surprised gasp, he added, "Well, the dog wasn't in it. We were supposed to be dismantling it to build a new one," he explained with a shrug.

"The explosion just sort of hurried the project along," Thomas added with a wave of his hand, his expression showing no humor and certainly no sign of guilt.

Christiana stared at the two men. "Oh!" And with that, she hurried out of the room.

Gregory rolled his eyes and excused himself as he hurried to follow his wife. As he passed Emma, he brushed his hand against the hand that wasn't holding onto Ariel's. Her fingers felt the small parcel he held for her, and she took it, carefully hiding it in her palm.

With her parents taking their leave of the library, Ariel begged to be let down and crawled out of the room after them. "Bye-bye," she waved, not giving her aunt and uncle another glance.

Emma watched her niece take her leave and smiled broadly. When she turned to face Thomas, she shook her head. "I do not think Christiana was very happy to learn of your experiments," she said as she wrapped her arms around his waist and hugged him.

"I'm quite sure I mentioned that incident to her in the past," Thomas replied as he grinned and returned Emma's hug. "Are you all right?" he asked in a quiet voice, kissing her temple.

"Mmm," Emma murmured as she buried her face in the small of his shoulder. "I am just a bit tired is all," she admitted. "Perhaps I'll take a nap before dinner."

Thomas kissed her temple again. "All right. In the meantime, I am going to write a letter to Mr. Vandermeer," he said with a nod. "How much more can we afford to pay him, do you suppose?

Emma considered the situation. "If we offer too little, he may be offended. But I still have no idea how much he was paid at East India," she replied as she continued calculations in her head. "I remember Deborah once implied that he could have left his position at the John Company if they moved to a smaller house, so he must have some income from somewhere else," she reasoned. "Investments, perhaps?"

Thomas nodded. "He has investments in many of the same ventures as Gregory," he said as he pursed his lips. "On a smaller scale, of course."

Biting her lip, Emma took a deep breath. "What about a raise to sixteen-hundred pounds plus some kind of commission on the amount of business he manages on the Continent?" she suggested.

Thomas visibly winced. "Can we afford that?" he asked, his brows furrowing.

Smiling, Emma leaned back in his arms. "Yes. In fact, you can go as high as two-thousand if you think it necessary, but it would be a poor example to set for yourself."

Furrowing his brows, Thomas replied, "Whatever do you mean?" he asked, his expression turning to one of worry.

"I pay you seventeen-hundred-and-fifty a year," Emma replied, surprised he didn't seem to know his own salary.

Startled, Thomas released his hold on Emma and stepped back. "You do? Since when?" he asked, giving her a look of disbelief.

"Well, since I started doing the payroll. Right after I married you," she replied with an arched brow. "Your articles of incorporation say that you are entitled to a compensation commensurate with the profit from the company. So, that is how I determine how much to pay you, as well as all the employee owners, each month."

He angled his head and smiled. "And how much do you pay yourself?" he asked mischievously.

Emma rolled her eyes at his implication. "I receive the same salary as Mr. Peabody did—"

"Which was two-hundred, twenty-five per annum as I recall," Thomas interrupted as he crossed his arms and regarded his wife.

"And fifty extra for my share in the company," Emma added happily. "Which I plan to use to buy exquisite gifts for Christmas."

Thomas stared into space for a few moments as he considered the information. "So we could afford—"

"To travel, yes," Emma said with an enthusiastic nod, but her smile waned when she realized that travel was not really on her husband's mind.

"I was thinking of hiring another person or two for the household staff and the stables," he finished, immediately regretting the statement when he saw his wife's reaction.

"Oh," Emma replied with a sigh, disappointment evident in her face. "Would they be in addition to the housekeeper, and maids, and footmen that Gregory is planning to hire?" she asked before she bit her lip. She rather wished the new staff had already started.

Nodding, Thomas pulled her back into a hug. "You do too much around here," he whispered. "And we need to start raising horses for the company."

Emma's face brightened. "Raising horses?" she repeated. "What a capital idea!" They had spent a good deal of money investing in more horses for the overland transport part of the business. With the death of two horses and several coming up lame, it had been necessary to replace those horses at great expense. Raising their own seemed a more affordable option.

"It was Gregory's idea," Thomas said with a shrug. "We have good stock from all over, so we don't have to be as concerned with inbreeding. And the stables out here are large enough so that we don't have to build on just yet. So I was thinking of hiring someone to manage the horse breeding and training," he explained.

Wrapping her arms around his neck, Emma reached up and kissed him. Her tiredness overcame her though, and Thomas held her up as the kiss ended. "Let's get you up to bed," he suggested, reaching down to lift her knees. He half expected her to protest, but Emma sighed and allowed him to carry her up the stairs and to the bed.

She was sound asleep before Thomas even left the room.

CHAPTER 53

AN ATTEMPT AT SEDUCTION

Later that evening

A clock chime sounded, and Emma woke with a start. She felt for and found the item that Gregory had given her, the package still in one of the pockets of her gown. Relieved to find it still in one piece, she unwrapped the tissue paper and discovered two pieces of rectangular glass inside.

Rewrapping them, she pondered where to leave them. Somewhere Thomas wouldn't notice them, she decided as she placed them on the dressing table in the bathing chamber.

She proceeded to don a dinner gown that she knew Thomas would find appealing. The peach chiffon set off her coloring to good effect and allowed her to wear her best jewelry. Then she redid her hair, pinning it up so most of it was loose and wavy on top. One thick lock fell down onto a shoulder, and a cascade of ringlets framed her temples.

Glancing at her reflection in the cheval mirror, she wondered if she was trying too hard at seduction. No sooner had the thought formed when Thomas entered the bedchamber to change for dinner. Upon seeing her, his eyes widened.

"Are we... are we going to a ball? Or the theatre?" he asked, wondering if he might have forgotten an evening engagement.

"No, darling. Just dinner, unless you're of a mind to go back to town," she replied, hoping he wouldn't want to make the trip.

Despite her nap, she doubted she could make it through an evening at the theatre.

"I am not," he countered. He moved to stand behind her, his reflection appearing in the mirror as he lifted a finger to the earbobs she wore. "Are these—?" he started to ask.

"They are," she replied with a grin. "The ones you gave me before we were married. So inappropriate," she added with an arched brow, even if they were meant to be a 'thank you' for having helped him survive the night he'd had the bad fever.

Thomas sighed. "It was," he agreed. "I was," he added. He glanced down at her gown. "The last time you wore this gown, we went for a walk in the gardens after dinner," he remarked, a hint of longing in his voice.

Emma angled her head to one side. "I remember," she agreed. "Would you like to again this evening?"

His eyes darkening as he considered the question, curious as to what she was up to with her fancier than usual dinner gown and jewelry, Thomas finally nodded. "That sounds lovely." He sobered. "Is today my birthday? Or yours, perhaps?" he asked, his brows furrowing in concern.

Emma blinked. "I don't think so."

It was Thomas' turn to blink. "What's going on, Emma?" he asked then, his expression betraying his suspicion.

Her shoulders sagging, Emma allowed a sigh. "I wanted this night to be like that night. That night you proposed in the gardens," she whispered. "We haven't had a night like that in... well, ever since all the babies were born."

His lips were on hers in an instant, but only for a hard, quick kiss. "Oh, my dear Emma. You had me worried there for a moment. I thought perhaps..." He allowed the sentence to trail off.

"Perhaps?" she prompted.

He gave a wan smile. "I thought you wanted to go to the theatre," he hedged. "And any other night, I might have agreed, but not tonight."

Emma sighed and allowed a grin. "Well, I was also hoping we might—"

"Make love?" he finished for her, a hint of hope in his voice. Over the course of the past few months, the frequency of their couplings had dropped to just a few times a week.

She sighed again. "I am being obvious, am I not?" she asked meekly.

Thomas grinned. "Well, now that I know an evening at the theatre wasn't your motive, I suppose that would have been my next guess," he admitted sheepishly. He sighed and regarded her a moment. "Any time, Emma. If it's the middle of the day, and you wish to be tumbled, all you need to do is... " He paused, wondering what she could do to indicate she her desire. "Tell me. Not in front of anyone else, of course. Just... arch a brow, or give me one of your *deadly* 'come hither' looks, and I shall be at your beck and call," he murmured.

Emma could swear his ears were bright red. "Thank you," she whispered. "I promise I shan't do it often." She stopped speaking when she noticed his sudden disappointment. "And I will give you the same consideration, of course," she amended with what she thought he meant by her 'deadly come hither look'.

Chuckling, Thomas pulled her into a hug and held her for a time. He would have continued doing so but for the sound of the dinner bell ringing somewhere down below. "May I escort you to dinner?" he asked as he offered his arm.

"Of course," she replied with a sigh of relief. Despite everything they had discussed, she was relieved they hadn't discussed what she was most worried about.

Babies.

CHAPTER 54

DECEPTIVE SEX

Later that night

After dinner and a brandy in the library, and a rather lengthy discussion about servants and horses with Gregory and Christiana, Emma and Thomas took their leave of the library. Making their way to the back of Woodscastle, they regarded one another for a moment before opening the back door and stepping out into the gardens.

With the addition of another gardener, the grounds around the house had elevated the look of Woodscastle to that of a proper English estate home. Shrubs were trimmed into pleasing shapes, autumn flowers grew in colorful clusters, and the single, large arched arbor sported a flowering vine where none had grown before. Although the back gardens had never been formal, the path through the blooms suggested they might one day become so.

"I wrote the letter to Todd," Thomas stated as they made their way through the arbor.

"Will you give it to him tomorrow?"

Thomas gave Emma a look of surprise. "Tomorrow is Sunday, dear heart, so I will wait until Monday to do so."

Rather embarrassed she had lost track of the days of the week—these past few days had her struggling to remember the simplest things—Emma angled her head. "Of course," she murmured. "Which means we can remain in bed as long as we wish tomorrow."

Thomas gave his wife a sideways glance. "We can," he agreed with a grin, wondering if her comment was meant as the hint that they should head straight to the master suite. When she made no move to turn around, though, he continued following the path through the shrubs and flowers.

"Are you happy?" Emma asked.

Blinking, Thomas paused and regarded Emma for a moment. He gave the question a moment of thought and then bussed her on the forehead. "I am," he replied. "I don't think I would be if I weren't married to you, though."

She regarded him with a look of concern. "Oh?"

Managing a grin, Thomas added, "I fear I would be a busy, bored man," he murmured. "I wouldn't have anything to look forward to every day." When Emma turned to stare up at him, he added, "I rather look forward to waking up to you every morning. It may not always... seem like it, but, trust me, I prefer waking up to finding you in my bed than to being alone." He took a few more steps and then paused. "What about you?"

Angling her head to one side, Emma was quite sure he would notice how she blushed despite the dim glow from the west. "If I am to answer your query honestly, then I must admit to the same. I love you, Thomas. I cannot imagine my life without you. I could not abide waking up... alone."

Once again, Thomas had her gathered into his arms, his lips coming down onto hers in an urgent kiss. "Then let us go to bed now," he whispered.

The two turned around and headed back to Woodscastle, nearly running as they burst through the back doors and up the east wing stairs.

As Thomas began to undo the buttons of his waistcoat, he felt Emma's fingers undoing the buttons of his breeches. She stood behind him, pressed up against his back with her arms wrapped around his hips. His first reaction was to still her fingers—he feared his release would occur even before he could get her stripped and onto the bed. Even if she hadn't indicated her desire with what she wore or her suggestion to walk in the gardens or her seductive moves and the soft kisses on the back of his head, he certainly would have made his move when it came to helping her out of her corset.

"Your fingers are so warm," he whispered as he took one of her hands from its mission of pulling his shirt out of his breeches and kissed it.

"As is your entire body," Emma countered, her free hand sliding beneath the fabric of his shirt and lightly stroking his chest. "You were chopping wood this morning," she whispered, and then kissed his neck before pulling the shirt over his head.

Thomas arched his head back and smiled broadly at the reference to chopping wood. "So, you noticed that?" he said as he turned around to face her and wrapped his arms around her. Pressing against her, he knew she would feel his hardened manhood through the fabric of his breeches and her gown.

"Oh, yes," she breathed. "And my corset nearly burst," she claimed with a raised brow and a suggestive smile on her face. Turning around in his arms, she presented her back to him so that he could undo the ties on the corset.

Reaching down the back of her gown, Thomas found the end of the tie and pulled it. Grabbing a handful of her peach chiffon dress, he pulled it up and slid it over her head, her arms rising over her head as the gown's sleeves were the last to come free. Before she could lower her arms, he loosened the corset ties and slid his hands under the chemise and to her breasts. Cupping them with his warm palms, he noticed their larger size as he gently rubbed his thumbs against the sides of her hardening nipples.

Gasping, Emma pressed her back against him and rested her neck on his shoulder. She moaned softly as the ripples of pleasure coursed through her body.

When he was sure she was ready, he pulled the corset and chemise off of her body while keeping the front of his body pressed against the back of hers. Placing his hands on her hips, he slid them between her skin and her pantaloons. With one hand, he cupped a globe of her bottom and with the other, he stroked the side of her leg. Moving the hand around to the space between her thighs, he grinned at her quick intake of breath. Pressing one finger against her womanhood, he smiled when her body jerked in response. Kissing her neck, he moved his body so that she fell into his arms.

Surprised and delighted, Emma wrapped her arms around his neck as he carried her to the edge of bed. Lowering her onto the mattress, he regarded her with a mischievous grin as she pushed the pantaloons off of her long legs and dropped them seductively to the floor. He sat down on the edge of the bed and slowly removed his boots and stockings whilst she circled her long, slender fingers over his back. When he stood to remove his breeches and smalls, he turned to find her languidly stretching her arms above her head, a beatific smile on her face and her body ripe and ready for him.

"Oh, dear," he murmured as he moved to lie on top of her.

"What is it?" she whispered as she opened her eyes to find him staring at her.

"I will not last long this evening with you all... sensuous like this," he accused quietly. Emma smiled and opened her legs for him, lifting her knees just enough so that he could enter her slowly. Once his manhood was inside, he kept still, suspending his body over hers by leaning on his elbows. "I wanted you so badly today," he murmured before he kissed each of her nipples.

"So, why didn't you take me?" Emma whispered in reply, her breaths coming faster as he blew on her nipples and watched with delight as they responded.

"We were at work," Thomas replied, and then suckled one of the hardened pebbles.

"You allowed that to stop you?" she whispered mischievously, inhaling as a wave of pleasure coursed through her body.

At that, Thomas let go of her nipple and regarded her with a startled look. "You wicked woman!" he said in mock dismay.

Why didn't I? After what they had just agreed to before dinner, he supposed he could have easily talked her into the scandalous act.

Emma moved her hands down his body to grasp his buttocks. Arching her back and wrapping her ankles around his back, she pulled him into her as hard as she could. His sac slammed against the moist folds between her thighs, and she gasped at the sensation, her body shivering and her sheath tightening around him.

The quickness of her move surprised Thomas, and he let out a yelp as the pleasurable spasm from his release gripped him. Burying his face into her shoulder, he continued to jerk in reflex to the shivers he felt as his body pressed against hers.

When at last the sensations faded and their breathing returned to normal, Thomas lifted his body off of her. Emma wrapped her arms around his shoulders and held him against her. "Lie on me. Stay in me just a moment more," she pleaded.

Thomas relaxed and remained on top of her, the weight of his torso pressing her into the mattress. "I'm crushing you," he whispered.

"I don't mind."

When she finally unwrapped her legs from around his back, he lifted himself from her and rolled onto the bed. He was asleep even before his head hit the pillow.

When she was sure Thomas was sleeping, Emma carefully moved off of the bed and hurried to the bath. Taking one of the slides from the tissue, she pressed it against her inner thigh as she felt his seed dribble down her leg. She pressed the other slide on top of it, wiped herself with a bath linen as quickly as she could, and donned her dressing gown. Before leaving the bedchamber, she listened a moment to be sure Thomas was still sleeping. Hearing his soft snores, she hurried out the door and down the steps to the library, cradling the pair of slides in her palm.

She had arranged for Gregory to leave one lamp lit in the library. She used it to light several others and placed them around the microscope. Removing the slide that was already in the microscope, she positioned her slides under the tube. At her first glance through the lens, she recoiled in horror and then forced herself to look again. Trying to focus her eyes, she realized it was the microscope lens that needed to be adjusted. It was several tries at moving the gears surrounding the tube before she found the one that changed the focus.

When at last she could see clearly, she was repulsed at the sight of tiny ovals with wiggling tails. Pulling herself away from the instrument, she took a deep breath. Leaning over again, she forced herself to watch the creatures squirm in their thin liquid pool. *Sperm!* she realized as she marveled at the sign of life trapped in the glass prison. Unconsciously, she placed her open hand against her abdomen. I am pregnant, she thought, not quite sure if she should rejoice or feel despair at the realization.

Moving to one of the sofas, she sat down and contemplated what to do next. *How do I tell him? And when? What if he doesn't believe me? What if he thinks I have been with another man?*

Emma was still running scenarios through her mind when she realized she wasn't alone. Thomas stood at the library table, peering through the microscope. His reaction to the image in the slides was much the same as hers at first. But he continued to stare through the tube for a very long time.

Finally regaining her feet, Emma moved to where he stood and wrapped her arms around his chest. Pressing the front of her body against his back, she waited for him to say something.

When at last he turned around in her arms, he had a huge grin on his face. "Are these what I think they are?" he whispered as he motioned with his thumb over his shoulder.

"If you think they're your seed, then yes, they are," Emma replied, relieved at seeing his expression.

He wrapped his arms around her and pulled her close. "But why... what made you... ?" he started to ask.

Emma pulled away from him and regarded her husband as he looked down at her. "I have not had my monthly courses for over three months now, so I thought perhaps... I was barren," she whispered, trying hard not to cry.

Thomas pulled her against him again, hugging her hard. "You're not barren," he whispered in reply. "You're pregnant," he said happily.

In the candlelight, Emma watched her husband's face. "You

say it as if... as if you already knew it to be fact," she accused, wondering how he would know such a thing.

Thomas chuckled at the comment. "Of course I did," he replied. "Your entire body is... ripe," he said as opened her robe and ran his hands down the sides of her body. "And... you positively glow!" he added as he placed a warm hand on her belly.

"I do?" she asked, surprised at his enthusiasm. Why, he seemed positively happy about the situation.

"Oh, yes," he replied assuredly. "I must admit, I was concerned when I first noticed, but I knew you couldn't have been with anyone else." He noticed Emma's sigh of relief and her hand against her chest. Pulling her into a hug again, he asked, "Is that what this is about?" as he motioned to the microscope. "Truth be told, I thought that's why we went to the gardens tonight. I thought you were going to tell me then," he said in a hoarse whisper. "And then, when you didn't, well, why didn't you?"

Emma shrugged, not sure what to say. "If you weren't sterile, then it would mean that I was barren," she finally replied, her voice quiet. "And I don't know how I'd feel about that," she added, tears finally escaping her eyes and flowing down her cheeks.

Thomas hugged her harder. "I remembered something you said to me after you had your way with me during the summer."

Emma raised her eyebrows, wondering what she had said.

"You said I tasted different," he reminded her. "And, so I saw the doctor again, and he told me I was no longer sterile. Apparently high fevers have only a temporary affect on one's ability to father a child."

Sniffling, Emma frowned. "Why didn't you tell me?" she asked, feeling somewhat betrayed. Knowing that bit of information would have saved her from several weeks of questioning and grief. And it would have saved Gregory from having to purchase the microscope.

"I... I wasn't sure... you said at one point that you didn't want... no, that's not right," Thomas amended as he tried to remember their afternoon discussion about children and adoption. "You said the idea of giving birth scared you to death. And, I know that I said I didn't want children then. And, at that point in time, I didn't."

Emma wiped the tears from one of her cheeks. "And now?" she asked as she watched him gaze at her.

"Well, now I would very much like us to have a child. Or two," he replied with a grin.

Smiling despite her tears, Emma buried her face into the space between his chest and arm and hugged her husband. "Me, too," she whispered.

"It's just that, I will miss you terribly if you don't come to the office with me every day," Thomas whispered into her ear.

"Of course, I'll still come to the office," she replied. She remembered how round Christiana had been with her pregnancy and added, "Well, I may have to ride in the carriage instead of on horseback at some point."

"I was thinking of having Tilbury make us a new curricle," Thomas countered with an arched brow. He had actually been considering a sporty phaeton, but couldn't imagine how she would reach the high bench when she was round with child.

Emma pulled away to give him a quelling glance. "You were thinking of a phaeton, I'm quite sure," she countered with an arched brow. "Yellow? Or red?"

Thomas rolled his eyes. "Red," he admitted with a hint of guilt. "But there's no reason we can't get both a curricle and a phaeton," he reasoned. "I used to love watching you when you arrived here driving the Simpson's phaeton," he murmured. "I remembered thinking I should respect any woman who could drive such a conveyance with the confidence you displayed."

Emma gave him a look of surprise. "And did you? Respect me?" she asked in surprise.

Thomas nodded. "Indeed. I probably would have proposed weeks earlier than I did, except you informed me it wasn't yours."

Arching an eyebrow, Emma managed a grin. "Bounder," she accused.

"I was," he agreed, pulling her back into his arms. "I

remember having the most scandalous thoughts about you just before I fell asleep every night."

"Indeed?" she countered.

"Oh, yes. And several of them involved this very library table," he murmured just before he kissed her on the temple.

He grinned when he felt her jerk in his hold. "Whatever were we doing on this library table?" she asked. Her eyes darkened. "Was I... bent over it?"

Thomas frowned. "Of course not. You know I don't like doing it that way," he replied.

"Liar."

Blinking, Thomas gave a shrug. "You were sitting on the edge of it..."

Emma was suddenly out of his arms and perched on the edge of the table. "Like this?"

He blinked again. "Well, yes, but you had more clothes on."

She gave him a quelling glance before she undid the tie of her dressing gown and allowed it to fall open.

"Oh, that's far better than what I imagined," Thomas said as he moved to stand before her. When Emma wrapped her legs around his back and hooked her ankles together, he took a deep breath. "Oh, God."

He undid his robe and thrust his hardened manhood into her without another word, reveling in how Emma's arms wrapped around his shoulders as her gasp of surprise filled the otherwise quiet library. His arms wrapped around her hips, his splayed hands grasping the globes of her silk-covered bottom to steady himself as he thrust into her over and over again.

When he felt her body spasm and watched as her front arched into him, he allowed his own release and finally buried his head into her shoulder.

The feel of her fingers spearing his hair finally had Thomas straightening. "We have an audience," Emma whispered, giving her head a nod toward the library door.

Thomas' eyes widened before he dared a glance to his left. "Why, how do, Ariel," he managed to get out between gasps for breath. He struggled to retie his robe despite his member still firmly entrenched in his wife.

"I tirtsy, Aunt Em," the baby said in her quiet voice. She went from her hands and knees to a standing position, one hand gripping a table for support.

"I'll get you some water," Emma replied as she hurried to tie shut her dressing gown. She gave Thomas an arched brow when she determined he wasn't doing anything to remove his manhood from where it had sought refuge only moments ago. "Where's your nurse?" she asked as she slowly lowered her legs from around Thomas and gingerly touched her bare toes to the carpet below.

"She's with Mister Lars'n," Ariel replied, her face breaking into a huge grin. "Kissin'. Like you," she added happily.

Rather wishing she had one of the linens from the bath, Emma managed to extricate herself from Thomas' hold and moved to join the toddler at the threshold. "Let's..." She spun around, remembering the decanter of water on the sideboard. On the salver with the decanters of brandy and claret stood a decanter filled with clear liquid. "Come over here," she said as she lifted Ariel into her arms and moved to the sideboard. She filled a tumbler with water and held it for the child as the girl gulped down half of it.

"Did you get enough?" Emma asked, rather startled her niece could drink so much.

Ariel nodded and then indicated she wanted down. Once she was back on her hands and knees, she crawled out of the library. "Good night, Ariel," Emma whispered.

"'Night, Aunt Em. 'Night, Unc' Thomas," Ariel managed before she disappeared. A moment later, Emma could hear the girl's *thumps* as she crawled up the stairs. Emma turned to stare at Thomas. "Mr. Larsen and the nurse?" she whispered hoarsely.

Her husband allowed a shrug. "First I've heard of it, but I can't say I'm too surprised," he admitted before moving to join her. "They're the only unmarried servants... *younger*, unmarried servant in the household," he clarified.

Emma rested her head against his shoulder. "Have we scarred her for life?"

Thomas allowed a chuckle. "I'm sure her parents have already managed in that regard." He took a deep breath. "Come. Let's get back to bed, shall we?"

Sighing, Emma allowed a nod. "I am so glad we're spending most of tomorrow there," she whispered with a teasing grin.

"Oh?"

Emma's eyes widened. "Well, of course. I don't wish to face Ariel's parents if she tells them what we were doing here in the library—"

"She thought we were kissing," Thomas interrupted.

"—And I was under the impression you were going to spend the day in bed, too."

Grinning, Thomas gave her a hug. "That I am," he agreed. "That I am."

CHAPTER 55

EXPECTING

The following morning

Thomas woke up with a start and immediately moved his right arm out seeking to touch Emma. Not finding her in the bed, he lifted his chest, his elbows tucked beneath him, and listened intently. Perhaps she was in the bathing chamber or dressing somewhere nearby. But only the sounds of the early morning came to him—a bird chirping in a tree, the doors of the stables being opened by one of the grooms, and the very faint sound of water being pumped in the kitchen. A piece of paper lay on her pillow, though, and he reached for it. *I am in the gardens,* it read in Emma's even script.

Thomas lay back on his pillow and considered the message. *This is unusual. It was good of her to let me know*, he thought, *But is it an invitation to follow?* Intrigued, he threw off the bed covers and pulled on his robe, vaguely aware of her scent from when he had held her the night before in the library. *She's going to have a baby,* he remembered with a grin.

Hurrying down the stairs, he nearly collided with Humphrey as he turned the corner from the main hall to the hall leading past the dining room and kitchens.

"Good morning, sir," his butler said as he stepped out of the kitchen.

"It certainly is, Humphrey," Thomas replied with a smile, barely slowing in his quest to get to the back gardens.

"Would you like me to bring coffee, sir?" the butler asked before Thomas could get to the back doors.

"No, but a bath would be most welcome," Thomas said as he left the house.

"Very good, sir," Humphrey replied, a bit too late as Thomas had already closed the doors behind him. The butler, left wondering where his master was off to wearing only his robe, returned to the kitchens to begin the task of hauling hot water to the master suite.

The October sky was nearly clear and the sun was just over the horizon as Thomas made his way along the garden path. If the night had been chilly, there was no hint of it now. The air was already surprisingly warm. He was nearly running when he reached the far part of the path where the stone bench was located. It was where he had proposed to Emma, and he found her there now. Barely wearing her dressing gown, she was seated with one hand loosely holding the fabric closed at her waist and her head held back. Eyes closed as if in prayer, her face looked peaceful bathed in the golden light of morning. Her shoulders were bare, the robe having slipped down around her arms at some point while she sat waiting for him. Waves of golden blonde hair fell down behind her, the ends nearly touching the stone.

Stopped in his tracks, Thomas inhaled sharply as he took in the sight of her. *She is glowing,* he thought as he regarded her. Just the way she was sitting oozed sensuality, and he felt his loins respond.

As he was about to move to her side, Emma smiled and opened her eyes. "I am so glad you have come," she said quietly. In a fluid motion, she stood up from the bench and glided into his arms, her robe opening in the breeze to reveal her naked body. Kissing him gently, Emma wove her hands through the opening of his robe and slid them down his back and around the swell of his buttocks.

Thomas tensed at the sudden sensation. "Are... are you well?" he whispered between hungry kisses.

"I am," she replied, her eyes watching him through lowered lids. "And are you?"

He could only nod his reply as he continued to kiss her. His hands gripped the sides of her ribs as his thumbs brushed along the bottom of her breasts. Before he realized what was happening, she had backed away from him and spread her gown on the grass next to the path. And as fluidly as she had stood up from the bench, she was lying on her dressing gown, naked and reaching for him with an outstretched arm.

Sensing her need for him, Thomas dropped to his knees next to her. Drunk with passion, he was unaware of their surroundings as he stroked the length of her torso with the back of a finger. He took notice of how her nipples were already pebbled. Despite the earthy odors of the plants around them, he could smell her wetness and knew she was already ripe for him. Her arms stretched out to either side of her body and she spread her legs for him.

Thomas swallowed hard as he knelt between her legs, the still-sane part of his brain realizing he had best cover her nakedness with his own body and the robe he still wore. The aroused part of him knew she was ready—he couldn't help but notice her engorged womanhood, its red-pink color deepening before his eyes. *I have never seen her like this*, he thought. *Outside, in the light of day.*

Leaving his robe on his body, he opened it to provide some coverage and lay on top of her, his breaths coming in short gasps as he entered her. She was wet and warm and begging him to hurry.

Responding to the sense of urgency, Thomas pounded into her over and over, amazed as he watched her breasts heave, amazed at the sensation of how her cocoon tightened around his manhood, and amazed at the sensation of his balls pounding against her wetness. He groaned as he felt his own oncoming pleasure, trying hard to keep his eyes open so that he could watch the ecstasy on her face as the first wave of pleasure passed through her. His own spasm of pleasure gripped him, washed through him, and finally left him satiated and breathless.

Emma's arms, wrapped around his shoulders but under the robe, pulled him down to her, even before her pleasure had passed.

It was several minutes before he lifted his head and glanced about. Realizing where they were—realizing what had just happened—he allowed a slight chuckle. He placed a hand along Emma's face and stared at her beautiful features, marveled at her parted lips and the look of contentment on her face. Lifting his weight from her body, he gazed down the rest of her, and his body shivered at the remembered pleasure.

Her eyes still closed, Emma slipped her arms into the sleeves of her dressing gown while he watched. Sighing deeply, she opened her eyes and smiled at him. "Thank you," she whispered happily. She made no move to let go of him, nor did she lower her legs from around the back of his legs.

Thomas regarded his wife and wondered how he was going to get her back into the house. "You're very welcome," he whispered in reply, and then kissed her on the nose and the forehead. "May I take you inside now?" he asked quietly, wondering how much longer she expected they could stay out in the gardens without being noticed by a servant or their relatives. He was rather shocked to find a cow standing not twenty feet away, munching on the lawn and regarding them with an expression of boredom.

Noticing the direction of his glance, Emma turned her head and smiled broadly at the sight of the bovine. "Oh, my," she whispered. Reluctantly, she slid her arms down and off of his body. "I suppose... I guess we should go in now," she admitted, her gaze on him unfocused and her actions almost lazy.

"Are you well?" Thomas asked, his concern increasing as he watched her.

Emma's face flushed red as she glanced first to her left and then to her right. "Are we truly in the gardens?" she whispered, trying to lift herself onto one elbow despite his body covering most of hers.

"Yes," Thomas answered slowly, "By the stone bench," he added as he continued to watch her with growing concern.

Falling back onto the grass, Emma sighed and shook her head. "I just had the most incredible dream," she whispered as her eyes widened and she came fully awake.

"Indeed?" Thomas replied as a mischievous grin appeared on his face. "I rather enjoy your dreams. You must tell me all about it in the bath," he insisted as he rolled off her body and at the same time, covered her by gripping the front edges of her dressing gown together as quickly as he could. He wrapped his own robe about his body and secured it with the tie before pulling her up to stand next to him.

Unsteady on her feet at first, Emma waited a moment before allowing him to lead her on the path back to the house. "How long have I been out here?" she whispered, gripping his arm hard.

Thomas kissed her temple. "Not long. You left a note, so I knew where to find you," he added with an amused expression.

Turning to give him a look of shock, Emma gasped and then bit her lip. "*Where* did you find me?

Kissing her again, he replied, "On the stone bench. You were a vision to behold."

At that, Emma swallowed. "I remember now," she said with relief. "I woke up to watch the sunrise and thought of the garden. I must have fallen asleep on the bench," she added with a sigh.

As they climbed the steps to the master suite, they passed Humphrey. He seemed taken aback at the sight of his master's wife in her dressing gown, at least outside of their bedchamber. "Good morning, Mrs. Wellingham," he said as he nodded.

"Yes, it is," Emma replied happily.

The butler turned his attention to Thomas. "Your bath is ready, sir," he said. "Would you like assistance dressing this morning?"

Thomas glanced at his wife and shook his head. "That won't be necessary, Humphrey."

"Very good, sir," the butler replied.

Once in the master suite, Thomas removed his robe and helped Emma out of hers. "You look spectacular, you must know," he said, taking her hand and leading her into the bath.

"I do?" she replied, her eyes wide at his comment.

He dipped the back of his hand into the water, testing to be sure it wasn't too hot. Assisting her into the large copper tub, he waited for her to sit down and to lower her head back into the water to soak her hair before he got in behind her. He sat down and stretched his legs out on either side of her body. Soaping his hands, he began washing her hair and rinsing it by pouring cupfuls of water down the golden cascade.

"You must tell me about your incredible dream," he teased as he washed her hair.

Emma relaxed against the front of his body. She used the soap to wash his legs. "I dreamed I was expecting a child," she whispered as she turned to watch his reaction.

"Indeed?" he replied with a smile, thinking at first she was teasing him. *At any moment, she'll remember being in the library last night*, he thought happily. He frowned. *Or did I dream that?* he wondered, his heart skipping a beat when he doubted what he had seen was real.

But even as he watched her, he could see the reaction on her face changing. Her attention was redirected to some tissue paper on the dressing table. Thomas reached over, his fingers barely able to pull the empty papers to the edge of the dressing table.

He gave them to Emma, and she held them for a moment. "So, it wasn't a dream?" she asked as she turned to look at him, her face betraying concern. "I am expecting a child."

"You are," Thomas replied with a grin as he nodded his head, wondering what the tissue paper had to do with it. "At least, that part wasn't a dream," he assured her.

Emma's eyes widened. "How long have you known?"

Thomas blinked. "Well, I suspected something a couple of months ago, when you didn't have your monthly courses. And then when you didn't have them again, I knew for sure," he reasoned.

"I never felt sick," she said.

"But you've been tired."

Sighing, Emma agreed. "My corset feels tighter than usual."

Thomas moved his hands to her breasts and cupped them from beneath the water. "I should say so," he agreed with a chuckle. He kissed her shoulder. "You've been scatterbrained, too," he accused.

"I have," she agreed. "At least I'm not so much at work," she added quickly, hoping he wouldn't think she couldn't do her job.

"You get lost in the numbers," he murmured.

"I do."

"You must have thought you were dreaming in the gardens, but I assure you, that wasn't a dream," he said happily. "I don't believe I have ever seen you quite so *insistent* on being bedded."

Emma gasped and turned to regard Thomas a moment, grinning as she did so. "And, you, no doubt, were more than happy to oblige," she teased.

"Indeed I was," he agreed with a mischievous grin. After a moment, he remembered her comment just before Deborah had given birth, and his grin widened. "I will be," he added. "Your wish is my command."

Arching an eyebrow, Emma settled back onto his chest and considered what she might have him do next.

EXCERPT

*Read on for an excerpt from Linda Rae Sandé's Book 3 in The
Widows of the Aristocracy* series
The Secrets of a Viscount

May 5, 1818 in St. James Street

The moment she realized she was walking in St. James
Street, Miss Diana Albright wondered if she could turn back.
Wondered if she could simply stop, turn around, and begin
walking in the opposite direction. For in her few moments of
introspection, or what most would refer to as daydreaming, she
had made the turn onto St. James, completely unaware she had
done so.

She wanted to go in the direction the street would take her,
of course. She just didn't want to pass by the window.

The bow window.

The one that had been added onto the front of the building
that housed one of London's most notorious men's clubs.

White's.

As much as she supposed the men therein didn't know their
secret was out, it was. Even her students at Warwick's Grammar
and Finishing School knew what went on in the bow window at
White's. Apparently, before his departure to the Continent the
year before, Beau Brummel occupied the table in front of the

window, his status as a socially influential gentleman his ticket to watch the world go by.

Or rather, the women of the world.

The ones that dared walk down St. James Street, either because they didn't know any better or because they did and were curious as to how they would be rated by him—or those, should he have others in his company,—who watched.

She knew there was some discussion as to what constituted a rating of 'one' versus a 'ten'. Were 'ones' given to those young ladies deemed most beautiful? Or were those 'tens'? For unless one knew which was considered the better end of the rating spectrum, only the women deemed a 'five' knew exactly where they stood in the ratings.

That is, if they actually overheard the numbers being called out by the young bucks who ruled the roost of the bow window.

She rather imagined there were times when no one was in the window, or when older gentlemen managed to claim the seats closest to the window simply because whoever was deemed most socially influential wasn't in the club at the time. Certainly an older gentleman would be more discreet if he bothered with the practice at all.

Given it was entirely too late to simply turn around and walk the other direction, Diana held her head up and continued her walk toward Jermyn Street. If her hips swayed any more than usual, she wasn't conscious of it. If a slight smile played at her lips, it was only because her daydreams were rather pleasant. Anything was better than thinking about the never-ending days spent attempting to teach spoiled rotten girls basic arithmetic and dancing. Well, the dancing she didn't mind so much—at least the chits wanted to learn to dance. That was their ticket to an advantageous marriage, after all.

The fact that Diana wasn't married and probably never would be was the only reason she was teaching arithmetic and dancing at Warwick's Grammar and Finishing School.

When the hairs on the back her neck suddenly seemed to move, Diana nearly paused in mid-step. Something skittered down her spine, and she was quite sure it wasn't an insect.

And then she did pause. Her head turned at an angle and her attention immediately went to the bow window.

A man was watching her. A rather handsome man, in fact, gazing at her. He didn't even try to hide the fact, nor look away when he realized he'd been caught staring.

Diana was suddenly conscious of every piece of clothing she wore. A peach muslin gown, sprigged with tiny embroidered flowers over which she wore a darker peach spencer. Not a fan of poke bonnets—she was quite sure a gust of wind would send an especially light chit sailing away down the streets of London —she preferred hats with silk flowers. Not the large, overpowering silk flowers which festooned some lady's hats, but rather small, delicate flowers that merely lined the edges of where a brim met its crown. And none that featured feathers. Goodness! Some of those hats sported ostrich plumes that nearly grazed a ceiling and required their wearer to duck down when passing through a doorway.

The one she wore today was just such a hat, peach with peach and green flowers. A shade of peach that showed off her charcoal black hair to its best advantage. Her half-boots were well-hidden beneath her skirts, a reticule that matched her hat hung from one wrist, and brown kid gloves hugged her fingers almost too tightly.

I'm at least a five, she found herself hoping as she stared at the gentleman. And then, quite before she realized what she was doing, she approached the front door of White's and rang the bell. Reason arrived far too late to have her stepping away. Stepping away and running down the street in an effort to get away before anyone could answer the door, for an older, liveried man did indeed open the black-painted door. He regarded her with a set of gray eyebrows that were rather high on his forehead and combed into elaborately shaped fans.

"My lady?" he ventured, as if he were seeing a woman for the very first time in his entire life. Well, he probably was seeing a woman at this particular door for the very first time, she realized. White's was a men's club, after all. Women were not allowed.

Diana bobbed a curtsy, the action so automatic she didn't realize she needn't have done so, given a servant answered the door. "Could you please inform me as to the name of the distinguished-looking gentleman who is currently presiding in the bow window?"

The butler's eyebrows seemed to go even higher and fan out wider, if that were possible. "I... cannot," he replied carefully. He seemed to reconsider his answer and then said, "One moment," as he held up an index finger. The door closed and Diana was left on the stoop feeling ever so much a fool.

What the hell am I doing? she wondered, not bothering to chide herself over the curse she used. Why, if the daughters of the ton she was responsible to teach six days a week had any idea of her inner thoughts just then, they would certainly swoon from shock.

She was about to step away, turn around, and begin running toward Jermyn Street when the black door suddenly reopened. The same butler, his voice kept low, said, "I'm to tell you to wait one moment as the gentleman retrieves his coat and hat."

Diana's eyes widened. "But... ," she started to protest, realizing just then it was entirely too late to make her escape. If the man was retrieving his coat and hat, then what did he intend to do? Before she could even consider the possibilities, he was suddenly standing in front of her.

If she thought him handsome through the bow window, she didn't know what word to use to describe him without a pane of glass and the reflections of the buildings lining St. James Street in front of him. He wore his nearly black hair cut quite short, a hint of gray highlighting his temples. His sapphire eyes were lined with black lashes and tiny crinkles, a testament to a life filled with amusement and perhaps a bit too much drink. The straight nose suggested he had never been punched at Gentleman Jackson's boxing saloon. His square jaw held a mouth with lips she could imagine saying any number of words and doing rather wicked things to a woman's lips.

And other body parts.

A frisson shot through her and nearly had her allowing an audible gasp. Instead, she managed a curtsy.

Realizing she was staring, she blinked. Before she could get a word out, though—she thought to simply apologize and claim she thought him to be someone else—the man said, "Oh, my sweeting, I apologize profusely. Do forgive me. I completely lost track of the time." He turned and gave the butler a quick nod before placing his top hat upon his head.

ABOUT THE AUTHOR

A self-described nerd and student of history, Linda Rae spent many years as a published technical writer specializing in 3D graphics workstations, software and 3D animation (her movie credits include SHREK and SHREK 2). Getting lost in the rabbit holes of research has resulted in historical romances set in the Regency-era as well as Ancient Greece.

A fan of action-adventure movies, she can frequently be found at the local cinema. Although she no longer has any tropical fish, she follows the San Jose Sharks and makes her home in Cody, Wyoming.

For more information:
www.lindaraesande.com
Sign up for Linda Rae's newsletter:
Regency Romance with a Twist
Follow Linda Rae's blog:
Regency Romance with a Twist